STANDING
ON THE
CORNER
OF
LOST
AND
FOUND

Jan Marin Tramontano

ISBN: 1463520255
ISBN-13: 9781463520250

for Ron
and
the joyous bonds of sisterhood

Lost

1975

∽

Shadowbox: Bolt from the Blue

A foil lightning bolt tears a heart-shaped candy box in two.
One side is bright yellow. A baby doll pillow is surrounded
by Hershey kisses. The other side is black. It is littered with a
pile of crumpled candy wrappers.

Some late October days have that good-to-be-alive feeling. The air is crisp but not cold, the colors are vibrant and the slightest breeze sends the burnished leaves tumbling to the ground. Indian summer, nature's cruel trick, makes the biting winter wind off the Charles River seem impossible. The golden sun low in the sky was the last reminder that gray, endless winter was close at hand. But Lisa could not have cared less. Today was perfect.

She loved her walk home from work, from Kenmore Square to Brookline which took her past the Charles River University campus, then across the bridge to Babcock Street to Coolidge Corners. Crunchy brown leaves and showy reds and oranges reminded her of home. The big oaks and maples lining the street, as well as the two-family houses with big open porches, were just like the street she grew up on. Her walk took her to Harvard Street in Brookline. The fish market, deli, bagel place, and temple gave the area character. There was a movie theatre, bookstore and a Pewter Pot Muffin House. Over gallons of coffee, Lisa and her friends voiced their hopes for the future.

Lisa was bursting to tell Mac that two of her shadowboxes had been accepted by the Boston Arts Co-op. He'd been right to encourage her to submit her work. But he had appointments out in the country so her good news would have to wait. Mac had driven to Concord hot on the trail of a Fitzgerald first edition for his collection. Later in the day, he was meeting an antiquarian bookseller somewhere near Northampton.

As she trudged through thick piles of leaves on this warm October afternoon, she thought about the past summer. Everything seemed more vivid; the grass seemed greener, the flowers more fragrant. Had she seen this as her future on days she felt listless or despondent, perhaps she would have had a happier childhood.

The life she lived with Mac was beyond the expectations she'd had for herself. Charismatic, smart, dreamy Mac, who loved her completely, supported all her cockeyed ideas, her social issue of the week, her shadowboxes and her work. Their life together as partners, lovers, best friends, and soul mates was perfect. Together they formed the nucleus in an orbit of moving and shifting light.

As she strolled home, snippets of memory passed randomly through her mind. She thought about the first time she woke up next to him — the pleasure of their lazy lovemaking in the early morning, their sleep, how they read newspapers to one another over coffee with croissants in bed. The first morning he said, "You complete me." She smiled thinking of Mac's arms around her waist, his kisses on the back of her neck while she'd washed the dishes just last night.

Days seemed particularly bright after nights spent wrapped in each other's arms, safe and warm. Happiness puts luminous color into your life. Losing her grandmother last year was hard but being with Mac was beyond anything she'd ever hoped for. As Grandma said, there's always bad with the good.

When she rounded the corner and saw two policemen standing in front of their apartment, she didn't think anything of it, even when they asked her if this was the residence of MacKenzie Taylor. "He should be back in a couple of hours," she said. "Do you want to come in and wait for him? Can he call you when he gets here?"

"Yes, Miss. We'll come in. What's your relationship to him?"

"Relationship?" she repeated. One of the officers took her arm, while the other held her trembling hand.

They sat down in the living room. Lisa stared at the painting over the sofa. They'd bought it from an artist their friend Phil had dated. It was abstract and they were in deep disagreement about its subject. *Mac, I see it your way now. Wait until I tell you.*

The two policemen were trying their best to soften what they came to tell her. She was afraid of what they might say. She had to keep them from saying it. Once they did, they wouldn't be able take it back.

"Would you like some coffee or soda or something?"

"No, thank you. What's your name?"

"Lisa," she whispered.

"Lisa, who can we call for you?'

Her legs buckled. She couldn't catch her breath. She felt like she'd swallowed broken glass. Her heart lay so heavy in her chest she thought it would crush her diaphragm.

The other policeman repeated, "Lisa, who can we call for you?"

They called Phil and he called her old roommate, Amy. They came within minutes of one another. The detectives explained to them what had happened. Lisa couldn't think about the facts. They didn't make sense. How could Mac be taken without any warning, so quickly and alone? Bleeding out in a crash of steel and glass? Wrapped around a tree while she was enjoying the afternoon? What was their last conversation about? A movie he wanted to see? Getting dinner with Phil and his latest girlfriend? Reminding him to take out the garbage? She didn't know.

The police speculated he might have swerved to miss a deer. They found one dead up the road. Treacherous, those narrow country roads.

In the days that followed, Lisa was in shock. The only thing she was aware of was that she called the police station every morning, her heart beating, praying for a different answer. That maybe they made a mistake. That Mac would come home.

She was put through to a man with a patient, composed voice. "I'm sorry, Miss Stern. We'll never know exactly how it happened. There is nothing to investigate. There were skid marks on the road. The car smashed into a tree. No one else was involved. We're sorry, miss. It was an accident, an unfortunate accident." Sorry, sorry, sorry.

The funeral was a blur. His mother wouldn't let her see him. She said it was better that way. No one would see him, not even her. They had to remember him as he was.

He grew up in Reading, a picturesque New England town outside of Boston. His town reminded her of a Currier and Ives image of a town square with a white church and slender steeple around which there was a cemetery with the grave markers of the early settlers. A minister, who might have known Mrs. Taylor but certainly not Mac, spoke in generalities; he could have been eulogizing anyone.

Everyone who knew him knew Mac scorned religion. He would have wanted Phil to tell some of his best stories, to have him go out as he truly was. But he wasn't there to plan it as he would have been in life, meticulously attending to every detail.

She sat propped up by Phil, stiff with grief. She didn't want to look at the coffin, yet she couldn't take her eyes off it. She whispered to Phil, "No cemetery." He nodded and squeezed her hand.

She didn't know how she would get over this. The only thing clear to her was that the course of her life was forever changed. There would never be another Mac.

Chapter One

Race Point or the End of the World

Lisa pulled her shawl and blanket tightly around her. The bottom of her skirt was damp. She stood on the beach at the very tip of Cape Cod, where the ocean and bay dissolve into one another. At the horizon, there was an emptiness suggesting she was at the edge of the world.

She was unaware that another sleepless woman inched toward her, in case the girl walked into the water. The woman had seen that happen before and knew it would happen again. But not on her watch.

The blackness of night faded to gray. Crashing waves sizzled and swallowed the beach. Grasses and scrub pine rooted in sand resisted the northwest winds that sculpted them. The dunes shook themselves free in the wind, shaped but not beaten by the assault. Lisa knew she was not a dune.

She looked down at the dark silkiness between her toes at the water's edge. The water slapped her shins and then pooled around her feet. Mac's sudden death was incomprehensible. What should she do with herself now that he had been ripped away from her? Lisa sat on the wet sand, amidst kelp and shells washed ashore. Close to the surf, she grabbed her knees tight to her chest, rocking slightly and crying first in waves of hysteria, then weary sobbing.

Her dead grandmother's voice broke through Lisa's haze. *What are you doing, kinde? Get away from that water! Mach schnell. Right now. Don't be such a big baby. You should have known this was coming. What did you expect? I told you over and over. The goniff is always waiting. He takes. I'm sorry for you, Liselah, but that's life. You think you've had a loss. Let me tell you about loss.*

Lisa grew up with hearing that no matter how good things seemed to be, there would always be the inevitable appearance of the *goniff,* the lurking thief ready to strangle peace of mind and replace it with trouble — *tsouris.* Lisa had always imagined her personal *goniff* as a wrinkled troll who would silently creep up from behind and snatch her happiness. But when the thief had finally arrived, he'd caught her entirely by surprise. She had forgotten all about him when she was with Mac. But he came anyway. Lisa never imagined grief to be physical. It was hard to breathe and her broken heart had jagged edges. Body and soul were marooned in the replay of memory.

"Good night, Grandma, go away." Lisa mumbled, covering her ears.

Moving toward the water, the woman approached Lisa. Hands on wide hips, she wore a man's coat with a scarf wound around her neck. "It's a bone-chilling night," she said. "You must be freezing." She spread a blanket away from the surf and pulled a thermos and a mug from her straw bag. "Come, have some coffee to warm you up."

Lisa looked up at her, sniffling. "No thanks. I'd like to be alone, if you don't mind."

"The coffee is free. No strings." She sat down on her blanket, poured coffee into the top of the thermos and handed it to Lisa. The only sound was the water lapping the beach and the wind. "I thought maybe you were thinking about taking a walk into the water. So no," the woman's thin lips half-smiled, "I don't expect conversation."

"Why are you here?" Lisa took a soggy tissue from her pocket to dry her face.

"Probably the same reason as you. Can't sleep."

Lisa looked into the woman's lined, ruddy face. "The nights can be endless."

"For an old woman." She sipped from her mug. "Have some. It'll warm you." She looked out at the water and then back at the disheveled girl. "I'm Isabela."

"Lisa."

Isabela pulled a wad of Kleenex from her bag. "Need these?" She tossed them to her.

"Thanks. The coffee is good." Lisa blew her nose hard.

They sat quietly side by side, watching the rush of the waves. The sun was rising; vague puffs of pink and gold signaled the start of another day. What should she do now? Go back home to their empty apartment, the place where Mac still filled up every space? Call one of her friends who didn't know what to say anymore? She didn't even have a job to go back to. Ruby told her not to come back to the day care center until she pulled herself together, and her other job had not yet received funding.

"It's too cold for you to stay out here. You really should go home." Isabela pointed to quick-moving swollen clouds. "The sky is clear straight ahead but look over there. A storm is moving in and the air smells like snow."

Lisa shrugged, her eyes filling again. "I can't go home."

Isabela hesitated, and then said, "Come with me then, come to my place above the bakery. You can sleep for a while until you decide what to do or where to go."

"Brinca's Bakery?" Lisa's eyes widened.

"Yes. I like to come down while the bread is rising. Not much of a sleeper myself. I usually stay closer to home but tonight I felt a pull to come here to Race Point."

"I can't go there. No. Not there." Lisa shook her head, tears rolled down her cheeks.

Isabela let a few moments pass. "You liked my cinnamon raisin bread and your boyfriend always wanted lemon cakes. Don't look surprised. You two never seemed to notice there were other people in the world. I don't know what happened but you have a choice to make. You can freeze out here or you can choose a warm bed. Just come take a nap. The salty air, the aroma of bread baking and rest might do you some good. "

Lisa knew she probably shouldn't go home with this stranger, but Isabela smelled like raw dough and sugar. That was good enough for her.

Chapter Two

Asleep or Awake, the Nightmare is Real

∽

A recurring dream brought Lisa from her apartment in Brookline to the beach in Provincetown. Its repetition drove her crazy. Did she think she could change the ending by going there? Maybe she'd be able to bury it in the morning silt.

The ocean gleams sapphire on this sunny morning. The wind is strong and Mac is pulling her along. She's the rope in a tug of war between Mac's firm grasp on one side and gusting wind on the other. There is no stopping him. He has a surprise and he is not going to let a little bit of wind discourage him. They are high up on the dunes. A thin strip of sand several feet wide sparkles with bits of feldspar, mica and quartz. Most of the beach has disappeared and become ocean.

Mac finds a space sheltered by the dunes. He lays a rough blanket on a bed of sand sprinkled with tiny broken shells among thickets of bayberry. The gulls are squawking, looking for their morning feed. The wind is trying to tell her something. She strains to make sense of it but only hears a sad howling. Mac tells her he'll be right back, that he's forgotten something. Lisa calls after him, "Mac, don't go down there."

He doesn't hear her and slides down the dune. The wind warns him back. He is pushing against an invisible wall. Fat strands of wet seaweed catch his feet and ankles, but nothing holds him back. He is determined. As he gets closer to the shore-line, he turns to face her and waves with his back to the water. A rough breaker overtakes him. She screams out to warn him but he can't hear her through the bel-lowing of the wind. He disappears into the ocean.

She told him not to go. Why didn't he listen?

⤳

Shadowbox: Remains

The back of a wooden cigar box is painted black with spirals of burnt orange, red and gold fire. A gray floor seeps into green relief painted with dots of purple grapes, overturned miniature boxes of glued-together toothpicks, a paper doll, and a cut-out of silver candlesticks.

Lisa woke to the sound of the waves rushing the beach. She looked around the unfamiliar room — a tall gouged dresser, a lamp with a seashell base, pictures of a man and boy holding up a fish and standing on the beach with blowing dunes behind them. The woman had been kind to bring her here. What was her name? Ella? Ellen? No. Isabel. Isabela. She thought of her grandmother. She would have done the same thing, take in a stranger like a stray puppy who needed a good home or, at the very least, to get out of the cold.

She wasn't sure whether she wandered down to the beach again last night or thought she did. She must not have. How would she have found her way back to this hard, narrow bed? Her random thoughts took her back to her family. Her grandmother, mother, and aunts lived in perpetual worry about tempting fate. They knocked on wood. They said *poo-poo-poo* after a compliment. It was bad luck to go to a baby shower before the birth. How do you know the baby won't be born dead?

But, the belief that made the biggest impression on Lisa was *you sing in the morning and cry in the afternoon.* Waiting to embrace the worst seemed to be in the genes. Lisa never wanted to believe them. But maybe they knew better.

*Look what happened when I was only sixteen and what about when I came to this country and…*yes, Gram, tell me your story. Remind me how lucky I am. Lisa lay stiffly on her back, pulled the quilt up to her neck and closed her eyes, ready for her Grandma's life of misfortune to wash over her. *Remember this: somebody always has worse troubles than you.*

Grandma would always begin her story the same way. *Mama and Papa whispered to each other late at night over their tea. Papa's big warm hands covered Mama's. Ach, the words we didn't know: riots, soldiers, Cossacks, pogrom. We learned fast that it meant neighbors killing Jews, village by village. It's all anyone talked about. What to do? Where to go?*

The week before my sixteenth birthday, Papa was reading us a story — the eight of us gathered around him. His voice was thick as honey, but the firelight showed deep lines of worry across his forehead and between his eyes. I wasn't really listening. I wondered if Mama would make me a new dress for my birthday. All at once, we heard distant rumbling in the night, different from thunder. Papa's voice was drowned out by the sound of the Cossacks on their galloping horses, drawing nearer.

Lisa's heart always beat in sync with her grandma's rhythmic smacking of her palm on the table, gaining speed, the stampede of horses, the sound reverberating, loud to her even then, decades later. The sound of a life pummeled and then pounded into the earth.

Grandma's life disappeared in the crackling of their burning home. All of her Papa's wealth was in his grapes. Now, with his land charred and vines hacked apart, he had nothing. He scraped together passage to America for his children by doing menial jobs, bartering the little that was left, making deals so that two by two, an older child with a younger one could get out. In his own Noah's Ark, the children would be saved.

It was years before they were a family once more. Except for Grandma's sister Tati. America turned its back on her.

So she had a little infection making her eye pink. What was the big deal? Imagine being sick and having to take that filthy boat back to Romania alone. Vey is mir. We never heard from her again. Grandma being grandma was sure Tati jumped overboard and was eaten by sharks. What else could she do?

Liselah, you can't imagine the stink of the sick vomiting and doing you-know-what all over the place. Down below you couldn't breathe. We were packed in like

6

rotten fish. The water seemed to be angry with this boat we were on. Throwing us around in the big black water that sank the Titanic. Did you know I had never seen such big water? And swimming? How you did that, I didn't know. We were afraid to eat the little that was offered. What kept us alive, you wonder? Same as everybody. Hope. We owed our families. We believed that in America, we would survive. No one would want to kill or rape us just because we were Jews.

When they saw the Lady, Tante Golde and Grandma hugged and danced right up on the deck. If they'd known they were going to be herded around and examined like goats for sale, maybe they would have jumped overboard during the voyage like so many others. They stood in lines for a doctor, to have their teeth inspected, to wash off the filth of the trip. They couldn't even keep their names. Not such a good welcome, but thank God, she'd never have to get on a boat again. *God forbid I should ever take a ferry to Staten Island. Never. Never. Never.*

"That's enough, Grandma. Cut. It's time for you to *sha stil*," Lisa whispered softly, "I don't want to hear anymore." Lisa put her hands over her ears, rolled over and fell into a troubled sleep.

Sweet Breads and Lemon Cakes

Lisa woke up in the late morning and went into the kitchen to make a pot of coffee. While waiting, she wiped a circle of condensation from the back window. She couldn't see Commercial Wharf or the dark, turbulent ocean beyond it, but, she could hear it growling. Waves rushed the beach, gulls shrieked. Lisa hoped none of the fishermen were going out that day. She opened the back door to breathe in the air. It felt moist and smelled like snow. In Provincetown, a lacy carpet of silent flakes would fall and disappear as quietly as it came. She heard Isabela trudging up the steps.

"I didn't expect you'd be up yet." Isabela put on the sweater that was draped on the back of her chair.

"How many days have I been here? I've lost track."

"Just two."

The coffeepot on the stove stopped percolating. "Do you want a cup of coffee?" Lisa asked.

"Sure." Isabela lowered herself slowly onto the kitchen chair. Lisa put a cup of coffee on the table and Isabela took a sip. "Ah. You make a good cup of coffee. Strong." Isabela massaged the base of her spine.

Lisa asked, "Did you hurt yourself?"

"With the snow moving in, my arthritis is acting up." Isabela winced.

"Why don't you rest this afternoon? I can work the counter," Lisa offered.

Isabela arched her eyebrows, looking at the girl whose hair was a tangled mess, with puffy purple circles under her eyes, in an old flannel nightgown washed so often the little red cherry pattern was a faded pink.

"Why so surprised? If I'm going to stay a few more days, let me at least help you." Lisa said.

"You sure? You don't have to."

"I want to. I'll go wash up, get dressed, and go down. Thanks for the nightgown."

Isabela nodded.

Lisa stood up. "What do I need to know?"

"Mary is there. She has an hour left on her shift. Go down and tell her you'll be working the counter when she leaves. It's not that busy this time of year. Make sure she shows you how to wrap things up proper. I don't want any of the pastries smushed up."

Lisa raised one hand and put the other over her heart. "No smushing, I promise."

"I'm serious. Things have to be done just so. And if any kids come in, give them broken cookies. They always ask so don't be giving them anything we could sell. I know Mary does, but don't you start. When Martin Cross comes in this afternoon, he will expect his party order to be ready. It just needs to be boxed. His order slip is next to the register. He is very particular and comes in every day, so do it right."

"Anything else?" Lisa put her coffee cup in the sink.

"No, that's all. I'm going to take some aspirin and lie down."

With no tourists, Provincetown was quiet and relaxed. Lisa liked filling trays with cinnamon sweet bread, anise cookies, and almond biscotti.

One of the display cases was filled with linguica and cheese, a Portuguese croissant; and torta de laranga, orange tortes. In the slow season, Isabela made her assortment of pastries once a week. All the locals knew that, so they'd sell quickly. For the rest of the week, she only baked bread.

Martin ordered bolinos de bacalhau, salted codfish cakes, and shrimp pies for his party. When he came in for his order, he invited Lisa.

"You must come. I'll introduce you to everyone." Martin said.

Lisa forced a smile. "Thanks, anyway. I'm not in a partying mood."

"I know. I know. You're a mermaid and you washed up ashore. You must come and tell us the story of your life at sea. We all love a good story. This time of year is so boring."

"I can't, Martin, but thanks for the invitation."

"If you change your mind, this is the address." He scribbled on a slip of paper he found in his pocket.

"I'm sure it'll be a great party. Have fun."

"Thanks, doll." He waved goodbye.

Lisa turned over the closed sign and locked the door when the bread was gone. She was tired but it was a good tired. Maybe her fatigue would keep the *goniff* of her sleep away and she could pass through one dreamless night.

When she went upstairs, Isabela was at the stove. "I made fish chowder. Want some?"

"It smells great."

They sat down at the kitchen table. The steaming bowls held a creamy mélange of cod and vegetables. They broke off chunks of bread, browned on the bottom, which they couldn't sell. It came out dark, but the inside was light and delicious.

"We must talk," Isabela said, sopping up the last of the soup with the bread.

Lisa's eyes welled up with tears. "I suppose you must be ready for me to leave."

"No, child, that's not it." She looked past her. "I found you mourning like fishermen's widows who go down to the beach before dawn and walk aimlessly as you did. The wailing is heartbreaking. The ocean absorbs their tears, just like it took their men. It's our way of life but not yours."

Lisa swirled her spoon from one side of the bowl to the other. "Martin said I was a mermaid you fished out of the sea."

Isabela shook her head. "Gossips."

Lisa once again felt tears rising up in her. "Do you do this often? Rescue wailing widows?"

"What do you take me for? I've got enough on my own." Isabela straightened her back. "I have never done this before. You can be very sure of that. Do I strike you as someone looking for trouble? I've got plenty without taking on more."

"I'm sorry, I didn't mean anything."

"It's odd, though. I almost never take the car to Race Point when I can walk to the Harbor."

Lisa wiped away her tears with the back of her hand. She could taste her saltiness and swallowed her hesitation. "Isabela, I'm going out on a limb. But here goes. What do you think about this? I liked working in the bakery this afternoon and I'd like to learn to bake Portuguese bread." She looked straight into the old woman's eyes. "When I was a little girl, my grand-mother taught me. We'd bake challah every Friday. It's the sweet, braided Jewish bread for Sabbath. I'd love for you to teach me, too. The bread you bake has a sweet taste to it. It's just wonderful."

"That's because it's simple bread. Flour, sugar, eggs, milk, butter, yeast and a touch of lemon."

"Like my Grandma's: few ingredients but lots of advice. Sometimes I think the stories she told were baked right into the bread." Lisa paused. "Now she is gone, too. Just last year."

"I like it quiet so you can hear the bread, its bubbling yeast, the slap of the kneading, the hollow sound it has when it comes out of the oven." Isabela filled the kettle. "Don't you have a job, a home, friends, family?"

"Of course I do. But I think that everyone would be happy to have a breather from me. My good friends don't know how to comfort me and are tired of trying. Ditto for my family." Lisa's eyes misted and her voice cracked. "My boss put me on leave until I can pull myself together. I work with children and seeing me upset isn't good for them. My other job is on hold. I was also doing some research for our friend who was on sabbatical. But he also wanted to get as far as he could from Boston for awhile. He and Mac were like brothers." Lisa pushed her hair from her face. "Phil is so distraught he's wandering across the country. He asked me to go with him but I couldn't. Being with him, without Mac, was out of the question."

"What happened to Mac if you don't mind my asking?" Isabela asked.

"Car accident." Lisa looked down. "He hit a tree trying to avoid a deer."

"I'm very sorry." She paused. "You're right, though. Running doesn't help. I've seen more than my share of that. So what limb were you talking about?"

Lisa's head was bowed and she took a deep breath before looking up. "I paid the rent for our apartment. I like the idea of banging around the dough and making beautiful sweets." Lisa got up to clear the table. "When I went into the back room, I was amazed at what you can turn out in such a small space, with the mix of pans and mismatched bowls, hanging pots and a work surface just the size of a kitchen table. I bet you have the same pans you've always used."

"Of course. You can't buy anything as good now."

Lisa smiled. "I can help with other things too. Take care of the apartment, pitch in with the cooking."

"Wait a minute." Isabela put her hand up to stop her. "You don't have to sell me on your usefulness. I just don't want you hiding here."

"How long do the widows go to the beach?" Lisa poured the boiling water into two heavy mugs for tea.

"The teabags are in the small canister on the counter and the honey is in the cabinet to the right." Isabela floated the tea bag over the water and put it in Lisa's mug, then stirred in a heaping spoon of honey. "The widows? They mourn for as long as it takes to run out of tears. They live with fear. Lost fishermen are a fact of life, but it doesn't make it any easier. We help each other and everyone pitches in. It's an unspoken tradition."

"Did you lose your husband that way?"

Isabela shook her head. "No. When we were first married, my husband and his brother bought a fishing boat. But Stefan was no fisherman. He couldn't stand the smell. He'd scrub and scrub but the fish stink went right through his pores. He said he felt like the dead fish lived in his body.

When the bakery came up for sale, we took a chance. At first, he didn't even know how to bake a cupcake. But he took to it — especially the pastries. When the tourists came, they'd buy us out. We couldn't keep ahead of them. They sold as soon as we brought them out. The line was out the door," she smiled. "Mine are pretty good but nowhere near his."

She sipped the sweet tea. "Ah, my Stefan. He loved everything about it but the hours. He had a heart attack right in the bakery as he waited on a customer. He was gone before the ambulance came. We'd been married thirty-nine years." Isabela twirled the narrow gold band on her finger. "We owned the bakery for thirty of them. I had to carry on. I'm not the kind of woman that can go to Florida and play cards. I like the ocean, cold and rough. It suits me." Isabela sighed. "For him, I'm glad it was fast. His brother had a terrible cancer."

"I'm so sorry, Isabela." Lisa reached over to lightly touch Isabela's hand and then cupped her hands around the warm mug. The day's broken cookies were left untouched.

A few minutes later, Lisa said, "I feel a different kind of tired today. It's the first time I've had a stretch of peace since Mac, since that day that ... I'm not thinking about anything but whether or not I can fit the turnovers in the box so they don't get smushed."

Isabela didn't answer right away. Lisa let quiet sit between them, leaving her space to think. "How about if I pay you to work the counter three afternoons a week and bake with me two nights? I can't take away from Mary. You won't be staying that long."

"No pay. I'd like to work in exchange for my room here."

Isabela frowned. "Don't be ridiculous. Nobody works for free."

"I wouldn't be. I'm working for room and board. So, do we have a deal?" Lisa asked.

Isabela shook Lisa's hand. "Now, call your mother. You must have a mother worrying about you somewhere. Let her know you haven't been kidnapped or swallowed by a whale or something crazy like that." Isabela took her soup bowl and mug to the sink. "I have plenty of old nightgowns and socks. Both the thrift store and general store stay open all winter so you can pick up the clothes and toiletries you need." She fixed the pins holding up her hair. "I'm going out for awhile to visit a friend."

"Can I hug you?" Lisa walked toward her.

Isabela shrugged. "You want to hug me because I'm putting you to work?"

"We already shook hands to seal the deal. I want to hug you because I want to hug you."

Lisa came around the table to put her arms around Isabela and when she hugged her, she thought she heard Isabela sigh.

"Hi, Mom. It's me."

"Lisa, I've been calling and calling. Even Amy doesn't know where you are. She said she hadn't been able to reach you in days. You're not even at work."

"I'm sorry I worried you."

"I tried to stay calm. I was giving it one more day and then Daddy and I were coming to knock down your door."

Lisa laughed. "What a picture! You don't have to knock down any doors but it's a nice thought."

"What's so funny?"

"The image of you kicking open a door!"

"Always with the jokes. If you're not in your apartment then where are you?" her mother asked.

"I'm in Provincetown and I'm going to stay here for a few weeks. I'm working in a bakery. The woman who owns it lives upstairs and is letting me stay in her spare room."

"That's *mishuganah*. How did this happen? You're going to live with a stranger?"

"No, Mom, it's anything but crazy. I can't focus on anything. The routine of the bakery is good for me. She reminds me of Grandma in some ways, except she's Portuguese. Baking and selling bread is what I need to do right now. It's good for me to do methodical things like packing boxes of pastries and bread. It's physical and I don't have to think. "

"How about when you start to think again, you think about coming home."

"Mom, I don't know what I'm going to do. Let me give you the telephone number. Got paper?"

"Just a minute."

She heard her mother rustling papers. Lisa gave her mother the phone number and address. "Don't worry, Mom. The worst thing that could happen to me already did. Maybe I don't have to worry about any more shoes dropping."

"Ah, your grandma, may she rest in peace, filling your head with all her silly superstition."

"You don't believe it?"

"What I believe is this. You've had a terrible thing happen. Everything in Boston reminds you. If you come home to Albany, you can start fresh. Get an apartment, find a new job. Your family is here."

"I'll think about it, Mom."

"Thank God you called and are all right."

"Give my love to Daddy." Lisa blew a kiss into the receiver.

Chapter Three

Mac: A Man with a Plan

∽

After five years of teaching, I'm already asking myself how people do this year after year, class after bloody class. During all those years of coursework, research, and writing my dissertation, it never once occurred to me that I'd be teaching kids who had no interest in learning anything. So far, the majority of my students could care less about school. They're not dumb. They have good minds but they're distracted. Fire trucks and police cars, flashing lights and screaming sirens blaze down Commonwealth Avenue, pulling students out of bed and into the street while the dorms are searched for bombs. The girls stand in the street in provocative T-shirts and coats thrown loosely over nightgowns, giving the boys hard-ons. And then they come to class either tired or stoned or wasted from the night before.

They are preoccupied. I can relate but there is a limit. I sweated bullets wondering if I'd keep my student deferment year after year, but when they instituted the draft lottery, I got lucky for once in my life. My April 20th birthday was number 345.

Man, I know what it's like to be in the middle of the action. I went to Columbia, a hotbed of political protest. Militant groups like the Weathermen and Students for a Democratic Society planted bombs and occupied buildings, planned rebellion on campus, at Army Recruiting Centers, and downtown on Wall Street. The rhetoric was blistering; anger spilled into the crowds and across the country.

One Sunday afternoon, I was walking with my girlfriend, Sandy. We were going to see a flick in Times Square called *The King of Hearts*. It was a French movie set right after World War I about a soldier opening the door to an insane asylum, giving the patients freedom to take over the town. It was so cool. Showed who was really crazy. As we walked toward the train after the movie, Sandy said to me, "What's that horrible smell? It's like rubber or burning hair or something." She was right. A crowd was gathering on 42nd street at Eighth. I pushed through the crowd and saw the horror of a guy who set himself on fire. I was so shaken I couldn't console her. My eyes stung from the smoke. What possible good could come from that? Talk about crazy.

Don't get me wrong, I went to some volatile protests and rallies myself. The war was wrong and we were angry. Violence would escalate really fast – some ending with kids being arrested, dragged by the hair by the fuzz who were angry about being jeered at, or flipped the bird, or just plain sick of the hassle. The worst I suffered was some tear gas. I focused on my classes. After all, I wasn't slogging through the jungle, running away to Canada, or rotting in jail. I wasn't forced to do those things because I was a student. Had to respect that.

The war was on the TV news showing pictures of body bags, burning villages, and swampy rice paddies. It was all so pointless. Just like a kid's body smoldering on a beautiful Sunday afternoon.

❧

I know what it feels like to have people you love vanish. My father died suddenly when I was ten and my life went dark. My father would dance my mother around the kitchen, whisper to her, and she'd exhale a peal of laughter that drifted toward me. Our house was alive; beams of light shimmered through us. When I was small, Dad would hoist me up on his shoulders, walk in the woods, and tell me the names of trees, rocks, streams. We went fishing and on trips to see aunts, uncles, and cousins.

When he died, my mother's high spirits were buried with him as was our world of fish and deer and spotting birds, naming flowers and reading books together. My mother did the things required of a mother, I suppose. My clothes were clean, she made my lunch (I can still smell the tuna fish sandwiches switched off with peanut butter and jelly) and dinner. We'd sit across the table from one another, her eyes staring past me as she sat on her chair, stone-faced, picking at her food, while the TV wailed to fill up the room.

A couple of months after my father's accident, I picked up the phone extension to hear who she was talking to. (My mother's friends had dropped off one by one, unable to console her.) At that moment, I knew I would be completely alone. Dad's sister, my Aunt Mary, was on the line. "Let him stay with us until you pull yourself together. You can barely take care of yourself, let alone a young boy. We'd love to have him. James would want you to..."

My mother, the woman who barely had the breath to ask a question, screamed into the phone, "You're not taking my son. Never, ever call this house again!" She slammed down the phone, ran into her room and sobbed into her pillow. I stood in the doorway watching her, hating her more with each passing minute. I pleaded, "Mom, please let me go for a little while. I promise it won't be for long." She didn't answer. I screamed, "Mommy, I don't want to stay here with you. Please let me go live with them for just a little while. Please."

She turned her head to look at me, not saying a word. An odd look passed across her face and she turned away from me. With that single phone call, everyone I loved evaporated.

My father had been a high school English teacher and his study was lined with bookcases. He read books to me and would laugh and say by the time I got to college we'd have read every book in the room. It was stuffy now but still had the lingering scent of his pipe tobacco in the air. I remember watching him puff out the smoke and tap his pipe on an ashtray to start fresh, with new tobacco and a new thought about something he was reading to me. I took his pipe and the tobacco. Since my mother couldn't bear to go in there, she never knew.

Time passed. My school years flew and summers dragged. College would only be possible with financial help. I wanted to go to the best school. I wanted my father to be proud of me, to know that I'd made something out of my life.

When I started high school, I calculated how I would make myself well-rounded, attractive to colleges. I became editor of the school newspaper, played football, and was senior class president. My plan worked and I never deviated: scholarship to Columbia, doctorate in literature, dissertation published, and be the best damn teacher my students would ever have.

It was the teacher part that stymied me. How could I take my students on a journey when they resisted getting in the car? I was teaching in the days of free love and Haight-Ashbury and war protests that were always a stimulant for getting laid; there was no sex shortfall. But Christ, I didn't expect offers to barter for a better grade. I was on tenure track and would never risk that for a piece of ass.

Last semester, I had three freshmen and a sophomore offer themselves up braless and panty-less. Cop a feel for a B? All the way for an A? There was no possible misunderstanding. They were direct, coming into my space, touching me, leaning over my desk. Did they really think I would give a grade they didn't deserve for a roll in the hay? What they didn't know about me is that if they'd come into my office to actually talk about a book, I might have considered it.

My college buddy, Phil Rhoades, who came to Boston with me, warned me to lighten up. "Mac, you aim too high. Reaching one kid a semester is a reasonable goal. What do you think? That everyone lives and dies by the novels they've read?" I'd tell him, "That's easy for you to say. Science is definite and it draws a different kind of student."

"Not true but I don't want to debate it with you. At least you don't have any intro classes this semester. How you talked your department chair out of assigning you the lecture hall scene is amazing. Be grateful."

☙

I looked at the clock and then at the last student in. She slid into an empty chair in the middle of the classroom, third row, third seat, probably to avoid my direct line of vision. Wow. She was a beauty. A head of messy black curls, some escaping from the clip at the nape of her neck, high color in her cheeks, clear, sharp eyes and a tall, angular body.

"Nice of you to join us, Ms?"

"Stern. Lisa Stern." She looked up at the clock on the wall behind him. "It's only 9:59." She pointed to the clock and smiled.

I looked over my shoulder. "It seems Ms. Stern is correct."

I waited for the minute hand to jump and I smiled. "Okay, then. Let's begin. I'm Dr. MacKenzie Taylor and this is ENG 450 Section A29, Seminar in Contemporary American Literature. Are you all in the right class, right section?

Good. Here is the short version of the first day of class drill. I do not lecture. This is a discussion seminar and I expect you to be ready to discuss each book on the syllabus. I'll assign frequent short papers to help you develop your critical thinking skills. If this isn't for you, now is the time to make up your mind. I have a wait list. Questions?" I paused and looked up. Only Lisa looked back at me, her eyes bright, attentive.

"Good, then everyone got the reading list in advance and re-read *The Great Gatsby* and I'm sure you realized that this wasn't the book you thought you read in high school." I loved this book. Everything about it except the car accident. Whenever I read the scene when Myrtle was killed, it made me go cold. But, I had to get over it. I'm sure my father would say it's the perfect book. Don't go soft on me. It had to happen that way.

I scanned the room at the faces in an array of expressions all seeming to say *are you kidding? Just give us the syllabus and dismiss us like any other professor on the first day.* So, here we go again. You think their parents know they're throwing away their money?

A blonde sitting next to Lisa snickered at the thought of having finished a book for the first day of class. Two boys, one with a blonde ponytail, the other with a head of red curls and a bushy beard, slouched down, their legs stretched out, staring down at their notebooks. The others had different versions of *please don't call on me* etched all over their faces.

I set my gaze on each student assessing how vacuous they were. There had to be intelligence in some of those faces. But only Lisa Stern looked at me. Leaning against the front desk, I rolled up my shirt sleeves.

"First, let's get out of these rows and pull the desks into a circle." The students moved the desks into some semblance of a circle, trying to avoid where I might sit. Except for Lisa. She positioned herself directly across from me, rolling up her own sleeves as if to signal that she, too, was ready for work.

"Why do you think I wanted to begin the semester with this book?" I scanned the faces in one sweep. "No ideas? Don't you see this story as America's story? It's about the American dream!"

Lisa murmured, "Of course, dummy us."

"Ms Stern, a comment?"

"No, sorry."

"Anybody?" I waited. "Come on. Is it a love story, a rags-to-riches story, a tragedy? What?"

Lisa flipped through the book looking for a clue. What did she remember? Not much. Gatsby in a white suit throwing big parties, Daisy not being worth all the trouble, and Myrtle being run over by a car.

I looked at her, longing to hear something intelligent. "Lisa, what do you think?"

"Um, what I think is..."

"Yes?" Our eyes locked. I wasn't letting her off the hook.

"I think that, well, aside from it being a story of the American Dream, it's about possibility. Yes. Possibility."

"Go on," I coaxed.

"Maybe Gatsby reinvents himself just as all the immigrants coming here did." She hesitated. "Immigrants believe if they work hard enough, they can attain their dreams. The streets of America are paved with gold and everybody thinks that they can be a millionaire. Gatsby is like most of us. Big dreams he thinks he can make happen. But it isn't always so easy to break into social groups."

"Not in the in-group in high school? Their mistake." I smiled and looked around. Her face flushed. "Who else?"

"I'm Nina. I sort of think Nick was a little obsessed, too. Everything he did revolved around Gatsby. Gatsby this. Gatsby that. Who is he? What is he doing? He is obsessed."

"Yes, Nina, good." I got out of my chair and walked around the circle.

"It's a sad story, I think," chimed in a blonde girl, sitting taller in her chair.

"What makes it sad?"

She shrugged. "Nobody gets what they want."

"True." I scanned the students' faces. "Didn't the language pull you right in? Fitzgerald is masterful in painting word pictures. Turn to page thirteen. Nick Caraway first arrives at Tom and Daisy's house."

I couldn't keep my eyes off her as I recited the passage. "Are there any parts that particularly struck you?"

A boy half-raised his hand. "I was kind of reminded of what's happening now with the war."

"The class divisions never end," chimed in a skinny boy in an army jacket.

"Tell me more." I sat down and stretched out my legs.

"Who is getting drafted and who is getting deferred? If we were in Gatsby's time, would Tom be drafted? Probably not. His father would only have to make a call or put him back in school. If he went into the military, it would be by choice and then he'd go as a commissioned officer. But Myrtle's husband wouldn't have the same choice."

"Excellent point. Anyone else?"

The fire alarm rang. The shrill sound set off chaos. Outside the classroom, the halls were filling with students making their way out of the building. I shouted over the clanging, "For next time, I want you to write a paper on an obsession you have. We all have them. Three pages. Okay, let's get out of here."

We rushed down the stairs out onto Commonwealth Avenue. The fire trucks, police cars, and an ambulance stopped in front of the building; their sirens were earsplitting. Lisa scowled.

I walked over to her. "What's the matter?"

"I hate this. We had alarms at both three and six this morning. I almost didn't come out the second time."

I shook my head. "It's costing the University a fortune."

Lisa shrugged. "Dr. Taylor, can I ask you something?

"Of course."

"Have you memorized the entire book?"

"No," I laughed. "But more than I'd admit to!"

She grinned. "And the others on our list?"

"You'll just have to wait and find out."

"I guess I will."

I knew I was standing too close to her but I couldn't help it. She smelled like wild strawberries. "I'm taking your class because my roommate, Amy Wilson, insisted. I think it's fair to say that you got her hooked on reading. Now she reads fiction to relax in between labs. Total transformation. I'm more social science than humanities. In fact, I am starting an internship soon at Bridgeton Prison. But, I have a feeling your class may change me somehow too. If Gatsby is any example, your love of books is..." she flushed. "Oh, listen to me blubbering like an idiot. I'm sorry. Words have a way of falling out of my mouth."

I laughed. "Please blubber on. It's the reason I teach. You've given me a reason to live."

"See you next time." She smiled and I watched her as she walked down the sidewalk and disappeared into the crowd.

∾

"Good morning, everyone. This is my suggestion for today's session. There are twelve of you in this seminar. We don't have a lot of time together and I want you to get to know one another. You know where I'm going with this. I can see you sliding down the chairs." I laughed. "You can run but you can't hide, as they say." The students looked everywhere but at me.

"Everyone reads their paper. The rules are that you listen, you make no judgment, you think about how this particular obsession affects their lives, whether you can relate to it, whether you think it is honest. Who wants to go first?"

Lisa raised her hand. "Since we all have to read, I'll go first. I want to get it over with."

"Good philosophy."

"Okay, here goes."

> If you'd asked this question to anybody in my family they'd say, without even thinking about it, that I am an obsessive person. I don't think it's the right word for what I am. But maybe it is.

22

Here is an example. I love art and I love the idea of being creative. The problem is that I really have no talent for traditional mediums. That is an understatement. I stink.

She stopped and looked up. "Go on," I said, laughing along with the rest of the class.

The results of my efforts were abysmal. My mother has a collection of uneven ashtrays, lopsided cups and watercolors that don't seem to resemble anything recognizable. My violin teacher suggested I try dancing. The teacher in my Israeli dance troupe asked me if there was something wrong with my ears that prevented me from hearing the beat of the music.

But I was undeterred. I knew in my heart that I was an artist and nobody could tell me otherwise. Sometimes things happen for you. Sometimes you have to make them happen.

One day, I was in the library and I read something about an artist named Joseph Cornell. He wasn't a trained artist. I think he worked in textiles or was a salesman or something. He was a quirky collector of objects, picking up other people's discards and creating something new from them. He imagined and arranged new worlds inside boxes. The book had beautiful pictures. They were so interesting to look at – movie stars, birds, paper cut-outs, postcards. Many of them were finished worlds sealed with glass panels. Others were called *Explorations* because he kept the collected material loose in the box for people to sift through and interpret their own way.

He was called a visionary and what he did was called assemblage art. While I was short on talent, lack of imagination was never my problem. That was it. I would become an assemblage artist. I've been told that is a very pretentious name so let's just say, I make boxes with different themes and messages.

I knew then I had found a medium that would be perfect for me and I began collecting. I'd wait until an idea formed in my mind. Using my father's wooden cigar boxes and jewelry cases from my uncle's store, I created little worlds.

I titled my favorite box, *Possibilities*. I covered the box with bits of a world map and overlaid it with pictures from exotic places. Then I decoupaged the box to give it a lacquered, shiny finish. Inside I found women's faces – all ages, races, nationalities from my uncle's *National Geographics*, and laid them out inside the box. My mother gave me a broken miniature china doll that she played with as a child and one of my father's marbles. I anchored the torso of the broken doll, holding up a beautiful white marble stone. Strewn around her was a tiny doll, a painted briefcase and books I made out of cardboard. I felt I was creating something to help me understand my view of the world. I'm sure no one would consider me an artist but it's the closest I can come.

I think that obsession is tenacity that comes naturally. You can't help but be who you are. I admire Gatsby for trying to make his dream come true. Isn't that the best definition of obsession? If you really want something, you have to have tunnel vision. Forget the distractions around you and go for it. I have very strong opinions about things that I want to change and once I make up my mind, I work hard. I don't know if you call that obsession or not. But if it is, I think it's a good thing.

She looked up. "That's it."

Intriguing. Joseph Cornell. I'll have to look him up. Maybe she'd raise the bar for this class. "Yes, I, too, think it is a good thing. Thank you, Lisa. Who's next?"

Chapter Four

∿

Shadowbox: Ships of Hope

A cardboard cutout of Noah's Ark is anchored to the back of the box.
In the foreground, pairs of giraffes, lions, and monkeys separate pairs
of people- a mother is separated from her child, a man and woman
lose sight of one another. Both the animals and people look toward a
spot of sandy ground and tall grasses. A sign over
the land reads: Survival.

Isabela didn't have a lot to say. She didn't ask many questions and made it clear she wasn't going to join any pity party. The yeasty smell of bread rising, the kneading and shaping of the bread was a tonic, filling up desolate spaces with melt-in-your-mouth sugar cookies and warm cinnamon buns.

You think life is easy, Liselah. Well if you think that, you are wrong. Don't be such a baby. Here I come all across the big ocean, thinking that was the end of my misery. Then what happens to me and Golde? We're taken in by family who make us feel like we're taking the food out of their mouths. Oy, they were fatsos and couldn't share a few potatoes? Hazzers they were. Greedy pigs. I knew I had to do something quick. So I married Herschel. Not such a great idea but I had to take a chance. And you should too. Gnug. It's enough.

Her grandmother's incessant chattering in her head wasn't the only reason Lisa was groggy and lethargic. She slept on and off, in and out of dreams, with no sense of time or memory or of leaving her bed to wander. Maybe she only imagined getting up.

Her dreams played out as movies, all different but with the same panic — being separated from her Grandma on the ship to America; becoming separated from her roommate, Amy, as police on horseback rush the crowd during a war protest; walking a labyrinth, unable to find the way out, Mac outside the maze in gradually fading shadow.

But then, she'd pull herself back into the semi-conscious mix of dream with reality. She picked out vignettes to handle gingerly, wanting to tread lightly, leaving a path that would always lead back to him.

Lisa flipped through the neat pile of magazines that Isabela subscribed to and customers left for her. The variety — *National Geographic, Bakers Quarterly, Provincetown Journal, Yankee Times* — stimulated her to start working on her boxes again. Isabela gave her pie boxes but when Lisa told her they were too flimsy, she found shoeboxes. Her subjects weren't pretty, her frame of mind still dark; a woman crouching over a dead child, kneeling among blood streaked newspapers; a woman's arms pulled off as she is stretched between a baby doll and a dancer; a drawing of a plump woman and a young girl standing together on a fissure, the background painted in uneven gray blocks; and one that would stay unfinished for now — a crumpled car ad, a brown papier-mâché log, and an unclear brown shape in deep background, alert, standing tall.

As Lisa finished them, Isabela put them out in the bakery on a ledge on the back wall. The librarian came in one morning and asked if she could take them to the library. Wouldn't Lisa like to have a reception where she could talk about them? People look forward to getting out in the winter.

That was fine but she longed for an idea to germinate and take root. Her mind was dull and for the first time in her life, she considered herself slow-witted. A few short years before, life was breaking open. Thrust into the protest against the Vietnam War, making abortion legal, and working with kids, Lisa planned to be someone who changed things, someone doing something that mattered. That was what Mac loved most about her. Who was she now, consumed with thoughts about widows and shadows and dead ends? Would her mind-numbing bleakness be permanent? She had to pull herself out of the wreckage of Mac's crashed car.

Get Ready World, Here I Come

True, she had false starts and wasn't as brave as she hoped. But at least Lisa tried to overcome her fear of falling into Alice's rabbit hole. She cringed when she thought back to her first internship in a maximum security prison. Sociology courses in deviant behavior had made her want to see a prison firsthand. But her experience there was a total bust. Who was she kidding? Her roommate, Amy, knew it wouldn't work, but there was no convincing Lisa otherwise. Her professor, Dr. Kessler, didn't want to place her there either, but she insisted.

Back in her room after her first day, she fell apart. "Amy, as soon as I heard the door click shut, I got so scared. You know Kevin and Sean, who are doing this internship with me, would be no help if I needed it. I probably weigh more than Sean and Kevin is a pacifist."

"You really wanted to do this. Dr. Kessler warned you. He said that Bridgeton State could be rough. You wouldn't consider going to that minimum security prison."

Irate, Lisa asked, "And what would be the point of that? What would I do for tax cheats? Clean their cells?" she fumed. "I hope I never see the inside of a prison again. I don't think I'm going to any more demonstrations."

Amy groaned.

"No way will I be a social worker or a public defender," Lisa ranted. "And who exactly would choose to work in a prison?"

Amy sat down on Lisa's bed with her. "As a matter of fact, my cousin Dick does. He thinks his work is important and so do I. Calm down and tell me what happened."

Dr. Kessler transported the three students to the prison. They drove up a long gravel road to a sprawling building with crumbling bricks and blacked-out windows with bars. The few plants around the entrance to the building were brown and withered. Lisa thought if she went in there, she too would come out looking like a dried-up shrub. To her, it looked like the set for a horror movie. Marlon Brando dragged in chains. The evil prison warden waiting to ... well, never mind that.

The warden came out of his office to welcome the new interns for the eight week rotation. Lisa's heart pounded so loud she thought it might jump out of her chest and fly across the room.

As an experiment, the prisoners were all mixed up at Bridgeton. The violent repeat offenders were mixed with first-time robberies. Lisa asked if she should be told who she was working with. Maybe she didn't want to teach a rapist to read. The warden told her that her question was inappropriate and she would be supervised so there shouldn't be any problems.

Sean went to the health clinic and Kevin to the shop area. Lisa waited for the warden to take a phone call. When he was finished, he told her not to worry. Agitated prisoners were calmed with medication. They walked down a bright hallway to the library and met Cora, the prison librarian. Lisa thought she might have been a linebacker but now was completely round with at least four chins sprouting black whiskers. Her ankles were fat and folded over on themselves. It was probably her only chance to be with men.

The doors slid shut when the warden left. The split second of silence was broken by Cora sneering, her voice raspy from bourbon and cigarettes. "What's your name again?"

"Lisa."

There were five men in the library. Their eyes were glazed over. Lisa was sure she was in the midst of *Night of the Living Dead*. The library was small. Bookcases lined three walls but the shelves were half-empty. One man stood staring at the shelves; three others each sat at separate tables and appeared to be reading. A fourth prisoner sat with Cora.

Cora yelled, "Charlie, get over here. You're going to get your GED if it kills one of us and it's not going to be me. You, Georgie take your book and...what's your name again?'

"Lisa."

"Lisa will listen to you read and don't give her any crap."

She was mean. Lisa didn't know who scared her more, Cora or the prisoners. Either way she was sure she'd be chopped liver in no time flat. Charlie went over to Cora, muttering under his breath. George had a book in his hand and sat next to Lisa.

He was tall and skinny with round watery eyes, his nose large and flat across his face. The drugs slowed him down and there was dried spit in the corners of his mouth. He mumbled his story to Lisa. He held up a grocery store to get money for his family. Nobody was meant to get hurt. He didn't mean to shoot the grocer. It wasn't supposed to go down that way. He licked his lips.

Sure, George. Things happen in a split second, Lisa thought.

Cora shouted, "George, shut up and open the book."

Lisa didn't care what he'd done as long as he didn't mind reading his book to her. When he got off track, he muttered or stared at Lisa or down at the book. He could hardly read. Maybe it was the drugs. It was a fifth grade level book and he could barely sound out the words.

Cora hollered, "Pay attention, George, or you're out of here. You'll go straight back to the kitchen."

"Yes sir," he tittered at his own joke.

"These do-gooders are a big waste of time. Useless," Cora scoffed.

Lisa felt useless. She couldn't get George to focus on the reading. The book, donated from an elementary school with *Property of* stamped all over it, was about twelve-year-olds on a treasure hunt. Lisa asked Cora if they could try another book, something he might relate to.

"Like what, Elise? You're here ten minutes and you're telling me how to run my library?"

"My name is Lisa." She was sorry she'd opened her big mouth. "Books like *The Autobiography of Malcolm X* or Eldridge Cleaver's *Soul on Ice.* Books like that."

"Are you out of your friggin' mind?" Cora roared. "You want to start a riot? Just do what I tell you to do."

"Sorry." Cowed, Lisa bent back over the book, pointing to the line she wanted George to read.

Cora snorted. "You sure are. A sorry pain in the ass."

Charlie snickered. George stared at Lisa's boobs, or lack thereof. A nightmare. It was the longest afternoon of her life. Lisa choked back tears during the silent ride home.

A girl with sense would not go back there. Mishuganah. What do you need to be working with killers and robbers for? They should deserve you? Take it from me. There are some people worth helping and some not. You should never know from being robbed.

Not now, Grandma. Do you have something to say about everything?

She went to Dr. Kessler's office the next day. "Lisa, I told you the prison assignment would be tough. If you don't feel safe, I don't want you there." He opened a file folder and pulled out the top sheet.

"I'm sorry, Dr. Kessler. I had no idea that I'd feel that way."

"It happens every year. We try to have the internship match the student but it doesn't always work at first. I had something else just called in today." He looked at her over his half-glasses. "A daycare center with a federal grant to train welfare mothers to be daycare providers."

Lisa shook her head. "A daycare center? No way."

"Didn't you tell me you volunteer at the Center for Legalizing Abortion? This is a perfect tie-in."

"How could babysitting do that?" she asked, incredulous.

"It will give you some experience with women, some of whom may not have become mothers by choice. And it will give you an opportunity to see how a grant works. It's a federal demonstration project, and if it works they'll be trying it in different areas around the country."

"A daycare center, Dr. Kessler? Come on. That's it? No other choices?"

"I know you had other ideas but the whole group has been placed. If I have to start looking for something else, you'll lose a couple of weeks. This is a full credit course and you might not have the time to log in the required hours."

Lisa looked down at her lap.

"Is your silence a yes?"

"I don't really have a choice. I guess if it's the daycare center or the prison, I'll have to take the daycare."

As Lisa opened the door to leave, he called after her, "Give it a chance, Lisa. Keep an open mind."

Yeah, right.

Disappointed in herself, in Dr. Kessler, in everything, she walked back to her dorm defeated.

I'm a quitter, she thought. *Big ideas and no moxie add up to a big zero.*

The daycare center was in Jamaica Plain. Lisa had never been there before but she knew that it was one of the original streetcar suburbs. It was home to a significant portion of the Emerald Necklace, an 1100 acre chain of parks, linked by waterways. Like Arbor Hill in Lisa's own hometown of Albany, Jamaica Plain had once been a thriving community. The many classic three-story houses that define nineteenth century New England architecture and commercial areas were abundant. Later on, it became an immigrant community for the Irish, Italian and Germans. But then many houses and commercial buildings were demolished for a federal road project that never came to pass, leaving the surrounding property devalued.

It was now a marginal, mixed area rather than one defined by single ethnic or racial groups as was commonplace in many Boston neighborhoods in the 1970s. It wasn't like Irish Southie or Italian North End, or black Roxbury. Rather it was more like Dorchester — a bit of a melting pot. It wasn't a great neighborhood, but Lisa thought that anything other than going into the projects would be better than the prison.

From the closest trolley stop, the Center was a six-block walk, across the turnpike bridge and then two more blocks. Lisa walked down streets with broken asphalt and cracked cobblestone, lined with dilapidated brown-stones. The daycare center was on a block of boarded-up storefronts and low-rise housing on one side and a mix of houses on the other. Four boys, who probably should have been in school, lounged on a stoop drinking beer. She walked fast to get past them but they didn't seem to notice her.

Lisa stopped in front of a small brick building. Brown butcher paper decorated the front of the Animal Crackers Day Care Center. *Suck it up, kiddo.*

The door was locked. She rang a bell and a girl about her age let her in and directed her to the office. Lisa tiptoed around children sleeping on blankets. She didn't see any adults at first. *Maybe they take naps too. That wouldn't be half bad.*

Around a corner was the small office. Lisa knocked on the door and opened it. Four women sat around a table.

"Excuse me for interrupting. I'm Lisa Stern. I'm looking for Ruby Williams. I was assigned here as an intern."

"Oh yes, Lisa, I'm sorry. I forgot you were starting today," Ruby said. The women gathered their papers together.

"Ladies, Lisa will be helping out on Tuesday and Thursday afternoons."

"Jesus, another college girl? What do you know about babies, anyway?"

Lisa looked at the tall woman wrapped in a swath of red and brown material. She had clear, mocha skin and wore a turban that matched the dress. "Excuse me?" Lisa asked.

"I asked you what you know about babies."

"Marika! Show some manners," Ruby said.

"What do I know about babies? Let's see." Lisa thought for a moment. "I was one?"

Ruby and the two other women laughed. "We need a sense of humor around here. Some people don't have one." She gave Marika a warning look.

"Lisa, I'm the director. And this is Virginia, Vera, and Marika." Marika was drawing in her notebook and didn't look up. "While we finish up, go into the kitchen. It's right around the corner. Pour apple juice into the Dixie cups — three quarters full — and put two boards of graham crackers on each napkin. We have twenty-five kids today. You will be with the three- and four-year olds."

The first day wasn't bad at all. The children were great and she liked reading to them and coloring apple trees which she later tacked up on a big bulletin board. Thereafter, she went every Tuesday and Thursday after class and arrived during naptime. She enjoyed getting the juice cups ready, portioning out the graham or animal crackers, squares of orange cheese, waking them up, folding up their blankets and stacking them out of the way.

Lisa was assigned to help Marika. Bad luck. She was angry at Lisa all the time regardless of what was happening. Vera was great with the children. Her soft-spoken commands sounded like drippy syrup. You couldn't help but want to do what she told you. "Don't you worry, honey," she whispered to Lisa. "Miss Queen Tut is just a big mouth, she can't help herself. Don't take it personally. Marika doesn't have a chip on her shoulder; it's more like a boulder." They laughed together.

Marika was always dressed regally. She wore bright turbans and long cotton dresses in primary colors with African designs, animal prints and other totems. Lisa wanted to say, *I get it. You're African royalty. Excuse me for living.* She was stiff and pissed off to begin with and having to work along-side a stupid, white college girl was obviously too much for her. And she was bossy. Lisa's stomach would turn to knots when she heard the swish-swish of Marika's dress coming her way.

"Lisa, mop up the apple juice over there. Lisa, did you make Isaiah cry again? Pick up the crayons and straighten up the paper, girl. Quit staring at me and do it."

She did as she told because she needed to keep this internship and was a little afraid of her. But Marika pushed too far. One afternoon after Lisa had been there about a month, Marika told Maurice, a little boy who was just potty trained, that he couldn't go to the bathroom until he finished his snack. He pooped right there sitting at the table and started to cry.

"Stinky, stinky," said the little girl sitting next to him.

Another boy held his nose. "Yuck, P. U."

Marika said, "Shame on you, Maurice." He sobbed, afraid to move. Annoyed, she yelled to Lisa, "Get him out of here before he stinks up the room."

"How could you?" Lisa countered. "You take him, Marika. It was your fault. And you should tell him that so he stops crying."

"Don't give me any back talk. Just do it."

"Marika," Lisa's breath was ragged, "get over yourself, will you? This is your fault. Just admit it and take care of him."

The Queen glared at Lisa and said nothing. The little boy hiccupped. Lisa wiped his face gently with a damp washcloth. She whispered to him, "It's okay, Maurice, Marika will take care of you."

"Out of my way, Lisa." She picked up Maurice with rigid arms so the smell didn't stink up the yards of material rustling around her.

Lisa whispered *fuck you* under her breath.

When Marika came back with him, he ran to sit in Lisa's lap and buried his head in her chest. Marika didn't talk to anyone the rest of the day.

Chapter Five

Marika

⌒⌒

Shadowbox: No Child Should Live Here

The back of the box was scribbled with graffiti. Crayon bubble letters
read Mary and Michael Forever, Fuck You Asshole. The floor had
gray lines of broken sidewalk, roughly drawn brown-shaped bottles,
crumpled paper as trash. On the side was a door hanging on an angle,
not quite fitting the door jam.

I didn't always live in a shithole. My father owned a package store in
Roxbury and my mother was a teacher. We lived in a brownstone with big
wide steps I used to play on. My mother made all my clothes and taught
me how to make a pattern.

Good thing she didn't wait to teach me things. Mama helped out at the
store on busy Saturday mornings. A junkie got his hands on a gun and came
in shooting. I was twelve.

Mama had one sister and Daddy didn't have anyone so I went to live
with my Aunt Cassie, Mama's baby sister who was a sometimes addict.
I guess there is no such thing as sometimes but there were times when

Aunt Cassie was almost, but not quite, responsible. And fun. Every once in a while, she'd try to take care of me and we'd do cool things. Sometimes we'd listen to some musician in the park and she would dance with herself, attracting quite a crowd. And she loved to try on clothes and hats at really fine department stores. If we ever bought anything, it was from Filene's Basement or secondhand. But trying on clothes was free, she'd always say, and would make up wild stories for the snooty salesladies. The few times we went to the movies, she'd sleep. I'd squeeze her hand hard so she'd wake up but then back to sleep she'd go. She didn't have the qualities to be a mother, if you know what I mean.

Mama always worried about her. She would have died all over again if she knew I was stuck living with her. Aunt Cassie lived in a two-family house. She moved there with a boyfriend who was long gone. I knew that sometimes men would give her money but it wasn't all the time. The upstairs neighbor, Mrs. Daniels, owned the house and it was her flat that was my real home.

I would get so mad at Aunt Cassie when she didn't give any money to Mrs. Daniels. I once screamed at her, "We wouldn't even have a place to live if she didn't feel sorry for me. And what about my shoes?"

"What about 'em?" she whispered with her eyes closed. "Sorry, baby." She'd fall asleep right on the floor next to me. I'd cry and curse God for taking my mama instead of her. But, on the other hand, He gave me Mrs. Daniels. She was an angel on earth. I can still see her standing at the stove wearing a red-flowered apron, stirring something. She was always cooking so the house smelled like sugar cookies and red velvet cake and fried chicken and meatloaf. I would go there after school and do my homework on her big kitchen table.

We had supper together and she washed my clothes when Auntie Cassie was strung out, which was most of the time. Aunt Cassie's idea of a meal was cheese doodles and soda. But Mrs. Daniels fixed me slices of thick bread oozing with butter, chicken and biscuits, big fat sausage sandwiches. God rest her soul. She saved me from going to foster care.

In high school, I was determined to become a fashion designer. Be somebody. Design clothes for a black woman's shape. Make clothes that were the colors of Africa. Black was getting to be beautiful. Black was part of the women's movement, wasn't it?

I got an after-school job in Chinatown and Lily Chang, the shop owner, taught me how to tailor clothes and gave me remnants to practice on. Lily helped me make my school clothes on the sewing machine in the shop. When she bought a new machine, she gave me hers and stacks of remnants she couldn't sell.

I was in my last year of high school when I turned my own life to shit. Me, myself and I. His name was William and I met him at the beginning of my senior year. He was almost twenty-one, a neighbor's son, and the best looking man I'd ever seen. He had a close-cut fro, a wide smile, and eyes that seemed to look right inside of me. His skin was the blackest black I'd ever seen, making his white teeth gleam — he'd flash a smile that could melt a frozen heart. I couldn't believe he wanted me — shy, awkward, me. Mrs. Daniels warned me. She said she knew men like him and he had trouble written all over him. The worst kind of trouble. But I didn't listen. Not even when she pleaded with me not to ruin my life. Not even when she asked me to stop for her sake.

William worked construction sometimes and had money; at least I thought he did. I was an innocent babe headed for slaughter. I thought if he wanted me, it made me special. Problem was I got pregnant with my Amber and had to leave school. Aunt Cassie disappeared on me and Mrs. Daniels helped me through the pregnancy, sadness all over her face. I had the baby and went on welfare. Mrs. Daniels passed when Amber was a couple of months old. A daughter, who'd never called or visited her, inherited the house and I was out.

I'd seen both sides, and was trapped like a wild animal. I'd lost everything — my Mama and Daddy, Mrs. Daniels, my future.

From the time she was a newborn, Amber was a smiler. That was William's only gift to her. I'd be mad as a hornet and she'd just smile and smile. I couldn't resist that. And William? The bastard couldn't handle what he called the do-mestic scene. After a couple of days, he was like a trapped wasp, stinging everything in his way.

I was no better than Aunt Cassie. Soft and stupid.

So that's what brought me to learning how to become a professional babysitter. Ruby's good. She's smart. But Vera and Virginia. The V-girls. I hate those big fat black asses of theirs. And they are dumb. They sit and take down notes in the fucking training classes. Morons. What does it take to watch kids, anyway? And then she came. Whoa, baby. The last straw. Another white brat.

I never thought I would get over myself to make friends with that white college girl. Fuck her. Why should I? Serving juice and cookies to kids, thinking she's hot shit for helping poor people. Well, you know what? It doesn't work that way. I've seen it all. Holier than thou. Protesting like they really care about peace-on-earth when the demonstrations are really one big love-in. An excuse to listen to free concerts, score dope, and pat themselves on the back.

That Lisa bugs me more than the others. I don't know why but she does. Ruby assigns her to me for spite, I'm sure of it. Babysitting the babysitter because I don't smile and kowtow to her like the Vs- Vera and Virginia. Fuck them all. I hate the way Lisa stares at me. And what really pisses me off is that she gets me. Saving all that scut work and keeping her on poop patrol doesn't do a thing for me. Makes me feel bad but I just can't help myself. The kid didn't do a thing to me except volunteer to help out. So what am I doing? I couldn't seem to cut her any slack.

So I invited her to dinner. I wanted to see what would happen when she came into my world. Let her get off the T and cross the line into another country. She can see my neighborhood with the stately brownstones you might see on Commonwealth Avenue or Beacon Street — only here they're abandoned, vandalized wrecks. I want her to walk past the man who is always lying in one of the doorways with a crumpled brown bag by his side. I want her to pass the teenagers hanging out on the corner who make her feel afraid to walk past them as they're passing a joint and laughing like hell at nothing. Let her see what Amber passes every day on her way home from the daycare center and come to our building where the buzzer doesn't work and the front door is too warped to close and the stairway smells of garbage and urine and soured wine embedded in the walls.

I came to the doorway with a plastered smile on my face, all decked out with an apron like Betty Crocker but with leopard spots. I didn't really think she'd come but there she was with a jug of wine and a bouquet of daisies.

Amber loved Lisa for some reason I didn't understand. She took Lisa's hand and pulled her into her bedroom, proudly showing her small bed covered with a bright pink blanket, a room barely big enough to hold a bed and dresser, with drawings hung haphazardly to cover up some of the peeling paint, cracks, and stains on the walls. I watched Amber lead her around the tiny apartment and winced when I saw her notice that my couch was covered with the same material as one of my dresses. Oh well. C'est la vie. Nothing to be ashamed of. It is what it is. I watched her smile when she saw my sewing machine piled with the colorful fabric I wear to cheer myself up.

"This is Mama's room." They pushed through the beaded curtain into an alcove furnished with a mattress on the floor, an upside-down milk crate covered with a swatch of fabric, a clock, lamp, and some review books. I knew she wanted to see what they were but was too polite to get a closer look. I didn't want her to know I'm spending more time studying for my GED than that stupid daycare certification. I was only there to give Amber a good start. Not like the ass-kissing V-girls.

Amber asked, "Where do you live, Lisa?"

"Not far from here, sweetie."

Amber brightened, "Maybe we could come to your house next time!"

"That would be fun, wouldn't it?"

Yeah, right, not far from here. Maybe not miles-wise. But I bet at Lisa's there aren't any jerks, high as a kite, sitting by the door scaring my child so bad she grips my hand for dear life every time we go out. He was too wasted to do any harm, just asked her for kisses. Four years old and already afraid of men.

Dinner was quick — macaroni and cheese, then brownies for dessert. Amber basked in the light of Lisa's complete attention. I put her to bed and opened the bottle of wine Lisa brought. I was about to pour the dark red liquid into two glasses but Lisa said she had to go, didn't want to get back too late, that she needed to study.

I called her on it. "Don't bullshit me, Lisa." I laughed my jeering ugly laugh (I couldn't help it). "Homework, my ass, you're scared."

She said yeah, maybe she didn't want to walk to the T after dark. I told her the one thing about her that pisses me off the most is that she's a liar, mostly to herself. That blows. Come to think of it, I told her she reminds me of William, Amber's so-called father, who thinks he has to bullshit his way through life. But he's sexy as hell. At least he had that going for him.

Lisa pouted. "You don't think I'm sexy? I'm crushed."

I had to admit she had a sense of humor. I couldn't help but smile and talk faster with each glass of wine, giving Lisa an earful about being a poor woman. Ranting about not needing any white woman to help her and then go home to her easy life.

"That Louisa Henry from the city school committee might be talking out her ass about integration and bussing but I agree with the racist bitch. I don't want Amber on a bus for hours every day, leaving our neighborhood for the privilege of going to school with white kids. Any dummy knows she'll still get the leftover books with pictures of Dick and Jane White-bread living in a house she doesn't recognize."

And then Lisa cracked me up. "Marika, you're not a happy drunk, are you?"

I laughed. Gotta hand it to the girl. She never backs off.

"That's the hard thing about you, Marika. One minute you talk to me like I'm the scum of the earth you'd like to flush down the toilet and the next minute you're sweet. Not truly sweet, maybe semi or dark chocolate sweet."

It was true, I might not know if I liked her yet, but she had guts. I couldn't take that away from her.

We clinked our glasses. By my third or maybe fourth glass of wine, I didn't care what the hell I gave up. Barfing out my sad story mainly because I'd never had anyone over. Pathetic. Not a single woman friend. My eyelids were too heavy to hold open.

I leaned against the wall and said, "Lisa, you think a woman can take care of herself because you haven't had to yet. But you are wrong, wrong, wrong. Once a man gets between her legs, she gets soft and stupid and stays that way."

"I don't believe you."

"You'll see. What about you, Lisa? Have you ever had any misery?"

Lisa looked away. "Not by your standards."

"Oh c'mon, fess up." I knocked over my empty glass.

I poured what was left in the bottle and took another gulp. "Ruby's good. She's smart. But Vera and Virginia. I hate them and I'm nothing like them. They are dumb kiss-ups. Fucking morons." Did I already say that? Well, what if I did?

"Hey, I love this song." I stumbled over to the radio to turn up the sound. "Barry White — so low and sexy. Dance with me Lisa. C'mon." I pulled her up and we danced. Lisa had some good moves, and wasn't drunk like me. We were swayin' to the music but then the room started to spin and I fell toward her. I think she caught me. I might have let her hold me. I might even have wept.

When I woke up during the night, I realized I must have passed out; my head pounded. I got up for aspirin and poked my head into Amber's room. There was Lisa snuggled up to her. Ah, the two of them sleeping together brought tears to my eyes and I cried myself back to sleep. This time for real.

Good lord, why Lisa didn't walk away from me after the way I treated her is a true mystery. But I'm not gonna argue.

Chapter Six

Bricks, Valentines, and Politics

୧୬୦

Lisa and Marika were cutting out red paper hearts for the children. Marika frowned. "This project will be a mess. A teacher from the school down the block dropped off all kinds of art supplies. Big favor. Last time we used glitter, we were all covered in sparkles for days."

"That's the spirit, Marika. Always thinking on the bright side. You're someone who could use some stardust."

"Yeah, right." Marika squeezed glue into egg cartons.

Ruby walked in. "How are you girls doing with the hearts?"

"We're just about finished." Lisa stood up with the stack of red construction paper hearts. There was a crashing sound of shattered glass, then a hollow sound and a thud. Lisa went down. Blood spurted from the left side of her head. Marika cradled Lisa's head in her lap. She yanked off her turban to stem the bleeding and rocked her. "You'll be okay," she crooned. "Don't worry. You're gonna be okay, I promise."

Ruby made a quick assessment of which children were bleeding and took them into her office. The others cried, sucked thumbs, and clung to teachers. One little girl peed on the floor.

"V, don't just stand there. Get the kids out of here and calm them down. Will you? They don't need to see this." Marika's voice was shrill, quivering. "Where's the friggin' ambulance? You did call, didn't you?"

Lisa opened her eyes, looked up at the ceiling and then at Marika. "Marika, you have hair!" She closed her eyes again. "What happened? What's going on?"

"Some jerk threw a brick through the window. The corner caught you. But the way you fell, I think you might have hurt your foot, too. The ambulance is on its way. Some of the kids were hit with flying glass. Ruby has them. But you got hurt the worst. Be still. It's a pretty deep cut. I think you might need stitches."

"In my head?"

"I'm going with you. I'll make sure you're okay," Marika whispered. "It's about damn time. The ambulance is finally here." Marika squeezed her hand.

"So are we friends now, Marika?" Lisa whispered. She closed her eyes and when she opened them again, she was in the ambulance. She was whisked into the hospital but didn't feel awake. She was vaguely aware of Marika talking to the doctor, and then whispering to her that she would probably need stitches in her hair line. They had to dig a piece of glass from her scalp. She also had a sprained ankle. She was going to be admitted to watch for signs of concussion.

When she got to her room, Amy, Marika, Amber and her professor, Dr. Kessler were there. Amy's face was streaked with tears.

Dr. Kessler put a large bouquet of flowers on the table.

"Am I hurt that badly?"

He smiled. "The least I could do. You probably would have been better off at the prison."

"Doubt it. The flowers are really beautiful."

"Take good care of yourself and come see me when you're better, okay?"

"I will. Thanks again for stopping by and bringing me flowers."

When he left, Lisa asked, "Has everybody met each other?"

"Yes. But it's not as if we're strangers. We've been trading secrets so we know how you talk about us behind our backs." Marika said. "Amber, give Lisa your picture."

Amber held on to Marika's leg. "Here, Lisa. I made you a card."

"Honey, don't be afraid, It's just a big bandage." She read the card. "Will you look at this card? It's beautiful. A Valentine get well card. Thank you, Amber."

"Everybody made you one. But I'm the only one to get to come here."
Amber hesitated but came a bit closer to the bed.

"Will you be my Valentine?"

"Silly. You should ask a boy."

"I guess you're right."

"I called your parents," Amy said, holding her breath.

Lisa grimaced "You're kidding, right?"

"I had to. But I told them you just needed a few stitches so they wouldn't
be too worried. Your mom was upset anyway and they'll be coming as soon
as your father closes the store."

"Oh, great." Lisa closed her eyes.

"It will be fine. Maybe when you're discharged, you could stay overnight with them in a hotel. Get some pampering."

"Yeah, maybe. My head is starting to hurt. Can you ask the nurse for
something? I have a really bad headache."

"I'll go," Marika took Amber with her.

"How bad is it?" Amy sat on the edge of the bed holding her hand.

"My head really hurts. Not where they stitched me up. More like a
headache. I don't really remember anything, Amy. I know I heard the crash
and then I was on the floor with Marika pressing her turban onto the side
of my head. Her beautiful turban that she wears all the time was soaked in
blood. Were any of the kids hurt?"

"From what Marika said, some had a few cuts from the glass but they
were mostly scared. You know how heads bleed. They saw all your blood and
they freaked. Poor little things were crying. It was just lucky that nobody
got killed. Marika can probably tell you more, but it seems a drunken
homeless man — a vet, they think — started throwing bricks from a pile
in one of the empty lots."

"I have to close my eyes. But don't go, Amy, please stay for a while."

Amy squeezed her hand. "I'm not going anywhere."

The nurse came in and gave her a shot. She didn't know how long she
slept. When she woke up, she thought she saw Mac in the doorway. But
then, there wasn't anybody there. She thought it might be the drugs. There
was no way he'd come. She was only one of his many students. Lisa closed
her eyes but couldn't sleep. Everything felt weird. She had a big bandage on

her head and felt fuzzy. Maybe that's what a concussion feels like. She heard her parents outside her room. Eyes still closed, she called out, "Hi, Mom. Daddy. It looks worse than it is."

"That's my trooper," her father said. He bent over and kissed her forehead and gave her a single rose.

"Thanks, Daddy. But I thought roses were reserved for your Rose."

"I didn't think she'd mind. Do you Rosie?"

Her mother dismissed the question with a wave and turned her attention to her daughter. "You're going to be just fine. The doctor said it was a deep wound but you shouldn't have much of a scar. They're keeping you overnight as a precaution."

"I'll be okay? Not all fuzzy-headed like I am now?"

"No, *kinde.* No worries. You won't even know this happened to you. We're going to take you home for a few days and you'll be good as new." She fussed with the sheet and blanket.

"No, Mom. I don't need to come home. I'm fine, really. I'll take it easy for a few days and then it will be done with."

"How can you stay here? I can't take care of you in the dorm."

Quietly, Lisa said, "Once I get out of here, you won't need to, Mom."

Her mother folded her arms across her chest, "You're coming home and that's that. It's settled."

Lisa looked to her father for help. "Rose, let's talk about something else. Who did you get the pretty flowers from?"

"Dr. Kessler. He was so funny. He said I would have been better off staying with the prison. At least there the glass is bulletproof."

"Sending you into dangerous neighborhoods, flowers are the least that he should do. You'll have to find something else for that class."

"Mom, I don't mean to sound ungrateful but...."

Rose interrupted. "Already, she's starting, Jack. All I want to do it take care of my daughter when she's hurt and keep her safe." Her eyes teared.

"Mom, I'm a big girl. I have to learn how to take care of myself. I'm careful. This was just a fluke. I didn't feel safe in the prison and didn't go back. Right?"

Her mother sniffled into her father's handkerchief. He was always at the ready. "Why can't you be normal and do regular things? I worry about you day and night because you have no *sachel*."

Exasperated, she said, "Mom, please stop. I have plenty of common sense. Wanting to learn about other experiences and maybe help out doesn't make me abnormal."

"That tone. Even now." Rose clenched her jaw.

"I can't argue, Mom. My head hurts too much. I think the shock to my head brought on a migraine. The nurse gave me something. I'm happy you're here. Mama, can you just hold my hand?"

"That I can do. I can hold your hand."

Lisa closed her eyes. While she slept the doctor had stopped by and told her parents she had a slight concussion but if she felt up to it, she could go home in the morning. He thought after a couple of days she'd be fine and should come back in a week to have the stitches out.

When she woke up, the headache was better and she was hungry.

"Look what we brought back for you," her mother held it out. "A cheeseburger and fries."

"Are you kidding me? You actually bought me a cheeseburger. Did the doctor tell you I was mortally wounded?"

"No, smarty pants, just the opposite. He said you are probably fine and if you feel well in the morning, you'll be discharged."

"So, why the cheeseburger?"

"Because I know you've been eating them all along and that you love them. It's not such a *mitziah* to put cheese on meat. And it's not as if we're bringing *traif* into the house. So, eat while it's still hot. Here's some ketchup."

Lisa's eyes widened. "Are you my mother?"

Rose smiled and smoothed the top sheet over her daughter's legs.

Jack said, "We thought maybe it would be better for you to stay in Boston than take the long trip home. Uncle Ira will cover for me tomorrow. We have a room at a hotel in Kenmore Square, right near school. This way, we'll have a little vacation together and your mother can make sure you eat and rest. She'll see for herself that all is well."

"Thank you both so much."

The cheeseburger was the best Lisa had ever had. *Amazing*, she thought, *how pungent guilt can taste.*

⁓

Lisa worked on campus organizing protests against the war but she was also passionate about the struggle to make abortion legal and safe. When she was still in high school, her best friend's sister nearly died. Lisa's stomach still turned when she thought about it. It could have happened to anyone.

Maddy sobbed and hiccupped when she called. "Lisa, something awful happened." She blew her nose.

"Have your father drive you over."

"I can't," she said. "He's at the hospital with Marlene."

"He is? Is she okay?" Lisa asked, picking at the skin along her thumbnail.

"I don't know. She came home from school sick and bleeding. She and Tommy were doing it and she got pregnant."

"Oh my God. Why is she at the hospital?" Lisa whispered.

"She went to some woman on campus that does abortions right in the dorms and she did a really bad job. Marlene's fever was 105 and she lost a lot of blood. Mom and Dad rushed her to the hospital."

Lisa pictured Marlene lying on bloody sheets.

"What if she can't have any babies now? What if she'll never be a mother and I'll never be an aunt? What if she dies?" Maddy sobbed.

Marlene didn't die but she didn't go back to school either. Lisa once heard of a girl who was so desperate she used a wire coat hanger on herself to get rid of the baby. She didn't know if the story was true but she sometimes thought about it when she hung up her coat. Once she pulled a hanger apart and stretched it into a long straight line. With the sharp end, she scratched her leg. Boy, did it smart. She knew no matter what, no matter how desperate she was, she would never be brave or stupid enough to stick it up there. And if she did, what then?

When Marlene came home from the hospital, she had a look on her face that Lisa had never seen before. Whatever had happened to her made her smaller somehow. She certainly didn't look like the old Marlene, the big sister who teased them until they cried.

Weeks later, Lisa promised a very angry Maddy that when she got to college she would work to make abortion legal. The time was right. The Supreme Court was considering a case that could legalize abortion. Lisa volunteered for a grassroots organization, the Center for Legalizing Abortion — *CLA* — working to raise awareness and garner support.

The case to legalize abortion was like a well-packed suitcase whose contents had been strewn over the sidewalk to lighten its load. When the case began, there were three claimants from Texas: the first was Jane Roe, who wanted her pregnancy terminated by a licensed medical doctor under safe clinical conditions; the second was a doctor who was facing a trial for having performed an illegal abortion; and the third was a couple who wanted access to a safe procedure should the wife, whose medical condition would put her life in danger, become pregnant.

Two of the cases were thrown out because their situations were determined moot. However, Jane Roe's case stood up because she could become pregnant again. The decision would soon be argued as a right-to-privacy case, not one to be decided on the *when does life begin* controversy.

The Court needed to know that women across the country wanted legal, safe abortion available to them. Lisa usually volunteered once a week, but was working extra days to prepare for a big rally. They were in the middle of a mailing that had to go out the next day.

The CLA, organized by Bill Barton, was in a small, grungy storefront close to the Boston Gardens. Several years earlier, he was arrested at Charles River University for handing out one condom and one package of contraceptive foam to an unmarried couple. Convicted for violating a Massachusetts law against chastity, Barton took his case to the Supreme Court. He was exonerated when the Court threw out the verdict. This center was a continuation of his work to give women the right to privacy when making decisions about their bodies.

"Ah muchacha, what are you doing here today? It's Tuesday, isn't it?" Alma, the campaign director, had deep-set eyes, a bronze complexion and an ageless face. She might look fragile but she was a warrior. This was a battle she was going to win preferably with the help of others, but if not, she'd do it on her own. The volunteers speculated about what might have happened to make her so dedicated. They figured she was a victim of an illegal one rendering her sterile or maybe one of her sisters or friends died at the hand of a butcher. Maybe she was having an affair with Barton. They had no idea what motivated her and they knew she'd never tell them. Alma had the strength and energy of ten women and the volunteers laughed amongst themselves, glad to be on the same side.

"Glad you're here." Alma pointed to a desk of flyers and envelopes. "Lisa, this mailing has to get done tonight. We want the print materials to arrive before we start the phone banks. Everything you need is there and when you finish that, work on the press release for next week. If you need help Pamela will be coming in but I'd like to have her work on something else."

"Aye aye, Captain." Lisa saluted.

"You are fresh, girl. Get to it!"

Lisa sat at the desk by the door. She draped her jacket over the desk chair and began folding yellow flyers announcing next Tuesday's demonstration. It was scheduled to coincide with the legislators coming back to town for the fall session. The goal was to flood Boston Common across from the State House with a cross-section of people — young, old, black, white, rich, poor — to make clear this issue was not partisan or age-related, that the repercussions of illegal abortion touched everyone.

The opposition consisted primarily of religious-based conservative women's groups who were in a minority but well organized. Barton's strategy was to attract women who might scare politicians into action if the case bounced back to the states. The plan was to target women who had no access to legal abortions themselves just about the time their daughters were becoming sexually active. The abundant sex of the sixties and seventies was a mother's worst nightmare.

Lisa was surprised by the number of older women who came to the center to help out. She expected support to come mainly from sexually active young girls but that wasn't true at all. Maybe Lisa should call her mother to invite her to the big rally for women's rights and tell her how mothers and daughters would be standing together. Yeah, that would go over well. Her mother saw activism as putting the rest of your life in danger.

Not the other way around. Wild horses couldn't drag her to a political rally. Lost in her thoughts, she didn't hear the door open.

"Hey, Alma!"

"Hey yourself," Alma called out. "It's about damn time you got here. I need you to rework a speech."

"Don't worry. You'll have a new speech. It will bring tears to your eyes. Where's the boss?"

"Springfield. He made notes but said 'Mac never pays any attention to our conversations and I've never sounded better. So just tell him schmaltz is good.' Try to get it done within the next couple of days, okay?"

Lisa looked up. Dr. Taylor. Mac. What was he doing here?

Mac looked over and saw her. He grinned. "Hi, Lisa. This is a surprise."

She smiled back. "How are you?

"Fine. Just fine. But what about you? I heard that you were hurt during an internship last semester. You okay?"

"You knew about that? I'm okay. I have a hard head." She knocked on it.

"So glad to hear that. Wouldn't want anything to interfere with that quick mind of yours. I was hoping you'd be masochistic enough to take another class with me," he teased.

"No, I couldn't take it." She brushed the hair off her face. "Seriously, with my double major, I can't take many electives."

"Sure, sure. Are you a new recruit here?"

"No, I usually come on Mondays. I'm just putting in some extra time to get ready for the rally."

He stood at her desk with his dark eyes fixed on her, long enough for her to feel awkward.

"I better get cracking. Lots to do tonight." He started toward the back office and then turned around. "Lisa, maybe you'll look at my draft. A friend of mine is meeting me for coffee later to punch it up. We sort of work as a team but we could use a woman's perspective. If you're finished with what you're doing, maybe you'd like to join us."

"Really, I'd love to. I'll get the mailing done." Lisa nodded.

"Never doubted it," he laughed, walked into Barton's office and closed the door.

Alma nodded and smiled as Mac and Lisa left headquarters at about nine-thirty. They arrived at the Pewter Pot before Mac's friend arrived.

"Sorry I'm late, Mac. Well, hello. And who might you be?" He was the physical opposite of Mac — a short, slim man with thinning blonde hair and wire rimmed glasses.

Mac said, "Lisa Stern. Phil Rhoades."

"Nice to meet you, Lisa." Phil extended his hand. "Even though he's bossy, he's the closest thing I have to a brother."

She laughed.

"Let's get down to business." Mac motioned for the waitress as they all sat down.

"Coffee all around?" the waitress asked. "Anything else?"

Phil said, "Blueberry muffin for me."

Lisa echoed, "Me too."

Mac ordered a sandwich. "We're doing really well with the media on this event and I think we're going to get the mix we want," he said, slurping his coffee. "Bill left me some notes so the speech pretty much wrote itself."

"Did you get a first draft done?" Phil asked.

"Here." Mac handed him the pages. "The notes in the margin are some of Lisa's ideas. And we need to talk about the conclusion. It has to be hard-hitting and quotable. We have to keep the State House listening and create some strong undertow that will catch on nationally. The Court might decide Roe's case as a first amendment issue, a right-to-privacy issue, but we have to be prepared and get ready for Act Two: Legislation."

They went to work, going over each paragraph, smoothing the rough edges, making sure they pounded the theme home. Mac wanted to make clear that it was an exercise in choice and that was the point of living in a free society. Lisa's stomach was doing flip-flops at first, but somewhere along the way forgot who she was sitting with and went into overdrive suggesting changes Mac and Phil thought were dead-on.

She looked at her watch. It was eleven-thirty. "Oh, my God," She stood up, gathering her things. "Much as I hate to go, I've got to run before the T stops running."

"Don't be silly. You think we'd let you go back alone?" Mac asked.

"You have a car?"

"We do." Phil and Mac said in chorus.

"It is getting late," Phil yawned. "I'm done in. I can't do anymore tonight. And I have all those fresh young wide awake faces to deal with for an eight o'clock." He snickered. "Don't I wish?"

"You teach also?" Lisa asked.

"Bio." Phil threw some money on the table.

"My roommate's a bio major. Do you know Amy Wilson?"

"I teach at Newton College. Sorry."

"Excuse me, you two," Mac interrupted. "Let's just figure out a plan. Okay so... I'll make the changes we talked about. Phil, you write a better ending and pull together the media list. And Lisa, do you think you have the time to finish the press release?" Mac asked.

"Sure."

"We'll need it for Thursday," Phil said.

"Consider it done," she said as she put on her jacket and fixed the collar.

"How about meeting here then on Thursday. Six sharp. That will give us enough time to get the speech in good form and get it to Alma for typing," Mac suggested.

"Fine," said Phil. "You want me to take you home, Lisa?"

"No way, Rhoades. She's mine. Come on, Lisa." He steered her out of the restaurant holding her elbow.

They walked to his car, a red Kharmann Ghia convertible. "This is yours? I love these cars!"

"Yup. My pride and joy." He tapped the hood. "You live in the Zoo? I mean the 700 Towers?"

"It is a zoo. No getting around it. How did you know that?" she asked.

He shrugged, opened the door for her, and she slid in. They rode silently down broad, elegant Commonwealth Avenue. "Here we are, Madame."

"Thanks for the ride, Mac. See you Thursday." Lisa said.

"Count on it." Mac said, shifting into gear.

Lisa watched him pull away.

She tore into her room and bent over Amy. "Amy, wake up! Please wake up! I have to tell you something."

"I have an early lab tomorrow. This better be important," Amy complained.

"It is. I mean it's not urgent but if I don't tell you right now, I'll burst open."

Amy rolled over onto her back, rubbed her eyes. "What?"

"I'm in love. I'm absolutely in love."

"You woke me up for that? So what? You've been talking about Bill Barton since I met you." Amy yawned, closing her eyes.

"Not him. With Mac. Mackenzie Taylor."

"Yeah, right. I'm happy for you." She rolled over and faced the wall.

"Sorry I woke you." She got ready for bed. Lying on her back with her hands folded under her head, she looked up at the ceiling with a big smile on her face. He'd said: *She's mine.*

Chapter Seven

Thinking Her Way to a Future

∽

Isabela rushed into Lisa's room. "It's all right, child. It's all right. You're dreaming. It's just a dream," Isabela cooed as she took Lisa into her arms. Lisa couldn't catch her breath; heaving sobs wracked her body as Isabela held her. "There, there, child. Take it easy. You're awake now. It's okay. Hush."

Lisa hiccupped, and then whispered, "But it's not okay. I mean I know it's a dream but what I'm dreaming about is real." She put her head in her hands.

"Come, lie down now. I'll stay with you." Isabela rubbed Lisa's back while she fell asleep, her eyes resting on the picture of her husband and son.

Lisa's mind slowly awakened during her long walks along the shore. She was more conscious of the life on the beach, both unseen energy within the dark waters and what lived on the sand and in the air. Watching two terns momentarily in sync with one another triggered thoughts of transitory moments, perfect in a split second of time, then gone. Ideas floated in and out of Lisa's head much like clouds tossed by the wind, one form morphing into another. She had no answers because she wasn't sure of the questions.

In the silence of night, Isabela and Lisa worked side by side, rarely speaking. When they did, it was about the task at hand. In those quiet hours, she still thought about Mac, still cried, but not all the time. During her waking hours, she was preoccupied with what to do next. Isabela wouldn't let her stay forever. She wasn't sure she wanted to settle in Provincetown. Boston was out of the question. Maybe it wouldn't be such a bad idea to go back home to Albany. That had never been a possibility before. She spent her childhood thinking of ways to live anywhere else. But maybe she'd changed and that was no longer the case.

"Well, girl. We are finished. The bread is rising, the cakes cooling. Do you want to take some coffee down to the beach?"

Isabela, wearing her oversized cable-knit sweater and nubby wool scarf, grabbed her straw bag holding her thermos, mugs, and a wool blanket. They walked together in comfortable silence. Lisa liked that — not having to fill the air with mindless chatter. She'd never let quiet happen before and found it comforting.

There was a local tale that the dead wander across the dunes on moonless nights, guided by the light of their candles. Aware or not, Lisa kept watch. She liked to think about Mac hovering over the beach, not touching ground. Maybe Grandma would appear holding her Grandpa's hand.

As the dark night dissolved into day, Lisa realized that day didn't quite break. It rose slowly in thin bands of color from the horizon so as not to startle. Early morning showed what the ocean gave back — shells and stone, crabs, clams, fish. Gulls waited to pick at tangled seaweed, and sanderlings scurried at the water's edge, running in abbreviated starts and stops, patrolling the shore, pecking at fly larvae, beetles, and mollusks. A golden retriever trotted along the shoreline, his owner hardly keeping up with him. An ocean full of life, giving as well as keeping, what did not belong to her. It was time for Lisa to look at the waves washing up as forecasting the future, not reliving the past.

Isabela said she was thinking about selling the bakery. "But what would I do? I hate cards. I never was one to sit around making small talk. I just can't sell until it becomes clear to me what to do next," she ruminated. She bent to pick up some broken shells and stones and skimmed them across the cresting waves. Lisa admired her stocky, strong body, long gray hair carelessly pinned on top of her head, proud and strong.

Vaguely, Lisa thought about developing some kind of center for women, a place for rebuilding their lives. Women wanted change now. The times were uneasy. Civil rights and big catastrophic events caused ripples of change at home. More needed to happen besides endless talk, talk, talk and weirdness when it came to women's rights. Feminism, Lisa chuckled to herself. Making friends with your vagina seemed a little bizarre to her. Taking a mirror, parting the lips and looking inside might be a beginning of a feminist life. But not for Lisa, who saw feminism as practicality.

Lisa jammed some paper in her coat pocket to write down her ideas while walking on the beach. She also kept a running list on the pad next to the cash register.

Isabela said, "These notes don't look like no cookie order."

"No. Or bread." They stood together behind the counter. Lisa wrapped her arm around Isabela's waist.

"So you have something going on inside your head?"

Lisa smiled. "Finally. Yes. I think I'm ready to say it out loud. Let's go out to eat tonight. My treat as long as it's the diner."

"Big spender." Isabela smiled.

They slid into a booth near the window. A storm was imminent. The clouds were bloated and the breaking waves snarled at the beach.

"I hope no one is out there tonight," Lisa said.

"Probably not. The water's been choppy all day." Isabela signaled to the waitress to bring coffee.

"I've started to think about things. I think it was fate that you rescued me."

Isabela opened the menu. "It was fate, was it?"

"You know it's true." Lisa said. "Do you think you can braid my hair and pin it up like yours?"

"Whatever for?" Isabela absently smoothed the strands of hair that had slipped out.

"I think you're beautiful."

"You, my dear, are daft."

The waitress brought over the coffee. "What will it be, ladies?

Lisa said, "I'll have the fish and chips."

"Make it two," said Isabela, "and I'll start with a cup of chowder." They were both famished and attacked their dinners with gusto, focusing on the food, eating at the same pace so that they finished together.

Isabela said, "Let's have it."

"This is the thing. We're in the 1970s. Women expect to have both careers and families. But at the same time, there is a war sending husbands home disabled or dead; others are abandoned, through divorce and death, and many have neither skills nor money. Welfare doesn't help women become independent. It's predicated on the man saying sayonara. Who is going to watch out and support women except other women?"

"We do that already. Look at us. One taking care of the other. I'll give you this much, it was strange that I went to Race Point that night. I rarely do. It's too far."

"So, let's say it was a fortunate coincidence. But what if I'm in my thirties, got married out of high school, never worked, have three kids and suddenly my husband decides he wants out. What do I need?"

"A good divorce lawyer!" Isabela laughed.

"Isabela!"

"All right. Tell me what you think she needs. I'm listening."

"She needs a place to learn job skills, how to interview, how to dress, how to find or afford someone to take care of her children." Lisa reached into her pocket, took out a crumpled paper and flattened it out with her palm.

"You don't need that. I see where you are going with this. So, say you go ahead. What do you do first?"

Lisa slowly stirred her coffee, thoughtfully swirling it in one direction and then the other. "I don't know. But this thought occurred to me, Isabela. If you had a support center, someplace you could go to, maybe you'd sell the business. Maybe you could volunteer at a Center and teach women how to run a small business or teach them how to bake, or maybe just slap them around and tell them to snap out of it and start looking ahead."

"I've never slapped anyone in my life." Isabela snorted.

"You don't have to. One look is enough."

Isabela chuckled. "That's what Stefan used to say. And Mark. He'd say Ma, no fair. Don't give me the evil eye." She took a breath and tried to shake the thought from her head. "So how are you going to do this?"

"Mark?"

"My son." Isabela furrowed her brow. "He's gone, too."

"Oh my God! Isabela, I'm so sorry."

"He was killed in Vietnam six years ago. One of his buddies told me he died in his arms and didn't suffer. I don't know if it's true, but I like to believe that."

"I'm so sorry. I should have realized. The boy in the pictures on the dresser."

"Yes. You are the first to stay in his room. It's what killed my husband, I'm sure. His heart was broken."

Lisa reached across the table to hold her hands. "Isabela."

Isabela was still for a minute, then pulled back her hands and straightened her spine. "Now where were we?"

Lisa picked up her coffee cup.

"Where will this Center be?" Isabela asked.

Lisa shrugged. "I don't know."

"Do you have any idea of how to start?"

"Not yet."

The women were silent for a moment. Isabela furrowed her brow and put her hand up for Lisa to be quiet. "I'm thinking."

"Okay." Lisa downed the last of her coffee and signaled the waitress for a refill.

"Wait a minute. First, you should talk to Martin. He started the gay men's center in town."

"That's a great idea." Lisa stirred more sugar into her coffee. "There is something else I wanted to talk about. I was wondering if I can stay another month or so while I figure some things out."

"How can you? I'm not throwing you out but… "

Lisa explained she planned to call the landlord to tell him she wouldn't be coming back and also would contact Mac's mother to see what she wanted to do with his clothes and furniture. She didn't want to take much —

Gatsby with all his notes, a couple volumes of poetry and some of his record albums.

"I'm going to ask Amy or Marika to help me. I know one of them will. I can't be there alone yet and I don't want to backslide."

"You have steam coming out of your ears, my girl." Isabela half-smiled.

"There is nothing like walking on the beach in the wind to get you thinking."

"That's the truth. Of course, you can stay with me for a while longer. You can stay with me as long as you need to. Martin will be helpful and so will Sandra Davis. I don't think you've met her yet but she opened that book and craft shop — a consignment deal."

Lisa grasped Isabela's hands across the table. "Isabela, you saved my life."

"For heaven's sake, child. I did not."

"Oh, but you did."

∽

Isabela pulled her bathrobe tight around her. There was a chill in the morning air that blew in through the windows. Lisa wrote on a legal pad. The kitchen table was covered in paper — notes, books from the library, copies of Martin's grants and research. What he was doing for gay men was not that far off from her idea. He created a hub of activity.

"How did you start the bakery?"

"Do you want another cup?" Isabela held the pot in her hand before putting it back on the stove.

Lisa covered her mug with her hand. "I've had enough. Thanks."

"A bakery went up for sale at the time Stefan and his brother wanted to get away from fishing. We bought the business by scraping together a thousand dollar down payment. Can you imagine? We didn't have much money beyond that. We rented the building for five years until we were doing well enough to buy it. In some ways, things were a little easier then. No big deposits, help in gaining government business loans at good rates for GIs."

She put down her coffee and buttered a roll. "First, we baked in the kitchen because the ovens that came with the place were unreliable. The ovens we bake in now came later. To make enough to sell, we baked round the clock. Can you imagine four adults living and baking in this apartment? Mother of God! We did what we had to."

"Were you ever sorry?"

"I wished life was easier but anything was better than fishing. The ocean takes more than it gives up. Besides, Stefan always smelled like dough."

"Better than fish." Lisa smiled. "Is it okay with you for me to make some calls?"

"Sure. Go ahead."

"It's me, Marika, how are you?"

"Where the hell are you?" she asked.

"No hello?" Lisa chuckled.

"Still sassy, I see. Where did you go? Amber asks about you every day."

"Kiss her for me."

"Kiss her yourself. Are you back? Please tell me you're back now. How could you disappear like that? We're all worried sick," Marika chided.

"I'm in Provincetown. I had a terrible nightmare and drove here one night. I tried to wash away with the outgoing tide but was saved by an angel."

"An angel. Good lord. Have you lost your mind?"

"I know you won't believe me but I'm much better and I'm working in a bakery."

"Start from the beginning." Marika's tone softened.

"It's too long a story to tell over the phone. I'm coming on Saturday to get my things out of our apartment. I've been thinking long and hard and I want you to wrap your head around this idea. I think I'm going to go home to Albany and I want you to come with me."

"Don't be crazy. You couldn't wait to get out of there, have you forgotten that? And me go there? Now why would I go to the hick town you couldn't wait to leave?" Marika's voice squeaked.

"When I tell you my plan, you'll see what a good idea it is. I also want to see Ruby on Saturday. Okay?"

"You want her to move to Hicksville, too?"

Lisa said. "No, love. Only you." She paused for a moment. "Life is so grand for you now? Things looking up are they?"

Marika exhaled. "Okay, smartass. We'll talk when you come in."

"Don't forget to tell Ruby."

Marika muttered, "Shit, Lisa. I guess getting brained in the head with a brick was worse than we thought."

Lisa laughed. "You'll come to the apartment? One o'clock?"

"Yes. I'll be there. And then we'll go to see Ruby," Marika said.

"I'm sorry I worried you. I just couldn't call. It was as if I just needed to remove myself from everyone if I ever would get past... "

"It's okay, Missy. You did what you had to do. See you Saturday. One o'clock."

Lisa dialed again. "Hi, Daddy."

"Lisa!" he said.

"I'm sorry I worried you, Daddy. I was a total mess and had to get away." Lisa said.

"Your mother said you are thinking you might come home? I told her not to get her hopes up."

"Good. I want to ask you a favor. Will you get me a listing of city-owned buildings that have gone into foreclosure? I'll need to know how long they've been empty, what the city plans to do with them. Mr. Doherty still living on the block? He should be able to get it for you."

"What? Are you going into real estate or something?" her father asked.

"Not exactly. I don't want to tell you so you don't have to tell him. What's the good of having a councilman on the street without ever asking him for anything? I know he asks plenty of you."

"The price of doing business. Don't get me started." Her father paused. "I don't want to talk you out of it. Nothing would make your mother and me happier than having you here but it's opposite of everything you've always wanted. Honey, sometimes it's not such a good thing to make big decisions when you are still sitting *shiva,* so to speak," he counseled.

"Daddy, I cannot go back to Boston."

"That's the *now* talking."

"I have an idea and I want to see what happens. I'm going to stay here for a few more weeks and while I'm here, I'll go into Boston to get my things from the apartment. So when you get the information, mail it to me here at the bakery. Go get a pencil. Okay?"

"Okay, princess. I'll call him tonight."

"Thanks, Daddy."

"Honey, are you sure you're all right? You hardly sound like yourself."

"I'm fine. Really, Daddy. Don't worry."

Chapter Eight

∽

Shadowbox: Life for Rent

A shoebox is partitioned with cardboard. It is an empty apartment. The walls are painted blue. There are lighter blue rectangles where pictures may have hung and holes where bookshelves and curtain rods were nailed to the walls. Silhouettes of a man and woman stand off to the side.

"Mrs. Taylor, thank you for meeting me here." Lisa reached for her hand. It was both limp and dry. The slight, worn woman sat down on the edge of the couch, perched like a bird ready for flight. Lisa sat down next to her.

"I'd like to take care of this as soon as possible. I won't be coming back here." Her words were labored and she spoke just above a whisper. "You know you can stay here through the lease if you'd like. Mackenzie would have wanted that, I think. Wouldn't he?" Lisa leaned in to hear her. "He did tell me about you. Not directly about you, really, more as an announcement that there was a young woman in his life, the woman he'd always dreamed of." She shook her head. "My poor darling boy."

A stream wound its way down Lisa's face and neck onto her shirt. Mrs. Taylor stared at Lisa, seemingly without seeing her. "How could I have lost them both? Both suddenly, in the same way?" she asked her, eyes brimming, eyelids red. "Ah, look at the two of us." They sat quietly together, lost in their own thoughts, grieving side by side.

She straightened her back, lengthening herself. "Dear, let's get this over with." Mrs. Taylor patted Lisa's hand so lightly she could hardly feel her touch.

The apartment smelled musty. Their scent, commingled with incense and candles and pot, had been replaced with stale, oppressive air. Lisa opened the front window. The children were playing in the school playground. The little freckled redhead was jumping rope. Mac used to marvel at her quick feet. She'll be a track star, he would say. She was there with some other girls doing double skips. How could they still be there jumping rope when the world had changed?

"Mrs. Taylor, I'm going to take Mac's research notes from his office. I don't know how far along he was in his book but I'd like to bring it to the dean to see that someone finishes it and gets it published."

She arched her eyebrows. "He was writing a book? What sort of book?"

"About obsession in American literature. He was expanding his thesis."

"Really? Mackenzie was doing that? He was always a fine writer. He wrote a poem for me on Mother's Day when he was only six years old." She trailed off and picked invisible lint off her navy skirt. "Did he tell you his father died suddenly? He was there one morning and gone by the afternoon. I still listen to the cars drive down the street around suppertime, hoping one of them might be James. After all this time. It's silly of me, I know. But I can't seem to give away that one second of hope."

"I can understand that. Mac said losing his father the way he did made him realize that you never knew if you were living your last day. And he tried to live that way. Mac lived big, Mrs. Taylor. "

She didn't seem to hear Lisa. "When I lost one, I lost the other. MacKenzie was still a boy when his father died but after that time, he changed. It was my fault. It took me too long to tend to him. By the time I realized my boy needed me, it was too late. MacKenzie lost patience with me. He thought I was weak. To him, that was a sin he didn't want to be around. You must be one of those independent women, those new women's libbers." She finally directed her gaze toward Lisa.

Mac described his mother's difficulties to Lisa but she never understood her to be pathetic. He said she had never recovered from his father's death, that she lived with a mosquito net covering her. She'd depended on his father completely and when he died, she never bounced back. With her long thin neck and bony body, she looked like a wounded swan. Graceful and lost. Even though he kept his distance from her — for survival, he said — she was, after all, his mother. He rarely talked about her. Now Lisa could see why. If he'd have let her, she'd have grabbed onto him like a raft in a changeable sea, hanging on, pulling him down along with her.

"I'm sorry, Mrs. Taylor."

Mac's mother looked straight through her.

Lisa offered, "We could get some of the things packed up. Maybe give Mac's clothes to Goodwill? What do you want to do with the furniture? Mrs. Taylor?"

"Lisa, dear, will you get me a cup of water, please?"

"Of course." Lisa was glad to go into the kitchen until she saw how she'd left it. She'd forgotten she was living like an animal in those days after. There were stars of cream floating on top of cold coffee, plates with toast crumbs and curdled cream cheese. Sitting on the windowsill was Mac's father's pipe and an ashtray with a mess of paper and ash. Lisa quickly tossed the ashtray and put the pipe in her pocket, let the water run cold to soak the plates and poured water into two glasses.

Liselah, take a good look at her, sitting shiva her whole life like she's the only one who ever lost a husband. You have your whole life ahead of you, kunahurra, you should live to be a hundred. Now go, give her the water before she faints dead away in your living room. Pack up and get out of there.

Lisa smiled. Good old Grandma. Always pushing her forward. She brought Mrs. Taylor the water. She touched her lips to the cup and stood up. "Take whatever you want and I'll hire someone to dispose of the rest."

"I know. It hurts too much to be around Mac's things. The only things I really want are the two paintings we bought together and some books. Maybe I'll be able to look at them someday."

"Very well, then. Take anything you want," she murmured. Lisa had the urge to hug her to see if she was real or a ghost. If she didn't have the same shaped mouth and eyes, she would never have thought this to be Mac's mother. She was a brittle, prim twig. No wonder he never went home. "Good luck to you, dear," Mrs. Taylor stood and shook Lisa's hand.

"Thank you. Take care."

"Good-bye." Mac's mother sucked out what little air there was left in the apartment. It seemed like a mortuary without a body. Lisa stood in the doorway to Mac's office with a box in hand and noticed that the room seemed to have contracted. A room that always seemed to have its own buzz became just a room. The desk, a painted door on cinder blocks so that Mac could have wide workspace, suddenly looked like a door. The shelves sagged under the weight of the books, and the cover of his turntable was thick with dust.

She walked over to it and saw the last thing he had listened to was Clapton. He loved the driving beat of *Layla* and he'd often play it before starting work. To psych up, he would say. Running her hands over the desk, she picked up stacks of paper and put them in the box. She took *Gatsby* and a few other books, willing herself to stop weeping.

Off to the side was another long surface with all Lisa's art supplies — boxes, a basket of collected materials, paper, toothpicks, sticks, twigs, paints, shellac, newspaper, dry leaves, and flowers. She had been working on a new box called Harvest, but she was having trouble sorting it out. She'd made two stick figures from Popsicle sticks and fashioned the cylindrical hats Vietnamese farmers might wear when harvesting rice. She cut out construction paper hats but hadn't gotten as far as putting them on the stick figures. What she planned to do was to have the farmers standing in rice paddies tinged in red. Around that, she'd add the golds and reds of a Northeast harvest season. It had been the box she was thinking about when she walked down her street into the end of the life she knew and loved. How sweet it had been working together. She knew it then, but now it seemed to her she didn't appreciate it nearly enough.

In the bedroom, she packed her clothes and toiletries, avoiding Mac's side of the closet. But then she couldn't help herself. She walked in and among his shirts pressing them to her face, inhaling what remained of the lemony scent mixed with bleach. She took his faded blue work shirt, held it, and then put it on over her clothes. There was a slip of paper in the front pocket: *Elena* and a phone number. Lisa shrugged. She was probably going to be his next teaching assistant.

It was her favorite shirt. It was the one he wore that first day of class and it was the shirt he covered her with one day after they made love on the beach. There had been many trips to the beach but there was something magical about that one day. They both knew they'd remember it, though not this way. It was to be a memory they would share when they looked back on how they began. Lisa hoped that someday those memories would not feel so much like a branding iron searing her soul.

They'd packed a lunch and headed out in Mac's convertible. A light morning rain brought out the spring smell of the earth; green shoots popped up, bare branches were dotted with buds.

Lisa closed her eyes to feel the wind on her face. The sun was warm. Mac had his arm around her, his other hand on the wheel.

"Open your eyes, Sleeping Beauty." He kissed the top of her head. "We're here."

He parked the car and they headed down the path to the beach. Lisa carried the blanket, Mac the picnic basket and wine.

"Over there." She pointed to a spot obscured by a dune's tall grasses and wildflowers. They set down the blanket and picnic basket. She looked up at the blue sky. "Thank you whoever is up there for giving us this perfect day!"

They lay down on the blanket, Lisa's head rested on Mac's chest. "Whenever I come here, I think of my father," he said. "I wish you could have known him. He gave me good advice from the time I was a little kid. He would say in his deep voice, 'MacKenzie, keep your life simple. Respect your instincts. Live every one of your days as if it's your last.' I wonder if he knew he was going to die young, without warning. He would never leave the house without kissing my mother goodbye. He started teaching me from the time I could walk. We went on hikes all the time. When I tired, he would hoist me onto his shoulders and name the birds, the trees, the flowers." Mac closed his eyes to feel the warmth of the sun. "He died on a day just like this one, on an early spring morning. He left the house to go to the store and died in the parking lot, mowed down by an old lady driving a Cadillac who confused the brake pedal with the gas. Gone. Just like that."

Lisa touched his face. "Your father was a smart man and he taught you well. You, too, live large, packed days."

"He was an English teacher in the best sense and never really treated me as a kid. He could always pull out just the right words to illustrate his point. One of his favorite quotes was Fitzgerald's, *there are no second acts in American lives*. How is that for motivation? I was young when he died, but I remember he had a way of seeing clear through to the heart of any matter. I only wish he could have known you."

They were quiet for a moment.

"You want to know the advice my father gave me?" Lisa asked.

"Sure."

"He offered me many pearls of wisdom but his best, the one that made him laugh every time he said it was, 'I've got something surprising to tell you, Lisa. Money doesn't grow on trees. You see those green things hanging from the maple out in the yard? They are leaves not dollar bills."

Mac laughed and rolled over on her. He kissed her hair, forehead, eyelids, cheeks, moving slowly toward her mouth for a long, slow gentle kiss. She threw her leg over his, pulling him closer. He kissed her neck, slowly working down her body, opening her blouse. Lost in each other they didn't care who might see them. After they made love, Mac covered her with that shirt she loved. For that moment, they were alone in the world of warm sun on a perfect spring morning.

"Lisa, you here?"

"In the bedroom." She quickly tossed the shirt into her suitcase, pulled a rumpled tissue out of her pocket and roughly dabbed her eyes.

"There you are. Stand up and let me look at you." Marika held her shoulders and looked at her for a moment before wrapping her in a tight hug.

"I can't breathe. Let go."

"Wimpy as ever! So where are we in the packing? No fooling around and no crying, Missy. We're gonna get it done and outta here." Marika took the two paintings off the wall and leaned them by the front door. She unplugged the lamps and put them by the door as well. "What about the kitchen? Never mind. Finish packing your clothes."

She quickly washed and dried the dishes and cups, opened one of the boxes she brought and layered the dishes one on top of the other cushioned by newspaper, wrapped the glasses and threw in the cutlery.

Lisa heard the clatter and went into the kitchen. "What are you doing? I told you I don't want to bring anything. Besides, my car can barely fit the two of us."

"Don't you worry about me, Missy. Just keep moving so we can get out of here. Ruby's husband, Charlie, has a truck and he is outside double-parked. So what do you say we take some furniture?"

Lisa frowned. "How many times do I have to tell you I don't want anything?"

"So, Mrs. Moneybags, you have the money to go out and furnish an apartment?"

"I don't want any reminders, Marika. Please. I can't bear it."

"Honey, it's okay." She pushed back the hair falling over Lisa's eyes. "You'll never recognize them. I'm making slipcovers. I got a terrific deal on gorgeous material in Chinatown. A special order got cancelled. All your favorite colors — purples, pinks, and blues in batiked swirls. Nothing close to this ugly green. Hush yourself. I don't want to hear about it. We'll store it until it's time."

"I don't want any of it." Lisa muttered.

"We can always ditch it later. You're taking the paintings, aren't you?"

Lisa had not intended to bring any of it but what did it matter? She could throw everything out later, couldn't she?

"Are we ready? Good. Let's get the couch in first. Pick up that end. It's light." Marika backed out the front door while Lisa got the couch through the doorway.

Charlie helped them quickly pack the truck. Marika stayed outside while Lisa took one long, last look. She walked through the rooms, each altered in some way: a missing couch, a wall with holes, an empty counter-top. All she had left was how she remembered him.

At that moment, life didn't scare her anymore. She had no place to go but up.

ॐ

Lisa and Marika followed Charlie's truck to their house. He cleared out part of their basement to store her things. "Charlie, how can I thank you?" Lisa asked.

He smiled, "Didn't Ruby tell you? You're paying me in cinnamon rolls."

"You bet. With pecans and raisins!"

"Speaking of cinnamon rolls, I'm starved," Marika said.

"When aren't you, Marika?" Charlie laughed as he and the girls trekked up and down the cellar stairs.

"Lisa!" Amber ran into her arms.

"Hi, princess. I have a treat for you after lunch. Did Mama tell you I've been working in a bakery? I've learned how to make the best cookies."

"Can we have them now?" Amber asked.

"Go wash up, silly." Marika patted her head. "Lunch before dessert and then after you've eaten, you can play in the living room."

Lisa shook her head. "Amber's getting tall. What are you feeding that girl?"

"Not enough. She seems to be hungry all the time."

"Lisa, it's so good to see you. You okay, baby?" Ruby asked, hugging her.

She nodded, "I'm getting there."

She squeezed her before letting go. "You are going to be just fine."

"You think so? I'm not so sure," Lisa admitted.

"I sure do. Ah, there's the doorbell. Amber, will you see who's at the door?" Ruby asked.

Amber held Amy's hand and led her into the kitchen. "Amy! I'm so happy to see you. Come here," Lisa hugged her.

"You gave us all such a scare," Amy said. "I'm relieved you're okay."

Lisa teased, "I know, *Mom.* I'm sorry!"

Amy grabbed her hands. "I'm glad to see you still remember how to irritate me. I'll forgive you this one time." She grinned. "Thank heavens you are returning to the land of the living. What's this I hear about a big plan?"

"Let's eat first," Ruby said.

"It's so good to see all of you." Lisa teared up.

"No getting sentimental." Marika stared hard at her, searching for internal breaks and bruises.

"Quit looking at me, will you? I guess some things don't change. Bossy as ever."

Marika smiled. "Count on it."

Once the dishes were cleared, Ruby poured the coffee and put out the pastry and cookies. "You can bake for me anytime! These are mighty good."

The others echoed Ruby's approval. "These are yummy. How many can I have, Mama?" Amber asked.

"How about one more?"

"Only one?" Amber scrunched up her face.

"You go on now. Ruby's daughter will be back any minute to play with you."

"Honey, there are toys on the shelf by the TV," Ruby added.

"Oh all right, they're small. Here take these." Marika put one of each kind on a napkin.

"Thanks, Mama."

"See you later, Amber," Lisa called after her.

"All right Missy, it's time to tell us the *big plan*."

Lisa took a deep breath. "During the early mornings when I was sitting on the beach feeling sorry for myself, I watched the sandpipers. Actually, Isabela corrected me and said they were sanderlings or piper plovers or something. But, they're all related. I still like to call them sandpipers because they remind me of the Pied Piper. You remember that children's story?"

"This is your plan? A lesson on birds?" Marika interrupted, frowning.

"I'm getting to it, Marika. Humor me, okay?" She covered Marika's hand with hers. "Where was I? Oh, right. They are small shore birds with long skinny legs. They travel in groups. You rarely see them alone. They run back and forth into the water, leaving tiny prints in the wet sand. They have so much energy. Back and forth, frantically running down the beach, they work at high speed. For some reason, they are always in a group even though they're each doing their own thing. One morning it occurred to me that many women these days are like the sandpipers. They have obstacles that would be less daunting if they were in a group."

"Isn't that the truth!" Ruby said.

"But what does that have to do with birds?" Amy asked.

"Nothing. It's a metaphor."

Amy rolled her eyes.

"I want to open a Center that helps get women on their feet. Job training, child care, for starters. Then I want to branch out to other things — maybe even an arts and crafts gallery, courses, the list could be endless. But first we'll focus on stabilizing women who are on the verge of a new life after the one they knew crashed."

"Sounds hard and expensive," Ruby said.

"Where would you even start?" Amy asked. "I'd be totally overwhelmed."

"I won't be alone. Marika will be my partner."

"You're still on that. I'm not going to any cow town." Marika folded her arms across her chest. "Moving back to Albany? The place you couldn't wait to leave? The place you never ever wanted to go back to?" Marika shook her head. "I'm sure as hell not going there."

"Maybe Marika has a point. You shouldn't be doing anything this drastic now," Ruby counseled. "It's too soon. Look at you. You're still in pain. Anyone can see that."

"I know. But Albany is the perfect place. The bigger cities have started programs but the smaller ones are behind. I heard that Albany has some empty buildings ready to bite the dust. It feels right to me."

"So where do I fit in?" Marika asked.

"A new beginning. A safer home for Amber. Good schools. It's a risk for me, too. But I think this will work. No, I know I can make this work. We can make this work but I can't do it without you."

Marika shook her head. "I am not moving." She slammed down her cup, coffee sloshed the saucer.

"It's scary, I know and it's going to take me some time to get start-up money. We'll do it right," Lisa half-smiled, unconvincing.

Ruby said, "She's right, Marika. Have you forgotten how hard it was with a baby, a good-for-nothing man giving you no help, bills piling up, afraid of taking Amber to the park? Think how things might have been if you had that kind of help." She paused. "You should trust Lisa. It's her faith in you that brought you to this table. Keep an open mind."

"Marika, quit glaring at me," Lisa said. "Maybe in time we can help women start their own businesses. You could become a dress designer."

Marika shook her head. "You're dreaming."

"Maybe." Lisa's eyes clouded over.

"Missy, I'm sorry. Please don't cry. But I don't think you know what you're getting yourself into." Marika reached over to touch her.

"I'm sold. If anybody can do this, you can," Ruby said. "Go for it, baby. It's time for things to go right for you. I think some of the grants we got for the mothers' program at the daycare center may be something for you to look at."

"I need to do this. I can't stay here," Lisa sobbed. Amy came around the table to put her arms around her.

"Yes, you can. Why don't you stay with Nina and me for awhile? Just as we always planned. You can crash with us as long as you want." Amy held her.

Lisa shook her head. "Here." Ruby handed her a tissue and Lisa blew her red nose and wiped her eyes.

"Thanks for the offer, Amy. I'm not sure of anything except I know that I can't stay here. I have to do something challenging and totally absorbing. And I don't want to do it alone. Marika, you have nothing to keep you here. Think about that. And you can always come back if it's a bust. Me too."

"The girl talks sense. Wouldn't you like to get out of the dump you're living in?" Ruby asked.

Lisa sighed. "Marika, just promise me you'll think about it. Please."

"Okay. I'll think about it," Marika conceded. "But don't count on me."

Chapter Nine

Lock up Your Sorrow and Throw Away the Key

∽

Lisa knew it would be hard to go home. Every week, she pushed back the date. Not yet, not ready, one more thing to do. Going back to her hovering family was not the best idea she'd ever had, yet she knew she had no choice; the alternative was not an option.

"You have to push yourself over the line, from the sand to the water. Pick a date and stick to it," Isabela advised.

Lisa nodded. "I know."

"It's nearly spring. Even Albany wakes up green eventually, doesn't it?"

Lisa agreed. "Yes. I have that to look forward to." She stared out the window. "Leaving you is going to be so hard."

"Child, look at me. We are in each other's lives now and we'll stay that way. Try not to get attached so easily."

"Am I too attached to you?" Lisa asked, her voice thick.

"I was giving you general advice. You make yourself too vulnerable. You know I'm right." Lisa didn't answer. "Listen to me. Mooning over what was is no way to live. And you can't let other people put you down. You have to go back home as the woman you are, not as the misunderstood child you once were. You've got to live as if you know what you are doing."

There was nothing Lisa could say to that.

❧

Isabela said, "I never realized how lonely I'd been. You've been good for me. Since you are looking ahead, so am I."

Lisa put her arms around Isabela. "I'm glad. I hate to think of all this as one-sided."

"No. You breathed life into this old girl. Now it's time for both of us to get on with it."

Isabela pulled her close. She promised she'd come visit when business was slow and in return Lisa said she'd be back to work in the bakery whenever she could.

"Ah sure," Isabela sighed.

"I will, you'll see," Lisa promised.

"You'll mean to."

"I love you," Lisa said, kissing her good-bye. "Thank you for rescuing me," she whispered in her ear. Isabela held Lisa's head between her hands and kissed both cheeks.

She got in the car, tooted the horn, and through the rearview mirror saw Isabela waving as she drove away.

❧

Shadowbox: Great Expectations

The box has an open door in its center. On one side are little girl items- a doll, a block, bike handlebar streamers. On the other side is a kaleidoscope of color. Paper doll silhouettes of varying shapes and sizes stand against of backdrop of buildings.
Confetti is strewn on the floor.

The time Lisa had been waiting for had finally come. She was on her way to college in Boston, on the way to start her life. As the Stern family approached the city, it seemed to Lisa that the buildings rose up across the river as testament to her soaring expectations. Stone buildings in grays, browns and brick, glass skyscrapers, buildings squat and tall, church spires juxtaposed art deco and modern buildings on narrow cobblestone streets and boulevards with tree-lined center islands. She believed that all of it held her destiny and could hardly contain her exhilaration.

See Liselah, this is how I felt when I finally saw the Statue of Liberty. The worst is over. I'm getting off the stinkin' boat and into a new, good life. Vey is mir. It was nothing like I thought. So don't expect too much. Life is no bowl of cherries no matter where you live.

Not even Grandma could dampen her enthusiasm. Sitting in the back seat of her parents' car as they passed through this mix of concrete and steel, highway and bridges and paths along the river, Lisa knew this was it. She could feel the vibration of Boston welcoming her.

The sound of her mother's voice penetrated her thoughts. "I don't know why you picked this. There were so many colleges. With your grades, you could have gotten in anywhere."

"Rose, please," her father said. "That's all water under the bridge."

"I worry about our daughter. It's so easy to get lost in a city. And the crime? What about the crime, Jack? Sue me for worrying."

"I'm still here, you know. You could talk to me about me," Lisa said, her nose pressed to the side window.

"A mother worries. It's natural." She took out a Kleenex and dabbed her eyes.

"Are you crying, Mom?"

"I'm just teary."

"I thought you'd be happy to get rid of me," Lisa said, distracted.

"How could you say that? I'm your mother. The house will be empty without you."

"I'll be fine, Mom. Don't worry. Look, there it is: Charles River University. Daddy, look at those three towers. My dorm. Wow! I'm finally here." They were greeted by college kids who loaded suitcases and odds and ends onto rolling carts.

They checked in and found the bank of elevators for her tower. "Room 513. Here it is."

The door was partially open. A lanky, brown-haired girl in jeans and a college sweatshirt stood in the doorway. "Hi. I'm Amy Wilson. Are you Lisa?"

"Yes. Hi, Amy. The room is great. I love your purple quilt. My favorite color."

Lisa and Amy lugged the suitcases in while her father carried the stereo. "Thanks, Daddy. Everything is in. Before you get on the road, you should look around the city. Maybe you could go to one of the fish restaurants we were reading about," Lisa said.

"Home? Already? Let me at least make your bed," Rose offered.

Lisa shook her head. "No, thanks. I can do it."

"What about the stereo? You want me to hook up your speakers?" her father asked.

"No thanks, Daddy. I'll do it later."

Her father looked at her mother. "She's a big girl, Rosie." He gathered Lisa in a big bear hug. "I hope this is everything you want it to be."

"Thanks, Daddy. I love you so much."

He kissed her cheeks. "I love you, sweetheart. You're a smart girl. Make the most out of it."

"I will." She snuggled into him.

"Bye, Mom." Lisa hugged her and pulled her close. "Don't worry, I'll be fine."

"You'll call every Sunday?"

"Yes. Every Sunday."

"Okay, then." Rose smoothed down her skirt. "Nice meeting you, Amy. Have a good year." She turned to leave but stopped just outside the doorway. "You should know one thing before we go. Lisa can be very moody. Miss Gloom and Doom, I call her. Don't take it personally. When she's lying on her bed in the dark in the middle of the day, she'll get over it."

Lisa said, "Mom! How could you do this to me?" She turned to Amy. "Now you know why I picked the biggest school I could find three hours from home. My mother hallucinates."

"Lisa, what a thing to say. I didn't mean to hurt your feelings. I just wanted Amy to know that when you're lying in bed looking at the wall, it's not over anything she's done."

"And what about my feelings? Do you ever think about my feelings? Goodbye, Mom."

Lisa slammed the door in her face.

∽

Maybe she should have taken Amy up on the offer to live with her. She smiled remembering Amy's calm reaction to her impatiently explaining something that she thought Amy didn't understand. Exasperated, she would say, "Lisa, I'm from Ohio, not Mars." She made Lisa laugh. Better than Miss Gloom and Doom. Well, Mom, if you think I was gloomy before, you're in for it now. Heading back, trapped in a jar like a lightning bug to be examined by the whole family. She shook her head thinking of how she'd plotted and planned to escape as long as she could remember and turned up the radio full blast.

The first sign she noticed said Albany eight miles. She didn't remember any of the drive past the Massachusetts towns. The town names she didn't know how to pronounce at first — Chicopee, Worcester which is Wusta, Leicester, Lesta. Belchertown was her favorite. She always wanted to get off the highway and give up a good burp. So much compressed into a few years. That first trip began her liberation and now as a twenty-six year old woman she was going back to the place she'd never really been happy. What was she doing?

She shook her head to throw off those thoughts. She would know soon enough if coming back was a mistake. At least it was nearing spring. She'd be home to see the magnificent flowers in bloom. Lisa always hated the bleakness of northeastern winters. But there was nothing like the earthy smell of early spring. She opened the window to breathe in the air. The air was still a bit chilly but not for long. It was the best time of year to be coming back.

So Liselah, here you are. You're lucky you have a family to come home to. Things are different for you now. Farshtase, understand? You're not a little girl, anymore. I won't be there to tell your mother to sha stil. You have to find your own way.

Lisa turned up the radio, sang John Lennon's *In My Life,* at the top of her lungs.

Home Sweet Home?

Getting off the Thruway, Lisa took the slow route home. Tulips were coming up, the daffodils, magnolia trees and lilacs were budding. As Lisa got out of the car and stretched, her mother ran to her, almost knocking her over.

"Mom!"

"Lisa, I'm so happy to see you," her mother said, one hand stroking her hair, the other holding her tight. She put her arm around Lisa's waist. "Come, let's go in. Daddy will unload the car later."

She made Lisa's favorite lunch: tuna, crunchy with green peppers, celery, and a touch of dill. Bagels slathered in chive cream cheese. "This is so good, Mom."

"It's only tuna." She looked her up and down. "And if it's so good why are you picking at it? You're too thin."

"I'm eating, not picking. I'm not that hungry and I brought dessert. Isabela and I made some Portuguese bread and pastries for you. I want to have room." She patted her stomach.

"All right, I'll make coffee. Why don't you put out some of the pastry?"

Lisa's mother poured the coffee and bit into one of the little cakes. "These are delicious."

"They're Isabela's version of Danish. Trutas. They're from southern Portugal. She usually makes them with a sweet potato filling and spikes the shell with whiskey but these are filled with lemon, sugar and cinnamon. Isabela wouldn't let me bring the whiskey trutas even though I told her you were all of age."

Her mother smiled. "Delicious. Isabela sounds like a nice person." She put down her coffee cup. "So? What's your plan?"

"Let's not talk about it just yet. First, catch me up on family business."

She said, "They're coming over for dinner tonight so you can hear it from them."

"No way, Mom. You've got to be kidding. I am not at all ready to see them."

Her mother pursed her lips. "Of course you are."

"I can't be here if it's going to be like it was when I was growing up." Lisa brought her dishes to the sink. "I can't do it." She started to cry.

Her mother stood behind her, wrapping her arms around Lisa's waist. "I thought they'd bring you comfort. If I call them now and say no, it'll be more trouble. A whole *mitziah*."

Lisa turned around. "Just let them all know in advance that the subjects of Mac and my business plans are off limits. I'm not up to an interrogation," Lisa sniffled and blew her nose. "Just tell them I'm fragile and can't be upset. Do me this favor, Mom. Please?"

"All right. I'll call them."

Lisa said, "Call Aunt Faye first."

"You're the boss. Just so you know, Aunt Faye is not herself. She has something wrong with her digestion that makes her afraid to eat. Salt and sugar are her big enemies. All she thinks and talks about is what she can eat, what she can't eat. 'How much salt did you put in the soup? You know I can't eat cake so why are you asking me?'" Her mother lamented.

"I can just imagine. Lot's wife turning into a pillar of salt every time she sees a shaker."

"Something like that." she smiled.

"You're feeling all right, Mom? You look tired."

"You have no idea how worried I've been about you... and losing Mama...what can I say about that?" Her eyes filled with tears. "Enough of that." She straightened up in her chair and sipped her coffee.

Lisa pushed away her plate. "So fill me in on the news."

"Let's see." Sitting back down at the kitchen table, she covered Lisa's hand with hers. "I don't know if you know this but Nicky's back home from Vietnam."

"No, I didn't. Thank heavens. I'll have to call him."

Her mother shook her head. "He's not the Nicky you knew. The war. Those poor boys. What they saw over there and what they had to do was too much. He was in the VA hospital for a long time. He needed four operations on his leg. He has a limp. At least he didn't lose his leg or God forbid get killed. But his head is all mixed up."

"Mixed up?"

"He's nervous. If you get within a couple of feet from him he gets all jumpy. He has bad headaches and black rings under his eyes. Sometimes he goes out and doesn't come home for days. Mrs. Ianelli is worried sick. She looks like she's aged twenty years. But, of course, she's relieved to have him home. You knew Johnny McGrath was killed almost right away?"

"Yes. That was awful. Where does Nicky go when he disappears?"

Lisa's mother shrugged. "Who knows? He's not the only one who came back like this."

"What does he do all day?"

She shook her head, "He hardly looks at you when you talk to him and if he does look up, his eyes are empty. Nothing's there." Lisa's mother sipped her coffee. "I hate to tell you this, my daughter, but it's like Nicky died too. I know how close you two were. But the Nicky you knew is gone."

Heat rose up on Lisa's face. "That pointless war. Poor Nicky. He was the sweetest boy."

Her mother murmured, "It's life."

The two women sipped their coffee. "So tell me what you're up to. You've had Daddy busy but he won't tell me a single thing. Never has he kept so quiet. So what's up? Or did you come back for my tuna fish?"

Lisa laughed. "Mom, you seem different."

"Maybe it's you who's different." She squeezed Lisa's hand.

"This is the gist. I set up appointments for next week with the mayor's office and some community groups to see what they are doing in the way of helping women get through some of the hardship in their lives." Lisa hesitated. "Mom, it's so weird sitting here without Grandma."

"I miss her every day. I haven't had the heart to rent the upstairs flat. But maybe you want to live up there?" she suggested.

"I don't think I could bear it." Lisa shook her head.

"Something to think about. You'd have your privacy and have time to get on your feet. Make some money."

Lisa couldn't believe her ears. She didn't think her mother ever knew there was such a concept as privacy. Her father must have talked to her. But her mother seemed different somehow. She couldn't quite put her finger on it. Maybe this would work after all.

The dining room seemed smaller than Lisa remembered. After hugs and kisses Lisa thought would leave bruises, they carried on as usual, Aunt Faye talking past her to Aunt Rena. They were all on their best behavior. Not one comment or question, except about the weather and Mom's delicious brisket and how happy they were to see her.

"A celebration for my daughter's homecoming. Lisa brought dessert. Cakes like you've never tasted," her mother announced before putting down a large platter of sliced meat surrounded by roasted potatoes and glazed carrots.

Her father held up a glass of wine. "I'd like to toast Lisa's homecoming. May this be a time for happiness."

"*L'chaim*. To life."

"So Lisa," Aunt Faye said. "Tell me what it's like to work in a bakery. We were so spoiled. The store bought doesn't come close to Mama's challah. Not that I'm asking you to do it. I know you'll be busy. But maybe you know how?"

"Isabela taught me some tricks to kneading and making sure the yeast mixture is the right temperature. It brought back my time as a little girl helping Grandma. I'd like to try to make it. The smell of the baking challah was something else, wasn't it?"

"Oy, only now I have to be so careful what I eat. At least if you make it, you know what's inside. How much sugar, how much salt."

Lisa and her mother exchanged glances.

Her father said. "Lisa will be very busy, Faye. She's starting her own business and I'm going to be her first investor."

"Daddy!"

"What are you talking about, Jack?" Rose asked.

"The drugstore is doing pretty well in its new location and I have to do something with some of the profit. Can't give it all to the tax man. I might as well say it here in front of everyone."

Lisa's cheeks were hot. "Daddy, please don't. It's not the right time."

"Sure it is. I had my accountant look at your business plan draft. He says it's solid, provided you can get help from the city."

Rose stood up at her place. "What is this all about? I want to know right this very second."

"I started to tell you this afternoon, but we got sidetracked, Mom."

"Sit down, Rose. Take that frown off your face. We have a smart daughter and one with a big heart."

"I appreciate your confidence in me, Daddy, but I really want to do this on my own. I'm going to get grants and corporate donations."

"For what? What are you talking about?" Aunt Rena asked.

"All right. This is it. But I don't want anybody to say a thing. Just listen, okay?"

They nodded, throwing looks — this time worried ones, not the usual rolling of the eyes.

"The general idea is to help women who are single, divorced, and widowed get back on their feet. I've talked to people. They think it's a good idea. It's certainly needed. And I want to do it right here in Albany. There is nothing like it happening here."

"After all you've been through, don't you think you should take it easy?" Aunt Rena said.

"No. It's because of what I've been through that I'm doing this. I've decided that I'm going to throw all my energy into this. But that's all for now. Okay? I want you all to catch me up on the news."

"Before we close the subject, don't forget the rest of us. We have a few dollars to put together for you," Aunt Faye said.

"And so do we," Uncle Ira said.

Looking around the table, Lisa started to cry. The aunts and uncles who always put down every idea she ever had, who called her the *Queen for a Day* after the show in which women competed to have the worst problems, now circled around her. Lisa knew she had to be careful but it felt great to be on solid, familiar ground — ground loaded with traps, maybe, but not today.

"Is it possible for any of you to be silent partners?" she asked. Laughter filled a room hungry for life.

Lisa sprawled out on her bed and called Marika. "Hello."

"Lisa! Hi! How was the family reunion?"

"Fine. No, better than fine. The whole family will soon be competing about who can invest the most money. My dad got the ball rolling, and then he just sat back and winked at me."

"You sure you want to be doing this?"

"Yes." Lisa twirled the cord around her finger.

"So what else? I know you. This wasn't just a hello, Marika, how's the weather call."

Lisa chuckled. "You don't let me get away with anything. You know my grandma lived upstairs. It's a three-bedroom with an alcove, living room, dining room, front and back porch, and eat-in kitchen. My mother said she couldn't bear to rent it so I should consider it. I was thinking..."

Grandma's voice filled her head, shouting. *Home for one day and already you're making trouble. Who do you think you are bringing a shvartzah to live in your parent's house. After what they did to your father. What's the matter with you? Once in a while it wouldn't hurt you to think about somebody other than you. Lisa Rachel.*

"Are you still on the line?" Marika asked.

"Yeah, I'm here. I couldn't hear you for a second." Lisa took a deep breath. "What would you think about us living together? That would get you here faster. The neighborhood school is three blocks away and it's a good one. There are kids to play with on the street."

"You're asking me to come now when we don't know if this idea of yours is going to fly and you've just gotten home?"

"It's going to work. I'm as sure of that as anything. But for argument's sake, say it's a bust. The worst that can happen is you go back. Or get a job here until we get it up and running."

"And what would your family think about you living with a colored girl who has a child and no husband. Excuse me, I mean *shvartzah* living with their daughter under their roof."

"You are planning to come! Brushing up on your Yiddish already!" Lisa exclaimed.

Lisa, you're so naïve, Marika thought. Brushing up on my Yiddish? Not exactly. Jews owned the stores in our neighborhood. When I went to the store with Mrs. Daniels, the store would get real quiet and they'd whisper to each other to watch the shvartzahs, overcharging us and treating us like thieves. So yeah, I know that word. And some others.

Lisa went on, "Anyway, the family seems different to me. And if it doesn't work, we'll move elsewhere. And it's rent free. We'll only pay for utilities."

"I don't know. It doesn't feel right," Marika faltered. "You just got home. Take things easy."

"Don't want to live with white folk?"

"Hmm. Maybe not."

"Okay. Just come for a visit. Please."

"I will. Give me some time to make arrangements for Amber. She could probably stay with Ruby for a weekend."

"Okay. I'll call you after I meet with the mayor and company."

"Good luck with that."

"Thanks. I think it will go well. My father gave me background material that he got from the alderman. This is democratic-machine country. For once I belong to the right group."

Liselah, before you bring troubles into your house, spend some time with your mama. She needs you. Can't you see that? Look around you for once.

Chapter Ten

People Get Ready

Curtis Mayfield 1965

෴

Like Lisa, Albany was in a state of painful transition. Forty square blocks, in the heart of the city were razed to make way for a new government center. Whole neighborhoods were reduced to rubble, leaving poor families crammed into too few apartments or with no place to live at all. The demolished houses were old and in disrepair, but home was home. When you lose that and your life is upended, it changes you forever — a constant in her grandma's stories. *So you try your best to make a home wherever you are, but it isn't the same, ach, you look for something you've lost but after a while, you can't remember what you're looking for.*

Lisa understood how unfair this large-scale demolition was and was surprised things didn't blow up sooner. A hundred years after slaves were freed and nearly fifteen years after school segregation became illegal, Albany was in racial distress. Not all, but many black students were shortchanged in how and where they spent their school day, and many of them were the same students who'd lost their homes to the wrecking ball.

She had a friend in elementary school who lived in a house slated to be torn down. Lisa had loved going there. She thought it was exotic and mysterious with its brocade and beaded curtains hung over the doorways, colored fabric thrown over lampshades, and the smell of cigarettes mixed with candles that she later found out was incense. She loved the dark shellacked wood and worn Persian rugs scattered on the floors. But the architects of the new government center and the bulldozers didn't share her view. Ninety-eight acres of city homes just like that one were destroyed. Urban redevelopment might sound like a good thing but as her father said, it's the kind of thing that only looks good on paper.

∾

Lisa's high school couldn't accommodate all its students. Property had been identified to build a much larger school. Lisa's class was supposed to be first to graduate from the new school but ground hadn't even been broken until she'd finished college.

The school was forced to use classrooms in nearby buildings. The main building was an old elementary school. A half block away were some college buildings that were part of the state university and further away on the next corner was a beat up red brick building called the East Building Annex. Window panes were cracked and taped allowing ice to form on the inside of the windows. At the other extreme, the radiators would emit so much heat, sweat dripped down the students' faces. The wooden desks were gouged and the books worn. Students had to walk back and forth between buildings because all the common areas — the cafeteria, the library, and the gym — were in the main building. Needless to say, it was an unwelcome hike during Albany's snowy winters.

College-track students were in the main building and took advanced placement courses in the college building next door. Others who were taking general or business courses and students needing special education were sent a block away to the dilapidated building. It was a situation waiting to burst wide open.

The tension was palpable, yet it was inert. When an ashen-faced teacher blew the whistle in gym class for the students to go sit on the bleachers, there was uncharacteristic quiet. Lisa feared the worst; somebody must be dead.

The teacher spoke softly "Something terrible has happened." Tears rolled down her cheeks as she told the class of Martin Luther King's murder. A low-pitched howl came from two girls sitting together on the top rail. Most of the kids were struck dumb. Stunned and weeping students stumbled through the day and groups congregated by race.

That evening, there was a downtown vigil. Lisa lied to her mother and told her she was going to a sleepover at a friend's house. She took the bus downtown and stood with the mourners. The crowd was large but quiet. Candles flickered. Lisa was in tears, overwhelmed by both sadness and dashed hope.

She heard a ruckus coming from behind her. "What's going on?" she whispered to the woman standing next to her.

"I don't know. But it doesn't sound good. Heaven help us all," she shuddered.

Four white men circled a black man while another beat him with a four-foot pipe. Several bystanders tried to break it up by wrenching the pipe free from the man's hand. There was a scuffle, tempers were red hot, and fists flew — both black and white. There was shouting and pushing. Before long, the police chief was on a megaphone telling everyone to disperse.

Most of the crowd went home. Some remained and Lisa stayed with them. They sang gospel hymns and Lisa hummed along: *We'll sing of the Shepherd that died, that died for the sake of the flock/ His love to the utmost was tried/ But firmly endured as a rock.* The vigil lasted until sunrise and Lisa went straight to school.

When she got home, she read the newspaper account of what happened. "Oh my God. Liars," she muttered. "How could they write this?"

Last night, an unruly crowd of Negroes gathered downtown. Police were called in to disband the crowd. The Brothers, a civil rights group, were allegedly responsible for the trouble. One Negro man, beaten with a pipe, was brought to the hospital in serious condition. No charges have been filed.

Student rage festered and, when it surfaced, exploded into fury. Black and sympathetic white students wrecked the East Building. They hurled chairs and desks through windows and overturned bookcases. Books were torn to shreds and set on fire.

By the time the police came, the auditorium in the main building was in ruins. Seats were cut with knives and scissors, the backstage area was decimated. All the stage props and music stands were mangled. Some of the costumes were set on fire. Police evacuated most of the kids.

"Anybody makes a move and off to jail you go. File out of here and go home if you know what's good for you,"

"Home?" a boy shouted. "You haven't seen anything yet. "

The cop pulled him by his shirt collar. "Anybody else have something to say?"

Lisa filed out with the others from her history class and stood on the lawn of the church across the street to watch as police wagons pulled up. There was a round-up of the kids who were still in the auditorium. They spent a night in jail before charges were dropped. Nobody knew who did what because all the students, black and white — and the teachers too — kept their mouths shut.

Lisa's father and Uncle Ira owned a pharmacy in the south end of town. The Royal Theater with its flashing movie marquee, Zuckman's Bakery, Goldfarb's Grocery, and Paragon Paint all closed. Jack and Ira knew they'd eventually have to relocate too. Their customers moved further uptown and went to suburban drug stores. The police called a couple of nights a week because the drugstore had been robbed or vandalized. One time, kids got in and broke bottles of mouthwash. The store smelled like Listerine for weeks, no matter how many times they washed the floor and shelves. Rose paced and worried; she claimed Jack hadn't had a good night's sleep in months.

When her parents, aunts and uncles got together over coffee, Lisa often overheard their conversation about break-ins and near misses at the drugstore and at another uncle's jewelry store. They were so loud, she could hear them sometimes even when her door was closed. It was usually boring gossip or they'd be talking about her or her cousins, but one night she heard her mother crying. "He could have shot you. Thank God, you had what he wanted. But, what if you didn't? You gotta get out of there, Jack."

Lisa sprinted out of her room into the dining room and threw her arms around her father's neck. "Daddy? Somebody pointed a gun at you? Somebody tried to shoot you?" She buried her head in his chest.

"What are you doing eavesdropping?" her mother reprimanded.

"Rose." Aunt Rena put a finger to her lips.

"It's okay, honey." He stroked her hair. "Looks like we'll be moving uptown too." He shook his head. "Nobody will be left. I'm one of the last holdouts. Then what?"

Chapter Eleven

❧

Shadowbox: Meeting the Boys

Six cardboard cut-outs of men sit at a table made of Popsicle sticks. The man in the center sits tall in his chair and holds a cigar. The scene is meant to imitate the appearance of the Last Supper. A girl, made from a paper doll mounted on cardboard, is facing them holding a megaphone and whistle. Stacked next to her is a pile of paper. As she speaks through the megaphone to get their attention, only one of the men looks her way.

Lisa stood at her closet pulling out hangers — a patchwork peasant skirt, an Indian print dress, a gauzy embroidered blouse. She had nothing to wear to a meeting. Why didn't she think of that before? She needed a suit or even a pair of pants that weren't jeans. Preoccupied with what she had to say, she'd forgotten to get something businesslike to wear. The hell with it. I'll look like me and they'll have to get over it.

She put on a black, brown and white-swirled shirt, a black gauze skirt, and made a headband out of a white scarf to hold her curls back, Black espadrilles, hoop earrings and a touch of lipstick. She looked in the mirror. Hardly a professional outfit for a meeting with the Mayor but what could she do now? She looked at the time. "Oh my God, worse than what I'm wearing, I'm going to be late," she said to the mirror.

Hitting every red light on her way downtown, she had about five minutes to find a place to park and get up to the meeting. Luckily, a Cadillac pulled out of a large spot right in front of City Hall and she maneuvered in on her first try.

The receptionist was on the telephone and pointed to a closed door. Breathlessly, Lisa opened it and walked in. Sitting at the wide conference table was the Mayor and his usual cronies. The joke around town was that the Mayor always had three people with him, not always the same ones. He rarely attended a meeting or chaired an event solo. They were referred to around town as his eyes, ears, and mind — better known as his Trinity. There was gossip that the mayor was a drinker who had blackouts. His entourage helped him keep up appearances.

"Excuse me, gentlemen. I'm sorry I'm a bit late. I'd forgotten how hard it was to park down here."

"That's fine, Lisa. We were chatting about abandoned city buildings and whether it was better to bulldoze or try to save them." The Mayor leaned back in his chair. "As you can imagine, our building inspector and restoration architect have differing viewpoints."

"To say the least." A youngish dark-haired man with a neat beard stood up and extended his hand. "I'm David Lerner, outnumbered. On the side of building preservation."

She leaned over to shake his hand. "So happy to meet you."

"Yes. Yes. Introductions," the Mayor said, "To my right is Charlie Moore, Deputy Mayor. Jimmy O'Connor, Deputy Commissioner of Social Services. I believe you've met Tom Sullivan, the City Building Inspector. Reverend Avery from the Baptist Calvary Church, David. And of course, I'm Mayor Connelly."

"Pleasure to meet all of you."

"Why don't you tell us all about your little idea?" asked the Mayor. "I know you've toured some of the possible building sites with Tom but start at the beginning for the others."

Swallowing the Mayor's patronizing remark, Lisa inhaled the smoky air. She'd never seen Tom without a cigarette dangling from his cracked lips.

"This is the abbreviated concept. I want to open a women's center to address work issues, child care, and training."

Jimmy O'Connor interrupted, "Honey, my agency already does that. If you'd checked, you'd see we provide all kinds of services. Adding on a separate women's center, outside of social services, is both unnecessary and redundant."

Reverend Avery interjected, "Excuse me, Mr. O'Connor, but I think you will agree that after the creation of the government center, there have been many people who have fallen through the cracks and have yet to find suitable housing, let alone job training. I think we can always use fresh ideas. If you don't mind, I'd like to hear what Ms. Stern proposes to do."

O'Connor rolled his eyes. "Go on then."

Lisa took a deep breath. "The city owns a vacant building on Clinton near Pearl. It was a single family brownstone but was carved into three apartments — one on each floor. In my unprofessional opinion, it's a disaster." She paused and smiled at them. She saw she'd better punch it up a bit. Not yet to first base and one was hostile. Tom was nodding out, his multiple chins holding up his head. The Mayor squirmed in his chair and kept checking the clock. But the architect was alert, never taking his eyes off her.

"Depending on whether or not it can be brought back to usable space without breaking the bank, there are other possibilities on Central Avenue near Lark Street. But if possible, I'd like to avoid a commercial building. I envision transforming the brownstone into a home for women with a reception and child care area. We'll contract out job counseling and skills training at first, and we'll procure clothing for women to wear in the workplace. As you can see, that tends to be a problem for all of us." She gestured toward her own clothing. She looked around but only David smiled.

"Our target will be wide. Young single mothers, older displaced homemakers, minority, immigrant women, recent widows, vets' wives and the like. In doing some research on city demographics, we could serve a range of women to help get them out of poverty. I'll pass around this summary sheet I've prepared for you."

Lisa passed out her information sheets and explained why job training and support was essential but, as they grew, she'd like to develop the space as a community center, an art gallery, whatever the clients wanted. She described leads for grant money and private donors. "So what do you gentlemen think?"

The Mayor smiled broadly, "Very interesting."

Tom coughed out, "That building is a mess. Why don't you put up a serviceable cinder block building on one of our abandoned lots?"

Jimmy crossed his arms. "What you are proposing is a duplication of service."

"I'm sorry, Mr. O'Connor, I don't mean to contradict you but when I did my research, I found that the job training grant had been severely reduced and there was no accommodation for children during the sessions, so women could not attend consistently."

He dismissed her. "That is a temporary problem we're working on."

The Deputy Mayor leaned in toward the Mayor. "This might not be a bad idea. We're still reeling from the fallout of tearing down all those old Dutch buildings. Never knew there would be a ballyhoo about stepped roofs, but there was hell to pay for that. And now we have this new historic preservation group to contend with."

"That doesn't mean we have to pour money into old buildings. They're condemned for a reason," said Tom. "We finally got rid of all those crappy buildings and we should keep on going. Get rid of 'em all."

Reverend Avery shook his head. "Gentleman, Ms. Stern is onto something. I live and work in that area. I'm sure some of my parishioners would want to help out as well. There are many tradesmen who are out of work right now. It is respectful to rebuild in the clients' community. These were beautiful buildings in their day and I would favor bringing them back. What neighborhoods are left after the city's wrecking ball should be preserved."

David Lerner said, "Reverend Avery is on target. We're hoping to move into a time of community rebuilding. I think Ms. Stern's proposal is both savvy and timely. When I was asked to attend this meeting, I called the chairman of the Historic Albany Board and they expressed interest. They also told me there might be money available from the federal government. As you know, my firm does pro bono work. While I can't promise it'll be a lot of time, what I can do is gratis." He looked at Lisa. "It seems to me, Lisa, that you've done your homework and could create something Albany could hold up as a model."

Tom Sullivan snickered. "Take this the right way, Lisa. You're pretty young and inexperienced to know what you are taking on."

"That's true. But I have long range goals," Lisa said. "I'm realistic enough to know we have to do this piecemeal. Although this certainly isn't my area of expertise, we first need to make the building safe — the roof, wiring, plumbing, all that. During this time, I will focus on fundraising and figuring out what I need to learn."

Mayor Connelly put his pen in his pocket without making a single note. "So it's a go, with caution."

The building inspector made a face as he doodled on Lisa's fact sheet. Jimmy O'Connor, from Social Services, slammed his briefcase shut.

"Don't look so glum, boys. We're still in the maybe stage. I'll have Mary set up a time for all of us to tour the finalists. We'll invite a photographer from the newspaper to generate some interest. In the meantime, David, if you want to go in and do an assessment of that building with the city engineers, go ahead."

He stood up. "Thank you for coming in. Jimmy, Tom, Charlie, stay put for a minute. We have some city business to discuss."

"Thank you, Mr. Mayor, "Lisa said.

Walking out with Lisa, Reverend Avery said, "Ms. Stern, don't be discouraged. What you are proposing could energize a community that has been defeated. Their initial reactions are always the same. But with hard work and good publicity, they can be persuaded." He put out his hand. "A pleasure meeting you."

"Thank you so much, Reverend. I can't tell you what it means to me that you are behind this."

He shook David's hand. "Good-bye, Mr. Lerner. Feel free to call me anytime. I live in the area we've been discussing and am familiar with most of the buildings."

"Will do." David turned to Lisa and smiled. "Don't you worry. We'll make this work. Can I give you a lift?"

"No, thanks. I'm parked right here."

Lisa got in her car. The meeting was over but her project was just beginning. She handled the politicos as best she could. Reverend Avery would be an important ally. David Lerner not only supported her ideas but volunteered his time.

The Center would happen, regardless of how the rest of them treated her.

Under Construction: Albany the Not so Beautiful

Lisa stood in the bus station waiting for Marika. She couldn't wait to see her and hoped she'd changed her mind about bringing Amber with her. Lisa surprised herself by how much she missed them.

"Marika, Marika! Over here!" Lisa ran toward her.

A wide smile crossed Marika's face and she put down her suitcase.

"You missed me." Lisa smiled.

"Not so much."

"I don't believe you." The two women walked arm in arm to the car. "By the way, where's your turban?"

Marika squeezed Lisa's arm. "All right. I did miss you. And Amber is missing you, too. She asks me every day when you'll be back. I haven't told her about the friggin' plan you hatched for us," she paused. "And the turbans, I think I want to give them a rest. Maybe wear them on special occasions. New starts and all that."

"Yeah, new starts. I'm starving. There is a really cute luncheonette nearby."

"Lead the way."

They were seated and ordered their food.

"So, are you okay, Li? The truth."

"Yes. I really am. I'm too busy to be brooding and, surprisingly, being back home with the family is better than I ever hoped." Lisa sighed. "When I was growing up, I was miserable because it seemed that they were always disappointed in me. My grandmother often told them they were hurting my feelings. She'd tell them to stop, and they'd say, stop what? What are we saying? She's exaggerating. But you wouldn't say that Gram was exactly the nurturing type either." Lisa sipped her coffee. "I could hear them in the dining room on Saturday nights when they came over for coffee and thought I was asleep. They'd talk about how overly sensitive I was, how strange it was that I was both a bully and a sap. They didn't get me."

Marika shook her head. "It sounds like you were a handful. And truth be told, I don't understand you a lot of the time."

Lisa frowned. "Really? I'm not that complicated! Anyway, I'm not sure if it's me or them who have changed. It's good. They seem more compassionate than what I remember. The weirdest thing is I hear my grandmother in my head telling me what to do just like she did when she was alive. It's almost like she's my conscience."

Marika shrugged. "It's not crazy. It happens. Have you told your mother your brilliant idea about us living together?"

"I mentioned it. Just to warm her up, but she didn't react. Just kept washing the dishes. She is looking forward to seeing you and has been obsessing over what to make for dinner."

"Did you tell her to make collards and black-eyed peas?"

"Didn't have to. She's making fried chicken and biscuits. As far as I remember, she never fried anything in her life so it should be interesting."

"That's nice that she'd want to do that."

Lisa rolled her eyes.

"I'd say any kind of mother is better than no mother at all, Lisa."

"You're right. I'm sorry."

The waitress put down the food. "Anything else, ladies?"

"We're fine," Marika said. "Soup's good."

"I told my mother we wouldn't be back much before dinner. I want to show you around. Give you a tour."

"That's good. You can show me where I'm going tomorrow," Marika said.

"What do you mean where you're going?"

"Ruby is as pushy as you are. She helped me schedule interviews at a couple of employment agencies. One is tomorrow morning. They have some kind of training program and I'm going to a temp agency in the early afternoon. I also want to go to some of the better department stores to see if I might find work as a seamstress. Are there department stores in this wilderness?"

"Are you serious? Cool." Lisa said.

"How many trips here do you think I can afford to take? I have to see if there is anything for me here. I thought about what you said, you know, that I can always go back. I've got to get Amber out of the hellhole we live in. And it's just too fucking expensive to go anywhere else. But," she paused, "there is more to consider than myself. There is William."

"William? As in Amber's deadbeat father?"

"I know he's lousy, but he is the only father Amber has. He sees her little enough now. I've told him what I'm thinking and he was a total asshole. He took the opportunity to tell me that my daughter now has a half-sister. He was gloating and I slapped him hard but it didn't make me feel any better. Only made my hand sting. Do I want to take her away from him altogether? I don't know how much that matters or whether she'll care more when she's older. But she'll never see him if we move. And another thing. Promise me you won't laugh."

Lisa put up her fingers, "Scout's Honor."

"I've never lived anywhere else," Marika muttered. Lisa stifled a laugh but couldn't contain herself. She broke out laughing and soon Marika joined her.

"Marika," Lisa sputtered. "What happened to the big bad wolf woman I first met and grew to love?"

"She was a tiring pain in the ass. I lost her somewhere and good riddance. So now that she's gone, I don't know if I'm more or less scared."

"Maybe starting over is just the thing. Maybe you could open yourself to meeting a man who loves and respects you. You once said I didn't know anything about love. I think I've learned at least this — that men should support, not diminish us."

"Blah. Blah. Blah. I know you like to say that but what does that even mean? It's one of those platitudes that sound pretty vague."

Lisa shrugged. She picked up her sandwich and then put it down. "Don't ever repeat this. Or bring it up to me. Promise?" Lisa searched Marika's eyes.

Marika crossed her heart. "What?"

"When I was going through Mac's things, I found phone numbers for two different women. I don't know whether or not they belonged to a student, a teaching assistant, or a cousin. I wish I hadn't found them. I don't think he was cheating but I'll never get to ask him."

"Ask Phil if he ever comes back from his running-away trip. Those two shared everything. Anyway, I know you, honey, you will obsess over this. Wonder if what you had was real. Trust me. It was real. And it will be real again."

"I can't think about it. I have to focus on Albany. I know I haven't been here long but it feels new and different. Things are happening here. I know just where I want to take you. But I have to be honest. With all the government construction, which I'll show you, it's not a good time to be poor and black."

"Is it ever? Well, stop talking and eat up. We don't have a lot of time to waste."

Lisa drove down to the new government center still under construction. "You want to hear a story?"

"Sure."

"Okay. I have the numbers in my head because I wrote them into my business plan. Are you ready? It's appalling. For this grand complex that the governor wanted built, apparently as badly as he wanted anything, this is what it cost: ninety-eight acres of inner city housing demolished. That translates to twenty-nine blocks of housing and another eleven with partial demolition; sixty-eight hundred people in thirty-three hundred homes; three-hundred and fifty small businesses; three churches; two schools; and a police station. I'll give you three guesses about who was displaced."

"Did they find places for them to live?"

"Let's say it's a work in progress. What we have here are four small tower buildings, one large tower, a performing arts center that will look like an egg if they can ever get it to stand up, and an education and cultural center. All marble." Lisa deepened her voice. "According to this governor of ours, 'Great architecture reflects the true worth of us all. When men and women have finished their daily toil, they yearn for higher meaning, the lifting of the spirit, the satisfaction of our inner selves.'"

"I'm glad to hear that all those people who lost their homes can look out their broken windows and find higher meaning. Will you look at that?" Marika whistled through her teeth. She rolled down the car window to get a better view of the tall buildings.

"Yeah, that's what you get when you are ruled by a king. The supposed story is that for the Albany Bicentennial Celebration, a Dutch princess came to visit as part of the festivities. She said something about the city being a slum and as a result the governor decided he was going to build something special. Who knew it was going to be made of solid marble and what it would mean to the people who lived there? So now I'm going to turn down Pearl Street. You see that store to your right. It's called Gold's and has beautiful dresses and what not. It's probably the best place to work. They do a big prom and bridal business. How about if we go in to see whether they need a tailor?"

"All right. Oh look, there's a space." Marika pointed to a small space between two station wagons.

"You've never driven with me if you think I can get in there."

"You're in a VW bug. That's one step up from a bike. I'll get out and direct." Marika waved her arms in all directions. When Lisa finally slid into the spot, she couldn't get out of the car; she was so close to the curb, the door wouldn't open. Marika pulled her suitcase out the other side, opened it and pulled out a large rectangular batik-swirled bag holding neatly folded samples of her work.

"You want to go in with me?"

"Sure." Lisa scooted over the shift and went out the other door.

Lisa hadn't been in Gold's since she was a girl marveling at all the jars of colorful powders that were mixed together on the spot to create the perfect shade for each customer. She marveled at the way tints of purple or blue or red mixed with beiges could become an exact match for your skin.

"Excuse me." Marika approached a salesperson behind the cosmetics counter. "Could you direct me to someone I could talk to about possible employment?"

The white-haired woman, wearing a charcoal gray dress with pearls, asked "Doing what, dear? Are you looking for custodial work?"

"Hardly." Marika attempted to smile, keep her tone of voice even. "I'm a dressmaker."

"Well, in that case, go up to the second floor. Behind the formal gowns is Mrs. Lewin's office. She heads up our alterations department."

"Thank you," Marika walked over to Lisa. "Are you coming or do you want to get yourself some makeup?"

"When did I ever wear makeup? I'll do whatever you want. I can go with you or browse around down here."

"Come with me." Marika reached for her hand.

On the second floor, there were racks of satin and silk, brocade, and chiffon dresses. Bridal gowns lined one of the walls. A velvet couch and two side chairs were outside the fitting room. Off to the left was an office with a closed door. Lisa sat down on one of the chairs. "I'll wait for you here."

Marika knocked and opened the door. She was greeted by a short, solid woman with platinum teased hair and heavy makeup. "May I help you?"

"I'm Marika Jackson. Are you Mrs. Lewin?"

"Yes, I am."

Marika extended her hand but the woman stood with her arms by her side.

"How can I help you?"

Marika exhaled slowly. "I'm relocating here from Boston and I'd like to talk to you about doing alterations."

Mrs. Lewin left the door ajar. There was a short rack with hangers standing by her desk. Marika opened her bag, hung up her clothes, and sat down in the chair next to the desk. "These are samples of dresses I've made to give you an idea of my work."

Mrs. Lewin stood at the rack looking at the design and workmanship on each dress. "You made these dresses yourself? The stitching is exquisite," she said, nodding her head, taking each dress off the rack, examining them carefully. "You don't work as an assistant?"

"No, ma'am. I made everything here. I design and make clothes when my daughter goes to sleep. I had a very good teacher." She pulled three dresses off the rack, "On those last three, I did a number of different hand stitches as samples."

"Why are you moving here from Boston?" Mrs. Lewin's laugh was high-pitched. "It's usually the other way around. Young people can't wait to leave."

"I have a friend who thinks it's a great place for kids to grow up. I have a daughter who will start kindergarten in the fall. I'm here now to make sure there is work for me."

"As you can see, our quarters are pretty tight," Mrs. Lewin said.

Marika looked around the large room with four sewing machine stations, three-way mirrors and platforms. "I see." Marika straightened her spine, calling up the dignity she felt slipping away.

"Do you have references? Who knows you here in Albany?"

Marika sighed, "The work references I have are people from Boston. For a character reference, you might want to meet my friend." Marika stuck her head out the door, catching Lisa swaying in front of the mirror holding a red gown. "Lisa, Mrs. Lewin wants to meet you."

"I know you, don't I?" Mrs. Lewin asked, surprised to see Lisa.

"I'm Lisa Stern. I used to come in with my grandma. She loved this store and I loved the lunch at Myers that we'd get after we shopped. But that was a quite a few years ago."

Visibly relaxed, she smiled warmly at Lisa. "Is Jack your father?"

"Yes. Do you know him?"

"I used to get all my medicine from him until he deserted us and moved to the suburbs."

"He didn't want to move but he was forced out. The new store is doing well but he misses the old neighborhood," Lisa said.

"Be sure to tell him how much we miss him." Mrs. Lewin turned her attention back to Marika. "Ms. Jackson, if your references check out and Jack Stern vouches for you, it will all depend on your ability to find space to work in. I hope we can work something out."

"I'm not sure where I'll be living." Marika blinked hard.

"The workload varies but we're coming up to prom time which is very high volume. Extremely busy for us. So I can guarantee work in the spring; afterwards, we'll reassess. Will you be here by mid-May?"

"Yes, yes, yes!" Lisa exclaimed.

Marika threw Lisa one of her *shut-up-right-this-minute* looks. "There are some details I have to tie up. Can I call you in a couple of weeks to let you know when I might move?"

"Here is my number. I'll look forward to hearing from you." Mrs. Lewin sat down at her desk.

"Thank you. Mrs. Lewin." Marika quickly emptied the clothes rack, folding up her samples and stuffing them in the bag.

"Did you make that bag also, Marika?" She raised her eyebrows.

"Yes."

"Beautiful. Lisa, ask your Dad to call me."

"Will do. Nice meeting you."

They ran down the stairs and out the door arm in arm. Lisa sang out, "This means you are coming and that you are going to have to live in the upstairs flat to do the alterations."

Marika sat down and closed the car door. She sighed deeply. Closing her eyes, she willed away tears, realizing it doesn't matter where you go, nothing changes. She felt a wave of fatigue settle in.

Lisa started to say something but stopped herself.

Marika, leaning her head back on the seat, said, "Let's go home and meet Mama."

Chapter Twelve

∽

Shadowbox: A Touch of Color

The box is painted white top to bottom. A small oblong table is made from a child's block. It stands in the center of the room and it's covered with a white piece of cloth. A cornhusk doll painted black is wrapped in bright fabric. A red silk cloth flutters in the doll's hand ready to float onto the table. A pale cornhusk doll, with her back to the table, raises both of her arms reaching for the colorful floating cloth.

"Here we are." Lisa rolled into the driveway.

Three boys played basketball across the street and a little girl walked her doll in a baby carriage.

"Wow," Marika whispered. "You hire those kids?"

"I wish I'd thought of that." Lisa laughed.

"This would be heaven for Amber. I bet rent is sky high just like everywhere else."

"I don't think so. But remember you can stay with me until you get settled with work and everything. So. Are you ready for Mumsy?"

"I look okay?" Marika patted her hair and smoothed her skirt.

"Like the African Queen! Lovely and regal."

"Did you at least remind her I'm black?"

"I wouldn't blindside you like that. Anyway, she seems to be at loose ends, maybe even lonely without my grandmother. She'll fall in love with Amber. It'll be good for her. She just might not know it yet."

Marika sucked in a breath. "Let's go."

Just then Lisa saw Nicky walk by. His head was down, his gait slow. She stared at him, not believing this was her Nicky. It was the first time Lisa had seen him since she was home.

He hardly looked like himself. His confident strut was a shuffling limp. She wasn't sure she'd recognize him if she hadn't known he was back. His hair was greasy and long enough for a ponytail down his back. He was emaciated.

"Wait here a sec, okay?"

Marika nodded, taking her suitcase out of the car. "Sure."

"Nicky, it's Lisa," she called out to him.

He stopped walking. He knew he should know her but didn't; her face kept changing, blurring so he couldn't make out who she was. He shuffled down the street to his house, picking up as much speed as he could manage.

Lisa watched him turn at his driveway and look back at her from a safe distance. "Fucking war," she muttered, her eyes watering.

"Who was that?" Marika asked.

"My first boyfriend, Nicky Ianelli. He was such a great guy. A happy-go-lucky kid who loved horsing around with his friends. In the summer, he'd play ball from morning to night. Now look at him." She opened the door for Marika and they went inside.

"Mom," Lisa called.

"In the kitchen."

Her mother wiped her hands on a dish towel and took off her apron. "Marika, welcome." She extended her hand. "Wait a minute. Now I remember! We met when Lisa had the accident at the daycare center. I didn't put two and two together."

"Yes. There we were, cutting out construction paper hearts and the next thing I knew, she was bleeding from her head and shattered glass was everywhere." Marika paused. "Think it knocked some sense into her?"

"Yeah, yeah, yeah. Very funny," Lisa interjected.

"Lisa's been giving me a tour. It's a very nice city. Has more going for it than I expected."

"Well, I hope you girls didn't eat too much. I want you to be hungry for dinner. Lisa, why don't you get Marika settled into the spare bedroom. I only invited Aunt Rena and Uncle Ira. I hope Faye won't be mad. But I didn't want Coxie's army here."

"Who?" Marika asked.

"It's one of Mom's favorite expressions for a lot of people. The exact number is under constant revision." Lisa said.

Her mother sniffed. "We'll eat around seven."

Marika opened up her suitcase. "I brought you a bottle of wine and a tablecloth I made."

"Manischewitz? You do want to make a good impression!" Lisa put the bottle in the fridge.

"Very thoughtful of you." Rose unfolded an oblong tablecloth with scalloped edging onto the dining room table. "You made this? It's gorgeous. We'll use it tonight!"

"You don't have to do that," Marika said.

"But I want to. I have nothing this beautiful."

Marika and Lisa went upstairs and sprawled out on Lisa's bed; Marika leaned up against the headboard, Lisa was on her side across the bed, propped up on her elbow.

"I think I can probably pass a typing test at the temp agency tomorrow," Marika said. "And I have my GED. Thanks to you. That'll help, I think." Marika played with the fringe on the bedspread. "So how are you? I've been with you for a couple of hours and no sign of tears. You seem like your old self."

"I'm doing better. The nights are still bad but at least I don't get in the car and go driving anymore. Some days are better than others. All day I'm consumed with the details of this project but nights are still hard. My mother comes to me and holds me. She doesn't say a word. Just rocks me. She never did that when I was growing up. Maybe things would be different, if she had." Lisa absently looked out the window. "My mother never could never really accept that there are no words for some things. I don't know what changed. Maybe it was Gram's dying. But she seems different."

"And so are you. What is it you always say to me? No looking back." Marika stretched out. "It was a good idea — your coming back here?"

"Yes, I suppose. The scary thing for me is that sometimes I don't think Mac was real. I'm afraid I'm losing him all over again. I can't always see his face or remember the sound of his voice. I keep trying to replay times when we were together and it's getting harder."

"You won't forget. I promise you that. You'll begin to remember again in time when it hurts less. Missy, you are doing better than I ever thought."

Marika stood up and opened her suitcase. "Here." She tossed Lisa a peasant skirt in shades of pink and purple.

Lisa twirled it. "Thank you so much." She hugged Marika. "Where are you getting all this gorgeous fabric?"

"I have my ways." Marika smiled. "Let's go see if we can help your mother."

They set the table while her mother hummed in the kitchen.

"It smells great, Mrs. Stern. What are we having?"

"Call me Rose, please." She smiled. "I made fried chicken, mashed potatoes, and a couple of vegetables. I hope I don't dry out the chicken." There was a knock at the door. Aunt Rena and Uncle Ira came in; Lisa's Dad was just behind them.

"Hi Marika. Great to see you again." He gave her a big bear hug.

Marika stammered, "Better circumstances. It was like being in a slow-motion film. Lisa and I cutting out paper hearts and bang. She's on the floor and her head is bleeding."

"Lucky for us she has a hard head." Her father smiled.

"No. Not you too, Daddy!"

"Let's eat." Lisa's mother brought out a large platter of fried chicken and bowls of potatoes, green beans, and carrots. There was a challah on the table and wine glasses.

Marika bowed her head and folded her hands while the others looked at Lisa's father. *Baruch ata Adonai*...the blessing began. Rose lit the candles. Marika thought, wouldn't Mrs. Lewin be surprised to see me now.

Jack said a Hebrew blessing over the bread. Everyone pulled off a piece and passed it. Then, Jack raised his glass. *Baruch ata Adonai elohenu melech haolam borai pri hagofen*. Amen. Marika, that means we can drink the wine. May I add we're so happy to have you with us."

"Thank you, Mr. Stern. Happy Sabbath, everyone."

"Marika, no need to be formal. Call me Jack."

Uncle Ira asked, "Lisa, how are things going on your project?"

"I have another meeting at City Hall on Wednesday. They aren't an easy bunch to work with. And they sure don't like working with me. I'm young. I'm a woman. And I've no experience. But they are going along with it so far. They've pared down potential buildings to three and they've said they'll make a selection by the end of the month. Daddy, will you take us to see them? You know the neighborhoods much better than I do. Marika set up appointments for tomorrow morning so maybe we could go after you close the store?"

"Sure, honey. Love to."

"Jack, Saturday afternoon is slow. I can handle the store. You'll be able to see more in the daylight." Uncle Ira offered.

"Marika, are you also involved with this?" asked Rose asked.

"You mean the Women's Center? I'm not sure. Lisa thinks I would be an asset in doing outreach. Since much of her target group is black, she thinks she needs me," she said, looking at Lisa.

"That's *A* reason, not *THE* reason," Lisa said.

"My dream has always been to make and design clothing. Anything that brings me closer to that is something worth trying. Besides, we live in the neighborhood near the daycare center where Lisa was hurt. I need to get my daughter out of there."

"You will." Lisa nodded. "Marika's amazing. She's here one afternoon and already practically lined up a job doing alterations at Gold's. Daddy, do you know a Mrs. Lewin?"

"Lena?" Jack raised his eyebrows.

"She wants you to call her to vouch for Marika."

He laughed. "I know who you mean." In a loud whisper, he cupped his hands around his mouth and said, "She's the first girl I ever kissed." He winked at them.

"Jack!" Rose arched her eyebrows.

"Rose you know you're my one and only love." He reached over to touch her hand.

Lisa groaned.

"A husband like Daddy is what I wish for you," her mother said.

"Don't hold your breath."

"How's the chicken? It's not too dry?" Rose looked anxiously around the table.

"Mom, dinner's great. Uncle Ira, I was wondering. Do you have any units open in your apartment house?"

"Not right now. I think there is a three-bedroom available in September though. I don't think the tenants want to renew. Why?"

Lisa turned to Marika. "Well, we'll find something."

"What's the 'we'? I thought you were going to move upstairs." Rose said.

"Mom, Marika and I want to live together. I can help out with Amber and we'll be able to work and plan better if we're together. Besides, I don't think I could live by myself in Gram's flat. But I was thinking..."

Rose cut her off. "Let's talk about this later."

Marika measured each word, "Mrs. Stern, there's nothing to worry about. I don't think it's a good idea either. I wouldn't dream of living here with Lisa in your home. Last thing you need is having a child running around overhead." She caught Lisa's eye and sighed deeply. What a day. Marika began to lift herself out of the chair. Lisa quickly grabbed her arm and pulled her back down.

"Give it a rest, Mom," Lisa insisted.

Aunt Rena glared at Lisa as she always did, but this time, Lisa stared right back, her lip curled. Marika moved the food around on her dish.

Jack said, "On to more important things. What's for dessert?"

Aunt Rena said, "I made Lisa's favorite coffee cake."

"Marika, it's to die for," Lisa said.

In a bland voice, she said, "You're spoiling me. Dinner was fantastic. Better fried chicken than my Mama's. Not that I really remember it that well."

"Did your family all live together?" Rose asked. "That's how it always was. Not so much anymore. Now, children can't wait to get as far away as they can from their families."

Marika thought, no, we haven't been on the plantation for a while. She answered warily, looking down at the table. "No, I went to live with an aunt when my parents died."

"Oh, dear. I'm so sorry."

"It was a long time ago." Marika stood up. "Let me help you clear."

Aunt Rena stood up. "I'll help you, Rose."

"Just sit, Marika. Talk to Uncle Ira," Lisa said, stacking the plates.

"Yes, sit with me." He patted the chair next to him and Marika moved closer.

"By tomorrow my sister will have you drying dishes, I promise. Don't take offense. She's like a lioness protecting her cub. Her bark is far worse and all that."

"It's okay. You might say I've run up against this before." Marika nodded and thought, it's one think to think you are liberal and fair minded and another to live it. She'd been in this position before. One of two black kids in her elementary school. A white girl on the playground initiated her the first day. Told her that darkies were stupid and punched her. When Marika punched her back, only Marika was disciplined. After her parents died, she was in an all-black school with ripped up books and tired old teachers. Second rate in every way. So what if integration was the law? You can't legislate acceptance. What did she want for Amber? Living in an all-white neighborhood had positives but did they outweigh the negatives? Lisa didn't know the world. How could Marika have thought one place would be better than another when her experience screamed otherwise?

Uncle Ira pulled her back to the conversation. "You know as you were talking, I was thinking. It seems you'd rather work with clothing than in an office. There was a tailor next to our drugstore downtown. He's still there. An old Italian guy. He's always saying that he can't hire any good help. He's well established but he has a lousy disposition. He makes men's suits but no ladies' wear. I'll call him tomorrow morning. I have to tell you. He has a puss on him like the skies are ready to pour rain down on his head, and he might be called a bigot. Yes. Definitely a bigot but I think you could hold your own with him and I have to say this for him, he admires skill."

"I don't know." Marika shook her head.

"Think about it. And don't mind Rose. She was wound up when Lisa was first living with that guy. She thinks that Lisa is back for good and doesn't even want her to move down the block."

"Oh, I think it's more than that. Look, I'm a *schvarzah* with a kid and no husband."

Uncle Ira laughed deep and wide. He put a hand on her shoulder. "And one who is a good friend to our Lisa and got her through her *tsouris*."

"Are there any blacks in this neighborhood?"

"There is a rental down the street, a black family lives on the top floor and I think they have two kids. And I think a Chinese family may have bought the house on the corner."

"So if I move in with Lisa, the property value takes a dive?" Marika twitched.

"Who cares? Nobody is moving anywhere." He gently squeezed her arm.

"Cake and coffee time," Rena announced, bringing in a tray. Lisa and Rose followed her in. Cake plates were passed, coffee poured, and the rest of table time was spent pulling out the comfortable and amusing family stories, one story reminding them of another, all at Lisa's expense.

Marika took it all in. The pace of the city, Lisa's family, the promised work by an employment agency, the Italian bigot who was so short she towered over him and told him she wouldn't even think about working for him if he didn't promise to shut his big mouth. And, she warned him at the first slur out of him, she would leave and take his customers with her. He mumbled something in Italian but was impressed with her samples. He never said yes. Just when you come?"

Lisa took her to the bus and hugged her tight. "See how good this will be. Two tailoring jobs and maybe part time clerical work. The Center. No more babysitting. Come as soon as you can."

Chapter Thirteen

The Architect Builds a House of Cards

∾

David knew he should have said no when Lisa called him to ask if they could talk about the building over coffee. But he didn't want to. What was the big deal, anyway? He was a free man now, sort of. Separated. Was he in the army to march to his wife, Ivy's, orders? Tuesday, Thursday, Saturday. Back by Joy's bedtime. Seven during the week. Eight-thirty on Saturday.

Ivy was crazed. She looked like hell. When he first left, all she did was cry and drink and shriek and sleep. She hardly took care of their daughter Joy, who had been the light of her life — that is, along with her husband. David's leaving was a seismic shock and shook the life out of her. Her beautiful eyes that had always sparkled were dead. Her sweet disposition was gone. He'd done that to her when he blindsided her. No warning. No explanation. Just a Tuesday night. He stood up from the dinner table and told her he was leaving, threw a few things in a suitcase and drove away. He even surprised himself. Not that he didn't want to. He'd thought about leaving for months. What surprised him was that he did it. The words just popped out of his mouth. He felt outside of himself, hearing the words that had been in his head. He didn't mean to be cruel. He just wanted out.

What he did was terrible. The least he could do was abide by her demands. Even if it meant leaving work early and having to go back later in the evening.

Yet, despite his guilt over having left his wife and child, here he was on one of his scheduled nights with his daughter. He didn't leave his wife for another woman. He just plain couldn't stand their life together. Ivy was a wonderful woman, but for somebody else. Somebody who might appreciate being her sun and moon. Her clinging made him run, but he knew in his heart that it wasn't her fault. She couldn't help herself. He just didn't want what he signed up for anymore. That was the truth of it. He would be the best father he could be for Joy. In time, Ivy would pull herself together.

Lisa was at a table when he arrived at the coffee shop, sipping her coffee, and reading from her file. She wore a black turtleneck and jeans with a long, silver peace sign pendant and dangling red glass earrings that caught the light. What a beautiful woman she was. It didn't seem like she thought about that, though. She wore little makeup. The long, dark curls she'd tried to tame for the meeting were now cascading down her back. David didn't sit right down. He watched her for a moment. She was totally immersed and when finished, she'd toss the page she was reading onto a stack on the floor beside her.

"One?" the waitress asked.

"No. I'm meeting someone. She's over there."

The waitress called out, "Lisa, you know this guy?"

Lisa looked up and smiled. "Sure do. Hi, David." She slid the papers toward her, clearing a spot at the table.

"You a regular?" he asked.

"I used to baby-sit for Janie. She thinks I'm cool so I get free coffee."

"I think you're cool, too," David said.

"Wait until you get to know me better. You'll see what a pain in the ass I am. I called because I wanted to give you a better idea of what I'm thinking, so we get it right."

"Sounds good to me. Most of my clients don't have any idea of what they want. Only what they don't."

"Crazy," Lisa said.

"I've never been very good with telepathy. But on a more serious topic, I love banana cream pie. Do they have it here?"

"Probably. I'd have pegged you as an apple pie man, David. Solid, not whipped. No pun intended," she smiled.

David laughed. "Very funny. Let's see. What would I say about you? Hmmm. You would be a chocolate fudge cake. Three layer."

"Why do you think that?" She arched her eyebrows.

"Chocolate cake is rich. It's dense but the frosting is shiny with beautiful swirls. Substance and beauty."

Lisa laughed. "Sounds like one of your buildings. I saw the one you did on Columbia. Gorgeous."

"Glad you think so."

"What'll it be?" Janie asked. "We have the usual but also a French apple today."

Lisa said, "David, you're right. The chocolate is my favorite."

"Yeah, she gets it every time. Coffee?"

"Absolutely," David said. "I'll have the French apple and coffee."

"You got it."

"Good choice. I worked in a bakery for a time and we made all kinds of apple desserts. My favorite was an apple raisin," Lisa said.

"You bake too?" David asked.

"I bake but I don't know what you mean by 'too.' This is a business meeting, right? I don't want you to think I asked you out on a date."

"No worries. But can't we just talk a bit before we get into business? It's been one of those days."

She set her papers aside. "What happened?"

David sighed. "We had a big client meeting today. Big enough for all the partners to attend. That rarely happens. I inherited a project that was started before I began work at this firm. I can't say much about it but it seems to me that two opposing things are going on so the client will never get what he wants. It's a concept for housing to get away from projects. But because its low-income housing and the grants are really just seed money, the client wants to skimp on everything."

"Dessert is just what the doctor ordered. Why don't you have the banana cream too?" Lisa asked.

"Rolling me out of here is not the impression I want to make on you."

"Did you have dinner?"

"No."

"So let's have a round of desserts!" She caught Janie's eye. "We'd like to amend our order."

"Okay." Janie took the pencil from behind her ear and crossed out the order. She asked David, "You sure you want to be near her when she's revved up on sweets? It's worse than when she gets drunk."

"Janie, don't tell my secrets," Lisa said.

She ignored her. "When my mother called her to baby-sit, she would ask what kind of dessert we had before the day and time."

"Don't believe her. She was just a runt. Still is. Bring us banana cream and let's see chocolate cheesecake. Oh and extra dishes so we can share." Lisa said.

"So you look like you do and you eat dessert?"

Lisa shrugged.

"I'm more of a bread person," David said.

"Oh yeah. My grandma made the best challah and bagels. Love bagels."

"You're Jewish?"

She gagged on her coffee. "Lisa Stern. Are you kidding? Jewish in the worst sense. Shaky beliefs. Hovering family. High drama." She chuckled, enjoying herself.

"Me, too. How do you like that?" David asked.

Lisa laughed. "I don't know whether to pat you on the back or give you my condolences! Ah, heaven." Janie set all the desserts down on the table. Lisa scraped the chocolate frosting with her fork. "I don't know whether coming back here is the best thing I ever did or the worst. Time will tell."

David stirred sugar into his coffee. "Where were you?"

"Boston. Hey, enough about me. What about you?"

"Let's see. I'm pretty boring. I grew up here. Went to school here. Got married here and have a beautiful daughter. Am somewhat of a workaholic. I love my work and have no complaints with my twelve-hour days." He drank some coffee. "Most days, anyway."

"Back up a minute. You're married?" She smiled. "What does your wife do?"

"I'm separated. What about you? You must have at least a boyfriend."

She shook her head. "Nothing to tell. This project is my life."

"Why don't I believe you?"

Lisa shrugged and dug into the cheesecake. "Taste this. It's divine."

"Definitely goes down easy." David smiled, pointing with his fork to the half dollop of whipped cream, crumbs from the chocolate crust and the small wedge of cake left. "C'mon, you take it."

"No, sir. I am done." Lisa slid the plates away from them and rummaged through her bag for her pad and pen.

"Does this mean it's time for business?"

"Yes." She pointed to the sketches he'd given her. "I don't think this building or location is right. It's too small and the adjacent property looks like a big headache. I want to know what you really think about the other building we saw last week. Do you think it has potential or is really just a wreck that can't be fixed?" Lisa asked.

"Anything can be brought back. All you need is money."

She sighed. "Since you know I don't have any yet, what do you think?"

"I think we have to go slow. Concentrate on making sure any building we consider is sound and we'll fix it a little at a time. That will give you some time to raise the capital we'll need. We can get you up and running after the plumbing and wiring issues are resolved. You might get some volunteers from the unions. And having the Albany Historic Foundation on board will help enormously. They can tap into some urban redevelopment money. The timing is just right. All the players are steaming from all that was lost when the government center was built."

Lisa glanced up at him. "Are you the donation from your firm?"

David mimed a dagger to his heart. "Is that how you see me? Your freebie? I'm devastated."

"Sorry." Lisa flushed. "I didn't mean that. I just wondered if they might contribute financially. I think you are right about going slow so it's done right. I think I have to play it that way and convince people this project is a prototype for others."

"Afraid I'm it for the firm. They are in the business of making money, not giving any way. Are your wheels always turning?" he teased.

"My best and worst trait."

They went over the pros and cons of each of the other buildings on the city's list. Lisa took careful notes and clipped everything together. She looked at her watch. "I didn't realize the time. I've got to run."

"Do you want to get together next week?" David said.

"I don't know. Call me."

David motioned to Janie to refill his cup. He looked down at the half-eaten desserts and licked the chocolate frosting from Lisa's spoon.

He pulled up his collar. The night air was raw for springtime and the wind at his back pushed him down the wide avenue. He looked up at the clear sky. The stars shone bright against a full moon. It suddenly occurred to him that he hadn't looked up at the sky in quite some time. He had been trying to teach his daughter to find the Big Dipper but she had lost interest. Since he moved out, there was a reticence in her that was new; a reluctance when he picked her up and dropped her off. She seemed uneasy. Maybe she was afraid he'd go crazy like her mother. But that wasn't anything he could talk to a four-year old about.

David rented an efficiency apartment in one of the old hotels on State Street — a euphemism for a shabby room with a small refrigerator and hot plate. He chuckled to himself. It was a beauty in the rollicking, vibrant days of Legs Diamond, but now it was a mess with cracked plaster, and mustiness from years of rain and snow soaked carpets. Mold grew on the walls. The toilet bowl was rusted, the sink had spiny cracks.

He worked long days and when he wasn't working, he spent time with Joy at the house. He certainly couldn't take her to the hotel. Sometimes Ivy left but most often, she slept with the bedroom door locked. He often tried to clean up the garbage dump his house had become but that was the last thing she wanted. Sometimes she'd come back and start screaming and throwing things at him. *You have no right...get the fuck out of here.*

It was a short walk to the hotel but he saw one of the partners standing on the corner talking to a client. Some of his colleagues knew he and his wife were separated; how could they not? The way she often called the office in hysterics was humiliating enough but he would be further mortified if anyone knew where he was living. So he turned around and squared the block. Thankfully, they were gone by the second pass.

Ivy had been a good wife. She remained the same girl she was the day they met. Fun-loving and sweet. What had happened was he was not that boy anymore. He was a man with appetite for more than what she could give. She was so totally dependent. He tried to ignore the irritation that was growing in his gut. He'd started working longer and longer days to avoid going home. In fact, he had exceeded what the firm expected and they promised to make him a partner. He was the youngest, the most ambitious, and the most requested by clients. David loved his work. To him, restoring the buildings was like resurrecting them from the dead. He was in awe of the detail and grace of old buildings and loved bringing them back to the gems they once were.

If he had left her for another woman, maybe Ivy would have reacted differently. But she was devastated to realize their life together was so wrong for him that he'd move out and sleep in his office rather than stay with her. In the state she was in, he worried about Joy but knew he could never take Joy away from her. That would be too much: too much loss for her and guilt for him.

He told her he'd completely support her until she got on her feet and Joy was in school. He was generous in giving her all the money she needed, but he'd open the refrigerator and see bare shelves, limp and discolored vegetables, soured milk and juice, oozing black bananas. He'd stop by the store on his way over, never knowing if Ivy would hurl the groceries at him or thank him.

David knew it would take time for her to become self-sufficient. She was incapable of doing the simplest things. "Let me go with you to the bank to open a checking account," he'd offer.

"Go to hell," she'd scream, and do nothing. Mail piled up. Bills didn't get paid. He'd find envelopes in piles on the floor, behind the couch, on the table when he came to get Joy. She seemed to be getting worse the more time passed. The house was a pigsty but Joy seemed oblivious. Didn't she remember what it was like before? Before Ivy slept around the clock? He kept track of the wine that was disappearing from under the sink. Maybe if he could get a decent apartment, he could pick Joy up when he finished work and bring her to nursery school in the mornings. Temporarily. To give Ivy a chance to pull herself together and adjust. The conversation would be difficult but maybe once he suggested it, she'd be relieved.

David looked around the musty hotel room he called home. He turned on the lights so the roaches who took up residence while he was working would disappear into the walls. He lay on the bed; his arms crossed behind his head, and looked up at the stained and peeling ceiling. It occurred to him that the forms changed shape the more he looked at them. He'd spent many sleepless hours trying to decide if he was looking at a malformed cloud, a unicorn, or just a random mess, like his life.

He thought back on his meeting with Lisa Stern. The buildings she suggested were disasters. He wasn't sure any of them were structurally sound. It would take a miracle to restore them. But he had no doubts she'd make it happen. She seemed like that kind of woman.

Chapter Fourteen

Good Mothers

∽

Marika swallowed her fear and uncertainty. She told herself there was no decision to be made. A good mother protected her children and she knew, if nothing else, she was a good mother. The move would give Amber a childhood and education she'd never have in Jamaica Plain. She wanted her to have the summer to adjust to the neighborhood and make friends before school began. Although there was reluctance on everyone's part, Marika and Lisa would move into the upstairs flat.

Rose had nothing against Marika. She was a nice enough girl. But did she have to live here with Lisa? She tried her best not to say what she thought, walking away from Lisa, biting her tongue. It was a blessing to have her daughter back and they were getting along much better. She'd waited a long time for Lisa to come to her and didn't want to ruin it.

Despite the armor Lisa wore each day, Rose knew her daughter was profoundly sad. She would fall into a light sleep, subconsciously listening for Lisa's cries. Her heart would break when she heard her daughter sobbing in her sleep. Lisa, always standoffish with her, now melted into her arms. She didn't say much, only that there were two dreams that she had over and over: she was either on a beach during a storm and Mac was overtaken by the waves or she was trampled when the mounted police stampeded the crowd on the Boston Common. What had she seen? Her heart ached to see Lisa this wounded.

It was Rose's nature to worry. She worried about the *mishugas* of this Women's Center and bringing the *schvartzah* with her child to live in her Mama's apartment. What was Lisa thinking? They robbed her father at gunpoint and could have killed him. They forced him out of business and here she was bringing that kind of trouble home. She knew this wasn't fair. But ashamed or not, there was no denying it was the way she felt.

Rose tried talking to Jack about Marika moving in. "Jack, what do you think Mama would say about Marika moving into her apartment?"

"I know what she'd say and so do you. She'd say 'Lisa wants to live with her so there is nothing to talk about.' She'd say, 'Now Rose, don't go blaming everybody for a few bad apples.' And she'd also say that Lisa's idea of this Women's Center is good. She'd *kvell* with pride about her granddaughter turning her tragedy into good work."

"She would not and you know it."

"Rosie. Lisa made it clear that she wouldn't move upstairs if you didn't want her to. You are running out of time. Make peace with it or tell her how you feel."

"How can you be so calm?"

"Because there is nothing to worry about. Go to sleep." He rolled over and was snoring within minutes.

Sleepless, she played devil's advocate in her mind. Jack was fine with it and he was the one who had looked down the barrel of the gun. Her brother Ira thought it was great. He really took to Marika. He said, "Who knows what Mama would have said? You'd think one thing and then she'd come out with something completely different. It's not such a big deal, Rosie. Marika's a nice girl."

So she's a nice girl. Would their neighbors know that? Sometimes words tumbled from Rose's mouth before she could stop them, an unfortunate trait that Lisa inherited from her. One that ironically strained their relationship.

By breakfast, she couldn't help herself. "What's the matter with trying to be normal once in a while? From the time you were a little girl, you would find the weakest drowned cats from school and try to fix them. It never changes."

"I don't get it," Lisa fumed. "Why is that a problem? I never understood why you didn't think that was a good quality. Being compassionate isn't a crime. Don't think that I didn't hear you week in and week out complaining about me to everyone in the family?"

Her mother shook her head. "Not complaining. I'm sorry you took it that way. Mama always told me to relax, that you were a good-hearted girl."

"See!"

So I said it. So what? But gnug. Liselah. This living in the same house with your friend wasn't such a good idea. Sometimes I think your mishugas spills over you, you don't know what's right from what's wrong. Oy, think for once. Not everything needs to be a tsimmis. Stop stirring up the pot.

"Grandma, your big champion. She would never think this is a good idea. Naturally, you'd find a *shvartzah* with no education to be best friends with, not Amy or Nina from college. You always have to do things the hard way. And why live here with you? Can't she find another place to live?"

Lisa glared at her. "Mom, stop right now."

"Why do you always have to make waves?"

"Because it's the way I am. And you know what? I found out that some people like that about me. Every time I think you've changed, you ruin everything." Lisa stood up.

"*I* ruin everything? Ha. Sometimes I think you just do these things on purpose. Just to upset me."

Lisa flushed, her eyes blazed, "I hate to tell you this but not everything is about you. That's always been the problem between us. If only Mac were here. He would find the exact words to describe what was right about me. He loved who I was. Mom, I'm not a moody kid you can change. This is me. Why can't you love me as I am?" Lisa turned to walk out of the kitchen but her mother grabbed her arm.

"Don't walk out on me, Lisa Rachel."

She turned around. "Let go," she hissed, prying her mother's hand from her arm.

"Sit down," she insisted.

Facing each other at the table, Lisa looked into her mother's tired eyes. "Okay, this is it. Our last conversation about the move." Lisa paused to take in a deep breath. "You can tell me that you don't want Marika and Amber upstairs and we'll find another place. Or you can tell me it's not what you want but it's okay and you will welcome them. We're down to the wire, Mom, so you'd better decide because she is packing as we speak. And you know what? Marika has done more for me than you can imagine. If only you could open your eyes once in a while."

"Okay, I'm the bad guy again. You win," her mother complained.

The phone rang.

Lisa said, "Not good enough. You have to make a decision. I need to know by tomorrow morning."

Rose picked up the receiver with her back toward Lisa. "Yes. She's right here. Hold on a minute." She put the phone down and walked to the sink.

"Isabela? Hi. It's so good to hear your voice! I miss you! How are you?"

Lisa's mother could feel her body constrict into a tight knot.

Collateral Damage

Ivy skimmed her hand across the scratched mahogany table, her fingers pausing to massage each nick as if it were a scar she had the power to heal. It was the only thing she cared about keeping. David could take whatever else he thought was his. But not the table. She was determined to keep it for what remained of her own family — for Joy and for her.

She never wavered. That the table was rightfully hers was the one thing she felt with certainty, despite the fact that it once belonged to David's grandmother. The celebrated moments of their lives took place around its worn surface. They'd announced their engagement and had drunk champagne in a dizzying moment with her new family laughing and hugging her. How many nights had she and David sipped demitasse and played backgammon? How often did he massage her neck as she typed his papers there? It was at the table that Ivy told him she was pregnant and also where her water broke. At that table, Joy built villages, tapped glasses of water to make music, and sang as Ivy cooked their meals.

David sat across from her at that very table to tell her their marriage was over. 'Sorry, Iv. I'm truly sorry. But this isn't working for me. I don't want it anymore."

"What do you mean? You don't want it? What it don't you want?" There was a strange pounding in her head and she thought her heart would leap from her chest.

He stood up and pushed in his chair, hands gripping the back. "I think we need to take a break."

"All those late nights when you were supposedly working. I'm so dumb. I believed you. Who is she?" Ivy recoiled as if her voice came through a tunnel.

"There is no one else. Let's not say any more tonight." He stood up from the table and went into their bedroom.

"Say more? What are you talking about? You haven't said anything." The tears splashed from her eyes, large drops of summer rain that would later try to drown her.

He packed a small suitcase, grabbed some suits from the closet, and kissed his sleeping daughter in the time it took for Ivy to understand what he said, to react to the pummeling pain in her head. Before she could beg him to stay, to explain, to do anything but this, he put some rolled-up blueprints under his arm, dragged out his drafting table, threw his bag into the trunk and was gone. He careened out of the driveway on two wheels and sped away out of the range of her wail.

She'd thought he was as happy as she was. Maybe he gave her warning in these past couple of weeks. But she never saw it. He had always been happy to come home; he'd embrace her, and tell her he missed her. But lately, he'd lost patience and tuned her out as he ate the late dinners she kept warm. He was quiet and answered in monosyllables when she asked him about the new project or whatever else she thought he might want to talk about. He said he was tired or stressed from a client, or distracted with a new design and didn't feel like talking.

Sometimes he was sarcastic. "There's a big world out there, Ivy. Don't you ever read the goddamn newspaper, or is Dr. Seuss the best you can do? I don't want to be your network news."

He'd never been mean. It was so out of character. She silently made excuses for him. She'd have to try harder. He was under stress wanting to make partner. But they'd get through it together. Of course they would.

Bushwhacked, she now spent her evenings at the table drinking wine she poured from gallon-sized jugs into juice glasses. One day dissolved into the next. The cycle of day, into night, into day was useful only as a way of knowing when to take Joy to nursery school.

She still helped Joy get ready every morning, but the care with which she and Joy used to put together her outfits gave way to what was clean or close to clean. She poured Cheerios into a bowl; sometimes adding soured milk, packed her a snack and drove her to nursery school.

Joy asked questions; each day she seemed to think of a new one. *Mommy, don't you have to get dressed before you drive me? Why do I have to eat yucky cheerios EVERY DAY? Why don't you talk to me about the birds we hear on the way? Can we sing the song about the watermelon dripping down our wrists? Is Daddy coming today?*

Ivy looked straight at the road, hands locked on the steering wheel. She wasn't listening to the little voice coming from the back seat. Instead, she yelled at the windshield, "That sonofabitch will not take the table. I don't care how many years it was in his family. Joy and I have to have it."

Joy put her hands over her ears. "Mommy, no yelling in the car! Remember? You promised. I hate that dumb old table."

"Sorry, baby." Ivy wiped her face with the back of her hand.

They stopped in front of the church that housed her nursery school. Ivy got out of the car and went around to the other side to get Joy out.

"Mommy, aren't you going to say it?" Joy demanded. "What you always say when you drop me off?"

Ivy was so tired, she wondered if she had the energy to drive home. "Say what, Joy?"

"What you always say when you drop me?" Joy's bottom lip began to quiver.

"Just go in, honey. Mommy's tired."

"Say it," Joy demanded. "I'm not going in if you don't say it." She crossed her arms across her chest. "See you later, alligator. Where's your smile?"

Ivy looked at her daughter.

"Come on, Mommy. You have to. Where's your smile?"

Ivy sighed. "Crocodile."

"Don't be late again, Mommy. They make me wait in the office when you're late. Promise?"

"Promise." Ivy drove back home through a haze of tears. Promise. What the hell good was a promise?

When she got home, she peeked into the dining area to make sure the table was still there and then went back to the bedroom, setting her alarm clock so she didn't get another reprimand from the nursery school director for being late.

Chapter Fifteen

We All Want to Save the World

෬෨

Shadowbox: A Home of Our Own

There is colored graffiti on the wall: Billy loves Tina in a heart crossed out; score me some Mary; black is beautiful written over a clenched fist. NO, NO, WE WON'T GO; ALL COPS ARE PIGS scrawled on the walls. The floor is strewn with junk — a bent bottle cap, paper, a broken crayon, and a needle. There is a prism of light coming from the top left side of the box, shining a rainbow on the floor colored with crayons, lighting up some of the garbage.

The original properties that the city was willing to consider for the Center fell into two groups: one option was to choose one of the empty storefronts on lower Central Avenue; the other was one of four vacant brownstones on Clinton Avenue on the block adjacent to the Palace Theater and busy Pearl Street. Lisa liked the idea of a house, as well as the location, access to business, and the bus line.

She waited for David at a coffee shop between the locations the city agreed were restorable. Sitting by a window, Lisa watched people hurry to work as they passed the magnificent stone cathedral across the street. David smiled when he saw her and waved.

"Hi, Lisa." David bent over to kiss her cheek.

Lisa jerked away. "Hi, yourself. Why the big smile?"

"Am I smiling? Maybe. It's a gorgeous day and here we are." David motioned to the waitress to bring coffee and a toasted roll. "Didn't have time for breakfast this morning."

"This is D-Day. As in decision, not David, in case you're wondering," Lisa said.

"Cute."

"Did you get a hold of the city brain trust? Mr. Triple Chins & Company make a decision?" she asked.

"I met with them yesterday. They have narrowed down the choices to two." David opened his briefcase.

"Which ones?"

The waitress brought coffee for David. "Refill, Hon?"

"Please." Lisa held up her cup.

"One on Central near Lark, and one on Clinton."

"Did they say how they chose?" Lisa leaned over to look at the forms with checklists to identify code violations and other safety issues.

"Yes. Both of them are in really bad shape. These are the best of the worst."

"Why?"

David described the condition of the roofs, water damage from leaks, the wiring and electrical work that needed to be done.

"Have you picked the one you like best?" Lisa asked.

"You first."

"If they are equally bad, I would choose the brownstone. I like the location better. It's closer to Arbor Hill, near downtown businesses, and accessible to the new housing they are supposedly building. But aside from all that, it's a home." She arched her eyebrows. "On the other hand, if the one on Central is near Phil's Bakery, that shines a whole new light on things."

David laughed, "Lisa, Lisa. Sell your soul for a piece of cake! Finish your coffee." He dangled the keys. "We're going to take a field trip."

"The architect picked the home?"

"Yup. Let's go." He threw some money on the table and they left.

Lisa and David walked side by side; he closed in as much as he could without actually touching her, thinking her hair smelled distinctly like strawberries. Lisa chattered away about how to get started and whom she should call.

"Here we are. After you, Madame?" he bowed.

As it turned out, they didn't need a key. The door was ajar. They walked among rolling beer bottles, dented cans and trash. The place smelled like excrement and urine; there were water stains on the ceiling, holes punched in the walls. David described to her what would be needed to get the building ready for a remodel, the building permits and other legal papers. Lisa walked through pointing: "This will be reception, this for the children, the back area for the job service, walls here and there for small offices, classes...."

David said, "Whoa. Slow down."

"Sorry. I'm just so excited. Is this the building that was a brothel in Albany's heyday?"

David laughed. "Yes, I think so. Is that good or bad?"

"Good. Time for the women to take it back. So what I'll need from you, David, is a budget for infrastructure. I know this is outside Historic Preservation's area, but I think we'll be able to get some help from them."

"My firm is going to love this. Have you ever heard the term *adaptive preservation?*"

She shook her head.

"It's the new buzz word in restoration. It means restoring sites of historical value in such a way that they have new uses while maintaining the original architecture. Now, after many of the city's historical buildings were razed to build the government center, people are outraged. This is a very good time to be doing this project."

He stopped a can from rolling with his foot. "Recently, a report called *Architecture Worth Saving* was published. It described the significance of locating and encouraging preservation, restoration, and maintenance of buildings with historical significance. There seems to be a groundswell of support for this. I think your building qualifies for the Common Council's ordinance which permits the city to make prepayments up to 60% of the purchase price of the condemned property."

"Good timing, for a change," Lisa said. "Does that mean some money will be available?"

"Possibly. In yesterday's partners' meeting, they decided to give me more time to work on this and, although I'm not promising anything, we talked about making some financial contribution if we could use it as a demonstration of architectural integrity with function. It's a great model the firm can use for rehabbing other condemned buildings."

"David, that's great news." She leaned down to pick up a beer bottle.

"Can't promise I'll deliver but I'll do what I can. Anyway, this I do know: the city will sell it to you cheap as soon as you see a lawyer to set up the business. Call this guy." He handed her a card. "He'll set you up gratis. Have you thought of a name yet?"

"I have a few possibilities. But I don't love them. Let me try them out on you."

"Okay. Shoot."

"For Women Only; A Woman's Place: Anywhere She Wants to Be — too long, I know, but says what I want it to. Women Helping Women, New Beginnings for Women, Sisters Under the Skin; do you want me to go on?"

"Just pick one. It's only a name."

"No. It's more than that. It's an attitude. Each of the names has pros and cons. For Women Only suggests that men won't ever help. A Woman's Place needs the whole long name because that's the beauty of it."

"Well, I'm sure you'll come up with something." He looked at his watch. "Gotta run. I have a meeting. I'll leave calling the city to you." He moved toward her, but then changed his mind, taking a big step back.

"David, thanks so much."

After David left, Lisa walked over the rolling bottles, her heels clicking across the wooden floors and in and out of the different rooms. The only sound throughout was the echoing emptiness. The sink and the toilet in the bathroom were shades of rust and greenish brown mold. One of the sink faucet handles was broken off. The toilet seat was discolored with splotches of dried urine and feces. The kitchen window was broken and the jagged pieces of glass were on the counter and floor.

Lisa spoke aloud in the hollow rooms, "Can we really do this? You're a broken, sorry mess. Look at you. Neglected. Vandalized. Moldy. Don't you worry. Help is on the way. We'll fix you up and make you what you were meant to be. Even the *goniff* can't interfere with this. Wouldn't be worth his bother. We'll bring you back to life, I promise. With less talk and more action."

What Is War Good For? Positively Nothing

When Lisa arrived in Boston, there was never a shortage of political actions to choose from. There were sit-ins, teach-ins, mass rallies, hunger strikes, and vigils. The nightly television news broadcast the horror of war for the first time. Never before had the public witnessed massacres, body bags, and burning villages of war on a daily basis. This kept the rage over our invasion of Vietnam stoked. Lisa joined throngs of protesters gathered across the country at peace rallies. She participated in vigils, wrote to Congress and the President, and organized leafleting.

A group on campus kept a tally of body counts. No one was certain of their accuracy but just seeing the numbers reach into the thousands, increasing every day, made the point. Flyers hung in every classroom building making them impossible to ignore. Every day when Lisa saw the new number, she'd say a quick silent prayer to keep Nicky Ianelli safe. She thought of him every time she saw a new number, a bloody newscast, or a wounded soldier.

Nicky, two years older than Lisa, was her first kiss, first flirtation, and first almost all-the-way. When he stood behind her to teach her how to hold a baseball bat when she was sixteen, she could feel herself leaning into the heat of his body, his breath on the back of her neck and his hardness. Together they swung the bat so she could get the feel of it. He only backed away from her when the other guys razzed him.

At the end of their dead end street, there was a thicket of pine trees. Behind them was a small clearing with a tree stump and a thick carpet of pine needles. Lisa discovered it when she was around ten and as far as she knew, nobody else went there. She'd go there for peace and quiet; sometimes to read, sometimes just to lie down and look at the clouds moving across the sky. It was the perfect place for her and Nicky to explore their bodies. They never worried about getting caught, and the summer before he graduated high school, they went there almost every day. It never got past heavy necking and petting but they were each others' firsts and often took parts of their clothing off to touch and look at one another. Lisa was often amazed at how Nicky's soft, shriveled penis, like the sagging folds of old lady arms, could become so smooth and long.

They both knew their time together was a high school thing. Lisa talked incessantly about college and the war and the world; Nicky tuned her out, let her words wash over him, conscious only of the smell of pine and Lisa's soft skin. He didn't think much about the future. He liked hanging out with his friends and wasn't much of a student. His dad just assumed that they'd work together as carpenters. Nicky was fine with that.

When they watched the TV news over dinner, his dad never talked much about his time as a soldier. Best forgotten, he would say. Hell of a way to see Italy. All he said was that his feet were cold and wet as they walked around Mount Casino to save Rome from the Germans. So cold, he was lucky to keep all of his toes. But when your country's at war, you have to do the right thing.

One night in June of his senior year of high school, just as they were sitting down for dinner, Nicky's father broached the subject. "When you joining up, Nicky? You know all those hippies hollering about peace don't know a thing. There is no such thing as a good war. It's all the same. You just gotta get behind your country."

His mother cried out, "Why should our only son go over there? I won't have it. War isn't for boys like my Nicky. Let the tough ones go. Tomorrow you go down to the junior college and get yourself registered for classes."

"Don't be saying that, Angie. You know he's got to go. He's either gonna join up or be drafted. There's no pride in waiting to be hauled off. Right, Nick?"

Nicky and his best friend, Johnny McGrath, went to the recruitment center the day after graduation. Inseparable since kindergarten, they went together to an abbreviated basic training at Fort Drum in northern New York and were shipped to Vietnam together. The army needed replacements fast and lost no time getting new recruits overseas. Once in Vietnam, the two boys were separated.

Nicky wrote Lisa one letter before Christmas, 1967.

> *Dear Lisa,*
>
> *I don't have much to say. Everything here is hard and strange. Basic was brutal but I'm gonna be a muscle man by the time I come back. I've never seen country like this — swamps, deltas, rice paddies, and villages like you'd see in National Geographic. There is dust everywhere and I always feel dirty, wet, and tired. We sleep right where we are out in the open, always listening for something. Sometimes just even hearing the wind freaks us out.*
>
> *Johnny and I were counting on being assigned to the same platoon but it didn't happen. He could be close by and I'd never know it. You make buddies pretty quick here, though. My closest buddy is a guy who grew up in Texas and he's a Yankee fan. Can you beat that? Some of the guys are pretty cool but there are a lot of big mouthed jerks always looking for a fight, picking on guys. I don't know why they can't chill out.*
>
> *I'm really ok. I have the charm you gave me. I need all the luck I can get. I also have your picture and the one I took of our place. If I don't make it, be there for Johnny. Okay?*
>
> *Luv, Nicky*

Johnny was killed within weeks of arriving in Vietnam, about a month before Nicky's letter arrived. Lisa was in Albany when his mother was told. She exhaled a sound that didn't sound human, a sound that hung in the air like dense humidity, lingering for days without moving. The neighborhood was shrouded in grief. Flags flew from front porches at half-mast. This was the closest any of them were to the war.

Lisa hoped Nicky didn't know about Johnny while he was still there. She prayed that the *goniff* wouldn't take away his life. More than anything else, she wanted him to come home and be safe. She wondered what he would be like. Whether his eyes would stay soft, if he would still smile crookedly to hide his chipped front tooth, if his touch would still be gentle after what he had seen and probably done.

⤫

In 1970, the Vietnam War escalated into Cambodia. Although not officially reported, the US was also fighting in Thailand. The war, rationalized by the domino theory that if one country fell to Communism, the contiguous countries would follow, was a pooling bloodstain slowly seeping across the map of southeast Asia.

Lisa had one more class before exams. Students shuffled into History of Political Action. The weather was mild and the sensation of being wrapped in the warm breeze was intoxicating. The semester was nearly over and budding flirtations popped up like crocuses and pansies after the winter cold. Sexually charged air whirled around them. Spring fever and new infatuations obscured the tension on campus surrounding the war.

Dr. Zinman pushed his shiny gray-streaked hair behind his ears. He never said anything personal but rumors flew that he'd worked in the South on voter registration, was nearly murdered by the Ku Klux Klan, and knew Martin Luther King personally. He brushed off the questions, neither supporting nor refuting the rumors. Rather than stand at the front of the class behind a podium, he talked and walked through the center aisle of the lecture hall, his wiry body in constant motion, engaging students in every part of the room.

He wasn't smiling today as he did ordinarily, wasn't greeting his students as they strolled in. Nor was he walking through the middle aisle of the large classroom stopping to chat with students, as was his habit. He didn't call them to attention, or tap his watch as he always did the minute the class had officially started. He scanned their faces and it appeared that he was looking at them as if for the first time. Most of the students didn't notice.

He cleared his throat. "Your attention, please."

The class quieted down immediately.

"Something happened this weekend, culminating an hour ago. Unfortunately, it's your birds-eye view of history in the making. We've talked a lot about acts of rebellion in this class. We touched on the Orangeburg Massacre of 1968 when state police opened fire, killing two students and injuring twenty-seven others at South Carolina State College as they protested a segregated bowling alley."

He walked down the middle aisle of the room. "What happened today will blow your minds." Dr. Zinman was standing in the aisle facing the door. He took in a long breath. "Here's the background: A large peace rally was planned for today at noon at Kent State, a college in Ohio. There was a permit, but it may have been rescinded without students knowing. Some of the students involved were demonstrating but others were bystanders trying to get to class."

Dr. Zinman took a deep breath. "The school administration was pissed off after a weekend of sporadic incidents, including a small fire in the ROTC building on campus and a ruckus Friday night at the bars in town. Over the weekend, they gave the Ohio National Guard carte blanche to control the students at today's noontime rally. Something must have spooked them and they shot into the crowd. Four students are dead, another nine injured. Maybe more. That's all we know now. In Ohio of all places. At Kent State. Anywhere, U.S.A."

The class took in this surreal news and reacted; girls and guys alike were either crying or stone silent as if paralyzed. They didn't really know what do. Anger, confusion, sorrow, and disbelief blew across their faces. After a year of bomb scares in the dorms and classrooms, noisy rallies that were mostly ineffectual but largely peaceful, there developed a detached quality to their protest. But the killing of students on a college campus changed everything.

"We'll be planning some kind of action. SDS — Students for a Democratic Society — is organizing a national student strike." His eyes brimmed red with rage. He couldn't speak for a moment and stared at the floor until he collected himself. "Do you understand what the Guard did? They shot into a crowd of innocents exercising their first amendment rights. Think about our conversations about government repression. That is exactly what happened. Get the hell out of here and make it right." Tears rolled down his face. He slammed down his lecture notes and walked out. A small group followed him.

Lisa knew if something like this could happen, all bets were off. Unlike flocks of birds that fly with precision, war protests up until then flew every which way, touching down and then changing course. There was always a cluster of other issues clouding the purpose of the gathering. Coalitions of Black Panthers, equal rights, and gay rights supporters took advantage of the size of the crowds to further their causes. What happened at Kent State — that college students could be shot to death without provocation — unified them.

Lisa hurried out of class alone and headed toward the river to a favorite spot. She went there often. If she felt claustrophobic, the river calmed her. She crossed Bay State Road and cut through the grassy area. "Damn," she muttered. A couple was making out on her bench.

She sat on the damp grass, knees pulled up, sadness and worry nestled in her chest. She sniffled and rummaged through her pockets.

"Here." Mac handed her a tissue.

She looked up. "Mac!"

Lisa took the tissue and blew her nose, then wiped her eyes. "Thank you." How long had he been standing there, she wondered. She must look horrendous, all red and blotchy.

"You mind if I sit down?" he asked as he sat down.

"I guess not," she half-smiled.

"It's a horror. I wish I could cry. I want to, but nothing comes but disbelief. Part of me wants to think that something like this could never happen." Mac said.

She agreed, "I know. How do you take that in? The Guard shooting carelessly into a crowd?"

For a moment, they sat in silence.

He said, "I often come here. I think, like Siddhartha, that the river will answer my questions."

"What does it say?" Lisa asked, again a faint smile brushed her lips.

"I'm not sure. Does the calm mean things are about to get better or does it mean it's time to cause turbulence? I sound like a Chinese fortune cookie," he grimaced.

Lisa didn't know what to say. If he were a fortune cookie, she could hide away inside of him. Predict a blissful life. *Happiness will be yours with a certain dark-haired girl.* She sighed. "No. You sound like an English teacher."

"I guess. I am comforted by drawing literary references in the face of a tragedy like this. Silly, isn't it?"

"No. I think it's called coping," she sniffled.

"Yes, I suppose you're right." He paused, started to say something and then changed his mind.

"I can't believe we aren't in some kind of dream. Who could ever imagine our own soldiers could murder students? Who knows what is really going on in Nam?" Lisa wiped her eyes again with what was left of the shredded tissue. He was sitting so close. She wanted to crawl into his lap.

"Are you sure you're all right? Do you want me to walk you back?" he offered.

"No, that's okay. I think I'd like to sit here a while. But thanks, Mac."

He touched her shoulder. "Don't stay too long. Once the sun goes down, it will get cold fast."

"I won't. Thanks. Take care, okay?" She watched him walk away. Gorgeous and sensitive, she thought. He must have a girlfriend.

As she walked back to the dorm, she began to feel the pulsing behind her right eye and the narrowing of her vision, signals of an approaching migraine. Lisa picked up her pace so she wouldn't do anything embarrassing like throw up in the dorm elevator. All she wanted to do was lie on her bed in a dark, quiet room.

Lisa played the scene over and over in her mind. She imagined standing in one of the crowds packed in so tight that shoulders touch, with no place to move, and then hearing distant fire, shooting, students falling, blood spraying, screaming. She learned some time later that one of the murdered students was shot from almost four hundred feet away. The guards didn't aim. They didn't care who they shot. The students were part of a peaceful protest; they were unlike the kids who set themselves on fire and made the choice to die. These students did nothing more than exercise their right to assemble.

Student action was planned at about nine hundred colleges and universities across the country. It was estimated that four million students would be flooding the streets, assembled in collective outrage.

The day America killed its children became the rallying cry. Some universities closed voluntarily, but at Charles River, the president issued a statement saying that there would be no strike and if students did not take their finals, they would automatically fail their courses. What he didn't count on was that most of the students and faculty would stay out. He couldn't fail out the entire school. School closed for the rest of the semester.

Lisa joined a spontaneous march down Commonwealth Avenue to the State House to demand the flag be lowered to honor the dead students. After a tense delay (they stood for hours), Governor Sargent finally agreed to lower the flag. The crowd was silent; many wore black armbands. Arms were raised to flash peace signs. To Lisa, it was the first time standing in the street counted for something. The crowd actually accomplished what they set out to do.

On the first day of the strike, local colleges came together for one large demonstration at Boston Common. The State House was the backdrop, sitting high on the hill, its dome sheathed in copper and gold, sparkling in the sunlight. Thousands of students stood together to rally against a government that sent soldiers into a death trap and silenced protestors with firepower.

With sound rushing toward them, in a roar of incoherent chanting, Lisa, her roommate, Amy, and their friend Nina pushed through the crowd to find a place to stand. They wedged themselves in midway down the hill, their backs to the walk where mounted police sat high up on their horses, batons in hand.

From this vantage point, they saw bobbing heads covering every square inch of grass. Police patrolled footpaths. As the Common sloped down from the State House hill to street level at Tremont Street, the sidewalks through the park seemed to blister and swell from the heat of the day. Several mounted police were positioned throughout the spiral of downward paths, giving them an overview of the crowd. They sat ramrod straight in their saddles, wearing sunglasses. Lisa found them alarming. She didn't think they were there to bash in heads but she knew they wouldn't think twice if provoked. She also didn't want to be caught in a melee of enraged kids throwing things or using their placards for a beat-down. She'd seen it in other places. Kids wanting to get arrested, doing everything they could to make a statement. But for now it was peaceful. The horses were still except for periodic snorting and stomping their hooves.

An emaciated looking guy stepped over Lisa and Amy to get to the path. He was pimply, with long greasy blond hair and sweat running down his face from under a bandana tied low on his forehead. He was probably high; a cloud of pot hung heavily over the crowd. When he reached the path, he looked right up at a cop on horseback, taunting him. "Get outta here, Pig," he shouted. Unsteady at first, propped up by the crowd, he found his balance. "We got a right to be here and we don't need any oinkers telling us we can't."

The cop didn't say a word, just slapped the baton into his hand, eyes invisible behind the dark glasses. The kid backed away from him and stepped back, pushing and shoving as he disappeared into the crowd.

"Jerk," Lisa whispered to Amy. "That's what starts all the trouble. Using the P-word."

Clammy, damp bodies squeezed together. If she lost her balance, Lisa thought, she'd be trampled. She wasn't thinking about the invasion into Cambodia or the dead students. Instead, she thought about getting caught in a stampede, being struck on the head by one of the many signs waving in the air, smacked by a baton, stomped on by a horse storming the crowd. What an idiot she was. How dare she be afraid? What if she were in Vietnam? She was a coward. It was true. She was just a big talker, as her mother always said.

Lisa watched a Green Beret limp to the podium, using a cane. He struggled up the steps to the stage. She thought she saw him holding a peace sign, but then it was gone. A kid on the platform screamed at him and others joined, *Baby killer, Motherfucker,* and kicked him down. One of the performers helped him get up, took his arm and led him away from the stage. Lisa hoped he was saying sorry, don't mind them, they're idiots. What would he be doing there if not arguing for peace?

Nina nudged her. "Look over there. Lisa, I think I see your sweetheart with a group from the English Department!"

There he was, standing on one of the footpaths. Mac looked like he was pressed close to a teaching assistant who was standing up on a park bench. Lisa had seen her before, petite with a blonde ponytail. She stood on tiptoes to try to see. Was his arm around her? They stood too far away to see. She forced herself to look away. He must have a lot of women. Anybody who looked like him probably had students offering themselves up during office hours. That's how it was. Her friend, Maddy, said it happened all the time at New York College. In fact, she'd screwed her acting teacher right on his desk, not even caring if anybody walked in on them.

While Lisa, Amy, and Nina were straining to see Mac Taylor, singing gave way to shouting. The crowd on the opposite side of the park was becoming reckless. Small groups appeared to be goading the police, taunting them. *Get outta here, pigs. You gonna kill us too?*

Near where they were standing, a group of about twenty were swinging their peace signs at the cops. Although they couldn't see it, the chatter running through the crowd claimed two boys were pushed down onto the path and a cop on foot beat them with his baton. It didn't take much to rev up the crowd.

There was no place to go. The crowd was unstable because of the numbers. One of the horses got spooked; he snorted and raised his front legs. Policemen on foot ran down the path talking into their walkie-talkies. Lisa, taller than Amy and Nina, got on tiptoe to see what was happening. She lost her balance because the crowd was packed together so tightly; as she fell over she caught the corner of a placard, *What If We Had a War and Nobody Came,* and bruised her shoulder. The scuffle of protesters with police was over quickly. There were enough police to handcuff the troublemakers and haul them off to jail.

A policeman on horseback shouted through a megaphone. "If there is any more trouble, the permit to assemble will be revoked and the rally disbanded," he threatened. "One more outburst and we'll haul in the rest of you."

Helicopters flew low; the choppy wop-wop of the blades was loud. Were they going to drop something down on them, Lisa wondered. She listened to the still crowd. There was a pause as if they took a collective breath before regrouping. She immediately felt a shift inside of her, from being a scared girl to becoming part of this living, breathing mass of people. As if others had the same idea, the crowd's energy transformed itself into a magnetic field all its own. Close to tears, she felt she was part of something profound. Tears welled up but didn't fall as Lisa chanted the slogans, quietly at first, until she found both the rhythm and strength to make her voice heard: *What do we want? Peace! When do we want it? Now!*

When Richie Havens sang *Freedom* in his low, gravelly voice, the word coursed through the crowd, resulting in stamping feet, shouting, holding clasped hands high in the air. The crowd swayed as a solid mass. Chanting reverberated through the crowd. *One, two, three, four! We don't want your fucking war!* The music was rousing — Richie Havens, BB King, Bonnie Raitt — but when Country Joe and the Fish played their *We're all Fixin' to Die Rag*, the crowd screamed and sang with them.

Lisa scanned the crowd. Students, whether Panthers or SDS, gay rights, or women's libbers, wore what had become a demonstration uniform — green army jackets, tie-dye, and black, a lot of black — despite the heat. There were young couples with babies, children on their fathers' shoulders, all for peace. Lisa saw a group of Gold Star Mothers, those whose sons had died in the war, holding a large banner listing their sons' names. *Stop the War Now.*

When the last speech was given and the guitars put away, the crowd dispersed quietly. Lisa overheard bits of conversations. One girl said to the other, "What are you doing this weekend?" The friend answered, "I heard James Taylor will be at a rally near Harvard Square. Can you believe it? James Taylor!" A group of guys were trying to score some hash.

The spell was broken.

Chapter Sixteen

How Do You Mend a Broken Heart?

Bee Gees 1971

∽

Several months after David left her, Ivy was still dazed. She drank too much wine at night and slept most of the day. Her sister, Caroline, didn't know what to do. Ivy was wasting away and her niece was scared and confused. She stood by, figuring Ivy had to grieve, never thinking her despair might not lift.

It shocked the whole family when David up and left. Caroline also married too young and her marriage fizzled pretty quickly. But, there was no surprise on either side — both of them agreed they'd made a mistake. But with David, it was different. He had been part of their lives since high school. Sometimes, when you watch other couples bicker and insinuate things about each other, the unraveling marriage presents itself in slow motion. You wonder how people sabotage those they supposedly love. David would have been the last person on earth she'd guess would desert her sister. It was a brutal hit and run.

Caroline had to act. She feared her sister would never pull herself together. As it was, Caroline thought Ivy may have had a nervous breakdown. She needed help to get her through this staggering loss.

She unlocked the front door, shaking her head as she scanned the living room. On her way to the kitchen, Caroline picked up plates crusted with peanut butter, petrified macaroni and cheese, cups of soured orange juice and milk, discarded clothes, and forgotten toys that were in the direct path to Ivy's bedroom. She peeked in and saw that Ivy was sleeping. "I'll give you another half hour and then, little sister, you are going to rejoin the world. At least for today," she murmured.

Caroline put on a pot of coffee, washed and dried the dishes, sighing at the number of glasses on the table and in the sink with varying levels of red wine; she hoped Ivy's drinking was temporary. She knew her sister would be mad, but she looked under the sink and found two jugs of wine and poured them down the drain. She also picked up a bottle of pills from the counter. Their mother's Valium. Caroline flushed them down the toilet as well.

Then, she went into Joy's room tossing dirty clothes into the laundry basket and throwing toys into her toy box. By the time the wash began agitating, its drone hummed its way into Ivy's dreams and she opened her eyes.

Ivy walked out of her bedroom and pulled her bathrobe around her. "What are you doing? I don't want you to clean up my house. Go home." And she went back to bed.

Caroline followed her, pulled back the covers heaped up over her listless sister. The sheet corners slipped off the mattress, Ivy nestled into the tangled sheets and quilt.

"Come on, Iv. Get up and take a shower."

Ivy turned away from Caroline. "Go away. I'm tired and I'm not getting up." She lay face down. "Go home."

"You've got five minutes to get up or I'm dragging your sorry butt into the shower. It's over. You've given that jerk enough of your life. It's time to get up and out."

"Who the fuck do you think you are? Get out. Leave me alone."

Caroline sat at the edge of the bed. Ivy clenched the sheet and quilt tight in her fists, refusing to look at her sister.

"Ivy, please, I'm only asking for one day. Just today. You are going to take a shower, get dressed, and have some breakfast. I picked up the corn toasties you like. Then we are going out."

"Like hell I am."

"I called Meg. She'll take Joy to her dance class after nursery school and will bring her back to play with Laurie. She's staying with them for dinner. That gives us the whole day."

"How dare you? Who said you could make plans for Joy?" Ivy pulled the covers over her head.

"Okay, Iv. You asked for it." Caroline went to the edge of the bed, pulled up the corners and yanked at the sheets and blankets as hard as she could. Ivy slid onto the floor.

"Get out of my house," she shrieked. "Nobody told you to come here."

Caroline dragged the heap across the bedroom floor. Ivy flailed, freeing herself from the twisted mess. She stood up, faced Caroline, punched her hard in the shoulder and clawed at her arm. Caroline grabbed her wrists. Ivy swatted at the air trying to break free. Exhausted, she fell into her sister and buried her head in Caroline's chest, sobbing.

She pulled back from Caroline, backhanding her dripping nose, willing the endless flow of tears to go away. She tasted them, breathed them, and thought if they didn't stop soon, they would overtake her completely. The tears rolled like waves at sea, gentle and slow at first, then picking up strength, leaving Ivy powerless. She was exhausted from anger and pain. Her daytime sleep was much better than the fitfulness of the long nights. Ivy, who never drank or smoked much, needed to dull her pain. Hills of cigarette butts and ashes filled ashtrays in every room.

Caroline put her arm around Ivy and walked her to the bathroom. Ivy nodded and closed the bathroom door. Refreshed from her shower, she reached for a pair of jeans and sweater from the floor and pulled her wet auburn hair into a ponytail. The smell and sound of percolating coffee drew her into the kitchen. Caroline scrambled eggs and set the table. "Feel better?" she asked.

"Yes. But I can't go out."

"Here, have some coffee," Caroline urged, putting a steaming mug and a plate of bacon and eggs in front of her.

She ate her breakfast in silence. Ivy focused on her plate while Caroline watched, relieved to see her eating.

When they were finished, Caroline cleared the table and washed the dishes as Ivy sat with her hands around her coffee mug. "Go get your coat."

"No. You did your good deed. Thank you for that. But I'm too tired to go anywhere."

Caroline sat down next to her and put her hands over her sister's. "We can find some new furniture or dishes or something wonderful to wear.

Your clothes are hanging on you. Or we can look at apartments. Dad gave me some money for you and he's told Mother to shut her big mouth."

Ivy looked up. "So this is a family conspiracy? Thanks, but no thanks. And I'm not so whacked out that I would believe Daddy would ever tell Mother off."

Caroline straightened her back, pursed her lips, and mimicked her father's deep baritone, "Margaret, I'm sick to death of listening to your holy matrimony nonsense. For Christ's sake, leave the girl alone."

Ivy smiled in spite of herself. "Pretty good imitation. That's as close to shut up as Dad would go. Maybe I can tell her the same thing. I put the phone down when she calls to ramble and she doesn't even notice. Particularly because I don't think she ever calls before having her little 'nip' of sherry. She's a broken record: 'He'll come back and everything will be just like before.' I think she liked David better than me anyway. He always was nauseatingly sweet to her."

Caroline said, "Daddy was upset when you quit art school to support David. He wants you to think about going back and I think he has someone in his law firm who specializes in divorce lined up for you when you're ready."

"Why didn't he come talk to me?"

"Because he's Daddy. Unlike me, he needs an invitation. C'mon. Let's go."

Caroline parked the car in front of a Tudor home with an estate sale sign stuck in the lawn. This one looks promising," she said.

Ivy slumped down in the seat. "I hate those houses. You never see any life in them, no children playing, nobody sitting outside. They're tombs."

"Ah, as Mother always says, don't just a book by its cover."

"Gag me."

"Maybe we'll find something here."

Ivy asked, "What exactly are we looking for? And why do you think this house will be any different from the other eight junk piles you've dragged me to today? The trash people collect over the years is pathetic. They have sales because they're too cheap and lazy to go to the dump."

Caroline groaned. "Only five, Ivy. We've only been to five. Just this one and then we'll get coffee. I have a feeling we'll find a table here."

"I don't need a table," Ivy said. "I'm not giving in to him. Why, of all things, does he want the table? I'll never let him have it."

"You know why. It's the Lerners' idea of a family heirloom. I don't get why you are raising holy hell about a scratched up old table. It's not an antique or of any quality. It's just old."

Ivy's eyes welled up.

"Look at me, Iv." Caroline gently tilted Ivy's chin toward her. "Why do you want the old stuff around you? It'll keep you stuck."

"It's rightfully mine. Joy's really. She's a Lerner." Ivy sank back into the seat. "You don't know what it's like. It's not the stuff that hurts. It's the remembering and the missing and not having the energy to do anything. I can't even have a conversation with Joy's teacher. She called me the other night to ask if there was anything she should know. I couldn't even answer her. What exactly should she know? For that matter, what should I have known? I never even knew my marriage was breaking up." Ivy blew her nose.

"What happened feels like a nightmare. I can't stand the way he looks at me. I hate him looking around the messy house. The fucker can only shrug when I ask him what happened." Ivy closed her eyes. "I pound on him and he just takes it, stands there like it's making him feel better. I have nothing now and I'm not even good with Joy anymore." Ivy sniffled. "Sorry."

Caroline squeezed her sister's hand. "I know, Ivy. But you have to start living again. Small steps. I'm warning you. If you can't pull yourself out of this for just one afternoon, I'll tell Mother you need her. She'll be over before you know what hit you."

"You wouldn't dare."

"Don't test me. Now, let's go in."

Ivy dabbed her eyes. They walked up a flagstone path to a front door of carved mahogany inlaid with lighter squares of wood. It was partially open and they walked in.

"Good afternoon, ladies. Come right in." A sturdy-looking woman greeted them. "Have a look around. I'll be happy to answer any questions you may have."

In the living room, Ivy whispered to Caroline, "Doesn't this remind you of Aunt Kate's house?"

Ivy played a few notes on the cool white keys of the baby grand piano. The room had a red velvet couch with matching Queen Anne style chairs and cherry coffee and end tables. The honey-colored hardwood floors were buffed to a shine. Rich abstract paintings in bold colors were arranged on the wall behind the couch. Her eyes brimmed with tears. Not again. She wondered if she would always see through a blur. The tears kept everything out of focus, dimmed her sight, and sapped her energy. She had to stop them.

The woman touched Ivy's shoulder. Startled, she jumped. "It gets better, my dear. Not for a while. But it will. I promise you."

A couple walked through the living room to thank the woman and say they weren't interested in anything.

"It looks like we're alone. I wouldn't have sold them any of my things, anyway. They were cold. You could see the way they touched things. Some people just can't see value unless someone tells them what its worth. Would you two ladies have time to join me for a cup of tea?"

Ivy shook her head. "Sorry. We can't. We have to pick up my daughter."

"Remember? Meg is picking her up."

"Oh, right," Ivy said.

"We'd love some tea. We were just talking about getting coffee when we left here. I'm Caroline Hunter, and this is my sister, Ivy."

"I'm Camille Walton. Come. Let's have our tea in the dining room. The kitchen counters are covered with things for sale. I don't have much use for all this stuff anymore but I don't want my things ending up in the hands of junk collectors. I'd rather break every single dish than have that happen."

Caroline said, "I like your spirit. Though the style of this house is different, it reminds me of our aunts' house in Woodstock. Actually, the home of our aunt and her good friend who died recently. She was like family so we called her 'auntie,' too. We used to visit on Sunday afternoons. Aunt Kate could really sing. Wow, what a voice! She could play anything on the piano. You just had to hum the melody. 'Aunt Mary' was a landscape painter."

Camille nodded, urging Caroline to go on.

"They were mesmerizing storytellers. No one ever knew what was really true. We called them 'auntie legends.' They claimed they were in vaudeville for a time, that they had love affairs with artists and musicians."

Ivy added. "We didn't care if they were true. They were always filled with romance and adventure."

As she poured the tea, Camille said, "Some mystique is always a good thing. Your aunts sound like women I would like very much. When I was first married, I was only seventeen. My husband was a musician. He played the trumpet and wanted to see if he could make a living at it. We went on tour with his band, The Eddie Paul Quartet. The band was named after him, of course. Like your aunt, I was the singer."

"So you were musicians and then just gave it up?" asked Ivy.

"I got pregnant when I was only nineteen. My husband had a family business to go to — a restaurant. Eddie had big dreams. He figured that he could expand the place into a nightclub or something. But he was restless. He couldn't stand having to go to the same place every day and wasn't too good at being a father either. In those days, divorce was a real stigma. Not as commonplace as it is now."

Ivy said, "Fine time to leave you with a baby."

Camille laughed, "You have no idea!" She looked at Ivy. "Or maybe you do."

Caroline reached over to hold Ivy's hand.

The woman continued, "I was a baby myself when I got married and didn't know how to do anything but sing and play piano. So after a lot of ranting and raving and crying and feeling sorry for myself, I decided I'd teach singing. I knew I was good at it. Nobody could take that from me. I lived in a three-room apartment and made the bedroom into a studio. I bought an old piano for ten bucks and gave lessons. See that wall? I've hung the sound board as a reminder of how far I've come. Ivy, go ahead. Pluck the strings. Make some noise. I realized not too long ago that I absently strum it every time I pass by. My goodness, girls, I'm sorry. You come over to look at some antiques and I go on like this. Shame on me."

Caroline said, "Please go on."

Camille looked directly into Ivy's face. "Later on, I got my turn at happily ever after. I married the widowed father of one of my students.

We lived a great life together. My Arthur always said the best part of his life started with me and he wanted me to keep him close." She patted the Chinese urn in the center of the table. "He passed last year."

Ivy and Caroline locked eyes and then looked again at the urn.

"What are you going to do now?" Caroline asked. Ivy's eyes didn't leave the urn.

"I'm selling and moving somewhere with a view this time."

"There are some things that you just can't get over." Ivy said. "There are some things that happen that are worse than death."

Camille shook her head. "I would be willing to bet that if we have a cup of tea in a year, you won't be feeling that way. This is what I've learned. If you can imagine doing something else, or being somewhere else, you can do it. Take it from a pro."

She stood up. "Someone's at the door. Why don't you girls look around?"

Caroline collected the cups and put them by the kitchen sink. Ivy said to her, "Nice try. Do you think I'm stupid on top of everything else?"

"Don't be ridiculous. What do you think? She ran an ad in the paper for an estate sale with free advice for broken hearts? I'm good but not that good. Maybe she has a point?"

Ivy hissed, "Her husband's ashes are on the dining room table for heaven's sake."

On the buffet behind them was a china tea set with tiny pink rosebuds. "Ivy, I'm buying this. I'll hold on to it until you want it. "

"Just like Aunt Kate's. Joy will love the little flowers." Ivy agreed.

"I know she will. Let's look at some of the furniture."

In the bedroom was a sleigh bed with matching dressing table and dresser. Ivy lay down on the bed, looked up at the ceiling, and then rolled over onto her stomach, then on her back again. "I wonder if I'd be able to sleep in a new bed. I could heave our bed out the window. I'd love to see the look on David's face with our mattress flattening his precious hedges." Ivy's hardy laugh dissolved into tears.

They went back downstairs to the foyer. Caroline said, "Camille, it's getting late. We have to get going. Thanks for the tea."

"Here is my phone number in case you want to take a second look." Camille said.

"Thank you."

"Take time to think about what *you* want, Ivy. We only have one go around in this life."

Ivy got in the car. She lit and took a long draw on a cigarette. Closing her eyes, she hoped when she opened them, she'd be someplace else, be somebody else. Or travel back in time to when she was happy. She saw herself drifting through clouds on her new bed, floating away.

The sound of Caroline opening the trunk brought her back. Ivy knew she needed to find her way back to something. She looked out the window. Camille pulled up the blind covering the living room window and waved. Ivy closed her eyes hoping Caroline would take her far away. She didn't care where.

Chapter Seventeen

∾

Shadowbox: Still in Saigon

The box is painted black and is overlaid with long gray shadows.
A GI Joe action figure stands up against the wall on the left side.
Stretched out before him is a pool of milky water. On the right wall
(opposite the soldier) are faces painted in garish reds — round heads,
closed slits for eyes, and a big O for mouths exhaling screams.

Sometimes Nicky would walk toward Lisa's house, stop at the front walk, stand sentinel, and then abruptly back up and return to his house down the street. Jack watched him guard the house. He recognized the erect posture taught by the military in this crumbling boy. He knew from his own experience in war that if a guy was spooked like Nicky, you had to go slow and not get too close.

Jack called to him. "Hey, buddy. I'm going to paint Lisa's apartment. Would you like to help me?"

Nicky didn't answer but followed Jack into the house and upstairs. First, they moved some of the grandmother's furniture into the basement. Together, they prepped the walls for painting. At first, they worked in the same room, spackling and sanding. Nicky worked methodically. Jack said, "Nick, you finish up in here. I'm going to start on the living room."

He didn't answer but kept rolling the paint on the wall, steady and even. Lisa brought him a glass of iced tea. "Nicky, thanks so much for helping us out. You must be thirsty." She set it on the floor.

Lisa washed and arranged Grandma's pots and pans, the enamel bowl she used to mix the dough for her challah, dishes, cups, silverware and glasses. Nicky stood in the doorway and put his empty glass on the kitchen table. She smelled him before she saw him, his perspiration rank from a body that seemed more corpselike than alive. She couldn't imagine when he had last changed or washed the clothes that now hung on him, stained and worn thin. "Want more? I'm sorry I'm making a racket in here. I'll try to be quieter." She put his drink on the table. He took the glass and slipped away.

Nicky worked steadily without a break. Lisa made sandwiches for him and placed them near the ladder with a pitcher of iced tea. Each morning, he stood on their front walk, waiting for Jack to come out and take him upstairs. Then, Jack would go to the pharmacy. When Nicky finished painting all the rooms upstairs, Jack talked Rose into having him paint their living room, dining room, and back porch. She told him she didn't want Nicky in the house; he scared her. Jack told her she was being ridiculous. It's the least they could do for the poor boy.

Jack tried to pay him but he backed away from the money. When he finished all the painting and cleaned the brushes and pans so well they looked new, he disappeared.

Nicky crouched down between the towering pines at the end of the street, the secret place he went with Lisa when they were in high school. *The village was quiet. Just women and children. I'm sure I'm sure. No men didn't see any. We should have let them be should have left them be but orders are orders yes sir even when you know it's wrong wrong wrong, orders to burn it to the ground, no good guys we're no good guys we are bad bad bad as you can be; torching straw huts in the villages, shouldn't have looked shouldn't have looked shouldn't have. Eyes pleading pleading scared eyes pleading eyes. I'm stuck can't walk can't move can't help, Gary evil bully mean grabbed her ankles she was running, running fast, not as fast as Gary and she fell on her face on her face. He yanked her legs to turn her over, ripped open her dress fell on her, ground her into the dirt. What are you looking at, asshole. Get your own, he shouted, gravel stones fire in his voice. The girl. Her face*

Lisa then Ma then Lisa then Johnny's sister then the one he can't forget. Almond eyes empty eyes blurry face. And then he got off her and left her there naked and bleeding from the hole in her heart, streaming red.

He crouched behind the low lying branches of a fir tree. *They hurt them after they were dead. STOP STOP STOP SCREAMING. Can't help you now. STOP.* He put his hands over his ears, pushing them flat to his head. *It's too late. I smell her breathe in her terror and fire and blood. STOP.*

Cowered in a fetal position, Nicky slid a thick pallet of fallen pine needles under the trees, and rolled himself into a ball as small as he could. He kept still as death, listening to the wind through the trees, to the snap of their branches, listening for her screams.

Easing into a New Life

Marika second guessed herself until she finally arrived in Albany, holding hope for Amber's future in one hand and doubt in the other. Amber ran up and down the hall shrieking happiness.

"Stop running," Marika warned. "You'll get us kicked out before we even move in." Marika and Lisa were on either end of the green corduroy couch Marika had covered with a swirling pattern of purple and blue batiked fabric. "See? I told you it would be like a new couch. Even had some extra fabric and made a couple of bags. Which wall do you want to put it on?"

"I think we should put it under the windows, don't you?"

"Yes, indeedy!" Marika chirped.

Rose hesitated, but after listening to the activity for a couple of hours, came upstairs. Before she could say a word, Amber ran to her and hugged her waist.

"You must be Amber!" Rose said starting to touch her head but stopping short. "I see things are shaping up."

"Do you want to see my bedroom?" Amber asked, pulling her down the hall.

"It's beautiful. Every little girl should have a pink room. How about coming downstairs with me while your mother and Lisa unpack?" she faltered. "I baked chocolate chip cookies and found some of Lisa's old toys for you to play with."

Lisa stared and caught her eye. Her mother shrugged.

"Goody, goody," Amber said. "Can I Mama, please?"

Marika nodded, "Sure, go ahead. Mind your manners. Thanks Rose."

Lisa said, "Mom, why don't you bring her over to Shirley's? I think her youngest is also starting kindergarten."

She glared at Lisa. "No, Lisa. We're not going anywhere. We'll be right downstairs."

Amber took Rose's hand, "That's okay. I like it in the house! Will you be like my grandma?"

Lisa and Marika exchanged looks.

"Just call me Rose."

After they left, Marika said, "I hope this transition to an all-white neighborhood isn't too hard on Amber. Or your mother."

Lisa fluffed up the couch pillows. "Amber will be fine. And my mother will be too. She just needs time. When we finish this, I'm going out for awhile."

"You going to meet David again, Missy?" Marika asked, arching her eyebrows.

"Yes. We're going over the invitation list for the fundraiser."

"Since when is an architect a party planner?'

"Marika, you worry too much. It's business. I have no interest in getting involved in anyone else. Not ever."

"Like I always say, you are the most honest person I know but you lie to yourself. Whoppers, as Amber would say."

"The event is next week and then we'll be finished."

"Until the next project. Don't say I didn't warn you. Don't you see how that man looks at you? He's obviously head over heels. He was so obvious in the few minutes we spent together."

"You're crazy!" Lisa laughed. "We're just working together."

Marika backed up to look at the couch, nodded and turned toward Lisa. "Yeah, Missy, you'll see how 'crazy' I am. Just go. You don't need my approval."

Chapter Eighteen

The Art Opening

∽

When Caroline and Ivy drove downtown looking for a coffee shop, they rolled passed a brownstone. People were clustered in conversation out front and all the windows were lit up. A sign above the doorway read *Park Art*. She stopped the car and started backing into a space.

"What are you doing? Ivy asked. "I thought we were getting coffee."

She fumbled in her purse and threw Ivy a brush and a lipstick. "Here. Let's be spontaneous. This looks much more interesting than coffee. Besides, we can do that later."

"I'm not going in." Ivy crossed her arms over her chest.

"Suit yourself." Caroline gave herself a quick look in the rear view mirror, pocketed her lipstick and got out of the car.

Ivy dozed off but a chill woke her up. What the hell was Caroline doing in there for so long? She got out of the car and slammed the door shut.

The gallery was packed. A mixed media show of painting, sculpture, and photography was displayed in two large rooms. She didn't see Caroline and pushed through the crowd to find her.

David was on the other side of the room talking to two men when he saw Ivy walk in. His scalp tingled and he felt hot. As soon as her back was to him, he quickly excused himself and found Lisa.

He touched her arm. "Lisa, I have to go. Bye, Marika. See you tomorrow?"

"Are you sick? You're flushed and your hand is clammy."

He quickly pecked her on the cheek. "I'm fine. Great crowd. I forgot I have to get something done for a breakfast meeting. Catch me up on everything tomorrow?"

Lisa and Marika watched him sprint out like someone was chasing him. Lisa shrugged and continued schmoozing.

Ivy found Caroline in the back corner talking to a man with clear blue eyes and a salt and pepper ponytail. She seethed, "How long do you expect me to wait in the car? I'm freezing and I want to go home."

Caroline ignored her. "Aren't you glad you came in? It's warm in here." She smiled, "Ivy, this is Dylan Barmore. Dylan, my sister Ivy. He's showing his photos here tonight."

"Congratulations." She turned to face her sister. "Are you ready to leave or what?"

"You sure you don't want to look around? This is a fundraiser for a Women's Center. Dylan was asked to take some photos of the gorgeous doors on Willett, State, and Chestnut for a logo. Women opening new doors or something like that. Look at them enlarged. Aren't they elegant?"

"Yes. Elegant." Ivy said, looking at her sister. "I'm going home. If you're not ready, I'll take the bus or call a cab. Better still. Give me your keys." She put her hand out.

"Just give me a few minutes," Caroline grumbled.

"Fine. I'll wait for you by the door." Ivy nodded to the photographer. She turned around quickly bumping into a woman holding two glasses of wine.

"I'm so clumsy." Ivy blushed.

"No, you're not. There are too many people," she smiled. "I dare not bring a half a glass to my friend. Here, you take it," she said. "Cheers." She walked toward a table with food and drinks.

Ivy downed the wine in one gulp. She closed her eyes, steadied herself and found a wall to lean against. She shook her hair out of her ponytail. Beside her was a small table with a list of artwork on a clipboard with opening bids for the silent auction. There were also some flyers about the gallery, the exhibit, and the Women's Center. Ivy stuffed them into her pocket. A man standing with his back to her was talking to another woman and the one who gave her the wine.

"Lisa, tonight is a smashing success."

"I'm so excited. Even my mother left smiling. Did you see Mr. Triple Chins, probably here for the booze! But we received $5000 in donations on their leads. It's finally going to happen. We've got start up money from the city and David put me in touch with a foundation that supports infrastructure projects."

"Speaking of the devil, where did David go?" asked the man.

"He rushed out looking like he saw a ghost. Didn't he, Lisa?"

"Marika! And you think I'm melodramatic! He just had to leave. That's all," Lisa said. "We couldn't get a better architect if we dreamed one up. He gets the whole concept. All of it."

Ivy felt bile rising in her throat. Coward, Ivy thought. She grabbed another drink from a waiter who suddenly appeared. She was pasted against the wall, paralyzed.

"David is a godsend. He did this space and it's glorious. It was a complete wreck. The city building people wanted to knock it down but the preservationists made such a big stink that the city gave in and this paved the way for us. Never did I think this space would come to life like it did."

"Yes, Kevin, you should be very proud of this space. You've done well," Lisa agreed.

"I think so, too. We're going to bring this city back to life, I can feel it!"

"I'll drink to that! By the way, did you see the work David did on that old building on Broad Street? He's the best thing this city could ask for in restoration," said a man who joined the conversation. "After the Rockefeller massacre, we have to save every building we can."

"He's a pretty good restoration himself," said a woman dressed in a black mini dress. "I hear he's available, Lisa. Left his wife not too long ago and from what I've heard, she's not taking it too well."

"Oh, stop it. Nobody knows the real story. I love good gossip too, but you don't know anything about him or her," Lisa protested.

"Ah, protective, are we?" Kevin gloated.

"My relationship with David is business and all my time is going to be spent making sure my Center opens. Oh, Marika, look. Robert Sinclair just walked in. Handsome, educated, and well-connected. Let me introduce you."

Marika said, "Another time. You go ahead."

"Excuse me. I also want to talk to the people from the Albany Trust before they leave."

Lisa turned around and there was Ivy, leaning against the wall. "Hello, again. I'm Lisa Do you know anyone here?"

"I'm here with my sister." She pointed to the back of the room. "She said a few minutes... and I'm still waiting." Her voice trailed off. Lisa strained to hear her. Ivy spoke barely above a whisper. "I couldn't help but overhear your conversation about fixing an old building for a center or something?"

"Near the Palace. Clinton and Pearl. The city sold me a wreck of a place for a dollar and then unexpectedly gave me one grant and some leads on others. Thank heavens! I'm going to have to raise a lot of money so anything I get helps. I'm excited about tonight. Look how many people are here."

"Yes. I couldn't help overhear your conversation. Who is the architect you were talking about?"

"David Lerner. Do you know him?" Lisa asked.

Ivy stammered, "I used to...there was a David Lerner, I think...from high school. Do you know him well?"

"Just working with him. He has graciously agreed to work pro bono."

"Is he here?"

"He left a few minutes ago. Too bad! You could have had a reunion if he's the same guy."

"Yes. Well. I think I see my sister. Can I make a donation?" Ivy murmured, blinking.

Lisa smiled. "Just look around and enjoy yourself. And if you think of a name for the Center, just slip it into the box."

"Thank you." Ivy put her glass down. She felt her lips twitch and clenched her hands into fists to keep them from shaking. "What kind of Center are you opening?"

"It's for any woman who needs some help starting over. You know, job training, daycare, a consignment shop for work clothes. I have tons of ideas but I'm starting with the basics. It's going to take many volunteers to make things happen, so if you have any time or interest, call me. Here's my number. We could use your help and it's a good way to meet new people." She handed Ivy a napkin with scribbles.

Ivy's hand shook so badly, she dropped it. Together, they squatted to pick it up. Lisa steadied Ivy as they stood up. "Ah, too many people crammed in here. So take care. Hope to see you again."

Ivy watched Lisa walk away toward the back room.

Smiling, Caroline took Ivy's hand. "Did I see you talking to somebody?"

"Yes." Ivy pulled away. "David is working with that pretty woman over there with the long black curls. His latest project. I'm so glad we stopped by. In fact, he was here. He must have seen me and ran like the chickenshit he is."

Walking to the car, Ivy said, "Did you have to stand talking to that guy for so long?" She got in and slammed the door shut. "Does he think having a ponytail makes him look artistic? Well, it doesn't. It's greasy."

"It is not. Why would you say that? He's an interesting guy. In fact, we're going to have dinner next week. Besides, I thought mingling might be good for you."

"You were wrong."

They rode a few blocks in silence. Ivy suddenly shrieked. Startled, Caroline slammed on the brakes. "This is what he is doing while I'm dying? My heart is broken and he's out going for drinks and gallery openings and God knows what else?" Ivy pounded the dashboard with tight fists. "I never pictured his clients to look like her. He's been screwing around on me and leaves me like I'm his albatross. I'm cooking for him, waiting for him to come home and he's out doing god knows what. BASTARD. He's with someone like her and then is disgusted to come home to me. Son of a bitch. "

Your Shadow Envelops Mine

"Marika, did you see the woman I was just talking to?" Lisa whispered.
"Who?" Marika asked, scanning the room.

"The one with the red hair, leaning against the wall? She's gone now."

"I saw her. Why?"

"She's heartbroken." The redhead had that empty look, so familiar to Lisa, milky eyes with red rims and little puffy pouches underneath.

"How can you say that after a two-minute conversation?" Marika asked.

"She needs us. She couldn't even stand up her knees were shaking so badly. I wonder what her story is."

"You know nothing about her."

"I know that haunted look. She's a version of what I was like after Mac's accident. Whatever happened to her was devastating. She needs an Isabela. And if she doesn't have one, she needs us."

Weariness overwhelmed Lisa as she thanked the last of the stragglers, who were reluctant to leave the party or the wine. Her brief encounter with that sad woman made Lisa realize what had never occurred to her before. Sure, she wanted to help other women. Of course that was her intention. But underneath it all maybe she was just selfish. She worked nonstop because she had to — so she wouldn't feel like that woman anymore.

Mac buzzed in her ear, like a hornet, unable to alight for his next meal. Maybe it was because he was a teacher or because they first met as teacher and student, but she was always looking for his opinion in the weather that crossed his face; an arched eyebrow for, *you've got to be kidding;* an unflinching gaze for *you're wrong but I'll let you try to convince me anyway;* and a bemused smile for *I think you're changing my mind.*

Mac pushed himself and had the same high expectations for everyone around him. He was unyielding in thinking she would never fail. She felt his energy — pushing her to go out, go on, do something. It was worse than her grandmother bothering her all the time.

The open wound in her heart might have scabbed over but he seemed wired to her brain. He was with her every night and didn't seem ready to leave. If he had to be stupid enough to die and leave her alone, he should get the hell away. She'd have to work all the time and then she'd be too tired to dream.

Lisa was thankful she had no memories of him in Albany. Had she stayed in Boston or even in Provincetown, she'd probably never get over him. Mac would dog her every step and she would keep reliving the scenes of their life together, like bad reruns. At least he'd never been here.

When Lisa's father called to tell her that her Grandma had a massive heart attack, she assumed that Mac would go home with her.

"Honey, she's stable for now but it was a bad one. The doctor doesn't think she has much time. I called the bus station. You can get a six o'clock and I'll meet you at the station at nine-thirty."

Lisa shook her head. "Daddy, it can't be. She was so well when I came home for Thanksgiving."

"She's been very tired. We just didn't think anything of it. She's comfortable now but things don't look good."

"I'm on my way, Daddy."

Crying, Lisa shook Mac. "Mac, wake up!" She pushed his hair out of his face. Even at this moment, she admired his tawny brown hair falling over his eyes.

He sat up. "What's up? Who called?"

"My grandmother had a heart attack. There is a six o'clock bus but... I'm going to shower and get packed."

"Come here." He put his arms around her.

Lisa sobbed, hiccupping as she tried to speak. "She has to get better. She's never sick." She hesitated. "I wish that damn mechanic fixed my car. But you'll come with me?"

"I'll get up and put on some coffee. I'll take you to the bus."

"Will you come with me?" she repeated.

"No, babe." He headed to the kitchen.

Lisa followed him. "Why the hell not? It's a Saturday and I need you."

"No. You need to be with your family," he said. "Go get dressed."

"Then, if you won't come with me, can I borrow your car?"

"Baby, I'm sorry but you know I made an appointment today to see that archivist in Amherst." He released her and walked toward the kitchen. "I'll make some coffee and we'll have plenty of time to get the bus."

By the time Lisa arrived in Albany, her grandmother had died. An angry flash passed through her. If she'd driven, maybe she would have gotten there in time, had the chance to tell her things. Had a last conversation.

Lisa sat with her mother in the waiting room drinking lukewarm coffee. She broke one of the long silences hanging between them. "I've been wrong about so many things. Mama gave me a good talking to this morning about how foolish and stubborn I am," she lamented. "Now you've got to trust me. As old as I am, I can't imagine living in a world without her. I want us to be close like that."

She blew her nose and was silent for a few minutes. "Maybe I was wrong not meeting this Mac. If you love this boy, that's good enough for me." She sipped her coffee. "She was a good Mama. I was never good at it."

Lisa said, "Oh, Mom. She just understood me better, that's all. In some ways, Grandma was more modern than you. Maybe just pragmatic."

"You have Mama's spunk."

She held Lisa's hand. The tears spilled down her mother's face. No one could comfort her. She couldn't even make the arrangements. She left them to Uncle Ira.

Lisa tried to reach Mac at various times throughout the day. She became more and more agitated as the day wore on. "Mac, finally. I've been trying to reach you."

"Hi, love. I've been in Amherst. I struck pay dirt. So when are you coming home?"

"Not for a week. The funeral is on Monday. When can you get here?" she asked, waiting for him to answer. "Mac, are you still there?"

"Lisa, I told you. I don't do funerals."

"What does that mean? It's being there for me, not anything else. You're supposed to be with me when something like this happens." Lisa heard her own voice become shrill.

"I'll be here for you when you get back."

Quietly, she said. "So that's it. I don't do family. I don't do funerals or hospitals. I'll only be there for you if we're in Boston and nothing bad happens." Lisa cried into the receiver, wanting him to dab away her tears.

"I'm sorry, Lisa. I'm really sorry about your grandmother. I know how much she meant to you and that makes me sad. But I don't do these conventions. What you had with your Grandma is what's important. The funeral is for those people who feel bad about what they didn't do in the person's life."

"That's ridiculous. I can't believe you're so cavalier. Maybe arrogant is a better word."

"I'll talk to you when you calm down, Lisa. I'm going to hang up now."

Lisa's crying turned to fury. He hung up on me. He doesn't do conventions. Grandma would tell me to kick you out the door. Or since it's his apartment, pack my bags. *So that's your Prince Charming, Liselah? Kvult.*

When Lisa returned home she was worn out and all she wanted to do was sleep. Mac was tender, bringing her tea and toast, stroking her hair. She didn't have the will to call him on what he had done. Instead, she let him fuss in an effort to take care of her. Too little, too late? She let it slide. Maybe he was still spooked from going to his own father's funeral.

Marika came over to make rice and chicken. Amber brought cards so they could play *Crazy Eights* and *Go Fish*. Amy brought chocolate cake.

"Mac, how do you like being surrounded by beautiful women?" Amy asked.

"Never mind the women. The food is something else!" he grinned.

"When women grieve, they cook and they bake. Anything to postpone what they are feeling. Mrs. Daniels always said women fight their grief with a wooden spoon." Putting the biscuits on the table, Marika said, "When Mama and Daddy were killed, people brought over food to my Auntie's for days. You will never ever see me eat another casserole. Come sit down. Let's eat."

After they polished off the chicken, rice, biscuits, chocolate cake and a half gallon of ice cream, they went into the living room to watch TV, but as it turned out, they all fell asleep together.

At least there were no memories in Albany. He'd never been here and Lisa had to keep it that way. She had to remind herself that he was part of another life, far from the one she now lived. Lisa's disappointment in Mac drifted away. She didn't know when the shift in her thinking about how he left her came about. In her thoughts, he was swept away by water and not crushed by the steel of his beloved Kharmann Ghia.

The Strength of a Woman's Fury

Caroline pulled into the driveway.

Hiccupping, Ivy said, "I can feel it. I know he left me for someone else. Not his lame excuses. He's a liar. A goddamned liar."

Caroline reached over to comfort her but Ivy pulled away.

"Go in and call Meg. Ask her if Joy can spend the night. I need to get a few things from the garage."

"Why? What are you going to do?"

Ivy snapped, "Just do it."

"Okay."

Ivy pulled open the door and saw all David's tools hanging neatly on hooks. She took down an ax, a hoe, and anything else that looked sharp from the wall and brought them into the house.

"Is Meg keeping Joy?"

"Yes. What are you going to do? Your eyes are bugged out."

"Stand back."

"Ivy, you're scaring me. "

"Just get out of my way." Ivy picked up the ax, swung it over her shoulder and down onto the table. She struck slowly at first, slashing shallow grooves into the surface but her pace grew faster and harder.

"Keeping your dinner warm while you're out wining and dining someone else." She gouged the table. "Saying 'it isn't working' like I'm a goddamned toilet." Whack.

Short of breath, she barked, "Eating without a care in the world and then leaving like you're going out to buy milk."

Whack.

"No more cooking for your obnoxious family. No more... no more putting up with your petty mother."

Whack.

"So much for your table, you demanding, overbearing sticking-your-nose-in-my-business nag, always telling me I wasn't doing things the Lerner way, whatever the hell that was."

Whack.

"Not even a phone call since her precious son walked out. Not a god-damned call after all the years."

She aimed for the center, slicing up the table into large jagged pieces. "Ha! So much for your family heirloom."

Whack. Whack. Whack.

Ivy's breath was ragged. "Double-crosser. Arrogant bastard. Home after you're with somebody else. Belittling me." The wood splintered. "Wiping your mouth, crumbling your napkin on your plate; used up and thrown out... Sorry, Iv. I'm so sorry. Sorry. Sorry. Sorry. Sorry."

She struck the same spot over and over. "I hate you. I hate you, hate you, I hate you," she screeched. Ivy cut off its legs and hacked through the table top until the wreckage was in small enough pieces to carry.

Caroline stood back, not taking her eyes off the ax.

Ivy's face was flushed. She felt lightheaded and dizzy but at the same time sensed a shift within her.

With the ax still in her trembling hand, she said, "There. The matter of the table is settled."

"So I see."

"Let's light a fire."

Chapter Nineteen

Smallbany

∽

Lisa met David for lunch the next day to savor every detail of the fundraiser. The silent auction was a success and they'd raised far more money than they anticipated. There was business interest — optimistic conversation about improving skills and making a better applicant pool for employers, or so they said. Both newspapers sent photographers and one of the local TV stations had a segment on the late news.

"We scored a home run last night, didn't we?" David was folding his napkin into pleats.

"So to speak. The Business Council could give us a big boost." Lisa took a sip of her coffee. "There was a woman I met last night. She was thin, had long red hair. Did you see her?"

David shook his head, looked down at his empty plate.

"She was a mess and she needs us. I can't wait to be up and running. Meeting her brought me back to our purpose. I've been too absorbed with the building details. God, I wish things weren't taking so long."

"How do you know that? What did you talk about? With that woman, I mean. To know this?"

"She said she remembered you. From high school. Do you remember her?"

He stirred his coffee. "I don't know. It was a big class. What was her name?"

"I don't know but I doubt there were many redheads with long beautiful hair and green eyes. She had to have stood out."

He looked away. "There were twins. Yes. I remember twins with long, red hair."

"Must have been her. She was there with her sister. Though I didn't see her." Lisa finished her sandwich.

"What did you talk about that made you think she needs help?" David shifted in his chair.

"All you had to do was look at her. So what happened to you last night? You ran out like you were Cinderella and the clock was ticking."

"I remembered something I had to finish for an early morning meeting." He looked past her.

"I thought it was probably something like that," she nodded. "How did it go?"

"How did what go?" he asked.

"The meeting, David. What's wrong with you today?"

"Nothing. I'm a little distracted. Sorry I wasn't there to help with the cleanup."

"No big deal. Anyway," Lisa yawned and stood up, "I've got to get going." David stood also. "I'll give you a ride."

She shook her head. "No thanks. I'd rather walk."

Lisa could feel him watching her as she left the coffee shop. She needed to clear her head. It was a cold, clear afternoon and the wind pushed her forward. Thoughts of David raced through her head. He seemed old-fashioned in a way, polite and solicitous — opening doors, pulling out her chair, finding ways to speed up work on the building, making sure the trades didn't shortchange her. Too proprietary though: *our* Center, *we* did, *we* will.

Conversation was easy with him, drifting away from the Center to politics, families, movies, books. But there was something vague about him that bothered her. She couldn't put her finger on it. Maybe Marika was right about him. That he was looking for more than friendship. But if he thought she was looking for a relationship, he was mistaken. No way was that going to happen.

Still, she couldn't stop thinking about him. She wondered why it mattered when he bolted out of the gallery last night, why the room seemed to lose some of its luster after he left.

Ivy Gets Her Groove

Ivy dropped Joy off at nursery school and then drove to her father's office. Theresa, his secretary for the past thirty years, brightened when she saw her. Always the professional, she wore a navy blue suit and crisp white blouse, her hair upswept into a lacquered, blonde French twist. Her father counted on her in matters that extended well beyond his legal practice. Ivy and Caroline talked endlessly about whether or not they were lovers.

"What a nice surprise, dear. How are you?" She walked around her desk and held Ivy's hands in hers. "I know you've heard this a thousand times, but it's true: you will get through this and be better for it."

Ivy nodded.

"Your timing is perfect. Your father doesn't have to be in court for another hour. Go right in."

"Thanks, Theresa." Ivy knocked on the door and walked in. "Hi, Dad."

"Ivy. What a nice surprise." He rose from behind his desk and came forward to hug her.

"I have news." She stood on her tiptoes to kiss his cheek and sat down. Her father knitted his eyebrows.

"Don't look so worried," Ivy laughed. "You'll be happy to hear I've decided to rejoin the living. Now, I'm working on rage. I'm so angry at him, I could kill him," her face contorted. "Poor Daddy. Don't look so stricken. I'm teasing. I need some legal advice."

"You ready to start divorcing him?"

"No. No divorce yet. For now, I'd be happy just to hurt him. I decided neither of us should have that stinking table so I chopped it up and am using it for firewood. It makes lovely fires."

"You chopped up the table?" Her father sat down. "I'll be damned. Where did the strength to do that come from?"

"I have no idea. It feels particularly wicked because David was so picky about the correct way to make a fire. The table wasn't even solid wood. Caroline didn't report back immediately?"

"No," he chuckled. "You hacked up his table. I don't believe it," he shook his head. "So what's next? As your counsel, I have to advise you not to kill the remaining chairs."

Ivy laughed. "Not yet. We still need to sit." Ivy paused to collect her thoughts. "Dad, I think I need a few things. A new dining room set for sure, and a new bedroom set. I thought maybe if I threw out our bed, I might be able to sleep. We're not legally separated or anything so can I use his charge cards?"

"No reason not to except…" he paused. "No. Never mind."

"He deserves this, Dad."

"I suppose he does. How about if I go with you later today? Call your mother and bring Joy to the house after nursery school. I should be out of court by three. Then, we'll all go out to dinner."

"Great. Thank you, Daddy. I'll meet you at Mayfair."

He hugged her tight, whispered, "My lovely, lovely daughter. See you here at three."

After shopping, the family met for dinner. "Hi, Grandpa! Hi, Mommy! Yippee! I love Hot Shoppes." Joy said. "Can I have a hot dog and French fries and ice cream too? Can I have a hot dog, please? "

"Sure, honey. Anything you want. But get it with milk, okay?"

"Chocolate? Please, Mommy."

"Chocolate it is." She turned to her mother. "Mom, thanks for watching Joy this afternoon."

"She's a sweet child, Ivy. Considering."

"I think you'll be happy to know that I've turned a corner."

"David's coming back?" Her mother clapped her hands together and she looked up at the ceiling. "My prayers have been answered."

"Oh for Christ's sake, Mother. I said I turned a corner. I wouldn't take him back if he came crawling on all fours and begged. How could you think I would? Why would you want me to?" Ivy snapped.

"What do you think? Marriage is easy? Sometimes you have to put up with things." She glanced over at her husband. "You should be thinking about your daughter."

"Enough, Margaret." Ivy's father warned.

Ivy noticed that the red lipstick her mother always wore didn't quite make it around her mouth. "Mom, you've been drinking! You drove my daughter here after you'd been drinking? How could you?"

"Margaret! Tell me you didn't drink and drive."

"Don't Margaret me, George. Whether or not I have a sip of sherry is not a crime and it's none of your business."

Ivy said. "That's just great, Mother."

Joy looked up from her coloring. "Grandma was drinking Kool-Aid! Can't she have sugar drinks either?"

Margaret shot back, "You're a fine one to talk. At least I get up and get dressed every morning,"

"Don't start with me and don't change the subject."

"I will not have you turn this on me. I'll not have my family thinking that I'm the one with the problem. Two daughters. Both marriages kaput. It's all I think about. Caroline is stuck up, one of those women's libber know-it-alls and you're spoiled, wailing *poor me* all day."

"Think about this, Mother. While I was being the good wife raising our daughter, my husband stood up one day and announced he couldn't do 'this' anymore. This, I'm to interpret is being married to me. So, Mother, if this doesn't change what you think about me or about him, what will?" Short of breath, Ivy took a gulp of water.

"Well, la-di-da. If you want pity, you're not getting it from me." Her mother's words hung limp in the air.

George glared at her, "That's quite enough, Margaret. Please. Watch your tongue."

Ivy turned toward her father. "Maybe you should be the one to tell her what we did today."

"Tell me what? What did you two do today?" Margaret commanded.

He hesitated, looked at his daughter and nodded. "We went shopping. Ivy and I went shopping."

"You went shopping with your father instead of me?" Her mouth trembled.

"We knew this would be your reaction so we thought it best not to include you. We went furniture shopping," George said.

"Joy." Ivy bent over to brush the wisp of bangs from her daughter's eyes. "We bought you a table of your own with blue and white striped chairs. Now, you can have tea parties and do puzzles and draw. All yours! And we got a new kitchen table with chairs that have cushy seats. And

Mommy got a new bedroom set with a dressing table. I've always wanted to sit at a vanity! And I can brush your hair at night. Like a princess!"

"That sounds like a young fortune," her mother squinted. "I suppose we're paying for this, George?" She glowered at her husband. "What do you think you're doing? Involved in her nonsense without the courtesy to...." Margaret's voice trailed off,

"Include you?" he finished her sentence. "Judging from your reaction, you have your answer."

"It's not Daddy's fault. My mourning is officially over and I needed a few things."

"So you finally came to your senses and will give back the dining room table? I ran into Dorothy at the store. She wants it back. Demands to have it. For crying out loud, it's been in their family for forty years. You know, I still have to live in this town."

"You can tell my soon to be ex-mother-in-law that her table is firewood. Joy, put on your coat. We're leaving."

"Firewood? What did you do?"

Ivy interrupted, her voice rising, "Don't go there, Mother. I'm sick to death of you sabotaging my every move. You are never on my side. By this time, you should be able to let go of your precious son-in-law after he deserted your daughter and granddaughter. But no. I should know better than to expect any support from you."

The restaurant's background chatter became strangely quiet as diners watched the quarrel.

"Ivy, that's not true and it's certainly no way to talk to me. In front of the child and everyone else."

"Well, don't worry. I'm not talking to you again until you remember who deserves your loyalty. And you can forget about watching Joy until you go to AA."

"As usual, you turn everything upside down. It's not loyalty. Marriage is a sacrament."

"Oh great. Excommunicate me, why don't you. Oh, right. I'm already out of grace for marrying a Jewish man in the first place. Joy, put on your coat right now."

"No," she screamed. "I want ice cream!"

"We'll get some on the way home."

"I want it here. I want it here. Please, Mommy, please. I want it here."

Ivy said softly in her ear, teeth clenched, "If you don't stop this right now, you won't get anything at all."

"I'm not done." Joy said, "I want my French fries."

In a single sweep, Ivy slid the fries into a napkin.

"Both of you. Stop. Sit down, Ivy. Stop wailing, Joy. Everybody is looking at us," Margaret pleaded.

"Don't worry. We're leaving." She planted a kiss on her father's head. "Thank you for everything, Daddy. Talk to Mother, will you?"

She pulled Joy's arm as they walked toward the door.

Ivy could hear her mother calling after her as she walked out the door.

Payback

David picked up his mail, loosened his tie, and headed straight for his room. He had no real time for a shower before he picked up Joy. With a few minutes to rest, he sprawled out on his bed and opened the mail. He sat straight up when he read his credit card bill. Mayfair Furniture, Little Folks (she never shopped there for Joy before because it was too expensive), Gold's Department Store, Kitchens and More, an art store, and tuition to the local junior college. All told, she'd charged nearly $7,000.

He'd paid for everything, hadn't he? He let her lie in bed for months and play Sleeping Beauty, the wronged princess. And he was happy to do it after what he'd done, leaving her so suddenly. He paid for every last thing and took care of Joy so she had at least one stable parent. What the hell was this? He dashed into the bathroom and splashed cold water on his face.

David sped over to the house. The front yard looked like the aftermath of a tornado. A mattress crushed the shrubs along the front of the house. The box spring had made it further into the yard; the dresser must have been leaning against it and fell. Joy was stepping onto the box spring, walking across it like it was a balance beam. He watched her do it over and over wearing a pair of Ivy's heels and a long string of beads.

"Daddy!" She wobbled on the shoes.

"Hi Joy. "What the... What is all this?"

"Re-decorating! Look what I found." She opened her palm to show him Ivy's wedding ring.

"Does Mommy know you have this?" he asked.

"She said I could play with everything!"

"Oh, great. So where is Mommy?"

"Inside. She said to wait for you out here. She said to tell you she doesn't want you to come into her house." Joy continued to balance on the edge of the mattress.

"Is that right? Her house?" David couldn't control his voice. "Her house?"

"Daddy, where are you going? Don't go in. Please," Joy pleaded.

"Why not, sweetheart?" David asked.

"Mommy's happy."

"I'll only be a sec. I promise. Put on your sneakers so we can go to the park."

"They're in my room."

"We'll go in together. But first take off the high heels."

She kicked them off and ran. "I'll beat you in."

David gave her a running start and chased after her. Joy ran up the stairs, "You can't catch me," she sang.

"Hurry up and get your things. Sneakers, jacket, and Puppy."

David walked into the living room and saw the uneven pile of chopped up dark wood and jagged table legs. The living room opened to the dining room. In it was a maple table and chairs and in the corner a matching child's table and chairs. He could hear Ivy in the kitchen and rounded the corner. So that's what was two grand. He'd have to check the bill. Call them to see if they'd take it all back.

Ivy didn't look up. "I told Joy to wait for you outside."

"She was wearing heels. I thought maybe sneakers would be better for the playground. What the hell have you done? Have you lost your mind? Is that my mother's table chopped up in the living room so maybe Joy could poke her eyes out with those jagged edges?"

Ivy looked at him squarely. "Nice of you to worry but you opted out of that right. And while you're here, since you came into the house uninvited, hand over your keys." She put her hand out. "Don't want you coming in here like you own the place. In case you hadn't noticed, you don't live here anymore."

"Dream on. It's my house. I own it." David clenched his teeth. "Check the deed."

"Only on paper. How do you like my new landscaping?" she smiled, egging him on.

David's jaw was working double time. "What happened to you? Have you lost your mind?"

"Just get out." She turned to continue washing her brushes.

David glanced over at her easel.

"Don't you dare look at my painting, you son of a bitch." She leaped across the room to turn it the other way.

Joy stood in the doorway. "Don't be mad, Mommy. Here's Puppy." She offered her mother the stuffed toy.

"No, honey," Ivy smoothed back Joy's hair. "You take Puppy with you, love bug. I'm fine. I'm going to have a nice time. I'm going to work on my painting and I'll probably go out for something to eat with Aunt Caroline." She hugged her tightly and kissed the top of her head. "You go have fun."

"Okay, Daddy, I'm ready. Let's go." She took his hand.

"We'll talk about this later, Ivy."

"There is nothing to talk about." Ivy slammed the door behind him and turned the deadbolt.

David fumed the entire hour they were on the playground. As planned, they went to his parents' house. At dinner, Joy said, "Mommy is so strong. She chopped up the table all by herself. Now, we'll have good fires in winter. Mommy said we could cook hot dogs and marshmallows in the fireplace!"

David's mother pasted a weak smile on her face. "Joy, are you talking about the dining room table?"

"Yes! We have a new table now and I have one too! When Mommy paints, I can draw and make Play-Doh food, and build blocks and..."

"David," his father said. "Didn't I tell you to take care of things? To protect yourself?"

His mother interrupted, "My table is firewood?" She frowned at David who was pushing food around on his plate. "David, look at me. Tell me it's not true."

"I'm sorry, Mom. I know how much that table meant to you. Who would ever have thought she'd do such a thing?" David shrugged.

"Joy, take this to the kitchen for Grandma, okay? It's light." David's mother gave her the wooden salad bowl. "My table is gone? Chopped up? How could you let this happen? I always knew there was something off about her. I never wanted you to marry her in the first place."

"Let's not get carried away. You didn't want me to marry her because she wasn't Jewish. Don't forget, she converted because of you."

"She was never on your level."

"Mom, I'm sorry about the table but let's not go there. Please," David begged.

"Did I raise a doormat? Someone who can't stand up for himself?" She stacked the dirty plates and went into the kitchen.

His father said, "This is unbelievable. You might think you're being a mensch by letting everything slide. But you're not. You're avoiding what has to be done. Do right by Ivy but protect yourself, son."

"Too late, Dad. She's already charged $7,000 this month. Today was the double whammy: I got the bill *and* saw the table today."

His father advised, "David, don't be a chump. Protect your assets. And for god's sake, cancel your credit cards."

David dropped off Joy and waited in the car for Ivy to open the door. The front yard was lit up. It looked worse under the lights. There was a sign, *Free Stuff.* Maybe it would all disappear.

He had just enough time to swing back home, take a quick shower and meet Lisa for a drink. What the hell was Ivy doing? First, the woman plays dead, then she goes psycho. Throwing furniture on the lawn? Chopping up tables? What was this going to do to Joy?

He headed straight for his bathroom medicine cabinet to take an Alka-Seltzer.

Chapter Twenty

෴

Shadowbox: What's Next?

The back of the box is painted with a row of nondescript doors. They are all painted the same- a brown door with a round brown handle. In front of each door is a single object – a bead, a colored streamer, a blank page, a dollar bill, a thimble, etc. In the foreground, tiny dolls (used to decorate cakes) stand in a line, looking at the doors. Between the dolls and the doors is a small ball painted like a globe.

Marika and Lisa met at their favorite bench in Boston Common. The day was warm and sunny. Bright beds of scarlet and orange tulips, sunlit daffodils and the fresh smell of cut grass brought out mothers and babies in strollers. Children played tag and hide and seek, running around full leafed trees. A long-haired musician sat strumming his guitar.

"What's up?" asked Lisa.

Marika beamed. "This!" She held up the paper just out of Lisa's reach.

"You passed! You passed the High School Equivalency Exam! I knew you could do it," Lisa said. "So what's next?"

"Isn't that enough? Can't I just be happy with that? You're worse than an old nag," Marika laughed.

"Sorry." Lisa choked back tears.

"I'm teasing. What's the matter with you?"

Lisa shook her head and wiped away the tears on her face. "I sometimes get sad. You don't know that about me."

"Tell Mama," Marika insisted.

"It just comes over me. I feel like I'm going to throw up and then I'm just too tired to move. At least this time, I know why. I've got a thousand reasons to be down. I don't have a job. I'll never see Mac again. I know it sounds stupid but I think I've been in love with him since that first class."

"Missy," Marika put her arm around Lisa. "You hardly know him."

"Tell my heart that. But I can't call him and say guess what? I think I love you. It probably happens to him all the time. To make matters worse, I don't know what I want to do about work. The only definite I have so far is from Ruby. She says she can pay me two days a week."

"Oh that's good. She'll probably pay you two bucks an hour and you can come live with me in Jamaica Plain. But..." Marika frowned, "at least it's something."

"I read Congress is developing program legislation to prepare low-income children for school — to give them a head start, so to speak. In fact, I think that's what they're going to call it. I'd love to get in on that," Lisa considered. "But who knows when or if that'll happen. I also have an interview at Planned Parenthood. They have an opening for a community liaison. The pay is crummy but I'm probably going to live with Amy and Nina, so I should be okay. My friend, Maddy, has also been calling me every other day to remind me I promised her I'd move to New York. That's all we talked about when we were kids. So that's also a possibility. I don't know what to do."

Marika raised her eyebrows. "No way. You can't be serious. Why would anyone want to live in New York?"

"Admit it. You'd miss me, wouldn't you?" Lisa smiled in spite of herself.

"New York's got nothing on Boston," Marika declared. "Whatever you can get there, you can get here, too, but it's better."

Lisa asked, "How do you know, Marika? Ever been there?"

Marika shook her head. "No, smart mouth. As a matter of fact, I haven't."

"Ha, you'd miss me. I knew it." Lisa squeezed her arm. "Admit it!"

Marika smiled. "All right then. I'd miss you a little."

"Come on. You can do better than that."

"Nope. That's all you get."

"Well then, I'll move and send you a weekly postcard to nag you about getting a certificate to learn how to operate a small business."

"Pray tell, what for?" Marika sighed.

Lisa locked eyes with her. "So you can design and make clothes, of course."

"You wear me out with your big ideas. I just got my GED. Give it a rest."

"Promise to think about it and I won't say another word." Lisa crossed herself.

Marika shook her head. "You don't even do it right. Your cross is upside down."

"It's the thought that counts, Marika." Lisa blew her nose and wiped her eyes. "Didn't you know that if you save someone's life, they owe you forever?"

"What are you talking about now, Missy?"

"You saved my life when I got hit by a brick. So I'm yours for life. It's Chinese."

"I did nothing of the sort." Marika shook her head.

"Sure you did. I would have bled to death if you didn't choose me over your favorite turban."

"That's ridiculous and neither of us is Chinese. Girl, you're talking like a crazy person." Marika was quiet for a moment, watching three little girls playing in the grass. "Lisa, you have all kinds of big ideas for me. Time to start being more positive for yourself. You look like shit. You can't let yourself get all bluesy. Not now." Marika put her arm around Lisa. "You are graduating from a really good college. From where I sit, that's very cool."

"It is. And I know that. But I can't help the free fall. When I think about school ending, I feel like I'm going to fall of a cliff," Lisa cried.

"Quiet now. Everything will be fine. I promise." Marika drew her close.

The day before graduation, Lisa slept through breakfast, went to the Union Coffeehouse, and nibbled on a muffin while reading a trashy romance novel. It was pretty racy, but even a bodice-ripper couldn't grab her. She couldn't stop thinking about Mac, wondering how to say goodbye him. Wondering if she would even see him to say goodbye.

Be real, she chided herself. *He probably thinks you're an idiot with a school-girl crush on him. But how can I leave the campus and never see him again?* The words started to get blurry. *Do not cry. Do not cry, you jerk.*

"Hi, Lisa. Are those tears? It must be one hell of a story."

She looked up and blinked. "Mac!"

"I called you and your roommate told me you might be here. You finished with your exams?" he asked.

"Yes. All I have left is the graduation itself. I'd like to skip it but my father says going to the ceremony is important to them. They're so proud of me." She shrugged and rummaged through her bag for a tissue. "You want to sit down?"

"Sure." He slid into the booth across from her.

"What's up?" Lisa asked.

Mac smiled. "What's up? So glad you asked." He took in a deep breath. "This is what's up. Here goes. Please hear me out. I've been practicing but what I want to say never comes out right."

"I doubt that. You are the most together person I've ever met." *Shut up. Did you really say that?*

"Okay. Here goes. You are extraordinarily beautiful. You are smart. You have passion. You have that small beauty mark by your mouth that is irresistible. You have the most beautiful curls I've ever seen."

Lisa didn't know what to say. Her hands trembled.

"Do you want the long story about how I've loved you for an interminably long time or the short version in which I have no more patience and I'm glad you finally got around to graduating?"

"What?" Lisa's mouth hung open. He covered her hands with his.

"I'm taking a risk here. Watch my ego, it bruises easily. I know I probably have lots of competition. I've tried not to think about that. I've been waiting for you to graduate so I could have dinner with you or a walk in the woods, or browse through the stores in Harvard Square. It seems to have taken forever. We can do whatever you want. If you want."

Puzzled, Lisa asked, "You want to go out with me?"

"I hope this doesn't overwhelm you, but I've loved you since you read that essay in my class. And then a little more when we worked on Barton's campaign. And again still more when you were hit with the brick and I had to see for myself that you were all right. I could go on. I'm a patient man. But, if you have a boyfriend, I'll have to get rid of him."

"Oh, my God!"

Mac smiled. "Okay. No violence as long as you take a walk downtown with me. It's a beautiful day for the Gardens and then we could grab some lunch."

"You came to the hospital?" she asked.

He shrugged. "Yes, but I felt awkward and didn't want to disturb you."

"You were there! I thought I dreamt you." Lisa smiled.

"It was me. In the flesh."

Lisa closed her book, hoping he wouldn't see what she was reading, and stuffed it into the bottom of her bag. "Wow."

"So what do you say, beauty?" He reached for her hand.

"Sure. We can go for a walk. You want to go out with me? Like a date?"

He laughed. "A date? Sure. We can start with that."

Chapter Twenty-One

True Confessions or the Sharing of Soap Operas

❧

Lisa would never let David pick her up at home and she only agreed to short meetings — a drink, coffee, an occasional movie. Nothing more. They talked mostly about the Center. It was casual; a toe dipped into what he thought was a very deep pond.

"Hi David, over here." Sitting at the bar, she motioned to him.

"Hi, Lisa." A bit breathless, he kissed her cheek. "Am I late?"

She backed away from him and took a sip of wine. "No, I'm early. I went to the library to research some funding sources and decided to stay downtown. I found a major corporate donor who does capital projects and one of its priorities this year is historic preservation. Can you believe it?" she gushed. "Who knows what will happen, but think about it. This could be just the transfusion we need!"

"Excellent. That's the best thing I've heard all day," David said.

"So I'm buying this time. What do you want?" she motioned to the bartender.

"You are, huh? In that case, I'll have a double scotch."

"Did you have a bad day or are you taking advantage of my generosity?"

He shrugged. "On second thought, after the day I've had, I need something soothing, not hangover producing."

"It's a great night. Why don't we walk?" she suggested.

"Good idea."

Lisa paid the bartender and grabbed her jacket. In the cloudless night, scattered stars illuminated the inky sky. "How I love these nights. Look at how the stars seem to shimmer. I've always wanted to learn how to read them. I guess it's just one more thing for my to-do list." Wistful, she pointed upward. "I think that's Orion."

"I bought Joy a telescope. I guess I was anxious to teach her the constellations. Silly. She is much too young. We should use it on the next clear night," David said.

"Yeah, maybe." She thought Marika might be right about him. Lisa stepped away.

He appeared not to notice. "Where to, Madame?" he asked.

"Let's head toward the park," Lisa suggested.

"Sure. I won't let anything happen to you."

She frowned. "Thanks for the chivalry but I can take care of myself."

David looked down at the sidewalk. "If you knew me better, you'd see how far I am from chivalrous."

"You're acting a little weird tonight. Why don't you tell me what's going on? I'm a pretty good listener," Lisa offered.

They continued walking, finding a comfortable pace.

David began, "I've made a terrible mess of things. I had a wife who loved me and a daughter who was totally happy. Ivy was a good mother from the time Joy was put in her arms. But now, she's a complete disaster."

"Don't tell me you cheated." She stuffed her hands into her jacket pockets.

"In some ways, yes, but not the way you'd expect. I cheated her out of the promise I made when I married her. Ivy was an incredible wife. Just not for me. I left her for no reason except that I felt like a caged animal when I was home. I was starting to hate her. She didn't do anything wrong but I couldn't stand our life."

Lisa said softly, "Isn't that a reason to leave?"

"Not when you destroy the other person."

"Is she destroyed?" Lisa asked.

They passed a couple kissing as they walked. Both David and Lisa looked away. Lisa steered him onto Willett Street, a block of brownstones bordering the park.

"Well, she went to sleep for a few months. Drinking cheap jug wine at night. Sleeping all day. Barely functional for our daughter."

"So your daughter is with you? How old did you say she was?" Lisa asked.

"Four. I couldn't take Joy." David shook his head, paused before he spoke again, "If I did, Ivy would really have no reason to get out of bed. That would be the last straw. What if she killed herself?"

Lisa shook her head. "That's pretty melodramatic, David. Women do survive divorce even if it takes some time."

He combed his fingers through his hair. "You don't understand my situation."

"I was only saying that sometimes recovering from a shock takes some time." Lisa slowed down their pace. "Doesn't she have a job? Friends?"

David shrugged.

"What happened today?" Lisa asked. She nodded to a woman walking her dog and stepped aside to give her room to pass.

"I went over to the house this afternoon to pick up Joy and the front lawn looked like Ivy went bonkers. She threw out our mattress and dresser. I mean threw. I don't know how she got it out the window or through the door, but she did. There they were, crushing the bushes. The neighbors must be thrilled. She gave Joy her diamond ring to play with. When I went into the house, I saw that the table we'd been fighting over, my mother's table, was hacked apart for firewood."

David sulked. "All those jagged edges. Joy could really get hurt. And so she buys a new table, charges it, along with stuff for our daughter, art supplies, and tuition. I guess she's going back to school. Charges all of it without saying a word. And then to top it off, she asks me for my keys. She doesn't want me barging into her house. *Her* house."

Lisa threw back her head and laughed. "I'm sorry, David, but it's good what she's doing. Sounds like she's coming back to life."

"By screwing me?" David whined.

Lisa softened her tone. "Maybe it's not about you. Maybe it's about her."

"If she asked, I would have figured something out. I just rented an apartment. Where does she think seven grand is coming from on top of everything else?" David clenched his jaw.

"I'm sure she's not looking at it that way. Didn't you say you didn't want to figure everything out for her?"

"You would never let yourself get to that point," David huffed.

Lisa stopped walking. "You don't know anything about me."

"You're right. But I'd like to."

"I'll make a deal with you. You tell me a little about you and I'll tell you about me but only on the condition that you never ever ask me about it again. I mean it, David. Never."

"Drink?" he pointed to the bar across the street.

"Yes. Definitely."

A heavy wooden door opened into a dark bar with sticky, wooden nicked tables. They headed to the back next to the jukebox.

"Get a pitcher and I'll find some suitably maudlin music," Lisa said as she walked over to the juke box.

"Beer?"

She looked around. "Look where we are."

"I see your point." Smiling, he walked over to the bar and came back with a pitcher, glasses, and a bowl of peanuts. They settled into the booth.

"I'll go first before I change my mind. This is my brief history. The abridged version." Lisa inhaled deeply. "I'm a moody, opinionated, unfocused rocket who always expected everything to go wrong. You're from a Jewish family, right? So you know what I'm talking about. My grandma was the only one I thought understood me but more likely I was just the perfect candidate to appreciate the drama of her life — immigration, bad luck and death. Her tales were colorful and I believed every one of them." Lisa smiled.

"I always expected disappointment, or unhappiness, or something bad to happen. I had unstoppable crying jags, which I think might have been depression combined with a mother, father, aunts and uncles who dissected my behavior at the dining room table whenever they came for dinner or coffee. Which was often." Lisa looked down, lining up peanuts in a row and then crushing them with her glass.

"I couldn't wait to get out. I knew everything would be okay if I got to live free without feeling all those eyes boring holes in me. It never occurred to me to figure out what I wanted. Instead, I focused on what I didn't want. But I suppose that's your job when you're a teenager. Rejecting everything familiar is standard fare, isn't it?" She gulped her beer and wiped the foam from her mouth. "David, please don't look at me like that. I haven't even gotten to the bad part yet."

"Sorry. But I know that clannish mentality all too well."

"Yeah. So where was I? I went to school in Boston. Fell in love with all the steel and glass and old churches, wide boulevards and cobblestone streets. Durgin Park and the Harvard Coop, sitting by the Charles River and the Boston Common. Peace marches, political campaigns, community programs, smoking pot, talking, talking, talking about everything in the world and nothing at all. I loved everything — the sense of infinite choice and change. I made wonderful friends while I was at school and in fact, I dragged a friend of mine here. Marika. "

"Yes, she's great." David agreed.

"I took a seminar in contemporary literature that changed my life. The professor thought life would be better for everyone if they exposed themselves to the ideas and passion of literature. His name was MacKenzie Taylor. He was tall and had brown shaggy hair, wide open dark eyes, and a contagious, mellifluous laugh. I mooned over him for three years and kept running into him. We worked on various campaigns together — our politics were the same — but that was all. Then the day before graduation, he told me he'd been in love with me and had been waiting all this time for me to graduate." Lisa smiled wistfully, looking past David.

"So we lived three happy years together. Not just happy — meteoric, shooting star, blazing fireworks happy and then poof. He swerved his car to miss a deer and crashed. Gone."

David reached over to cover her hands as they twisted a napkin tighter and tighter. She flinched and pulled away, weeping. "I'm sorry, David."

"Don't be. Cry. It's okay," he murmured.

Lisa reached into her bag for a tissue and wiped her eyes. "So I fell apart and I won't bore you with the whole thing. Through some odd circumstances, I went to stay in Provincetown and lived with a woman who owned a bakery."

"Ah. So that's where you learned to bake," David interjected.

"Partially. Anyway, some semblance of myself came back to life after I conceived the idea of my Center. And here I am. It's what is keeping me sane and alive."

"Oh, Lisa. I'm so sorry," he murmured, leaning toward her.

"Yeah, well, this is what I learned. I will never let myself get to that point again. Never ever will I allow myself to become so intertwined with someone else. I could never survive this kind of loss again. Besides, I had love deeper than I'd ever imagined possible. We were both very strong-willed and definite." Lisa chugged down her beer.

"Mac used to point out two trees when we went to the Common. They were two oaks, deeply rooted in their own space, but the sun tilted the branches toward one another. With the lush growth during the spring and summer they look intertwined but in the leafless winter they stood side by side. An English teacher. Clichéd or not, I loved his metaphor and spent hours leaning against the tree that was him after his crash." She blew her nose. "Anyway, I've had more than most ever have. Short as it was. I'm done with that."

"How can a beautiful woman like you swear off love forever? You don't seem to have the persona of a professional widow in black," David smiled.

"Just watch me. That's all I'm going to say. I don't like to talk about him. When I give voice to my memories with him, they feel hollow and minimize the truth of what we had together. I don't want to share him." She poured more beer.

"When did this all happen?" David asked.

She put up her hand. "Enough. I'm done, David. That's it." She looked into the sudsy glass. "My grandmother used to talk all the time about a *goniff.*"

"You mean as in thief?"

Lisa nodded, "Yes. She believed in him, had me picture him as a living, breathing troll, waiting to snatch my happiness."

David said, "That's just Jewish morbidity. The idea that whatever you build will be destroyed."

"Maybe. But if I had doubts about this happiness *goniff,* I'm a believer now. The thing is I have to figure out how to live in a world without Mac. At first, it seemed impossible, now I don't know. He'd be happy about the Center. It would be infused with his enthusiasm. Sometimes, I feel him pushing me forward. Crazy, isn't it?" Her eyes teared.

"Not at all."

"Okay now." She pulled her hair off her face and tied it with a ribbon from her pocket. "Your turn."

"Where to start? Here is a stripped-down summary of my life. Mine is a story of a fairy tale gone awry. But then again there always was a dark side to those stories, wasn't there? Ivy is Sleeping Beauty and I am Malevolence, for sure. The root cause of trouble in paradise."

"No editorializing, Mister. Just the facts." Lisa folded her hands on her lap.

He laughed. "Okay. This is it. Ivy and I met in junior high. We were textbook childhood sweethearts on track to realize the American dream. Football player, cheerleader, prom king and queen. She went to the community college to study art and interior design while I went to Union University. Ivy was all set to continue on to a four-year school when we decided we'd rather get married right then, instead of waiting until we both had our degrees. There was no question we would marry. The only question was when. So she went to work while I finished my undergrad degree and then architecture school. I never asked her to support me through school but she didn't feel the need to go on and thought this was a better plan." He paused. "I wonder if she remembers that now. Anyway, we had Joy after I graduated." He averted Lisa's eyes, ashamed to tell her any more.

"Ivy was the Good Housekeeping wife and mother without the housekeeping. Her days were spent with Joy and finding recipes to cook for me when I came home from work. The house was trashed most of the time but she never seemed to notice. She'd hang on my every word about what was going on in the world. I was her evening broadcast news. She spent her days with Joy making crafts, going to the library, attending play groups. Everything we felt she should do. But it infuriated me. She seemed to be lost in mommy world and then would depend on me for everything else — cleaning, news, decisions about which couch to buy, paying the bills, where to go on vacation. She seemed not to have any opinions anymore. I was hungry for companionship, not coq au vin."

He looked at Lisa but her face was impassive. "I'd take deep breaths before I went in the house, hoping to quickly get through my obligations. Appreciating dinner, relating an anecdote or so about my day, bathing Joy, the whole drill. I tried to encourage her to get involved in something, get a babysitter, take some time for herself. But what she wanted was another baby." He drained his glass. "Do you want me to go on?"

Lisa nodded.

"I couldn't stand it. She didn't do anything wrong but I found it harder and harder to face going home so I worked longer hours," he sighed. "One night, after an aggravating day, Ivy waited for me to eat some new recipe she tried. I couldn't taste whatever it was and had trouble swallowing. She was watching me eat. I couldn't take it anymore and still didn't know how to tell her. Or what to tell her. You're boring? Your love is suffocating me? I can't stand the pressure of coming home at night pretending? So I just blurted out 'I can't do this anymore.' And in the ten minutes it took me to throw things in a suitcase, I was gone. She ran out of the house when I got in the car, and screamed over and over, come back, tell me what's wrong." David bowed his head.

"Oh my god, she got bushwhacked too." Lisa exclaimed.

"Bushwhacked?"

"Yes. Blindsided. Never saw the crash coming. No wonder...."

"Now that you know the truly lousy person I am, can we still be friends?" David implored.

"I'm not your judge, David. But I need to go. I'm getting claustrophobic." Lisa patted his shoulder and he watched her walk out the door.

Lisa took deep breaths, glad for the cool air. Had she stayed in that place another minute, she knew she'd throw up. She calmed herself down, but felt ripped open again with remembering. The curse and the blessing. *Why, why, why have you taken him away from me?* She silently screamed into the black night.

She slowed her breathing down as she walked. But she headed down her tunnel of despair anyway. Tonight she was swept into remembering the happiness she never thought she was capable of having. Her nerves were calm, she felt smart and pretty and more than anything else, lucky. She couldn't believe a man like Mac loved her and what's more, he loved the very things about her that irritated her family and friends.

One morning, Mac had opened the bedroom curtains and woke her with a kiss and a cup of coffee. Soft tears rolled down her face.

He pushed the hair from her eyes. "What's wrong?"

"Nothing. Well, maybe not nothing. I just realized something."

"Uh, oh, that could be trouble."

"Very funny." She lightly punched his arm "This is the thing." She reached for his hand. "It just occurred to me that I have a lightness of being. The world doesn't seem so hard to slog through. Even my wretched *goniff* seems to be on vacation." She smiled. "My revelation for the morning."

He laughed. "It's about time you noticed."

Mac took the coffee and put it on the nightstand. He kissed her tears, eyes, mouth, and the spot of the back of her neck that always aroused her. He slipped her nightgown over her head, kissed her breasts before he entered her, and she floated into the swirling pastels of early morning.

Chapter Twenty-Two

I Am Woman

Helen Reddy 1971

⁓

Marika's days were full. Most mornings she had already walked Amber to school and was sewing by the time Lisa got out of bed. It didn't take long before word of mouth spread and Marika began to build up a clientele. Lena Lewin from Gold's, trusted and admired her work. If she had reservations about how Marika would work with customers, they were unfounded. Still, she didn't invite her to work at the store — Marika only took measurements there. It was the principle that bothered Marika, not the actual working at home, for at long last, she loved where she lived.

The old tailor was more of a poor slob who was angry at the world than a bigot. It seemed he hated everyone equally and she found it easy to tune him out. He was a reluctant teacher. *How many times I tell you? You hold loose, no to pucker fabric. More loose. Capice?* She learned from him and began designing jackets and dresses for some of his customers.

His shop was on Pearl Street in Albany's South End, the heart of a tight-knit black community, drawn closer by the litany of shared complaints — lousy landlords, layoffs, cockroaches, kids' back-talking, pitiful schools. Marika bought groceries at a small market on Westerlo Street and at a fruit market on Ferry, got her hair cut in a beauty shop on Morton, and stood on the bus stop at Madison and Pearl engaging people in conversation, listening for the heartbeat of the community.

She wanted Amber to grow up in both worlds — black and white. Her experience taught her that it would be a long while before Martin Luther King's dream would even come partially true. Every Sunday she took Amber to Reverend Avery's Baptist church, not so much because she was religious, but to give her the chance to make friends. Amber was happy at her new school but Marika also wanted her to plant roots among their own. She wanted the same freedom and mobility whites claimed as their birthright, while maintaining the respect and connection to their heritage.

Education had been a constant worry for her. From the time Amber was born, Marika was determined her daughter would go to good schools. No way did Marika want Amber's choices to be as limited as hers were. And she knew firsthand what happened when bussing was mandated in Boston. To equalize race, black children from poor, working class Roxbury were exchanged for white children from poor, working class South Boston. Figured. Poor kids always get a raw deal.

It was an exchange program rather than integration. No gains to be made, just more of the same nothing. The Irish in Southie were not the least bit interested in having their kids go to black schools and the reverse was true as well. Violent street scuffles broke out. She would never let her baby go there. The School Committee, headed by a woman who was adamantly opposed to the whole idea, made the bus routes as circuitous as she could without breaking the law.

But the other option in Boston meant long bus rides to white suburban schools. She couldn't imagine putting Amber on a bus at five in the morning only to have her come home at six or seven in the evening. That on top of enduring the adjustment to white world where Amber would see how little she had compared to her classmates. She was determined to get her daughter a good education. Her own dreams were shot. They evaporated the moment she let that sorry good-for-nothing charmer, William, into her life.

No, she knew firsthand what happens without an education. She never wanted Amber to live in another dump, to walk over broken bottles and used rubbers, past men drinking whiskey on their stoops, just to get home.

She often pictured the whacked-out junkie trying to kiss her little three-year-old Amber. It ignited her rage and blistering lava gushed from her. There she was, twenty-one years old, with no parents, no diploma, and not much of a job, unless you consider being a professional babysitter a good job. Hope drifted away from her, a kite's tail dangling above her, beyond reach. She never looked up. Instead, she'd become a ravenous tiger, ready to eviscerate anyone who got close.

All that worry was in the past. No Southie, no Mattapan, no Dorchester. No long bus rides into white land. Something inside of her knew to grab the lifeline when it was thrown to her. Maybe the yearning still burned in her heart and her dreams had just been capped for safekeeping.

Marika was disquieted by how well everything was going. At least now, she didn't worry about Amber's safety. The kids in school gave her attitude and teased her at first but it was never easy being black in a sea of white faces. These little neighborhood kids weren't tough, angry kids. They were just kids testing the water. Amber was making friends and developing the backbone she would need to be successful in a tough, inhospitable world. The church people welcomed them and Amber loved the potluck dinners and Sunday school. She even sang in the kids' choir.

Now Marika would lie in bed at night sketching ideas for dresses that she was confident would have the *Marika* label. How could it be that she'd traversed a field of hopelessness to find such opportunity? That she would move from dealers and dopers sleeping in doorways to a tree-lined street with schools that bought new books and took kids on field trips.

She winced when she remembered how horribly she treated Lisa, what she thought of her at first. But Lisa somehow knew that she wasn't really the cold-hearted, disappointed bitch she'd appeared to be. In her typical *act first, think later* way, she'd believed in Marika long before Marika believed in herself.

In fact, Marika might even be ready for love.

"Good morning, Missy. Late night?"

"Not really, I had trouble sleeping." The conversation Lisa had with David unsettled her, relegating her to another sleepless night, tossing and turning, with dreams and memories moving in and out of one another. She was back at school in Mac's class, thinking about that very first day.

"So, what's the story with you and David?" Marika didn't look up from the skirt she was hemming.

"No story. I've already told you that. It's just that last night I told him a little about Mac. I guess it just brought me back." She poured some coffee. "Want a cup?"

"No thanks, I've had enough. You're probably feeling a bit guilty. He's the new man."

"No. He's not." Lisa rifled through the papers on the table, not ready to make phone calls. She poured her cup back in the pot. "I think I'll go downstairs to have a cup of coffee with Mom."

"Wait a minute. I have the first focus group scheduled today. Do you want to come?"

"No. It's better if you do it. Just stick to the script. Push to see what they really want. Not what they think we want." Lisa said.

"Yes sir!" Marika smiled, saluting her. "Say hi to Mommy. I'm going to finish this hem and head out."

Walking down the stairs, Lisa heard her mother on the phone. "Faye, did you see Lisa's picture in the paper? With the Mayor and the architect? Yes, they got the money. Of course they did. Save me your copy, okay? Yes. I'll tell her. Bye."

"Morning, Mom."

"Hello, Miss Celebrity!" Her mother was smiling and held her arms open for a hug.

She kissed her mother. "Hardly. Do you have any coffee on?"

"Sit. I'll make you breakfast." She had a frying pan on the stove and butter melting before Lisa could answer her.

"Don't spoil me, Mom. I could get used to this." Lisa smiled in spite of herself. They sat down to eggs and toast.

"So, if things are going so good, why do you have black rings under your eyes?"

"Just couldn't sleep. That's all." Lisa shrugged.

"Did you see this gorgeous picture of you in front of the building? Here, take a look at this."

"Good publicity. Especially showing the Mayor is with us. After what he's done to the city, it's time to start making amends. But look at me. I look like a scarecrow."

"You do not. And the architect is handsome. Lerner is a Jewish name. I'm sure of it," her mother smiled.

"What difference does that make? David is a nice man that has become a good friend. He's donated many hours to the project. But that's it. Nothing more."

"A mother worries." She furrowed her brow, tucked her short dark hair behind her ears.

"No need. Everything is great."

"If it's so great, why so pale?" She poured more coffee and sat down. "I know I've been lucky and don't talk from experience. But look at your grandma. She found a truer love second time around."

Lisa stood up. "Bad example, Mom. Two husbands and both dropped dead." Her face darkened.

"There is always more than one way to look at things. One bright, one gloomy."

"I wish you could have known Mac. Then you'd know. You'd understand."

"Know what, my sweetheart?"

"There will never be anyone else for me. I'm going up to make some calls."

She kissed the top of her mother's head and hurried up the stairs two at a time.

Shadowbox: Work in Progress

Plastic wrap is taped to the back of the box. A small figure is pushing a Popsicle stick with fringe at the end toward a heap of crumpled spitballs. One section of the box is painted white, the rest is covered in scrawls of graffiti. At the center are black and white paper doll cutouts holding hands.

The grant from the Historic Trust was approved and work on the building began. At some point, Lisa's project hit a nerve. People were bitter over the homes that were lost. They didn't view themselves as a blight on the city, a stain forfeited to cold marble. Rather, they believed their neighborhoods and way of life were stolen from them.

The rehab was going faster than expected because of the skilled volunteers who lived in the neighborhood, in addition to the members of the Clinton Square Neighborhood Association and the Brothers.

In the early sixties, the Brothers formed to advance the strategy of the Southern Christian Leadership Conference's *Operation Breadbasket*. The crux of this program was to encourage the Black population to boycott businesses that denied them jobs. The group, influenced by the range of rhetoric — Malcolm X, Stokely Carmichael, and Elijah Mohammed, as well as the civil disobedience philosophy of Martin Luther King — modeled themselves on the Black Panthers when they supported local communities on bread-and-butter issues.

The summer that burned — 1967 — there were sixty riots in cities across the country. The bloody riots that swept Chicago, Newark, Detroit, and Watts in Los Angeles helped precipitate the racial violence that spread to upstate New York. While Albany escaped the magnitude of looting and destruction felt in other parts of the country, polarization was deepening. Community leaders and directors of poverty programs insisted the looters and rioters weren't 'their people' and in one instance when a poverty program sent their kids to stop the pandemonium, the police couldn't tell the 'good' ones from the 'bad' ones and arrested them all.

There was a mini-riot that summer on Pearl Street and forty-four black teenagers were arrested after looting and destroying the storefronts of business owners. Two years later, there was a racially motivated stabbing at the Palace Movie Theater.

During the early seventies, the city implemented its long awaited urban renewal plan. Nearly one-hundred and seventy acres were to be renovated, displacing over five-hundred families, more than half of them black. A new elementary school was built in Arbor Hill, but then Van Woert Street was bulldozed and rerouted. Three-hundred eighty-five houses were demolished yet only one-hundred were rehabilitated. The Ten Eyck Manor and Dudley Park apartment complexes were built, adding three-hundred units for low and medium income families and seniors. High rise apartment buildings replaced what had been Colonie Street. Somehow, though, the math never quite worked out and many residents were still without adequate housing.

The push toward urban renewal was a good thing and improved quality of life for many families. But it wasn't enough. Arbor Hill, bounded by Clinton Avenue (where the Center was located), Northern Boulevard, Lark and Swan streets were all in decay. Many of the homes were boarded up, gutted by fire, or otherwise uninhabitable.

The Brothers raged over the displacement and overcrowding of their community. Housing was scarce, despite newspapers filled with stories of urban development building projects. Landlords in Arbor Hill renovated their buildings to meet the large numbers of families needing housing. They jammed three families into one-family houses and cut up two-family flats into apartments. It was rumored that one of the Brothers, infuriated by what was happening, dropped a bag of cockroaches on a slumlord's desk.

They picketed the construction site at the South Mall government center in protest against unions for not hiring black men, and then graduated to more hot button issues: police brutality and the five-dollar vote (it was an Albany tradition for the Democrats in power to buy votes).

Police harassed and arrested them. With each defeat, the Brothers became more militant until they disbanded. Originally formed as a nonviolent group, there was discord among the members that couldn't be reconciled.

Lisa's father knew the Brothers from the days when their drugstore was downtown. Merchants, who were losing their customer base, were silent supporters of the Brothers' actions. Many of the leaders went on to get more education and jobs within the government. But Louis Vanderholt, one of the founders, still lived in the old neighborhood. Lisa's father admired him and thought he could be helpful, so Lisa called him. He was not enthused but agreed to meet her if she could come to his home.

Marika and Lisa could hear the slow steps approaching the door and the thud of his cane. He opened it and gave them a curious, hard-to-read once over. "So, who do we have here? Let's see. I'd say an Oreo and a wannabe? Who *will* come next?" He leaned on his cane, a worn-out man with gray stubble and a round, tight afro.

"No hello. No pleased to meet you. Welcome to the neighborhood! Would you like to come in?" Marika shook her head and frowned. "Did you have a Mama? Didn't she tell you when ladies come to visit you don't insult them?"

Lisa turned her back to leave.

He shrugged. "Yes, ma'am, you're quite right. I forgot my manners. I'm just a beat up old man tired of the parade of disappointments coming through my door. Forgive me, ladies. Please come in."

"No, thank you," Lisa said.

"Please, I insist." He held the door open.

Lisa and Marika moved into the foyer so he could close the door but didn't go any further. Lisa's often repeated blurb came out at warp speed. "You probably know we are rehabbing the building down the block for a new Woman's Center. We would like to make it multi-purpose but to start, we are focusing on job training. We hope to learn who in the community we need to reach, particularly women with little or no job skills. We've got the churches on board. This is not just for Arbor Hill. North Albany Irish and West Albany Italians are part of our target audience. And whoever else needs our services." She paused and said, slowly, "You know you don't have to be black to need help."

"Ouch. Whoa, slow down, girl. I promise I'll listen. That's a lot to say in one breath. Why don't you two sit down?"

"No thank you. We're fine right here." Lisa said.

"What do you want?"

"For you to be on our advisory board and help us do things right. Suggest some others, preferably women, who might want to sit on an active board," Lisa said, now breathless.

He smiled at Marika. "And, my dear, what do you have to say? I doubt this white woman acts on your behalf."

"I'm her bodyguard." Marika deadpanned. "Against the likes of you."

He laughed from his belly.

"Mr. Vanderholt, do you want to see the building? It's just down the block," Lisa asked.

"Maybe I will sometime," Louis said.

"Sometime? How about right now?" Marika asked.

"Now? Hm. I suppose I could. Let me get my coat."

He walked down the steps, slowly balancing himself with the cane on one side and the railing on the other. As they walked down the street, Louis looked down, slowly negotiating the broken sidewalks and chipped curbs. A carpenter was working in the dining room. Vanderholt said, "Hello, Franklin." Franklin nodded and continued nailing. "Good carpenter made me a table once. And who is the other man?" Nicky was sitting on a chair, staring into space.

"Nicky," Lisa spoke to him softly. "Nicky, there is someone I'd like you to meet."

"Okay."

"Louis Vanderholt, this is Nicky Ianelli. Nicky is helping Franklin build our cabinets and will finish the back room once we get electricity out there." Nicky looked at the floor and then stood to go back to work.

"Good to meet you." Louis said. As they walked away, he asked, "Nam?"

"Yes. I grew up with him."

Vanderholt shook his head and looked around each room, nodding, leaning on his cane. "What am I looking at?"

"Here is reception and children's playroom — half walls will be constructed and we'll paint it in primary colors; the dining room doubles as conference/ training room and my office. Kitchen stays as kitchen. Back bedrooms will be offices for community liaison and intake. Back porch will become all-weather and used as a clothes closet. The other two floors will also be made usable in time."

Marika added, "I am new in town and need advice on who to call and how they fit in. We need a board connected to this community. We want people who are open minded, not old warhorses stuck in the past."

"I guess I deserve that," he smiled. "Things are worse now than in the sixties...if that's possible. You girls have spunk. What the hell? I'll make some calls." He opened the door, then turned around. "Ladies, forgive my earlier remarks. Please. And call me Louis."

Community members from the preservation league consulted with David as the work progressed. All the original woodwork and hardwood floors would be restored. In addition to the grants the Center received, there was unexpected generosity from both private and corporate donors.

David worked with Lisa's concept and the final plans were very close to what she had originally suggested. The family also pitched in. They decided to buy office furniture, supplies and toys. Uncle Ira and Lisa's father painted; David, Marika, and Lisa sanded the floors and sealed them with a high-gloss finish.

Before leaving each night, Lisa walked through the rooms, noting the day's accomplishments, how much closer they were to opening. *What do you think about this, Mac? Pretty cool, isn't it? You're up there watching. Aren't you?*

Hello Anger, Constant Companion

Ivy painted on her back porch. It was a glass-enclosed room with tight storm windows. If nothing else, David had been a fastidious homeowner — caulking windows, fixing bathroom leaks, patching the pale stain on the bright white ceiling. The porch had good light and overlooked their well-landscaped yard. She decided that with a portable heater, it would be a perfect year-round studio. She practiced studies of changing light and shadow for one of her art classes.

The art supplies were more expensive than she had imagined but hell, David was an architect pulling in the big dough. If it weren't for her working all those years when he was in school, he wouldn't even be an architect and she'd have her art degree. But no, she put herself second, always second to him.

She moved Joy's little table back and forth from the porch to the dining area. Ivy was trying hard to get back to the way she'd mothered Joy
before David's departure. Her daughter was the centerpiece of Ivy's life
again, though not as it once was. How could it be the same? The damage
was done. But Ivy was able to swallow her heartache and try to make up
for those months of neglect. She needed to help Joy adjust from her happy
little life, living in the magic of a snow globe, into one where she lived
without her father and with a comatose, then volatile mother.

Ivy's bitterness burned through her. She was fully transformed —
impatient and ready to argue with anyone about anything. The newspaper
delivered too late for her morning coffee or a slow line at the supermarket
could set off fireworks. Anyone who got too close was vulnerable to her
punishing temper.

When she railed at Caroline or her father, they just let her go on. What
else could they do? They both felt that David's ultimate crime had been
destroying Ivy's sweet disposition. They both hoped this too was a stage of
grief on her path back to herself, and it was better than what she'd done in
the months after he left.

It was her mother who bore the brunt of her rage. "Mother, you never
cared about what was good for me, nagging at me all the time that I was
lucky to have David and I should quit school to support him," she railed.
"You never once said to me, Ivy, he's lucky to have you. No. Not you.
Always 'Does David like this, does David approve of that... '"

Her mother slapped her hard. "Mother of God, Ivy. I'm sorry. I'm sorry.
I didn't mean to hit you but I don't know how much of this you think we're
going to take," she whimpered, and added, "Don't put it on me. Face up
to it, you've made a mess of your life and there's no use blaming everybody
else."

Ivy's internal fire smoldered, ready to ignite.

The phone rang. Ivy wiped her hand on the rag and went into the
kitchen to answer it.

"Hi, Ivy." David said.

"What?" Ivy asked.

"What happened to hello?" David asked. "You doing okay? How's Joy?"

"What the hell do you care?" she sniped.

"Does it have to be like this? Can't we be civil to each other, at least for Joy?"

"You're the one with all the answers. You're the one who did this to us. You tell me," Ivy demanded.

"I'd like to take Joy tomorrow night, rather than tonight," David spoke quietly.

"Working late? I can only imagine what kind of work you're doing," she sneered.

"If this is the way you are going to be, then let's just keep to the subject." He kept his voice even, clenching his jaw to keep his temper in check. "Yes or no?"

"Yes. But don't make it a habit. It's important to keep Joy on a regular schedule. Be here right at six. I'm going out." She slammed down the phone.

Yeah, right. I'm going out, she thought. Or maybe she would. There was a woman in her class who seemed nice. Maybe she could ask her if she wanted to meet for coffee or dinner. When Ivy met new people she always looked down to see if they wore a ring and divided them into two groups, them and us. This woman appeared to be one of the ring-less us.

Ivy's father wanted her see a lawyer but she wasn't ready. It was only fair that David pay for her school and continue to pay until she was done. She knew she had to pace herself. After all, she wasn't a carefree college student as he had been. She had responsibilities. She was a mother. She hadn't been in school for many years and she could only manage one or two courses at a time until she got back into student mode. No matter how long it took, she promised herself, she would finish and David would pay. He owed her that.

Let him float on the windy seas for a change. She'd control the line. She'd decide whether to rein him in or let him go.

Ivy opened the door to Joy's classroom. "Mommy," she shrieked when she saw Ivy and ran right to her. Ivy smiled and picked her up for a minute.

"Put me down, Mommy. I'm a big girl!" Joy squealed.

"Okay, okay, but first a kiss." She kissed her daughter's nose.

Joy's teacher motioned to Ivy. "Mrs. Lerner, I want you to know Joy is doing much better."

Ivy straightened her back. "Better than what?"

"Well, for one thing, she's smiling more and has begun to participate again. She's told the class that she is an artist like her mother."

"Yes, she is. Aren't you, baby?" Ivy tousled Joy's hair.

"I was wondering if I could ask you to do something."

"What?"

"We are putting on a play. I wondered if you would make the scenery. I'm writing a script around *The Hungry Caterpillar.* Maybe the children could help you?"

"When do you need it? I'm taking a class right now and am pretty busy." Ivy hedged.

The teacher smiled. "There's plenty of time. I always ask months in advance."

"I'll be just as busy then." Ivy turned to leave. "Shouldn't you be making your own scenery? I mean it's your damned job, isn't it?"

The teacher reddened and forced a smile, "Forgive me, Mrs. Lerner. I thought the children would have enjoyed working with a real artist. We'll find someone else. We have many volunteers." She turned around and erased the chalkboard.

"Yes. That's probably best." Ivy countered.

"Mommy, did you just say a bad word?" Joy whispered.

She shrugged, "Sorry." Ivy grabbed her daughter's hand and they skipped out the door. "Daddy won't be coming tonight. He's got something bet.... he has to do. Why don't we go home, have lunch and then go someplace fun. Your pick."

"Yippee." They ran to the car holding hands.

Chapter Twenty-Three

What is the Difference between Rescue and Recklessness?

∽

Lisa kept everything moving — fundraising, writing grants, meeting with community groups. She breathed a sigh of relief when they received a grant to offset administration and overhead costs. It wasn't much, but it paid small salaries to Lisa and to Marika, who supplemented her income with sewing.

She sat at her desk in the early evening when the phone rang. "WOW. This is Lisa speaking."

"WOW? Lisa, it's Isabela."

"Isabela! It's so good to hear from you. Yes, we're calling the center WOW. It came to me after all that thinking about it — Women's Options for Work. Isn't it great?"

"Very nice. Upbeat." Isabela agreed.

"I miss you. How are things? Your hip okay? When are you coming to visit?" Lisa rambled on.

"Whoa, child. In a word, I'm fine. How are you?" Isabela asked.

"I'm fine. Except..." Lisa's voice trailed off. "I can't believe you called today. It's a year ago today that Mac died."

"Time does go by, doesn't it?" Isabela exhaled a deep breath.

"I'm okay, though. Mostly okay. Some days are better than others but on those bad days, I'm overwhelmed," Lisa said. "Things are coming along great here. But today? What can I say? I'm very sad. Mac's missed a whole year of living."

"You're going to be fine. You know something, Lisa?"

"What?" Lisa pictured her standing in her kitchen with her mug that had a chocolate cupcake with pink icing on it.

"We might be caught up in undertow, but we women are buoyant. We may kick and paddle our hearts out, flail and gulp too much water. But we always rise to the top and get past our troubles. You and I are living proof of it."

Lisa laughed. "If that were true, I'd have a real problem."

"And what might that be?"

"I can't swim!" Lisa laughed, shaking her head. "Only you could make me laugh today."

"You still have your sense of humor, I see. So to speak," Isabela observed. "So listen to an old woman who's seen a lot. We always find a way to move on. And you, my dear, are growing strong."

"I'll keep it in mind." Lisa absently sketched out a new shadowbox, with deep swirling high water with a bunch of bobbing heads. "So what's up?"

"I want to close the bakery for the two weeks around your grand opening." Isabela hesitated. "Would that be all right?"

"Two weeks! Are you kidding? Having you here will be terrific!" Lisa stood up, then sat on the edge of the desk.

"Good. I want to get there early to bake and then maybe take a little time to look around Albany. I've never been to upstate New York before. Maybe I'll go to Vermont, too."

She scanned her calendar. "We think we'll be ready at the end of the month. The workmen should be out of here by Friday but I want to make sure they are really done before we set the date. But now, at least I have a desk to sit at," Lisa said and then paused. "Isabela?"

"I'm listening."

Lisa closed her eyes. "Will it always be this hard?"

"No. I promise. Take it from one who lost everything." Isabela's voice softened. "You find your way and maybe then…. a new life emerges. It's different than before. But the new life might even be better suited to you than the life you left behind. Don't forget. You are buoyant."

Lisa sat and put her head down on the big desk. She couldn't focus. Her eyes burned and her mind wandered. It was getting late and she was tapped out for the day. But she wasn't sure she had the energy to go home. Maybe she'd try to sleep there. If she just flopped on the tattered couch Nicky'd found, she'd be fine. Mac, dead a whole year. She knew it in her bones before she even realized the date. She woke up that morning with dread, lead in her stomach. No diversion could keep her from thinking about him.

Lisa heard footsteps but didn't bother to look up. Take anything you want. I don't care, she thought. The footsteps came closer and she recognized them as David's.

"Lisa." He touched her shoulder. "Hey, wake up, sleepy head. I've come to take you to dinner."

She lifted her head. "Not hungry. But thanks, anyway." She put her head down again.

"You are working much too hard. We'll walk so you can work up an appetite."

"Not tonight, David. I'm too tired. Give me a rain check?"

"You need to eat. Just dinner and then home," David insisted.

"Okay, I guess." She didn't move.

"Lisa?"

She sighed. "Let me clean up a bit." She stretched as she walked to the bathroom to wash her face, fluff up her hair and put on some lipstick. There was nothing she could do about her swollen eyes.

They walked up the hill to Fiorello's, an upscale Italian restaurant. "Isn't this a bit much for a Tuesday night?" Lisa asked. "I'm not that hungry."

"It's perfect because it is Tuesday," David persisted, taking hold of her arm.

"It's pricey, I hear. You paying? Not that I want you to, but girls on my salary don't eat here," she yawned.

"Yes, I'm buying." He held the heavy wooden door open for her.

"With your wife squeezing you for money?" Lisa asked. "The diner would be fine," she said, turning around to walk down the front steps.

"Lisa, forget that. I want to eat here."

"Okay, okay. But not as a date even if you insist on paying."

"Call it whatever you want." Working to contain his irritation, he led her inside and they were seated.

Lisa felt much better after two glasses of wine. She recounted the visit with Vanderholt. "He actually called Marika an Oreo, can you imagine? He's lucky he didn't cross the old Marika. She would have skewered him." Lisa doubled over with laughter. "Do you think I'm a black wannabe? The idea never occurred to me. Maybe I am. In addition to wanting to be a Moroccan gypsy or an Italian from Tuscany."

David picked up the bottle to refill their glasses but she covered hers. "No more. I'm already tipsy. Yup, I'm definitely tipsy," she giggled. The sadness that had weighed her down all day was gone. *Isn't it fabulous to have such a good friend?*

She looked over to the dark oak bar. "Oh look, speaking of the devil, there's Marika with Robert Sinclair." She waved them over. "More friends! Marika! Robert! What are you doing here? Are you two up to something?"

"I might ask you the same question. Why are you so flushed?" Marika groused.

"Am I? It must be the wine. You know what happens when I drink on an empty stomach? I get drunk!" Lisa cracked up.

Marika was steely. "Then don't drink before you've eaten. You look like shit."

"Thank you, Marika. You're particularly charming this evening, aren't you?" Lisa smiled and turned to Robert, "I'm sorry. Robert Sinclair, David Lerner." David stood up to shake his hand. "He's the architect on our building. You too just missed each other at the art fundraiser."

Robert extended his hand. "Good to meet you, David. Great job. It's fascinating to watch it rise from its ashes, so to speak."

"Thanks. It's getting there. Don't you run the new community center?" David asked, avoiding Marika's glare.

Robert nodded. "Yes. I do."

"Would you like to join us?" Lisa asked. "It would be so much fun. Wouldn't it, David?"

He didn't answer her.

"No, thanks. We're just having a drink. I have to get home. Amber's plans with her friend fell through. Your mother saved the day but doesn't sound happy," said Marika.

"Too bad. See you later, then," Lisa said.

Walking away, Marika looked back at her and watched David finger Lisa's hair, which Lisa didn't seem to notice. She shook her head.

"I think I forgot to eat today. What should I order? Order for me, David. I have to go to the bathroom. Do you know where it is?"

"Around the back to the right. How about the chicken and pasta special?"

"Sure. That'll be great." She teetered as she stood up, almost losing her balance.

In the bathroom, she sat down at the marble vanity and stared at herself. Dark smudges accentuated her watery eyes. What a wreck. No wonder Marika was in a snit. *Mac, you'd want me to have a good time today, wouldn't you? Of course you would. In fact, I think I'll have another glass to mark the year you've been gone. A whole year since you had the audacity to leave me. Maybe I'll drink a whole damned bottle.*

Lisa walked toward what she thought was their table but David wasn't there. She shrugged. Maybe it's this way, she thought. Can't even find the table. Cheap drunk. Lisa laughed aloud at herself.

Before she realized it, David was behind her. He grabbed her and twirled her around so fast she nearly fell. He was handsome with his green eyes, wavy dark hair and neat beard. In a split second, his arms were wrapped around her.

"David, what are you doing?" She pulled away but he held her firmly against him until she relaxed. He inhaled her, lifted her chin, kissed her gently on the lips, then deeper. He held her tight but with tenderness. Swaddled in the heat of his body, she wanted to stay there with him in that moment, forever.

"I want to tell you something. Just listen. Don't say anything, Look at me." He tilted her chin. "I love you, Lisa. I'm sure you know that by now. I know my life is a mess and you are not ready for me. We don't have to rush. Remember that before you run away."

"David, this is a bad time for me. I don't know what just happened but it's no good."

He held her tighter.

"Don't pressure me or expect anything from me. I will always be in love with Mac," she slurred.

He kissed her to stop her from talking and then again because he was finally holding her, and they slowly walked, hand in hand, back to their table.

After dinner and yet more wine, Lisa and David drove to his apartment. She sat in the car, nestled under his arm. As soon as they moved inside, they began to kiss, unbuttoning each other's clothes, dropping them on the path to the bedroom.

He pulled away, holding her shoulders. "I want to look at you, I've dreamed about this happening but you are even more exquisite than I have imagined. Come to me." David laid her down on the bed and began to kiss her neck, her shoulders, her breasts, moving down her body inch by inch, her legs, her toes, touching her, every inch of her again, back up her body. She was burning, fevered with longing. The moment he entered her, all thought evaporated into the intensity of disappearing into each other. What had been pent up inside her was released. There was a rushing in her ears, her heart emptied of its weight, a surging river flowed from her ahead of him, and then again with him. He murmured in her ear but she didn't care if he meant what he said. It was the moment speaking through him, she thought. How could anyone else love her? Not yet. Not the way she was.

When he fell asleep, she gently pulled his arm from across her chest and slid out of bed. She had to find her way out and go home where she could feel safe. She called a cab and waited for it outside.

The house was dark when she got home. Relieved not to have to face Marika, Lisa fell into bed and into a deep, dreamless sleep.

Marika wasn't asleep. She lay in bed restless, her blood boiling over after the encounter at the restaurant, wondering if what she'd heard about him was true. She distrusted David completely. Although they were from different worlds, so much of David reminded her of Amber's poor excuse for a father, William. He was great at the chase, thrived on it, in fact. The principle reason he had children with different mothers. He'd stay until they threw him out or he got bored or found a new woman to chase. David seemed manipulative and for Marika, that was enough to write him off.

When Robert dropped Marika off at the house, Amber was watching TV while Rose was getting supper ready.

"Marika, is that you?" Rose called out.

"Yes, Rose." She kissed Amber on the head and walked into the kitchen. "Sorry I'm so late."

She covered the pot she'd been stirring. "It's fine. No problem. Your daughter has a sweet, easy disposition. I'm not used to a little girl being so agreeable."

"But your daughter grew into one fine woman." Marika smiled.

"Yes she did. I made extra spaghetti and meatballs. You two are putting in long days and I thought you and Lisa might be too tired to cook."

"Lisa won't be home for dinner, so why don't you save it for leftovers."

"Another night meeting? She's working too hard. And in that neighborhood..." her voice trailed off.

"No meeting tonight. I guess you could say she's on a date."

Rose smiled and held up crossed fingers. "With David, I hope?"

Marika tried to put out of her mind the way Lisa had looked at the restaurant. Drunk and vulnerable. "Yes. Afraid so." Marika sighed.

"Why would you say that, Marika? He's wonderful. I met him at the fundraiser. He's handsome and charming and — "

"Jewish?"

"Yes, Jewish! I'm not ashamed to say it. I never thought I'd see the day. Don't spoil it," Rose cautioned.

"For heaven's sake, Rose. Whenever I think we're getting along better, you find a new way to insult me."

"Don't take it that way. But, tell me this. Isn't it true that you have a lot to lose if David and Lisa get married?"

"What an outrageous thing to say to me. Nothing would make me happier than Lisa finding someone to love the way she loved Mac. But you have no idea. David is not that man. Heaven help her if she marries him. But luckily, he's not ready."

"Says who? You?"

"Amber," Marika called out. "Get your stuff together."

"I'm sorry. That was too harsh. I just don't want you to get in the way of my daughter's happiness."

Marika sighed. "I know you don't think much of me but I thought you'd learned by now that things aren't always the way they appear. Thanks for watching Amber."

It was past midnight when she finally heard Lisa open the door. *If he breaks her heart*, Marika fumed, *he's a dead man*.

Chapter Twenty-Four

Afterthoughts and Second Guessing

∽

It was barely dawn but Lisa couldn't sleep any more. She made coffee and took a cup to the back porch. There was a chill in the air but with a blanket wrapped around her and the warmth of her coffee, she felt snug. What the hell happened last night? Had she lost her mind altogether? Sleeping with David. How could she? And on the anniversary of Mac's death? She felt like a cheater. Listen to yourself, Lisa. How can you cheat on a dead man?

Face it, imbecile. Mac is gone and will never be back. Did you really expect you'd be celibate forever? Making love with David felt natural, even if she had way too much to drink and it was a huge mistake. It was astonishing how he seemed to know her body as if they'd made love a hundred times before; it was more like familiar loving, two lovers eagerly coming together after an absence, rather than a drunken first encounter.

She'd never thought about anything happening between them. Or had she? This sitting *shiva* for Mac couldn't go on. It would rob her of leading a full life. Did she want to become stuck in grief like his mother? How could anyone live like that? Mac would have hated it and been so disappointed in her if she never recovered and wallowed in self-pity.

It happened on Mac's *yarhzeit,* though, and that felt wrong. But since when did she care about those dreadful Jewish markers, anyway? What if it wasn't coincidence? What if it symbolized a line drawn giving her permission

210

to move forward, to edge her way toward a new path? It's not like she jumped in the sack with David right away.

It was so comfortable being with David. She always looked forward to their dates, whether she wanted to call them that or not. It didn't have to be serious. A roll in the hay was allowed, wasn't it? As long as it didn't happen again. Lisa closed her eyes, trying to sweep out all thought.

Marika wrapped her bathrobe around her and came out on the porch, coffee mug in hand. "You're up early." She pulled her chair close to Lisa's.

"I slept soundly, better than I have in a long time. No dreaming. So when I woke up, I was fully rested. Why didn't you tell me you were going out with Robert?"

"I'm not. It just happened. I was finishing up with a group at the community center — that went really well — when he came in and asked me if I'd like to go for a drink."

"You like him?"

"I like him fine. Let's talk about you," Marika snapped, her mood dark.

Lisa looked at the sky. The sun was just coming up and a soft gray light was pushing away the dark sky.

"You slept with David last night, didn't you?" she asked. "I know you did."

"How do you know that?" Lisa asked, picking the lint off the blanket.

"You were flushed and glassy-eyed at the restaurant. He got you drunk. Tell me what happened."

"I wouldn't exactly put it that way but it was a little weird. I didn't want to go out for dinner. I was tired and I think I was sleeping at my desk when David came in and insisted I had to eat, and it might as well be with him. I thought going to that particular restaurant was overboard but he insisted. It's a gorgeous place, isn't it?"

"Plotted the whole thing," Marika muttered.

Lisa ignored her. "You're going to think this next part is corny and clichéd. I went to the ladies room and when I walked back into the dining room, David wasn't at what I thought was our table; I turned to see if there was another room and there he was. He spun me around, kissed me, and told me he loved me."

"He said what? You've got to be kidding." Marika splashed coffee over her hands and lap.

"Here take this." She handed Marika a napkin. "Be like that and I won't tell you anymore." Lisa rearranged the blanket on her lap.

Marika softened, "Tell me."

"We went to his apartment and it happened. The strange thing is that it felt like I'd been with him before. As soon as he fell asleep, I came home. At first, I was feeling guilty about Mac. You know what yesterday was. But now I'm not sure what I feel."

"I knew this was going to happen. I knew it." Marika grimaced.

"What does that mean? Do you disapprove, Marika?" Lisa turned from her.

She raised her voice, "Somebody's got to look after you. Obviously, he got you drunk and then took advantage. Do you think that's fair?"

"What are you talking about? You've just never liked him."

"I like him fine but he's got no business messing with you. He isn't even really separated yet," Marika blurted out.

"Of course he is. What makes you say that?" Lisa asked, absently rubbing her forehead.

"Maybe he's separated physically but after all this time, has he done anything about it?" Marika barked, "No!"

"And you know the status of his divorce because?" Lisa asked.

"All I need to know is he is not divorced and he's been after you like a crow hunting for prey. I should have told you what I heard before this...."

Lisa retorted, "If you know something, tell me. Otherwise, shut up about it."

"I only know that when one of the partners came in to the Center, he joked that he thought David was spending so much time here to avoid his wife calling the office. Apparently, she calls to scream that she'll never divorce him, that he can go screw himself, and that he's going to rot in hell."

Lisa was quiet. "It's probably a lie. How would anyone know that? Do they listen in on phone conversations? Marika, did you pump this guy for information? That's not something that would come up in conversation with a client."

"What he said is the kind of thing that gets around an office and you know it." Marika said. "I only said that he's done a lot that seems beyond his job as project architect. That's all. He has business to settle before he starts messing with you. I'll tell you this much, Lisa. If he hurts you, I'm gonna kill him."

"And you tell me I'm a drama queen? Relax. I'm going to take a shower." Lisa slammed the door behind her.

࿓

Lisa was humming and sorting papers when the phone rang. "WOW, Women's Options for Work, Lisa speaking." She picked up a pen and slid a notebook toward her.

"Hi." David said.

"Hi yourself." Lisa smiled.

"Why did you run off?" he asked.

"I took a taxi home. The whole thing. What we did. I was overwhelmed." Lisa said, cradling the phone to her ear, smiling in spite of herself.

"Overwhelmed? I thought it was spectacular!" he exclaimed.

"Well, yes," she hesitated. "I can't deny it."

"Since you aren't sure, I think we should do it again? How about tonight?"

She scanned her calendar. "Not tonight. I have an evening meeting."

David complained, "But I'm free. Joy has something at her school tonight."

"Maybe we can get together tomorrow night?" Lisa suggested. "But what happened between us can't happen again."

"Tomorrow I'll have Joy. Want to meet her?"

"No, absolutely not." Lisa shook her head.

He pressed on. "You sure? She's a great kid."

"I'm sure she is but I don't want to get into your family life as it is."

"What do you mean?"

"I heard that you aren't separated from your wife."

"Of course I am. You were in my apartment," he said. "The legal stuff is harder. I want her to get back on her feet before she has to go through that. You can't imagine what she's like. She takes longer to process things than most people."

"How long has it been, David?"

"Not long enough. I'll take care of things. Don't worry."

"I don't understand. You're talking but you're not saying anything." Lisa started to feel a throbbing in her temple.

David ignored her. "I'll make it right. Don't worry. Look at my incentive. Come on. Change your mind about tomorrow," he urged.

"I have to go." Marika's words swirled in her head.

"Come on. It will be fun."

Lisa gently hung up.

Her meeting ran until about eight-thirty. As she locked the front door, she saw David sitting in his car at the curb. He rolled down the window.

He grinned. "Does Mademoiselle need a lift?"

"I thought I said not tonight." Lisa frowned.

"You got me. I have no restraint. All my discipline of the past months is gone. Out the window. Never more." David's eyes sparkled.

He got out of the car, grabbed the back of her neck and kissed her hard, bruising her mouth. He pulled her tight. In spite of herself, her nipples were hard and she was wet. She ached for him. He roughly opened her blouse, pulled her bra up over her breasts.

"Let's go inside," she whispered.

He opened the door and pushed her inside. He carried her, legs wrapped around him, hiked up her skirt and laid her down on the conference table. In one motion, he swept all the papers to the floor. His thrusting was strong and every push she felt inside her brought her closer to where she wanted to be. She wanted him to explode in her and take all of her. Afterward, they lay down quietly on the floor.

"You're a sight, my love. Would you mind standing up?" David's arms were folded behind his head.

"I don't think I can."

"Please. Take off all your clothes. I want to see all of you," he insisted.

She took everything off, throwing them aside, closing her eyes.

"Come closer."

She lay down next to him, legs splayed, and she came again.

A few moments later, Lisa spoke, "David, what are we doing?"

"I thought it was pretty clear." He brushed the curls away from her face.

"This is too dangerous. It's too fast. It's confusing me."

"No, it's not. It's perfect."

Lisa looked at him spot on. "Next time, we have to be careful. Promise me?"

"You mean no more public places?"

"That among other things." She buttoned her blouse.

"See me tomorrow with Joy?" he asked.

"No. And do not come here with or without her. I mean it."

"Why not?" David asked.

"Why not?" She was incredulous. "We're on a bobsled, speeding down a fast, icy track. I don't want anyone to get hurt. Not the kid and especially not me. I'm not ready for this. You know," she added, "maybe it's just sex."

"It isn't and you know it. Nobody is going to get hurt. I promise you."

"Don't make promises you can't keep. Whatever this is. I don't know. It may be love. Let's keep it between us until we know what it is and can name it."

"I can name it now."

Lisa objected. "Stop it. You can't. Don't even try. I'll see you the day after tomorrow."

"I promise. If I can stand it."

Lisa kissed him hard on the mouth. "Lock up after you and make sure the room doesn't look like it was ransacked."

Chapter Twenty-Five

Baby Steps

∾

David reached the house at precisely five minutes before six. He didn't want Ivy to have a reason to blow up at him tonight. Not that she needed one. Just as he turned off the ignition, both Joy and Ivy came out. Ivy was well-dressed. Since Joy was born, he could count the times Ivy had changed from her jeans, tee shirts and sweatshirts. Now, she wore a pair of brown slacks and a cream colored turtleneck. Her sweater was unfamiliar. For a woman who'd never spent money on herself, she was making up for lost time in spades.

He rolled down the window as Ivy marched up to the car. "Make sure you give Joy a bath and have her in bed no later than eight-thirty. Don't let her talk you out of it. You also have to make two dozen cupcakes for the class party tomorrow. I don't know when I'll be back."

She turned away and walked to her car.

"What do you mean I have to make cupcakes? How am I supposed to do that?" he called after her.

"Figure it out, smart guy." She turned away and got in her car.

"Hey, Joy. How's my sweetie?"

"Not so good, Daddy."

"What's the matter?"

Tears streaked her face." I fell in dance class."

"Poor baby, did you hurt yourself?"

"It was when you line up and one at a time you have to skip across the room waving pretty scarves. I fell down and everybody was looking. That mean old Jessica laughed at me," Joy sniffled.

"I'm sorry, honey. Just think about mean old Jessica falling flat on her face."

"Yeah, Daddy. That would be really funny," she laughed. "She's a fatso and looks like a pig in a pink leotard."

"Oh, honey, that's not nice. Don't say things like that. It's hurtful," he said.

"You're not nice. You're hurtful." Joy said.

"Oh, is that right?" He tickled her, turning the tears into squeals of laughter.

"Stop, stop, please, Daddy," she giggled.

"Okay. What do you say we find us some beautiful cupcakes and then go to Hot Shoppes?"

"No, Daddy. They have to be made."

"I have an idea! How about this? We'll bring them home and make them look homemade. Our secret." He put his finger to his lips.

"Can we buy colored sugar and chocolate chips?"

"Sure we can. Let's get going."

As Ivy was packing up her paint and brushes after class the day before, she worked up the nerve to ask the woman who sat next to her if she'd like to go out to dinner sometime.

"Sure, Ivy. Love to. When did you want to go?"

"My husb… my daughter's father has her tomorrow night. Is that too soon?"

"I was going to see a film. There's a Fellini Festival at the Delaware. Would you be interested in that?" Victoria asked.

"Sure. It's been ages since I've seen a movie that wasn't *Sleeping Beauty* or *Snow White*," Ivy smiled.

Victoria laughed. "There's a Chinese restaurant next to the theater. How about if we meet about six-fifteen?"

"Great."

Ivy arrived at the restaurant first. Her stomach lurched. The waiter brought water and she asked for tea. She tried not to look at her watch every other minute until finally, Victoria rushed through the door. "I'm so sorry I'm late."

"Hardly." Ivy smiled. "I'm glad we were able to do this. Shall we order our own or do you want to share?"

"Share. Definitely," Victoria said.

They ordered their food and Victoria looked straight at her. "It'll get better, honey. Been there and back." Victoria settled her large frame into the chair.

Ivy played with the cloth napkin in her lap. "How did you know? Is it that obvious?"

"There is a look we all seem to have at the beginning. It's a tired, startled look. One that says, *how did this happen? No way can I do this*. And most importantly, *how could you do this to me?* But it goes away and you've got a lot going for you."

"I don't think so." Ivy shook her head.

"You're young, you're pretty — a redhead, no less — and you've got talent," Victoria proclaimed.

She sighed, "Talent? Sure I do."

"Yes, ma'am, and it's about time your recognized it. Stop being so timid in class. You're better than half the kids in there. I heard the teacher whistle under his breath at that last still life you did. Ivy, let me tell you something. I was dumped when I was forty-nine. My dearly beloved hooked up with an old girlfriend at his high school reunion. Can you believe that? She'd conveniently left her husband and lost fifty pounds before the big event. I'm not going to bore you with my sob story but without knowing anything about your situation, I'm going to give you the best advice you'll get from anyone: make everything as difficult as possible, spend as much money as you can before he cuts you off and delay the divorce as long as you can, until you want it."

Ivy shook her head. "Victoria…that's tough."

"It's the only way to pick yourself up off the floor. Gives you some power. Does he deserve any consideration? I bet not. Let me give you the name of a great art supply warehouse for you to stock up before he cuts up the cards. And when you are ready for a lawyer, let me know. I used a real ball buster." She took a sip of tea.

Ivy didn't enjoy the movie any more than dinner. She didn't like anything about Victoria. She was hard edged and caustic. Not just about her divorce. It was her world. Ivy counted the number of grievances she had — with the waiter, the neighborhood, the girl who put too much butter on her popcorn, the tall woman with big head of hair sitting in front of her at the movie. Ivy was relieved to know that she was sane enough to see Victoria was a horror show. She saw her as a warning. Ivy was on that path and didn't want to become a woman like that.

Rather, she would try to believe she could be an artist — it was clear that Victoria, negative about almost everything, meant it when she said she had talent. When Victoria finally stopped talking to catch her breath, raving about the stupid movie, Ivy simply said she found it confusing, overrated and she thought Fellini was schizophrenic. She didn't know where that came from but she was pleased with herself for having said it.

Ivy came home around ten-thirty. She walked into the kitchen and saw the cupcakes.

"Oh my god, look at all that sugar. What were you thinking?" Each cupcake had mounds of pink frosting covered with blue sugar. "The kids will be maniacs." She hung up her coat. "You can go now, David."

He ignored her. "Glad you are getting out. I'll pick Joy up on Saturday morning at nine. How long can I have her?"

"Keep her overnight. I've got things to do."

"Great. I'll get her Saturday at nine." He hoped she couldn't hear his disappointment.

∽

On Friday night, Lisa and David went out for pizza. Lisa was famished and devoured one slice after another.

David sat back, watching her. "When is the last time you ate? How does a slip of a thing like you eat four pieces of pizza?"

Lisa wiped her mouth. "I think I forgot to eat today."

"Why do I waste my money at Fiorello's when you're as happy eating grease?"

Lisa grinned. "Because I'm a class act."

"That you are." He squeezed her hand. "You about ready to head out?"

Lisa laughed. "Roll out is more like it."

They went to David's apartment. Last time she was there, she didn't see much. The living room was small. A loveseat, TV, drafting table, and a bookcase filled up the room. The bedroom was also sparsely furnished. The alcove, painted lavender, had a mattress covered with *Strawberry Shortcake* sheets and stuffed animals; books and games were piled up in the corner — *Candy Land, Chutes & Ladders, Sorry*. Lisa remembered them all from her childhood.

"So this is it? Home sweet home." She picked up one of Joy's teddy bears. "What's it like being a part-time father?"

"Ouch," he winced. "Just because I don't live with Joy doesn't mean I'm not thinking about her and taking care of her as I did when I was home." He moved a pile of Joy's books and sat down. "Having a child changes everything; it brings up emotion you never thought you had. Fierce, overflowing love. Worry. Amazement. Uncertainty. Fatigue. Where you live doesn't minimize how you feel."

"Don't patronize me, David. Is she a happy child?"

"Joy was the center of our world. I think Ivy had some kind of breakdown when I left. I've made a mess of things and hurt her in a way I never intended. Now, she's high energy combined with a ferocious temper. I don't know who she is any more and I don't know what's worse, her sleepwalking or rage. Joy was a happy, secure little girl with nothing but imaginary monsters to fear when I pulled the rug out from under her. The last year or so has been rough." He shook his head looking miserable.

Unmoved, Lisa asked, "A year and you're not legally separated?" She walked away from Joy's toys.

"Sure I'm separated. Look around." His arm swept the room.

Lisa gasped, "Have you seen a lawyer? That's what usually happens after couples split up."

"No, not yet. I already told you. I want her to be in better shape before she has to go through a legal separation and divorce. She isn't ready to handle it now. In fact, I think it would be best if she filed. It would give her back some of her dignity."

"You're kidding me?" Lisa began to button her sweater.

"Leaving her the way I did was horrible. I hate what I've done." David shook his head.

Lisa shrugged. "How nice of you. Maybe even noble. Listen, David, I'm really tired, I'm going home." She picked up her bag and walked toward the door.

"What do you mean? It's only 8:30 and I have Joy both Saturday and Sunday. Can we do something together? Maybe take her to the park? Just a short walk?" David implored.

"Are you nuts? That's a terrible idea. Besides, I have plans."

He came toward her, held her face, and kissed her. She pulled away. "Please, David. Not tonight. I just don't have the energy. I want you too much and I don't know what that is, and it scares me."

"I love you and want to spend my life with you. You can't possibly want me too much."

She'd heard those words before and that lifetime proved to be very short.

∞

Saturday was unseasonably warm and sunny. Ivy was about to leave the house when the phone rang. She hesitated but decided to answer it.

"Hello, Ivy."

"Hello. Who's this?" Ivy asked.

"What do you mean, who is this? It's Dorothy, David's mother."

"What a surprise! I hardly expected you to call after all this time. Do you realize that this is the first time you called since he walked out on us?" Ivy took in a deep breath and exhaled it slowly.

"How could you?"

"How could I what?"

"Don't play games with me, Ivy. Have you lost your mind? That table was mine and you destroyed it. How could you do such a thing?"

"It was good therapy. I pretended it was your precious son's head I was chopping up into little pieces. As it turns out, it wasn't even solid wood. Some family antique. A fake just like your son. And though it would never occur to you," Ivy inhaled a breath and blew it out slowly, "Your table is insignificant compared to what he's destroyed."

"You have gone crazy. Joy should be with David."

"You're kidding, right? David doesn't want either one of us. And he sure wouldn't want Joy ruining his love life. I was so mistaken about all of you."

Ivy slammed down the receiver and reached for the Valium she stole from her mother. She laid down, still trembling but amazed at herself for speaking up to her mother-in-law.

By mid-morning, Ivy was on the road, headed toward Woodstock. When she told David to keep Joy for the weekend, she had no idea what she'd do. She just blurted it out as she did most things lately. Her internal censor was missing, she mused, like she had Tourette's.

And then it came to her. She would visit her elderly aunt in the country, paint, and walk on the lovely grounds. Maybe her Aunt Kate might feel up to going into town for dinner.

On the drive, she thought about that woman she and Caroline met, the one who had her husband's ashes on the table. Aunt Kate would love the story and a description of the house.

Aunt Kate met Ivy on the front porch. Hugging her, Ivy said, "I'm so glad to see you. It's been much too long."

"My darling niece, I was delighted when you called. You're here now. That's what matters. I brewed tea." She took Ivy's arm. "Let's drink it on the porch." Ivy always loved the big old wrap-around porch with its deep, cushioned wicker furniture. She'd spent hours on the swing as a child. She and Caroline used to come for part of the summer when they were kids.

"Remember how I used to sit here with my pad drawing brown lines, topping them with green circles and calling them trees? I love how Joy draws the same way... her yellow sunshine always in the same left hand corner." She laughed at the memory.

Kate smiled. "Most of them were the usual kid stuff, weren't they? But with a little instruction from Mary, you'd get it. Take them to the next level. Your talent and will were always there. So tell me, what's going on?"

Ivy frowned. "Dad probably told you that David left us."

"Yes. All he said was that it was a real blow to you, as I can imagine." Kate stirred her tea and looked up with a smile. "I've always thought men were overrated."

Ivy laughed. "How did you know enough to stay away from them?"

"Some choices are not ours to make," Aunt Kate's blue eyes twinkled.

"What do you mean, Aunt Kate?" Ivy asked.

Kate patted Ivy's hand. "Darling girl, you never knew that Mary and I were lovers?"

Ivy nearly choked on her tea, spraying it all over herself.

Aunt Kate laughed at her, handing her a napkin.

"Of course, you were always so affectionate with each other, but I never thought about things like that. I guess that explains some of Mom's comments." Ivy rolled her eyes. "But I'm embarrassingly naïve. Let me let you in on a secret. I don't have a clue about most things. David shocked me. I thought our lives were perfect."

The two women were comfortable in the silence that followed. "Mary and I were distressed when you quit art school to support David. From the time you were a little girl, you loved making art. Maybe this change in your life will help you remember your plans."

Kate took a sip of tea. "Most of us weren't meant to spend our lives in supporting roles. Yet, we do because it's expected. Mary and I were way ahead of this supposed sexual revolution and feminism. We were in an equal partnership. We'd never allow one to give something up for the other." She shook her head. "I have a surprise for you. The attic is filled with Mary's art supplies. She wanted you to have them. There is enough paint, canvas, brushes, and palettes to keep you in business for a while. I also pulled out some of her paintings to see if you'd like to take one home with you."

"You must miss her terribly," Ivy said reaching for Aunt Kate's hand.

"Every day," she sighed.

"I'm sorry, Aunt Kate. Having her art supplies is a wonderful gift. Thank you so much." Ivy leaned over to kiss her cheek. "Why don't we walk down to the pond? I can paint and you can sit in the sunshine. And if you're up to it maybe we could go into town for dinner."

"Lovely. The Woodstock Arts League is having an opening reception for a group exhibition. We can go, raid the free wine and cheese, and later go to the Inn."

Ivy hugged her. "Aunt Kate, you're the best." She cried softly onto her aunt's shoulder.

"Dear, it might not seem so now, but one day, you are going to think that this is the best thing that ever happened to you. Your time is coming, I promise."

Ivy came home refreshed and happy with some new sketches. She was buoyed by Aunt Kate's natural self-reliance. Look at her living all alone in that rambling old house. Content and unafraid.

When she got home, she made herself a sandwich and looked at the Sunday paper. There was a notice that the Women's Center was having a grand opening. An idea for a painting popped into her head. The woman in the gallery had been so kind to her and in an accidental way dried up the waterworks she'd been drowning in over David. If it turned out well, maybe she'd give it to her.

She headed straight for the porch. The phone rang every fifteen minutes for the next two hours. He's not too annoying, the jerk. She had no intention of answering the phone until she was satisfied with her sketches.

"Hello."

"Hello, Ivy."

"Hi, Mom."

"I've been calling and calling. Where have you been all day?"

"David took Joy for the weekend and I visited Aunt Kate."

"Damn queers," she said under her breath. "I hope she didn't put any weird ideas in your head. Living with that other woman alone in the country. They're lucky they didn't get themselves killed. I don't know why your father is so damned fond of them."

"Mother, don't start," Ivy warned.

"Don't take that tone with me, Ivy."

"Listen. I had a really nice weekend. Please don't spoil it," Ivy moaned.

"I'm a little tired of walking on eggshells around you. I am your mother and I think it's time you remembered that and showed me some respect," her mother sniffed.

"Okay, Let's start over. 'Ivy, did you have a nice weekend?' 'Yes, Mother it was great to see Aunt Kate.' 'Oh, what did you do?' 'Well, we talked a lot. She still makes that great date nut bread.'" Ivy continued before her mother had a chance to interrupt. "I started a painting. It's a view of the pond next to that big old oak. Then we went to a gallery opening and had dinner at the beautiful inn in town. This is where you are supposed to say, 'Sounds great!' or 'How does Kate look? Is she doing okay after Mary's death?'"

"That's quite enough. You are so different now. You don't sound like yourself."

"That's a good thing, Mom. I did get some ideas for several paintings. And a wonderful gift. Mary left me all her paints."

"Are they still good? They must be old and dried out by now."

"They are fine. Good as new. So how was your weekend?" Ivy chirped.

"Your father went to the office today. On Sunday, can you imagine? So I cooked. I have some soup for you. Do you want to stop by?"

"I'll call you when I have time."

"Come to dinner."

"We'll see. I have to go."

Five minutes later, the phone rang again.

David growled. "It's about time you got home."

"Hello to you too, David. Did Joy have a good weekend?"

"Let her tell you herself. I'm bringing her back now."

"Not yet. Give me another hour. I'm working."

"Working? At what? Did you get a job?" he asked.

"No, David. I'm an art student. Remember? "

"Whatever. We'll be there at seven."

David also called Lisa. No answer. No answer. Come on, Lisa, pick up.

"Who are you calling over and over, Daddy?" Joy asked.

"Mommy and a friend whom I was supposed to call today."

"Maybe he'll be home soon and you can see him when I go home. Wait until Mommy sees my new puzzle."

David wasn't listening. He opened the phone book and jotted down a number.

"Hello, Mrs. Stern? This is David Lerner calling. Is Lisa there?"

"Yes she is. We're just finishing dinner. Would you like to stop by for coffee?" Rose asked.

"Thank you. That would be great. I'll be dropping my daughter off at seven. Will that be too late?"

"Come anytime. It's just coffee. We'd love to see you." Her mother hung up and returned to the table. "Lisa, that was David. He's coming for coffee."

"Here?"

She smiled. "Of course, here. Where else?"

"Did he invite himself over, Mom?"

"Relax, will you? I invited him. What's the big deal?" Rose shrugged.

Lisa scowled and looked around the noisy table. She tapped a spoon on her glass. "May I have everybody's attention? David Lerner is a friend and colleague. Do not think it's more. Promise me you will not ask embarrassing questions or humiliate me with stories you seem to think are amusing."

"You worry too much. What do you think we're going to say?" Aunt Faye asked.

"I just want you to be low key. Keep talking about the best buy this week on orange juice. Or how you're doing in the stock market. Okay?"

The bell rang. "Okay. You promised me." Lisa said.

She opened the door and he lifted her chin to kiss her. "What are you doing here?" she whispered.

Unabashed, he shrugged, "What can I say? Mama invited me for coffee."

Lisa led him into the dining room and introduced him to everyone around the table.

"Thank you so much for inviting me over, Mrs. Stern."

"Are you hungry?" Rose asked. "We have plenty of leftovers. Maybe a brisket sandwich?"

"He just told you no. Why are you pushing food?" Lisa snapped.

David replied, "No, thank you. Joy and I went to McDonald's. Her idea of the best place in town."

"Ah, the children love it. How old is your daughter?" Aunt Rena asked.

"She's four."

"Such a sweet age." In an instant, Lisa's mother had coffee, cream, sugar, and a plate of rugelach in front of him.

"I haven't had rugelach since my Bubbe died. These are delicious, Mrs. Stern."

"Rena's the baker. I bake a little but not fancy like her. Did Lisa tell you we will be baking cookies and cakes for the Center's grand opening? Isabela from the bakery is planning to bake with us too."

"So I've heard." David nodded.

Lisa sat next to him watching the show. What was it about him that made you feel that you were telling him something he was waiting a lifetime to hear? He certainly was in his element. His Bubbe. Right. Even if he had one, it's doubtful that's what he called her. He was hanging on their every word and at the same time, his hand was under the table trying to pry her legs open. Was he out of his mind?

"So did you grow up here?" Jack asked.

"Schenectady. My family belongs to Temple Beth Shalom. My Aunt Ida lives in Albany, though. Do you know Ida Weinstein?"

"Ida! She's in Hadassah with us. Lovely woman." Faye said.

"Yes, she is. Also a great baker. So, Lisa. Do you want to go over the list tonight?"

"List?" she asked.

"The invitation list. The list you wanted to show me before the invitations go out? The invitations to the grand opening?"

"Oh, that list!" Lisa blushed.

David stood up. He glanced around the table. "Thanks so much for having me. It was a pleasure meeting you all."

By the time he stood up to say goodbye, Lisa's mother wrapped up rugelach in a package for him to take home.

"Don't be a stranger. Come over anytime," the family murmured in chorus.

So Liselah, the truth now. Is this David a mensch or not? Be careful with a man who talks out of both sides of his mouth. Sometimes a goniff can come to steal what isn't his to take.

David and Lisa went upstairs. He kissed her, "Don't be mad at me for calling your mother. I couldn't take another minute without you."

"Marika and Amber will be home in half an hour." Lisa said, looking up at him.

"That gives us plenty of time," he said.

"No, David. Not here. Not now."

Chapter Twenty-Six

∽

Shadowbox: Sisters Under the Skin

The inside of the box is painted as a rainbow. There are crepe paper streamers floating to add to the gaiety. A pyramid of women stands in the center of the box. The woman on top is looking away.

The grand opening day finally arrived. The day was bright and clear with a cloudless, sunny sky. The rainy forecast didn't materialize. Lisa's mother had superstitions for either event — rain was good luck, sun was better. Marika and Lisa were up early and went downstairs for breakfast. Isabela was teaching Aunt Rena how to work the dough for a pastry they'd be making.

Lisa was delighted the focus groups were in agreement about the name. The sign was engraved on a copper plate to match the period of the house. In elegant font, it read: **WOW** *{Women's Options for Work}*. The sign maker, a member of the community, had also made a ceremonial sign the Mayor would unveil.

Literature was stacked on the reception desk along with clipboards to track attendance, volunteers, and sign-up sheets for training. Lisa's conference table was pushed against the wall, covered with a tablecloth. Louis found folding chairs and David came early to help Jack set up rows. Lisa's mother, Aunt Rena, Isabela and the local bakeries had made enough cake and cookies for a hundred people. It was beginning to look like a party.

Lisa and Marika changed their clothes just before noon. Marika made Lisa a cerulean blue dress with a round neck, a cinched waist, and a skirt that flowed to her ankles. For herself, she made one of her bright African print dresses with a matching turban that had the same blue running through it. They looked at each other and laughed. "Aren't we gorgeous?" Marika said. They hugged.

Lisa's eyes were shiny, "It's really happening. I can hardly believe it."

"I always knew you'd do it, Missy." Marika said.

"Not without you. Never without you. The women all love you. And you've already helped so many of them."

"Dragged me kicking and screaming, you did," Marika glowed.

"Aren't you glad?"

"Yes, I'm glad. Enough sap. It's showtime." She grabbed Lisa's hand.

Invitations went out to anyone they thought would be even peripherally interested in the economic, social, mental, and spiritual health of women. Letters were sent to community activists, service agencies, church groups, educators, youth program directors, the media, and state and local social service agencies. The local newspaper had run a couple of stories charting the progress in renovating and opening the Center. With all the publicity, they hoped to bring women from diverse racial, ethnic, religious and economic backgrounds.

People began to stroll in. They walked around, nodding. Some women came from church wearing dresses and hats, others wore jeans; they came with grandmothers, grandchildren, aunts, and friends. The Mayor arrived with his entourage and city photographer. He posed for pictures with some of the community leaders, along with Lisa and Marika.

He cleared his throat, looked at his watch and then at Lisa. She nodded and asked everyone to sit down. She looked around at the crowd: her family, the friends she had made since she'd come home, the advisory board, people she needed to get to know, even grumpy Louis Vanderholt, who looked smugly satisfied and winked at her. Robert was there with some members of his community center. Reverend Avery came with his wife and congregants. Children were excited that they had a play area and were happily eating far too many cookies. Surprisingly, Nicky was still there. Leaning against a wall. But he was there. He helped Jack and David set up chairs. Lisa assumed he'd leave when the crowds came, but there he was, sitting off to one side against the back wall. Before she began to speak, she scanned the room again, this time looking for David. But she didn't see him.

Lisa welcomed everyone and introduced the Mayor first, who made some vague remarks about a thriving downtown and unveiled the sign. He suggested there might be more city funding but was noncommittal. After he and his associates left, she introduced the board members and community leaders. She was radiant as she talked about the concept of women having this home away from home.

"I want to tell you a story. Don't worry, it's a short one!" She smiled at the audience. "I know it's probably no surprise to anyone here that I was a peace activist."

Laughter erupted, heads nodded and she smiled. "I arrived at college thinking I was going to be part of this great movement. The day after I arrived at school, there was a sit-in to protest ROTC recruitment on campus. So, of course, I went. It was held on a narrow cobblestone street in front of the administration building called the Castle because of its architecture — turrets and all.

I had never seen so many people squeezed into a space that small. The shouting was loud and discordant. It wasn't communal chanting about military recruitment on campus that I'd expected. Sure there were signs that said GET ROTC OUT NOW and IN THIS BUILDING HUMANS ARE TAUGHT TO KILL. But, there were faction groups with their own agenda. Black Panthers raised clenched fists and carried signs to free Bobby Seale and Angela Davis. A group of women waved their bras on sticks and held signs that read OUR BODIES, OURSELVES. THE TIME FOR ERA IS NOW. Gay and lesbian groups protested as well.

I remember thinking that I could be sitting with any one of these groups. But if they couldn't rally around a single issue, no one would be heard. And this is true for us here and now. So much gets in the way to sidetrack us, doesn't it?" Heads nodded and the room was quiet except for the sound of the children.

Lisa went on, "When I hit bottom last year, the first thing I realized was how hard it is to try to get back on your feet alone. I couldn't move. I was paralyzed. All I knew was the door to my happy life had been nailed shut and I was totally immersed in my grief. It happens to all of us in some way. A door may gently close or be slammed shut. Then what? What comes next?

I couldn't figure out how to pick up the pieces of my life or even decide which pieces to pick up. I was a total disaster, but luckily, I had help to see me through. Everyone should have a friend like Marika. And in addition to baking the delicious pastries you will sample shortly, Isabela fished this pathetic soul out of her pond of despair." She blew Isabela a kiss. "A stranger did that for me."

Lisa swallowed, "Isabela believes that we women are buoyant. Even if we don't think we can swim, we either surprise ourselves or are smart enough to reach out to grasp a helping hand. If I hadn't grabbed her strong hand, I probably wouldn't be here today."

The audience was quiet. Lisa could see rows of heads nodding, really listening.

"Sometimes it isn't so easy to figure things out by ourselves. That's the reason for the Center. This is the place to come. Our doors will swing wide open and stay that way. Although we may be strangers today, we will form a sisterhood to give the love, support, and training needed to make everyone's lives a little easier. We will teach each other, learn from each other, and have a good time doing it. This idea carried me off my lonely road and I hope we will truly become a force, giving us all a WOW kind of life!"

At that, there was a lot of hooting and clapping.

Marika came up front. She spoke about the focus groups and community outreach and her intention to help with job placement. She said we had to figure out how to change the in-and-out-of-jobs syndrome for women with limited, sporadic work histories and whose expectations rarely moved beyond temporary, dead end jobs.

A stout woman in the front row called out, "You gonna help us find jobs? That'll be the day."

Marika paused, "What's your name, ma'am?"

The woman folded her arms across her chest. "Sylvia."

Marika breathed deeply. "Sylvia, let me tell you something about my own story. I had nothing, and I mean nothing going for me when Lisa and I first met. Nothing as in a big zero. Everyone I loved was gone. I had a job I didn't like that paid shit and a little daughter to take care of whose daddy was no help. Just like a bunch of you ladies could relate to, I would guess." Murmuring rolled through the audience.

"But here I am now. Standing up here." She looked around. "I felt like I had a hot poker burning me up. I was angry and mean and without hope. Odds were my life would be hard and unhappy. But, it's not," Marika beamed, looking at Robert. "And what you think is impossible, isn't at all."

There was applause in the audience. Amber was jumping up and down, grinning and clapping.

She looked at the skeptical woman. "So ma'am, if I could get out of my own way, so can you. Just try us out. But you have to want it real bad." She looked hard at the woman who still had her arms crossed over her heavy breasts, shaking her head. "Talk to me later."

Marika talked about plans for the Closet. They would collect donations of suitable work clothing from stores and individuals for women to borrow as needed. And if there was interest, she would hold sewing classes. "Believe me. I never thought Lisa could drag me to this Albany place or that she'd even wanted to after the way I treated her. I was mean and hostile. But she did and here I am. This is where hope lives, ladies! This is where you come to change your luck. Be part of it!"

There were many questions; the excitement was palpable. Children ran around in circles, in and around the chairs, in and out of the different rooms. Lisa was delighted as she walked past small groups of people engaged in animated conversation. She hoped that this building would become a part of their lives as it had become hers. But, she had a nagging feeling that something was wrong and couldn't shake it. The *goniff* troll, who had taken a vacation, was back sitting on her shoulder at a time when he should be far away.

Her mother hugged her. Looking upward, she said, "Who knows? Maybe Grandma and Mac are up in heaven together *kvelling.*" Still entwined, Lisa said, "Thanks, Mom. I'm happy you're finally proud of me!"

"Of course I'm proud of you." Rose dabbed at her eyes.

Aunt Faye took over the table, refilling trays and making more coffee. Even Lena Lewin, the dressmaker, came to pitch in. There was a lot of tumult and shifting in the crowd with people milling about, but David was nowhere to be found.

Lisa was talking to a woman who had a job interview the following Thursday and asked Lisa if she could come to practice her typing. She really needed the job. Lisa told her to come the next day. Could she bring her kids?

"Of course. We have some toys and books but if they have anything they like to play with, they should bring it."

"Thank you so much, Ms. Stern," the young mother smiled.

"Call me Lisa."

She felt a tap on her shoulder and turned around. "Lisa, hello. Congratulations. My... my name is Ivy Lerner and this is my daughter, Joy, and my sister, Caroline." She paused and swallowed hard. "I met you a while ago at a fundraiser. The new gallery near here?"

"Ivy, yes. Of course, I remember you. You must be the sister that kept her waiting." Lisa clasped her hands together, steadying them.

"That would be me. Good memory." Caroline said.

"You aren't twins are you?"

Caroline laughed. "Maybe you could call us Irish twins."

"Hello, Joy." She looked into the child's green eyes that were just like David's, down to the gold flecks.

"My daddy has a friend named Lisa. I heard him calling. Are you his friend?"

"Your daddy helped fix up the building. You should have seen what a mess it was."

"He did? My daddy is an arch-i-tect."

"Yes, he is. He was here. Did you see him?" Lisa asked.

"No. Mommy, can I go look for him?" Joy tugged on Ivy's sleeve.

"Sure, honey." Ivy looked down. "Your talk was so right on. I really could relate."

"I'm glad. Maybe we'll see you here once in a while."

Ivy shrugged. "I wanted to thank you in some way for helping me. I mean I know you didn't really do anything, but... I'm sorry. What I wanted to say is something registered in me the night I met you. I know you probably don't remember. You meet dozens of people all the time."

Just give it to her, Ivy," Caroline interrupted.

"Give me a minute." Ivy glared at her sister.

"As a matter of fact, I do remember. You looked like I did — haunted and dazed — until I threw myself into this." Lisa extended an arm to sweep the room but was wobbly, her knees buckled. She willed herself to be strong.

"I'm back in art school and I had an idea for a painting. I don't know if it's any good but it's my gift to WOW."

"A painting? For us?" Lisa asked.

"If you like it. Otherwise, if you don't it's okay. I mean I don't want you to feel that…"

Caroline sighed, "I'm going to find Joy."

"We will hang it. Of course we will." Lisa nodded, her mouth dry.

Lisa hadn't noticed the painting Ivy held until she handed it to her. It was a pyramid of women in a circle painted in soft pinks and grays. At the base of the pyramid stood three elders — one black, one white, one Asian. On their shoulders were several younger women and at the peak was a smiling child.

Lisa teared up. "Ivy, this is incredible. It will be an honor to hang it in the entryway. It captures our purpose perfectly. Thank you so very much." Her mouth quivered as she took the painting.

Caroline and Joy came back with cookies. "Mommy, I looked and looked. I don't see Daddy anywhere."

"Figures. He probably booked when he saw us," Ivy muttered. "Joy, look at all of those cookies. Did you leave any for the others?" Ivy laughed.

"There's a gazillion. Lisa, do you want one?" Joy asked.

"No thank you, Joy."

"Good luck with this." Caroline said. "Ivy, look. Doesn't that woman look like Camille Walton?"

"Who?"

"You know. The woman we met who kept her husband's ashes as a centerpiece on her dining room table. How could you forget that?" Caroline laughed. She pulled her sister away from Lisa.

A woman tapped Lisa's shoulder. Before she turned around, she said. "Ivy, the painting captures it all. Thank you so much."

Caroline pulled Ivy away from her, "Did you see her face? I could see it from across the room. She tried to hide it but she looked like she was ready to faint."

"What are you saying, Caro?"

"Be prepared. I'm sure they have more than a professional relationship."

Ivy shook her head. "No, I don't think so. She wouldn't."

Joy tugged on her mother's hand. "Let's go, Mommy. I want to tell Grandma about all the cookies."

Lisa told the next woman waiting to speak with her that there was something she forgot to do and she'd be right back. She held the painting against her and walked as quickly as she could, avoided all eye contact, and ran up the back stairs to the unfinished second floor.

Oh my God, that trembling woman with the hollow eyes was David's wife. How could this have happened? He must have run away when he saw her. Again. He lied to me so easily about leaving the gallery unexpectedly and then lied again the next day. But why? Why does he run? Sure it would be awkward, but at least it would be honest. Lisa was shaking from head to toe and couldn't catch her breath.

Marika saw Lisa move through the crowd and followed her. Before reaching Lisa, she noticed blankets tangled up in the corner of the room, and that next to them were wood scraps and a kerosene lamp. What the hell? she thought, shaking her head.

She took Lisa in her arms. "Who was that woman? What did she say to you?"

"Only her name. Ivy Lerner. And because she thinks I helped her, she made a painting for the Center. Here." Ivy shoved the painting into her hands but Marika didn't look at it.

"David's wife?"

"David's wife. Where the hell is he? Did he see she was here and run away? Why does he run like that? They're separated. I don't understand. What is wrong with me, Marika? What is wrong with me?"

"Nothing is wrong with you. He's a selfish, weak bastard. Does whatever he feels like. And you didn't do anything to his wife. Get that straight in your head, Missy. Pull yourself together. Right now. This is your day and I'm not going to let anybody ruin it for you."

"Marika, look at this painting. It's absolutely dead on true. Ivy was nobody to treat that way. She was nobody to run from without explanation."

"It's just a painting. Don't rush to judgment." Marika wiped Lisa's wet face. "Try to put this off. Try to think about this later. Wash your face. Keep thinking about the dream you brought to life and all the people downstairs who want to see you. And think about how blitzed we are going to get tonight."

The lively buzz of the party had petered out and they were ready to start cleaning up. Aunt Faye and Isabela shooed Lisa away. "We don't need you, girl. We're pros. You have to rest up for your first big day."

"You sure?"

"I haven't cleaned up the Oneg Shabbat for forty years for nothing. No cooking for us tonight, just linguicas and trutas tonight. Do I have that right, Isabela? I'm not going to worry one bit about what I'm eating tonight!"

Louis Vanderholt gave her a big hug. "You are a force, Miz Lisa. A force of nature. I didn't realize it but I might still have a little speck of hope left. Go home. I have some boys coming over to take the chairs back where they belong."

"Make sure you leave chairs. Ten around the table. And stack another ten in the back hall."

"Yes, Ma'am. I'll see you tomorrow after the first training."

She hugged him again.

"Now don't you be going soft on me. Get outta here. Get some rest. You'll need it."

Lisa saw Nicky was still there, leaning against the wall. She said softly, "Nicky, thank you so much for all you've done — helping set up the chairs, and well, just being here. When I was speaking, I was happy to see you."

She went straight to bed when she got home. Exhausted, confused thoughts twisted past with present. She did not want to be part of anyone's unhappiness, but she didn't have anything to do with David's leaving Ivy. She knew the raw pain of loss first hand and this made her feel sick. Who was he? Running. Evading. Passive. Yet, aggressively pursuing her. And waiting for Ivy to divorce him? What was that? Integrity or weakness? Or maybe, lack of intention.

Would Mac have become a jerk in the long run? She recalled that queasy, sick feeling at the pit of her stomach when she emptied his pockets to do the wash. On a slip of paper was a woman's name and number. It had a Key West area code. Mac was going there for a conference the following week. If she asked him about it, he'd be pissed and turn it into a harangue about trust. Besides, if he was having an affair, he wouldn't leave evidence for Lisa to uncover. He'd probably tell her. She never asked and talked herself into believing it was the number of someone he was on a panel with or something otherwise explainable.

Mac was the opposite of David. He was strong-willed, opinionated, and confrontational if he had to be, in every aspect of his life. He argued on principle and was unyielding. You always knew where you stood with him. It might anger or upset you. But you knew. Mac would never slither out of a room or avoid a fight. In fact, if he did have a thing with someone at a conference, he would probably tell her and convince her it meant nothing. If he were going to leave Lisa, she would know exactly why, when he discovered he needed to do it, and how she failed him or possibly how he failed her. Maybe that was unfair. None of that ever happened and probably never would have. Had he lived.

David on the other hand might be warmer, more charming, and more attentive. It seemed he had a split personality. He could also be aggressive. But passive, too. No wonder Ivy didn't know what hit her. He just disappeared into the night without explanation. Had he left her a note it would probably say: *Sorry hon. this isn't for me. But we did have a good run.* Yet at work, he would argue a point relentlessly, never giving up until he won.

How could David disappoint her on today of all days? Mac would never have done this. He would have been there no matter what and he wouldn't have let anything personal keep him away. David was *not* Mac. Lisa had to get this under control. She wasn't going to see him, wouldn't let him touch her again, until he dealt with his life and showed her respect. She faced the wall and fell asleep.

When she opened her eyes the room was dark. Marika tiptoed in.

"We have a coffee table full of cookies and Robert brought a pizza. Just your kind of meal. We're all going to snuggle up on the couch and watch movies. Come on. You haven't eaten a thing since breakfast."

"Give me a minute."

"Okay." Marika shut her door.

Lisa washed her face, put on a nightgown and robe and joined them. "Yay, pizza. My favorite food!" She plastered a smile on her face.

Amber said, "We're all squishing together on the couch. Can I sit on your lap?"

"Sure. As long as you don't grab any of my pizza."

Amber rubbed Lisa's arm and whispered. "You know what? I've decided that I want to be just like you when I grow up."

Lisa kissed her. "You'll be anything you set your mind to. Not me. Not Mama. You'll just be cool Amber."

"Since it's movie night and we don't want any interruptions, the phone's off the hook," Marika said, looking at Lisa.

"Good. What are we watching?" she asked.

"*It's a Mad, Mad World*!" Amber shouted.

"My pick," said Robert.

'Really. I never would have guessed!" Lisa looked over at Robert. "I would've figured you more the John Wayne type but no, not you, the sillier the better!"

"You bet! Li, you made us all proud today," Robert said.

Lisa nodded, "Thanks, Robert." She thought she heard steps on the front walk. "Nobody answer the doorbell."

It rang once, twice, three times, and then over and over. Amber put her hands over her ears. Whoever was down there was leaning on the bell. "Make it stop. It's hurting my ears," Amber cried.

"Don't be afraid, honey. I'll go downstairs and get rid of whoever is there, okay?" Robert said.

"Please," Lisa said.

Marika turned up the volume on the television but they could hear the loud voices.

Robert opened the door. "Roses and champagne? You've got to be kidding."

"Let me up." David tried to push past him.

"No way, man. She doesn't want to see you and neither does anybody else."

"Move out of the way," he said, pushing Robert into the banister.

David tried to get past him but Robert pushed him, and with his hands full, David lost his balance and fell backward.

"Get outta here." Robert started to close the door on him.

David growled, "I'd like to hear from Lisa herself that she doesn't want me to come up,"

"We don't care what you'd like, asshole. You mess up what should have been a perfect day for Lisa, after too many bad ones, and now you have the balls to come here. Get outta here, you fucking bastard. She is too good for you."

"What are you talking about?" David gasped. "What did I do?"

"You're a spineless prick. Leave now or I'll call the cops."

Lisa's father opened his front door. "You heard the man, David, get lost. If Lisa doesn't want to see you, who do you think you are trying to push your way in?"

"But Mr. Stern, I'd like to clear up this misunderstanding."

"I thought you were a *mensch* but I was wrong. If my daughter doesn't want to see you, that's it. Go home." He slammed the door behind him.

Robert pushed him out the door and locked it behind him. He came upstairs.

"He won't be back tonight."

David walked down the path shaking his head and stopped short, thinking he heard something. Maybe Lisa would see him after all. But when he turned to look back at the house, the door was closed and the lights were off. The street was eerily quiet. He shrugged. Walking toward his car, a rock hit him at the base of his neck and he fell, shattering the champagne bottle, scattering the flowers. In a split second, Nicky lunged at David and rolled him onto his back, wedging his forearm under David's chin, across his throat. Pinned down, David's face was an inch from Nicky's. Wordlessly, his hollow eyes blazed warning. David couldn't breathe. But then as quickly as he appeared, Nicky vanished. David lay on the ground in a puddle of champagne, bewildered and unnerved.

Chapter Twenty-Seven

෬

Lisa was showered and dressed by six the next morning. She poured coffee into a thermos, added a dash of cinnamon, and grabbed some of the leftover pastry. She knew Isabela would be awake and went downstairs to get her.

Sure enough, Isabela was dressed and waiting for the coffee to perk. "Good morning, Isabela." She hugged her. "I'm way ahead of you. Get your coat and hat. We don't have an ocean but there is a pretty park not too far from here for our morning coffee."

The sidewalk was littered with broken glass and trampled flowers. They both stopped to stare at the mess.

"Anything you want to talk about?" Isabela asked.

Lisa sighed, "I'll take care of that later." Arm in arm, they walked in silence, Isabela listening for familiar birdsong. Lisa thought about how to organize her day, trying to push down the bitterness caught in her throat, banishing thoughts of David or Ivy. Her mantra was to make Day One the best it could be. If David dogged her, she'd tell him to stop calling and hang up.

As they approached a bench and sat down, Isabela asked, "Are you sure you don't want to talk? Lover boy made quite a racket last night."

Grim, Lisa said, "Nothing much to tell, Just sorry you had to hear anything. I made a mistake. A really big mistake. I'll cry some more and work harder and it will be over. After Mac, this is child's play."

"I doubt it, but if you say so, who am I to add my two cents? It seems like you already have three mothers. With me it would be four. Far too many!"

"Now you believe me? I told you!"

Isabela smiled. "It's easy to see how much your mother and aunts love you. Is Faye the one who gave you the most trouble?"

"How'd you guess? She try to boss you around yesterday?" They laughed together. Lisa squeezed her hand. "It's so good to see you. How is Mary? Is she still working afternoons for you? And what about Martin? The help he gave me in starting the Center was the best. The bakery busy?"

"They're all fine. They send their love and want to know when you are coming back."

"Tell them I'll plan a trip as soon as I can take a few days off."

"There is something I do want to talk to you about." Isabela sat forward on the bench.

Lisa turned toward her. "Sounds serious. You're not sick are you?"

"Don't look so panicked." Isabela patted Lisa's hand. "I'm fine. I want to talk through what I've been thinking." Isabela sipped her coffee. "I'm not ready to sell the bakery but I think I may want to close for a couple of months in the winter."

Lisa arched her eyebrows. "Really? Have you changed your mind about Florida?"

Isabela shook her head. "No. I wasn't thinking of Florida. Someplace colder."

Lisa tapped her foot. "You're making me nervous dragging this out."

"I guess I should just say it. I'd like to rent a place here for part of the winter. I could help out at the Center. Maybe teach baking or how to operate a small business."

Lisa threw her arms around her. "Come here? That would be heaven!"

"I'm just talking. Wanted to say it out loud to you. Feel how it sounded. See your reaction."

"What did you think? Nothing would make me happier."

Isabela leaned over and kissed Lisa's cheek. "Let's walk."

They fell into their familiar habit of walking side by side in comfortable silence, each lost in thought.

As Lisa unlocked the door, the phone was ringing. The grand opening was covered on both the evening news and the morning newspapers. There were requests for radio interviews, inquiries from women, employers calling with vacancies. Lisa let it all flow, writing detailed notes so she could keep a list of everything she needed to do. She also prepared notes for the first training session on interviewing. She wasn't really qualified but she figured if she kept it to basics and talked about the kind of things she would look for in a new employee, it would be fine. Totally absorbed in her work, she was only vaguely aware that a couple of women from Reverend Avery's church were setting up chairs. Louis wheeled in a blackboard.

"Buy you a cup of coffee?" he asked.

"I'm dying for a cup. But sit down first. I don't want you falling. Where's your cane?"

"Right here, leaning against the desk. Don't you be worryin' about me."

Lisa smiled. "The phone's been ringing off the hook. You responsible for the women coming out of the woodwork to help?"

"I made a couple of calls but didn't need to do much arm twisting. You did good yesterday." Louis nodded.

"Thanks, Louis. It was a wonderful day! Excuse me a sec," Lisa answered the phone. "Listen, I'm very busy today and don't want to see or hear from you. Do you hear me? Don't come here." She hung up. Her hands trembled.

"Who was that?" Louis grimaced. "Who's giving you trouble?"

"It'll be all right." Lisa took a drink of water. "Hey, what did you think about the Mayor saying he might give us money?"

"He says anything he wants and then never follows up. But we can chase him on this one. We had enough witnesses, even if they are the wrong kind. We're not his almighty constituency." Louis got up. "Anyway, go back to work and if anyone bothers you, tell him he'll have to deal with me." He shook his cane. "I'm serious."

"Louis, you're a prince. Now, go on," she waved him off. "I'm fine and I'll see you later."

Before she locked up that evening, she hung Ivy's painting so it would be the first thing everyone would see when they came in. Women on the shoulders of other women. It should become their logo. If she could stand it.

❦

All week long, David came home from work and paced in his small apartment like a caged animal. He needed to talk Lisa. Tell her why he left. He did it to protect her. He had to make her see that. He'd helped with the set up. He planned a private celebration for the evening. So he wasn't there for the program. Why was that such a big deal?

When the apartment walls closed in on him, he walked late into the night, not knowing what to do with himself. Nicky scared him. As he walked, he looked over his shoulder and listened for steps behind him, thinking he heard something with every branch swaying or car gunning its engine. He didn't see anyone, but had the distinct feeling he was being followed. He couldn't understand why Lisa insisted on having this walking time bomb around her all the time. David had no doubt that Nicky was so far gone he could kill without a minute's hesitation.

Lisa was in the protective custody of her friends, lost to him. Louis always seemed to be around and wouldn't let him near her. He didn't dare go to her apartment because he didn't want to get on the wrong side of her father. She wouldn't talk to him on the phone. And that miserable Marika was probably buzzing in Lisa's ear, telling her what a louse he was. Was it such a big deal to want to avoid a public confrontation with Ivy? Especially since Joy was with her? Maybe he shouldn't have run but was it the end of the world?

Struggling to fill up his time, he called Ivy to see if he could take Joy out. "Hi, Iv."

Ivy grimaced. "Joy's not here."

"Where is she?"

"At a friend's house. Bye, David."

"Wait Ivy. Don't hang up. Please." He wiped the sweat from his forehead with his arm.

"What do you want?"

"You went to the opening of the Woman's Center?" David asked.

"Yes. I hear you did, too. Joy looked all over for her Daddy. But guess what? He wasn't there. He apparently left without telling anybody."

"I couldn't stay." David played with the phone cord.

"Yeah, right. So what do you want to know? That I met Lisa? I did and the unflappable Ms. Woman of the Year seemed unnerved by me. Just why was that, David?"

His heart was pounding. "Why did you go down there? It's not exactly in your neighborhood."

"It's none of your damned business. Listen, I'm going to take Joy with me to Aunt Kate's this weekend. Do you want to take her on Friday?"

David was silent.

"David? You still there?" Ivy asked, shaking her head.

"Yes, I'm here. Friday's fine."

"Be here on time. Joy gets nervous when you're late." She slammed down the phone. It seemed with every contact, she grew to dislike him more and more.

Rose was sweeping the front porch when Marika came downstairs carrying a garment bag. "You're out early this morning!"

"I have one last fitting to do on this dress."

"Can I see?" Rose leaned the broom against the railing.

Marika opened the bag. "A cocktail dress for some bigwig's wife in the Mayor's office."

"It's very pretty. Beautiful material. Your work is very good. I have some sewing for you, if you have time," Rose said.

"Sure you do. I think maybe you have some other kind of mending on your mind." Marika smiled.

"All right already. I'm sorry. I was wrong about a lot of things. Tell me what's going on? What happened with David?"

"Don't ask me. Ask your daughter. And if that is your idea of an apology, you've got a way to go."

Rose agreed. "I am sorry, Marika. I really am."

Lisa was curled up in a chair wrapped in an afghan, a book open on her lap, when the phone rang. She looked at it, willing it to stop ringing. Finally, she couldn't stand it and picked it up. "Hello."

"Lisa, please don't hang up," David pleaded.

"David, stop calling me." She looked out the window at some kids playing kickball on the street.

"I have to see you, talk to you. Please. Meet me at the coffee shop. Coffee won't hurt, I promise."

"No."

"Just a cup of coffee? Please. I have to talk to you."

"Talk to me now."

"I can explain everything. But I want to do it in person." There was a long pause. "Lisa, are you still there?"

"Just coffee. That's all. Saturday morning?"

"Whenever you want."

David couldn't sleep and arrived at the coffee shop around eight, an hour early. His leg shook under the table. He rehearsed what he would say, how to explain himself. He had to make her understand that he just needed time to figure out how to make everything right. That he loved her and only her. That he couldn't be in the same room with both women was something he couldn't begin to understand or explain. Better to focus on Ivy's irrationality and anger. That was the real problem.

It was nine, then nine-ten, nine-fifteen and then nine-thirty. She wasn't coming. She's never late. How long would he wait? All day if he had to.

Lisa rounded the corner and relief washed over him.

She sat down. "I wasn't going to come but here I am."

"I'm happy to see you. You want to order?" David smiled.

"Just coffee," she said.

"Are you sure? You love breakfast," he exclaimed.

Lisa snapped, "Don't presume to know what I love and don't love."

He reached for her hand but she pulled it back and folded her hands on her lap.

She glared at him. "David, explain to me why a man separated and presumably getting a divorce runs out the door every time he suspects he might see his wife — his soon to be ex-wife. Even on the day the new woman he supposedly loves is celebrating something really big. He slinks out in the shadows. Doesn't even tell anyone he's leaving." She looked down. "Truly bad form, David. The worst."

"I'm sorry. It was wrong. I love you and only you. You have to believe that. I thought I was sparing you. I didn't want a big scene to spoil your day," David insisted.

Lisa wouldn't look at him. "That's bullshit and you know it. Your wife doesn't seem to be the scene-making type."

"It's true, she never was. But lately, well...you don't know her," he faltered.

"Don't you have Joy today?" In picking up her cup, coffee sloshed all over the saucer. She sopped it up with a napkin and put the cup down.

"No, Ivy took her away for the weekend."

"She looks just like you," Lisa said, finally looking at him.

"Yes, except she has Ivy's red hair and freckled skin."

Lisa stood up.

"Please don't leave. I promise I'll take care of things. I made an appointment with a divorce lawyer. I'll make everything right. You'll see," he stammered.

"You did? For real?" Lisa asked

"Yes. I did. I'll fix things. Believe me. You have to believe me."

She just looked at him.

"How about this? Why don't we take a drive? It's a gorgeous day. Let's go to Vermont and have lunch."

She meant to say no. She knew she should say no. But she didn't. By the time they walked to his car, she found herself neatly folding what happened in the back corner of her mind. Anyone can have bad judgment, can't they? He is separated, after all, isn't he? Doesn't he deserve another chance?

Chapter Twenty-Eight

Life Goes On

∾

Lisa and David walked out of the Delaware Movie Theater. "What was that about?" David asked.

Lisa laughed. "What was what about?"

"The movie. The girl lived a terrible life. One bad thing after another. And there was no real ending. How could they leave us hanging after all her misery? What do you think happened to her?"

"I guess it's one of those movies they want you to discuss. Did she make it to the city or was she just going to stay and put up with her husband? He was a master manipulator, wasn't he?" Lisa mused.

David asserted, "A happy ending is the least they could do for us after all that unhappiness."

Lisa said. "There isn't always a happy ending. What do you think are the chances that she eventually got to Paris?"

"I don't think she was smart enough. She was a beauty, though, wasn't she?"

"Yes. She had the most amazing eyes. You could see her all her emotion in her deep, dark eyes."

"I guess I'm a simple guy. I like a story that starts at the beginning and has a clear ending."

Lisa slipped her arm through his. "Next time, it's your pick."

"Next time. I like the sound of that." He pulled her to him and kissed her.

∽

Lisa was making a salad to go with Marika's chicken paprika. "This is a pretty complicated dish for a weeknight, don't you think?" Lisa asked, chopping green peppers

"It's a special day." Marika smiled as she stirred the pot.

"Chicken paprikash means good news or Sunday," Amber said.

Lisa knew Marika well enough to know that she'd spill the beans when she was good and ready. Amber was setting the table. Undecided whether the forks went to the right or left, she kept moving them.

"Forks on the left, honey," Lisa said.

Marika called out, "Dinner's ready. Come sit down. Amber, please say grace."

Amber folded her hands. "Thank you God for making Mama smile so much and cook yummy suppers and make pretty clothes. Thank you, God for letting us live with Lisa in this big beautiful house and thank you for the *Good job!* I got on my test today. And that Jerry said he was sorry for shoving me."

"And," Marika said.

"Thank you for the good food Mama made."

"And?"

"Amen."

"Excellent," Marika said. "Pass your plates."

"Mommy, why are you so happy today? You've been smiling and singing since you walked in the house," Amber asked, taking a roll from the basket.

"I have very happy news and a lot of it. I wanted to tell you both together. First, business. I am going to design gowns for a big country club wedding. A bridal gown and six bridesmaids' dresses. They loved my sketches and said they wanted the finest silk for the bride. I shouldn't be concerned with cost. The bridesmaids' dresses will be in shades of pink, each dress different."

"Hooray for Mommy. Hooray." Amber sang out and clapped. "Yeah, Mama!"

"Marika, that's fabulous! Congratulations!" Lisa raised her glass. "To *Designs by Marika*! I can say I knew her when!"

"One step at a time." She looked over at Lisa's plate. "Why are you playing with your food? You love chicken stew. What's the matter?"

"Nothing's the matter. I'm digesting your news." She smiled, "I'm excited for you but not surprised. Pretty soon you'll have the cover of *Brides Magazine*! Congratulations, Marika. You really deserve this."

"What's after business?" Amber asked.

"This is mainly good news, mixed with just a thimble of sad. So I'm just going to say it fast. For the past couple of months, I've been thinking we should move to give you some privacy, Lisa. Your parents have been generous but I think it's time to move. I've been talking to Mrs. Cleary down the block and I thought we'd move into her house — that way we'd still be close as can be." She paused, looking at Amber. "But, something unexpected happened."

Lisa put down her fork. "What?"

Marika smiled, "I talked to Robert about my plans and he said he had a better idea. He asked me to marry him!"

"Robert's going to be my Daddy? What about my real Daddy?" Amber asked.

"It seems to me that Robert has been more of a real daddy to you than your blood daddy ever was. How many times has your real Daddy been to visit? Who helps you with your homework? Who reads you stories?"

"Robert!" Amber shouted, clapping her hands together. She ran over to sit on Marika's lap.

"Children who have two daddies are lucky," Lisa said.

"We're moving into his house? It's so big Lisa can come too," Amber said.

"Good thought, sweetie. But a married couple and their children need to live together without extras. We'll still see each other all the time. I promise," Lisa said. "I'll miss you as my roommate but I couldn't be happier for you. Robert is a good, good, man." She went to Marika and hugged her.

"Thank you, Missy. I know this is quick but when it's right, it's right. Now, sit down and eat something. You're as pale as a ghost."

"Only by comparison," Lisa forced a smile.

Amber ran around the table to Lisa. "I get it! You are silly."

"Let's get Robert over here. I'll call the family and David. We'll toast your happiness." Lisa choked back tears.

Marika, leaned over to her friend. "Nothing will change between us, Missy. Don't you worry."

After the family left and Marika and Amber were in bed, Lisa and David sat together on the couch.

"You'll miss them, won't you?" he asked, rubbing her feet.

"Very much. But we're family. That won't change. Marika is becoming busy. She'll probably have her own clothing line before long! I wonder how much longer she'll be able to stay with the Center."

David played with Lisa's hair. "She'll find a way. She's devoted to you."

"I'm bushed. Time to turn in. I'm so tired. I feel like I could sleep forever."

"I'll get going." He stood up. "I can't wait for the time for us to be together. Do you want to move in with me?"

"Where did that come from?"

"I've been afraid to ask," he said.

"You really should start conquering your fears, David. They're piling up. Let's see, have you talked to Ivy yet? No, don't tell me. Let me guess. Oops. Not yet. But you will. As soon as you figure out what to say. No, wait a minute; you're waiting for an appointment with a lawyer. I've got the script down. Go home, David."

Shadowbox: I Have Met the Enemy and She is Me

The back of the box is covered with smooth shiny foil. Two cardboard paper dolls are holding hands. One has curly black hair and the other straight red hair. Reflected in the foil are two faces. The dark-haired doll sees herself as the redhead and the redhead sees the dark-haired one.

"No, David. You aren't going to drag Joy into your social life. The little time you spend with her should be all about her." Ivy's voice rose. "Don't you realize what she's been through?" Joy ran to her and hugged her legs. "Ssh, sweetheart. It's okay. I didn't mean to raise my voice." She rubbed her daughter's head.

"Calm down, will you? I'm not talking about any big deal. Just to the playground or out for pizza," David huffed.

"You do not have my permission. Since you've abandoned us, I am responsible for Joy and she's not going anywhere near any of your girl-friends. How dare you even think it," she fumed.

"I have not abandoned you or Joy. If I had, you wouldn't be living in my house, you'd be working, and I wouldn't be seeing my daughter every other day."

"No, this is not your house. You gave up your rights the second you ran out the door. Don't you dare bring Joy within ten miles of any one of your girlfriends if you ever want to see her yourself." She slammed down the phone.

Ivy was spitting mad. She phoned Caroline. Come on. Pick up. Pick up.

"Hello." Caroline was breathless.

"Hi, Caro. You just come in?" Ivy drummed a pencil on the counter.

"Hold on a sec. I've got groceries on the front steps."

Ivy waited, doodling, unaware she was drawing a snake.

"Okay. What's up?"

"David just called."

"Obviously." Caroline said, cradling the phone on her shoulder as she unpacked boxes of cereal and pasta.

"He wants Joy to meet his girlfriend. I hit the ceiling and said no." Ivy flared her snake's tongue to breathe out dragon fire.

"That sounds right," Caroline agreed. "It is too soon. Unless it's a serious relationship which I doubt it is."

"You still think it's Lisa?" Ivy asked.

"Probably. She came unglued at the opening but maybe nothing had happened. Maybe she just wants something with him. Poor girl. Anyway, we only have circumstantial evidence. But why obsess over it? You've cried enough over him," Caroline said, putting milk in the refrigerator.

"Trust me, it's her," Ivy drew curlicues around the snake's head. "I'm going to call her," Ivy vowed.

"What for?" Caroline stopped putting her groceries away.

"Because if it is, I want to know. I have to figure out if I want her to be with Joy."

"That'll take *chutzpah*, to borrow a phrase from your mother-in-law."

"Lately, it seems I run on it." Ivy then drew a head with curly hair, with the face of a donkey.

"Little sister, I think you should choose your fights. It's a really bad idea. Meeting her will take too much out of you and when it comes down to it, what has to be settled is between you and David."

"I know. Maybe you're right."

"Of course I'm right. We're still on for the weekend? Aunt Kate is expecting us," Caroline reminded her.

"Yes. Can't wait. I'll pick you up at ten."

"Great. See you."

Ivy hung up the phone, wanting to call Lisa but instead she drew a pig, a greedy, snorting pig.

Ivy could think of nothing else. It was gnawing at her. Wanting to call Lisa. Not wanting to. Caroline thought it was unnecessary at this point. Aunt Kate advised her to call only if she knew exactly what she wanted to ask Lisa and why. She agreed that a confrontation would not be good for her niece.

Ivy knew the number by heart. She dialed and then hung up by the first ring, dialed again, and hung up at the second ring. Just do it. What the hell? She dialed again and forced herself to let it ring.

"WOW. Lisa speaking."

"Lisa. This is Ivy Lerner. I'd like to talk to you. Meet me at the Gateway Diner tonight at eight." She hung up before Lisa could answer.

It was so odd and fast, Lisa wasn't sure she received the call at all. What would the woman have to say to her?

When Lisa arrived at the diner, she saw Ivy seated in a booth toward the back. She waved and walked over.

"Hi, Ivy. Your call was so abrupt, I wasn't sure if it happened at all." Lisa took off her coat and slid in opposite Ivy.

The waitress came over. "What can I get you, ladies?"

"Coffee for me."

Lisa said, "I think I'll have tea. I feel like I'm coming down with a cold."

"My mother always gave me tea when I was sick. I still think that's the only time you should drink it." Ivy's attention fell to the spoon she was stirring round and round in the cup.

"No reason to make small talk." Lisa looked at her straight on. "What's up? Why did you want to meet?" Lisa asked.

Ivy's eyes widened. She hesitated, and then blurted out, "I want to know if you are having an affair with my husband."

Lisa answered slowly. "An affair with your husband? That's an odd way of putting it. You and David separated long before I came along."

"Let me tell you something. We are separated. Separated is not divorced. Separated is not neat and tidy. Separated is it's not totally over. So are you are the girlfriend? Admit it. You're the other woman and you're a hypocrite," Ivy's voice rose and in one quick movement, she leaned across the table and slapped Lisa hard across the face.

Lisa rubbed her smarting cheek, grabbed her coat and stood up. "Are you out of your mind? Let's get a few things straight and then this conversation is finished. In the first place, I don't know why you put me on a pedestal. So if I've disappointed you, it's not my fault. It's your own doing."

Ivy opened her mouth to speak but Lisa stopped her. "I'm not finished. I think it's a fairly reasonable assumption that when two people are separated, especially for the length of time you two have been separated, they are getting a divorce. Blaming someone who comes along later is lame. And … forget it. I lost it." Lisa flushed. "Wait a minute, yes. Questions. I have questions. Why wouldn't you want to divorce a man who doesn't want to be married to you? Why aren't you moving on? I'd be so pissed off if I were you."

"Stop," Ivy bellowed.

Lisa stood to leave when Ivy lunged at her and grabbed her by the hair. Lisa swatted at her, trying to free herself from Ivy's grasp. She dug her fingernails into Ivy's wrist so she'd let go. When Lisa was free of her, she held Ivy's wrists until she stopped swinging.

The manager ran toward them. "Stop this right now and leave. And don't ever come back here." He slapped down their check and walked away. "Show's over," he told the customers.

Ivy's face crumpled. Wounded, she sank back into the booth.

"Are you out of your mind? Punching me makes you feel better?" Lisa asked, tears streaming down her face. "Why are you doing this to yourself?"

"Yeah, I heard you. You don't think you are in the middle of anything. You think I'm yesterday's garbage."

"What a thing to say. Yesterday, yes. But, of course, you're nobody's garbage." Lisa bit her lip. Her scalp pulsed from Ivy's hard tug of her hair and her stomach churned. At the moment, she thought Ivy was one of the biggest losers she ever met in her life, but she composed herself to be careful with her words. She had to remember women like Ivy were the reason for WOW.

"Why are you so self-deprecating?" Lisa put on her coat and slapped a couple of dollars on the table. "You know, Ivy, before I met David I didn't know there were still women like you. Not finishing their education to support a man. Not wanting a career. When he told me about you, I couldn't imagine what it must be like to just take care of someone and that's all. This is the 1970s, not the 1950s.

Ivy sniffled, trying not to cry.

"I'm sorry. That came out wrong. But look at you now. You're a gifted painter!" Lisa exclaimed.

"Big deal." Ivy's bravado lay in shreds all around her.

"So I guess this is the part when you order one of those mile high meringues and smash it in my face?" Lisa's face twisted with mixed emotions.

Ivy laughed through her tears. "Oh, I've always wanted to do that. But you're safe. If I did, it would definitely be at David. And I'd make it rhubarb. He's allergic and his face would blow up into one red welt."

Lisa cringed when Ivy said that. She knew so little about David, none of the details that come with a shared life — a favorite color or dessert, whether he preferred the beach or the mountains, how he liked his socks paired. She knew all of these things about Mac. But David? None of the above. "So he's allergic to rhubarb."

"And strawberries and pollen and honor," Ivy added.

"What do you want from me?" Lisa asked.

"I want you to be good to Joy."

"Right now, meeting her is out of the question. I hope David hasn't suggested otherwise. But if and when I meet Joy, you have nothing to worry about. I am more than aware that a child needs only one mother." She rolled her eyes. "Sometimes even one is too much."

"That's for sure." Ivy shook her head. "You're a hard woman to hate."

"Why hate me at all?" Lisa asked. "Ivy, just so you know, I hung your painting by the reception desk. It's the first thing anyone sees when they come in the Center. Including me." She turned toward the door and walked out without looking back.

Chapter Twenty-Nine

Baby Talk

⟨∾⟩

WOW was a beehive of activity but the queen was still under the weather. Volunteers were in and out all day. Some helped Marika plan the fashion show to kick off the opening of *The Closet;* others worked on another project called *Job Connections*. There were enough children at the Center to warrant asking their older siblings to baby sit. Volunteers solicited merchandise from department stores, unclaimed clothing from cleaners, and set up donation boxes; others called employers to ask them to become part of the job network. Women also came in to practice typing on five donated typewriters.

The women talked amongst themselves, worried about Lisa. She was pale and quiet. Sylvia, the former skeptic, who worked with Marika to mend donated clothing, was chosen to broach the subject with her.

"Lisa, we have to talk," Sylvia said.

"Sure, Sylvia. Have a seat."

"I don't have to sit down. I'll only be a minute. This is what I want to tell you. I have five children and know what a pregnant woman looks like. You don't have no flu."

Lisa raised her eyebrows. "Don't beat around the bush!"

Sylvia laughed. "You get yourself a test so you can get rid of it, if you want. It's legal, you know."

"Oh, Sylvia. Are things that easy?" Lisa sighed.

"In my day, it was have the baby, try to get rid of it yourself, or try to find somebody to do it who wouldn't kill you. At least now you've got a safe choice."

"Is that what you think I should do?" Lisa crinkled her forehead.

"Hell no. I'm just telling you, if you don't face it soon, you'll be having yourself a baby."

Lisa shrugged. "Everybody's talking?"

Sylvia sat down. "We just want to help. Remember. We're all in this together. Sisters under the skin and all that." She looked around the room. "You said so yourself. Besides, without us, how you gonna manage with a baby?"

Lisa didn't need Sylvia to tell her what she already knew. Every time she had to pee and saw no blood was reminder enough. Lisa thought about little else.

᪥

On warm summer evenings, Mac and Lisa looked forward to sitting out on their front porch after dinner. They'd talk about the day and watch the busy street. There was an elementary school across from the house with a small playground and sandbox.

They both loved watching their neighbors, imagining their lives and speculating about their own. "Imagine how beautiful and smart our children will be. Look at that little curly top on the swings," Lisa said.

Mac nodded. "They would be if we were going to have any."

Stunned, Lisa asked, "What do you mean if?"

"Why do you think I worked with Barton?"

"I thought you believed it was the right thing to do," Lisa sputtered.

"Yeah. That, too. But I was motivated for my own reasons. I have no interest in becoming anybody's father." He looked down at the open book on his lap.

Lisa put down her wine. Incredulous, she asked, "You don't want children? Ever?"

"No, I don't. You are all I want." Mac turned the page.

"Mac, look at me. We need to talk about this. I never thought..."

Mac interrupted. "There is nothing to talk about."

"What do you mean there is nothing to talk about? There is everything to talk about." Lisa's voice rose to a crescendo.

He slammed shut his book. "That is one thing that is not negotiable. No way. I thought you felt the same way. Why were you there?" he asked.

"For choice. To keep women from dying in alleys. From..."

"Lisa, dial it down. The whole neighborhood can hear you," he chided.

"I don't care who hears me. You can't just make a decision like that and refuse to even talk about it. I thought we were partners."

He stood up. "I'm going in. There is nothing more to say. I don't want that kind of responsibility. End of conversation."

"You can't do that. Just proclaim something and walk away. Do you think I'm still your fucking student?"

"Watch me." He went in, banging the door behind him.

Lisa sat outside until the curtain of darkness slowly fell. The mosquitoes were dancing up and down her arms and legs, leaving pink bumps in their wake, but she didn't want to be under the same roof with him. She cried but she was angry — and stunned that she didn't know something that important. What else didn't she know? She hated his imperious, professorial tone. She didn't want to sleep in the same bed with him. Finally, she went inside, slathered her body in calamine lotion, and flopped onto the couch. It was the first time they'd slept in separate rooms.

She woke with the sun streaming into the front windows. Her sleep was restless, filled with fragments of dreams she couldn't remember. Her hair was tangled and she had the start of a headache. She hated that every time something upset her, a migraine followed — a relentless pulsing and crunching on the right side of her face and head. Coffee sometimes helped. In any case, she would take her ergot medicine, hoping that it was early enough in the headache for it to work.

The bedroom door was open, the bed made. Where did he go so early, she wondered. It didn't matter. She was glad he left. She made herself some coffee and brought it into bed. She didn't know what to think. Couples argue. That was only natural. Of course, there was the occasional irritation here and there. He wanted to go to a party, she didn't. The toothpaste on the sink, dirty dishes piling up on the floor by the bed, the things that didn't matter and could be fixed. But this? This was big. Could she give up the idea that someday, not now of course, but someday she might want a family? She remembered how sad Maddy's sister was when the abortion permanently ruined her chances to have any children. She didn't want a baby at the time. But after she was married, she did. That was the reason to work for Barton. Not to let some man think of it as birth control.

But life without Mac? Unfair. She never imagined she'd have to make that kind of choice. It shouldn't be an either/or. Would he be willing to let her go so easily? She didn't think so. It was far off anyway. Maybe in time he would change his mind. She finished her coffee, which didn't help her head at all, lowered the shades and pulled the covers over her head.

When the headache passed, Lisa cleaned the apartment and cooked dinner. Mac came home from class with a bouquet of daisies. He took her in his arms and held her. One thing she loved and counted on from Mac were his hugs. His big bulky frame encased Lisa's lithe body. They let the storm pass. Her disappointment in him drifted away, postponed until some later time.

◌੭

Lisa passed Planned Parenthood on her way into work every day but couldn't bring herself to go in. Sometimes, she thought she was delaying because she really wanted the baby. Other times, she thought everything about it was wrong. She was confused. She knew she loved David but her thoughts were more about her and the baby, rather than the three of them. She could imagine his face when she told him. Horror. He'd flip. And what about the Center? It needed her full time attention.

The morning after her chat with Sylvia, Lisa knew she couldn't put it off any longer. Marika went with her. "I'll wait here, Missy. And don't look like you're going to get executed. We're just collecting information. Sweet Jesus. I'm starting to sound like you."

Lisa sucked in a breath. "Okay. Here I go."

She had a physical exam and peed in a cup. She waited for the results in the soft-spoken doctor's office, staring at the model on the doctor's desk of a fetus in a uterus. She listened for his footsteps coming down the hall, her stomach lurching as he opened the door.

The doctor sat behind his desk. He folded his hands on her file. "Lisa, you are about seven weeks pregnant. If you want to keep the baby, I want to see you every month. If you want an abortion, we have to do it right away."

Lisa realized she was holding her breath "That's pretty straightforward."

"No reason not to be. I'm sure none of this is news to you." He looked at her over his reading glasses.

"No. It isn't. How many days do I have to decide?"

"The end of the week. The longer you go, the harder it is. Legally, you have another month, but I don't do them past eight weeks."

"All right. How about if I make the appointment now and then cancel if I change my mind?"

"Fair enough. Good luck to you," he stood and shook her hand.

When she saw Marika in the waiting room, she burst into tears.

"It's okay. Whatever happens, everything will be okay." Marika put her arm around Lisa's shoulders.

Lisa sniffled. "Let's go get some tea."

Marika and Lisa ordered their tea at the restaurant across from Planned Parenthood. Marika took out a steno pad and flipped past pages of dress designs. On a blank page, she wrote pros in one column, cons on the other. "Go."

"Pros. I want to have a baby sometime. I love David. Also sometimes."

"Cons?"

"David will flip. I am living in the same town as my parents. I make so little money. I'll make a lousy mother."

"So, you think you want the baby, regardless? And you are assuming that David won't be a part of this? I've been there, Missy. It's not easy." Marika sipped her tea. Putting down her cup, she covered Lisa's hands with her own and added, "But if anyone can do it, you can."

Lisa called David the minute they got back to the center.

"Hi, Lisa."

She could hear the smile in his voice. "Listen, can you come here when you finish work?" Lisa asked.

"Sure. Everything okay?"

"Yeah. About what time?" She pulled at the phone cord.

"I'm meeting with a client at six. Let's say no later than seven-thirty?"

"Great." Lisa hung up.

She was a wreck. She paced and talked to herself. I'll just blurt it out, she thought. Caught off guard, she'd see the truth even if he backpedaled.

The door opened and shut. She steeled herself for the worst, whatever that was.

"Hi, babe." He kissed her. "What's up? You sounded so serious. You're not having any problems here?"

"No. Nothing like that. It's something else. I don't know whether it's wrong or right, it just is." Lisa sat down behind her desk.

"Don't start haranguing me about the divorce again, okay? Things will work out for us. They will. I'll make it happen. I just need a little more time."

"No, David. It's about us but it's not about *us*."

"You're not making sense. What do you mean?" he asked, sitting down on the edge of the desk, leaning in toward her.

"I'm pregnant." The words lay between them on the desk. They both looked down at them to see how they might be reformed.

"No," he said. "You can't be. It's out of the question."

"Seven weeks."

David reached for her hand but Lisa pulled it away. "I'm so sorry."

"I don't know whether I'm sorry or not," Lisa said.

"What? You can't be serious?" David stood up.

"Dead serious. I have until the end of the week to decide." Lisa wouldn't look at him.

"What's there to decide?" He moved toward her. "Honey, we can have a baby sometime." He hesitated. "We will have a baby. But not now. It's impossible now. Out of the question."

"Why is that, David?" Lisa turned off her desk light and stood up. "I just wanted to tell you and see your reaction."

"We have to talk about it," he implored.

"Not tonight. Tomorrow is soon enough." Lisa shut off the lights. "Go home, David."

He called after her. "You have no idea about how a baby consumes you. You wouldn't even be thinking about it if you did. It changes everything. It will change *us*."

Lisa sighed. "Good night, David."

Lisa went home and laid on her bed thinking about the baby growing inside of her. She had no thoughts of a doctor scraping her uterus clean. Ah, those first times with David. How could she not have a baby born out of that sublime togetherness? She pictured a baby girl with David's green eyes and her dark hair. She knew she wasn't thinking straight and needed an ice water bath. She knew just where to go for that.

Her mother was at the sink washing the dinner dishes.

"Ah, Lisa." She turned toward her daughter and saw her gray pallor right away. "What's the matter? You look terrible."

"I need to talk to you and Daddy."

"Is something wrong? " Her mother dried her hands on the dish towel. "Daddy is in the living room. We'll sit in there."

He turned off the TV. "Hi, Princess."

"Hi, Daddy." She bent over to kiss his cheek.

"Jack, Lisa has something to tell us," Rose announced.

"What is it, sweetheart? Is something wrong?" Jack relit his cigar.

She stood to face her parents. "Yes and no," she paused. "All right. Here it is: I'm seven weeks pregnant."

Her mother gasped, "Tell me it's not true."

"No bug, no flu. Just baby," she added.

"David can't even marry you," her mother declared.

"True. He's not divorced," Lisa said.

"Thank God abortion is legal now."

"Rose, let her talk, will you?" Jack demanded

"I know the timing is wrong. I know better than anyone David's marital situation. But I do love him. And our baby was created with love. So I'm not sure I want to have an abortion."

"Isn't it enough that you work with *shvartzahs?* Now you have to live like them. Having babies when you aren't married," Rose cried.

"Mom! What a horrible thing to say."

"Rose! Stop it right now. Don't say another word," Jack ordered.

"Don't shush me, Jack, I thought she was finally getting her life together." Rose sat down, twisting her dish cloth.

"Lisa," her father said. "I'm behind whatever decision you make. Either way is hard but you have to decide on your own."

"And I'll be stuck babysitting," her mother said.

Infuriated, Lisa asked, "Do you actually think I wouldn't take responsibility?"

"You don't know what it is to have a child, let alone without a husband. And what about your future? If it doesn't work out with David, who is going to marry a woman with an out-of-wedlock child? What will people think? Think of the child being born that way. You have no idea what you are bringing on yourself and an innocent baby."

"Can you think of anything else to say? Because I want you to say everything right now. And afterwards, I never want to hear you say these things to me again." Lisa's eyes watered.

"Lisa, your mother is upset. Let's just sit with all of this. Your mother thinks you are making a mistake in even thinking twice. Me, I'm not sure. I think if you set your mind to it, you can do anything."

"Great, Jack," Rose sneered. "What do you know, anyway? You were always working."

He ignored her. "Does David know?"

"Yes. David knows," she sighed.

"What did he say?" Jack asked, searching her face.

"He said we'll have babies. But not now. The timing couldn't be worse."

Her mother's eyes burned through her. "He's right. I want to be a grandmother but not now, not like this."

Tired as she was, she couldn't sleep. In her mind's eye, Lisa was surrounded by children — the little girl with bright ribbons in her cornrows jumping double-dutch in the park, the girl pumping the swing high near the Brookline apartment she shared with Mac, and of course, Amber and Joy. Childhood friends became children again as they passed through her mind.

She sat upright in her bed. I'm in the same damn place I was with Mac, she realized. He would have the same attitude as David. She'd have to make the same decision. The men were so different but one similar trait popped out at her: they were both completely self-centered. She'd never dwelled on that aspect of Mac. But it was true. If she had become pregnant with their baby, would he have stayed, she wondered?

On the other hand, what would the world be like without an Amber?

She had to get out of bed just to quiet all the noise in her head.

The next morning, Lisa sat at her desk unable to concentrate. Her mind sifted through disparate emotional extremes. On the one hand, her heart quickened at the thought of a baby. She could see her beautiful baby girl with fair skin, a rosebud mouth, and dark hair. The next moment she chastised herself: *Who do you think you are? You can't even manage your own life, let alone care for a child.* And on it went for most of the morning. Yes. No. Yes. Doubt and self-pity, then a swelling of her heart.

She was oblivious to the dreary day until a cloud shifted, exposing a hazy sun. Through the window, Lisa felt the unexpected warmth on her face. She tilted back her head and closed her eyes. In that instant, she knew she wouldn't allow fear and insecurities drive her decision. She released the tension holding her body rigid. What had she ever planned in her life?

She thought back to the Barton days. She was naive, thinking that the decision would be a simple one. In medical terms, yes, it was good that abortion was legal. Now, anyone could go to a doctor's office or hospital and have a safe medical procedure, rather than risk sterility or death from an unqualified abortionist. She never thought about cells or embryos or eventual babies when she worked at CLA. It was all about keeping women safe. But now that she was one of those women free to choose, the only thing on her mind was a full picture of a baby girl. She was certain it would be a girl. Her baby girl.

She dialed David. She didn't want to see his face when she told him.

Lisa announced, "David. I've made up my mind. I'm having this baby."

"What about me? What if I haven't made up my mind?" David protested. "This is a decision we should make together, you know. You have no idea what it's like to have a baby. No idea at all. This will change your whole life, our life. It will ruin everything. My marriage went to hell after we had a baby. What am I going to tell Ivy and Joy? Have you thought about anything but what you want?"

"You don't have to tell them anything. Given your attitude, I doubt my baby will have any impact on them at all." Lisa's heart raced and her breath was rapid. "Goodbye, David."

"Lisa, we have to talk about this."

"You can talk all you want, but I'm canceling my appointment." Lisa gently hung up the phone.

Nu? More tsouris you bring on yourself. That boyfriend of yours. What a kvetch. Worse than my husband, Hershel. Some men are just schmoozers: talk talk talk. That's all he knows how to do except you-know-what. He needs a swat in the tuchus if you ask me. Listen to me, you stay with him, you'll have two babies to take care of — a little one and a big one. It will be hard but kindelah, you have moxie.

Thanks for your vote of confidence, Grandma.

During the next few weeks the nausea subsided. Her appetite was back and so was her energy. When she was beginning to show, she decided to tell the Board at their monthly meeting. Everybody seemed to know through the gossip network or because they recognized Lisa was pregnant before she did. They congratulated her and wished her happiness — at least to her face.

The family was a different story, Aunt Rena and Aunt Faye joined her mother in disapproval. Even though it was too late to change her mind, they nagged her anyway.

Aunt Faye had called her right away. "Lisa, why are you doing this? How could you do this to your mother?"

"No hello?"

"Pardon me. Hello, Lisa. It's Aunt Faye. Is that better?"

Lisa cradled the receiver on her shoulder, sorting papers in three piles. "So Mom has recruited the whole family to whip me into submission? I hardly think you are the person to advise me about children," Lisa snapped.

Stung, Aunt Faye said, "You know how badly we wanted a baby. But it was God's will it didn't happen. How could you say such a cruel thing to me?"

"I'm sorry. I shouldn't have said that," Lisa said. "It was uncalled for. But the God argument works both ways. What do you think God is saying now? Don't you think He, or maybe She, is sending me a message too? *Have this baby, Lisa. Love this child.*"

"There's never been any use talking to you. You are as pigheaded as they come. And what is this? You think God is a woman? *Mishuganah.* Where did you come from?'

"Same place as always. Mars," Lisa said.

Aunt Faye squeaked, "There is nothing I can say to you? What about David? Will he help you?

"No and I don't know."

Exasperated, Aunt Faye said, "So what you're telling me is not to waste my breath?"

"Bingo! Maybe you'll even baby sit once in a while? You'll be a grandma! How do you like that?"

Aunt Faye laughed. "Ah, Lisa, I give up. When if comes right down to it, you could convince a rock to roll over."

"I take that to be a yes."

Neither David nor Lisa were ready to see one another, each frustrated and angry with the other. When he finally called, she said, "David, I'll only go for a walk with you if the word abortion is off limits. It's too late, you know."

"Deal. I'll pick you up in a few minutes."

Walking on a path along the river, David asked, "Are you sure you're not too tired?"

"No, it feels good to walk after sitting at a desk all day. How was your day? You still working on the foundation rehab project?"

"Yes. It's big. I should be on it for quite a while. More important than that," he paused, "I went to a lawyer today."

Lisa stopped walking. "What kind of lawyer?"

"You know I want a divorce. It's just complicated."

"So what did he say?" She faced him squarely.

"Nothing very encouraging." He looked away. "He said I have no grounds because I abandoned my wife and child."

"Doesn't paying for everything count? How are they abandoned when the wife is still in the home, doesn't work, and the husband sees the child at least three times a week? I'll tell him what abandonment is. He should come visit WOW." Crestfallen, she turned around to walk back to the car.

"Wait. Calm down." David said.

"Great, David. This is why you wanted to see me. To tell me you can't get a divorce?" She crossed her arms across her belly.

"Absolutely not. I'm going to see someone else. A woman lawyer this time. Next Thursday. Maybe she'll have a different opinion." David bent down and kissed her belly. "I want you to know I'm trying."

"Right." Lisa rubbed her temples, willing away a headache.

"Having a baby now is a really bad idea. It makes a bad situation even worse, but I have to have you in my life, baby or no baby." He pulled her close. "Without you, my life is a flat line. I don't know how I'm going to make things right, but I will, I promise."

They walked silently. After a time, they talked about their days; the difficulties of returning vets; how pretty the river looked at sunset.

No one would have ever guessed they were anything but a happily married couple excited about having their first child.

Chapter Thirty

Fall Out

೨

The Yorkshire Pub, a new restaurant in town, displayed two of Ivy's paintings. Caroline and Ivy's mother wanted to celebrate by taking Ivy to lunch there. They arrived early and sat at a table looking out at the street. It was a warm day and people spilled out of their offices during their lunch hours to enjoy the sunshine. Caroline was people watching and gasped when she saw Lisa stop to talk to someone right in front of the restaurant.

"What's the matter? You look like you just saw a ghost," her mother asked, alarmed.

"I'm fine, Mother." Caroline couldn't take her eyes off Lisa and the round belly protruding from beneath her cardigan.

"Waitress," Margaret called, "Could you bring my daughter some tea and ice water? Also, bring me a glass of a sherry?" She gazed past Caroline to see what she was looking at. "Who's out there?"

"See that pregnant woman on the sidewalk? That's David's girlfriend. Sonofabitch. She must be five or six months pregnant."

"He has a girlfriend? Does Ivy know about the baby? You know she never tells me anything." Their mother swallowed hard.

"Let's not go there now, Mother. No wonder he stopped bugging her about letting Joy get to know Lisa," Caroline mused.

"Lord have mercy. Hasn't my poor daughter been through enough?" Margaret downed her sherry and signaled for another.

"Mother, let's change seats so Ivy's back is to the window and promise me you'll act like nothing's wrong until we figure out how to tell her," Caroline warned.

"What kind of fool do you take me for? I'm her mother, for god's sake. You better put on some blush. You look like a mummy."

Caroline sniped, "And your cheeks are flushed. I thought sherry was to be sipped."

"Don't be talking to me like that. It's fresh."

The front door opened. "Okay, Mother. Here she comes."

"Hi, Caro, Mother. I have great news!" She looked at Caroline, then Margaret, then Caroline again. "What's wrong? You two look like you just came from a funeral."

"Nonsense. We're fine, dear. Aren't we, Caroline? Tell us your good news."

Ivy sat down with her back to the window. "Remember the landscape of the pond I painted at Aunt Kate's? It won second place in the juried student show."

"Iv, that's wonderful. See? You've done well, kiddo," Caroline reached over to touch her hand. "The paintings here are gorgeous too."

"The autumn still life sold right away." She pointed to the painting on the right wall across from the bar.

"I'm proud of you. My daughter, the artist. That is something to celebrate!"

"Thanks, Mother." Ivy looked at her sister. "Caro, what's the matter? You look funny."

"Silly. I'm fine."

"No you're not. Come on you two. Something's going on. Tell me right now. I'll think the worst if you don't tell me," Ivy said.

"Later," Caroline said. Their mother was quiet, rubbing her hands together.

"Tell me now. It's about Shithead, isn't it?" Ivy demanded.

They both nodded.

"Is it that bad?" Ivy asked "How much worse can it get?"

Her mother grabbed her hand.

Ivy pulled away from her. Resolute, she turned to Caroline. "Tell me. I think I'm past the point of being shocked."

"No, you have one more. A big one." Caroline drew in a breath. "Lisa walked by while we were waiting for you."

"So what? Was she with David?"

"No, she was alone. But she stopped to talk to someone and I got a really good look at her." Caroline hesitated.

"And?" Ivy gripped the edge of the table with both hands.

"Ivy, there's no good way to say it." Caroline whispered. "She's pregnant."

"No way. She can't be. Maybe she's just getting fat."

"No, honey. She's not getting fat. She's having a baby."

"Ivy, I'm so sorry, dear heart. My poor daughter. I wonder how his mother is taking all this? I saw her at the movies last month and she looked terrible. She wanted to know why she doesn't see Joy more often. She never suspected..."

Both girls ignored her. "I can't breathe. I've got to get out of here. Now!" Ivy stood up and grabbed her purse.

"I promise you, Ivy. I will never say another word about him. Ever, As far as I'm concerned, he's dead," her mother said.

Ivy looked at her but said nothing.

"Are you sure you can drive yourself?" Caroline asked.

But Ivy was already gone. She sped home, ran into the house, went straight to the phone, and dialed his office. Her voice was thick.

"Hello, dear. How are you feeling? Tired, I bet." She chatted on. "David is in a meeting. Shall I interrupt him?" the receptionist asked.

Even his secretary knew. She thinks I'm her. What a laughingstock I must be. Ivy seethed, "No. Don't interrupt his meeting but tell him his wife called and that it is very important that he stop by the house right after work. Tell him it's urgent."

"Oh. I'm so sorry...well....yes... of course. I'm sorry. I thought you were somebody else. A client. Yes. I didn't recognize your voice at first, Mrs. Lerner, and I thought you were a client." she stammered.

"Obviously."

"I'll give him your message."

David rang the doorbell about an hour after she called. "What's wrong? I got your message and came right away. Is Joy all right?"

Ivy slapped him hard across the face, and then punched his cheek, his shoulders, his chest. When he put his hands up to protect his face, she punched him hard in the gut.

"Stop it! Stop it!" He grabbed hold of her arms. "Are you crazy?"

"You couldn't just reject me?" she screamed. "You had to reject Joy, too? Lisa's having a fucking baby? You are totally disgusting. When were you going to tell us? When the announcement was in the paper? Get out of here, Scumbag. Get out of here before I call the police!" She pushed him backward and slammed the door in his face.

Caroline came over right away. Ivy's face was wet with tears.

"It gets worse and worse. Down deep, I believed he couldn't take the responsibility of being a parent and that was the reason he left. Not that he doesn't love Joy. He does but he couldn't handle the changes that came with fatherhood. It wasn't me he was leaving, but the situation. Just when I think I'm making progress, when I'm finally beginning to cope, he does something even more outrageous to push me off balance. I'll show him. He'll never get a divorce from me so he can have his little bastard child."

"No, Ivy. Just the opposite. Go to that lawyer that Victoria mentioned. Get all his assets. Take him to the cleaners. Cruel and unusual punishment. Abandonment. You have many choices but do it on your terms. Honey, do that for yourself. Please."

Ivy rubbed her eyes. "I beat him up."

Caroline laughed. "I hope you kicked his nuts."

Ivy laughed and then dissolved into tears. "I think I gave him a black eye."

She stroked Ivy's hair. "Sweetheart, listen to me. He is not the guy you married. He is somebody else. He is not the David we grew up with. I don't know what happened to him. I don't know where the David we loved went. But he's gone."

"I keep hoping the real David, my David, will come back."

"No, little sister, he can't. Your David doesn't exist anymore. He's left our planet."

෬

David sat at the bar at The Larkin, nursing a scotch and soda. His cheek was bruised and his gut felt like someone stood on it and jumped up and down.

Robert sat down next to him. "What happened to you, bro? Tell me you walked into a door."

"Very funny."

"What's your deal? I wouldn't want to be in your shoes for anything in the world. Caught between two women who have every right to give you shit because you're an asshole."

David gulped down his scotch and signaled the bartender for another. "I don't remember asking for your opinion."

"I don't know your wife. But I do know Lisa and this is the way I see it. You're always around when you need her but when it's the other way around, it's a roll of the dice. You know what, David? You keep going this way and you're not going to end up with either of one of them."

"It seems simple but its not. I love Lisa and only want to be with her. But getting — "

Robert interrupted. "Spare me your bullshit. Hey, my table is ready." He put down his drink and slapped him on the back. "See you."

David knew what Robert said was true. Everyone who knew Lisa would say the same thing. What was his problem? He had a great woman. He loved her and she was having his baby. It sounded logical but they didn't know the whole story. David stared down at his drink. How had he ever let things get so out of control?

෬

The excitement before the fashion show was palpable. Seats filled up fast. The back office was transformed into a dressing room and Louis brought in wooden platforms to imitate a runway — more like a propped-up wheelchair ramp, but it would work.

Marika chose her models from the volunteers, in big sizes and small, to show business attire. They received donations of clothes, shoes, bags, and belts from downtown department stores and were negotiating a deal with Goodwill. David had insulated the back porch and installed clothes racks all around. He hung a few scrap cabinets and bookshelves for accessories and a curtain for privacy. After the show, the women would be invited to go through the clothing and try things on.

Marika and Lisa really hadn't been able to figure out how to lend the clothing. Should there be a charge or not? How would the clothes be cleaned? How long could one woman keep a dress or suit? They kept talking through the possibilities but hadn't resolved it yet. For the time being, they were going to run it like a lending library. If a woman was starting a new job, she could keep a suit and four blouses for two weeks. Then, she would return it clean for the next woman.

Aunt Rena and Isabela, who had been coming to visit Albany more frequently, did the baking. A supermarket donated all the paper products and coffee.

Lisa planned to welcome everyone and then turn the program over to Marika. Some women look haggard and uncomfortable pregnant. Not Lisa. Her cheeks were rosy, her eyes sparkled, and she carried the baby weight well. She wore a red dress and put her tumble of curls and a red flower on top of her head.

Ivy sat in the audience and stared at Lisa as she was speaking to the crowd. Lisa felt her intense gaze before she saw her. She stopped a moment, swallowed, and regained her composure. Finishing to applause, she sat in the chair reserved for her in the front row. Lisa knew Ivy had come to see her. She sure didn't need to borrow clothes.

Lisa tried listening to Marika as she described the idea of The Closet and what the women were wearing. They sashayed onto the makeshift runway like they were fashion models, turning around and twirling jackets over their shoulders. The audience clapped and whistled but Lisa couldn't concentrate. At least David wasn't there to be a jerk and run out when he saw Ivy. Ivy asked him to take Joy this afternoon. Now she knew why.

After the fashion show, small groups of women took turns in The Closet. Lisa stood up and turned around. She caught Isabela's eye and saw she'd be ready to pounce if Ivy caused a scene.

"Hello, Ivy."

"Lisa."

"I doubt you need to borrow work clothes, Ivy. Why are you here?" Lisa asked.

"I could have called you but I wanted to see you for myself. This is what I want you to know. David never told me you were pregnant. My sister saw you on the street. What do you think that means?"

Lisa's eyes filled with tears, but she choked them back.

"I want you to know what kind of a man you think you love." She spun around and walked out.

Lisa turned from her and walked straight to Isabela. Her grandmother's voice was in her head again. *I've been trying to tell you. He's no mensch. He's a goniff, I tell you. Taking, not giving. Life with him would not be easy. The way he acts. Shame on him. Listen to me. Think with your head for once.*

Her first impulse was to confront him but she didn't. She was sick and tired of his stories and excuses. It was more than the whole ridiculous Ivy-and-David show. Getting a divorce wasn't that hard if you had few assets and joint custody. Something was left out of the story and she doubted either Ivy or David knew what it was.

Somehow she controlled herself and never told David about Ivy's visit. She didn't know the reason. Maybe she was saving it. Maybe she was afraid that once she said it aloud, she might agree with Ivy. What kind of man did she love? Ivy had no reason to lie. It slowly occurred to her that she was using the wrong flight plan and if she kept it up she'd take a nosedive into a mountain.

These were her thoughts when she wasn't with David. When she was with him all her resolve vanished. They started Lamaze class six weeks before the baby was due. After seeing the birthing film, Lisa exclaimed, "I can't do that! Can I change my mind?" The other women in the class laughed with her. The conversation was easy. There were five other couples and she and David appeared to be just like them — a couple excited to be having their first baby. At least, for the hours of the class, she felt like it was true. He counted breaths, learned to effleurage her belly, rubbed her back. When they left class, the truth of their situation tasted like rotten fruit.

They got into the car. "Are you going to be there when I go into labor, David? Promise me you'll be there otherwise, we have to train Marika."

"Of course I'll be there," David said.

"And then? Don't answer that."

"What's wrong with you? We just come out of a couples' class and you're still carping at me?"

"I'm carping?" Anger rose up, burning her throat. "I don't think I want to see you for the last month. I want to get used to the idea of being alone with the baby. Better adjust to your absence before rather than after."

"Lisa, c'mon. Don't do this. We're fine. We're happy. Aren't we happy?" he asked.

"Respect my wishes unless you change the circumstances. I don't want to hear anymore about it. Ever. I don't care if Ivy never did anything to you. I don't care if Joy was the most perfect child who ever lived. I don't care that Ivy put you through school. I don't care about any of it." She swallowed. "You know what I've come to realize? The integrity I thought you had and respected in you is gone. The truth is you have no will and because of that, I have no respect for you." A moment passed. David looked away. "Look at me David. What is your excuse for not having told Ivy about our baby?"

She slammed the car door before he could answer.

Chapter Thirty-One

When One Door Closes, Another Opens

∾

Lisa believed all the Jewish superstitions and wives' tales about pregnancy and childbirth. No baby showers until you had a baby to need things. Fixing up the nursery was bad luck. What if something terrible happened? Lisa wholeheartedly agreed it wasn't worth tempting fate.

She was certain the baby was a girl. Perfect strangers in the market or on the street would touch her belly and tell her it was definitely a boy. With girls, you carry all around. Boys, in front. What are you going to name him, they'd ask? She'd shrug and say Lilith. Her name will be Lilith. I dreamt three times I was going to have a daughter named Lilith. They'd shake their heads and smile. Pick a boy's name too, just in case.

She told everybody to plan for a girl and if they were going to knit anything, it could be pink. But along with that certainty was her Jewish pessimism. The *goniff* started hanging around again ever since Grandma mentioned him. He stayed with her the days she was without David, a nasty troll with his sinister aura. What did the *goniff* have to do with babies? She hoped nothing. But for whatever reason, she'd felt better not daring him.

David stayed away about ten days before he came to the Center.

Louis saw him coming and put his cane across the doorway.

Marika saw him and came to the door to throw him out. "Did Lisa call you?"

"I have to talk to her," he insisted.

She frowned. "Go away. Lisa doesn't want to see you."

Lisa walked to the reception area. "It's okay. Hi, David."

"You look radiant," he said.

"I feel great today. It's not always the case, but this morning I've had a huge burst of energy."

"You know that means the baby is coming soon," David said, nodding.

Marika's hands were on her hips. "On whose authority? Your big experience?"

He ignored her and turned to Lisa. "I'd say tomorrow. Next day at the most."

Marika called out, "Hey, ladies. Listen up. The midwife, David, says Lisa is going to have the baby tomorrow."

"She's doing just fine without you. Go away." Sylvia moved toward him. Two other volunteers stood by her side.

"Can't I talk to you without the Secret Service?"

"What's there to say? Any news?" she asked.

"Don't forget I'm your Lamaze coach. Be sure to call me at the first sign of labor, Marika. My secretary knows to find me the minute you call."

From the door frame, he turned around and gazed wistfully at Lisa. She returned the look.

Lisa forced herself to stay busy. She set things up for the weeks after the baby was born. The Center was participating in a job fair at the Armory. Though she couldn't be there, Lisa organized the materials and staffing. The tiredness she felt at the end of the day dissipated after a good night's sleep.

Last night, she'd had a dream about Mac. It was different from the others. Mac was her teacher. The blackboard was covered with quotes from Fitzgerald and Hemingway. But a line from Emily Dickinson was circled: *Tell the Truth but Tell it Slant.* Lisa repeated it over and over. *Tell the truth but tell it slant.* Tell the truth. Tell the truth. To who? What truth? What does it mean? She couldn't understand. She didn't know why he wanted her to get it. Mac was annoyed. "Lisa, you are no fool. Admit the truth. Tell anything to anyone else. But tell yourself the truth."

It was so real she expected Mac to walk across the room. But she looked down and said out loud. Why can't I go back? Why can't it be then? Why aren't you here? Lisa was troubled by her dream. She knew she needed to understand it but couldn't.

Although she was adamant about not having a baby shower, the women thought a cake would be all right. Thelma Avery, the Reverend's wife, gave Isabela some competition. The cakes she made were heavenly and Lisa's favorite was her red velvet. Thelma decorated it with booties and rattles.

"Your time is near. Look how low you are," Thelma clucked.

"I can barely walk," Lisa admitted.

"All the signs are there. Your time is soon. Very soon." She nodded vigorously. "Yes, indeedy!"

That night, Lisa had dinner with her parents. She had devoured two huge bowls of macaroni and cheese when she had the first pain.

"Mom."

Her mother turned from the sink. "What is it, honey?"

"I think I just had my first contraction."

"First babies take a long time. Try to relax," she said.

Lisa ran from the kitchen into the bathroom. Her mother followed her to hold her head as she wretched into the toilet. "Come, I'll make you some peppermint tea." She handed her a cup of tea and a notebook. She sat down with her. "We'll keep track."

Lisa didn't know whether or not she was having contractions. She had excruciating back pain unlike anything she'd ever felt before. The pain seared through her on and off through the night and into the next day. She called the doctor and they told her to call back when the contractions were coming at short, regular intervals. Her water didn't break but she lost the plug when she went to the bathroom during the night. She rubbed her belly. She breathed as she was taught, but nothing prepared her for this brutal pain.

By the second day, she didn't care whether or not the contractions were still erratic. She couldn't take the pain and called David to take her to the hospital. The resident hooked her up to a monitor and examined her. "You can go home. You're only three centimeters dilated."

"No way," David told him. "She can't go home. She's been in agonizing pain for two days. Can't you see that?" David asked.

"Okay. You have one hour and if you show some progress, we'll keep you. Otherwise you're just not ready. Sorry. I'll be back later." He left the room.

"David, I can't go home. I can't take it. Why isn't my cervix effaced? I can't do this." Tears streamed down her face.

He said, "We'll just plan on staying. Concentrate on the focal point. Look at the watercolor of Race Point you like so much." David stayed focused on the monitor to watch for the contractions. "Here it comes. That's it. Breathe. You're doing great."

Her obstetrician came in about an hour and a half later. "Let's see what's going on here."

"Please tell me I'm more than three. Please. It hurts so much," Lisa cried.

The doctor smiled. "I'd say this baby is coming tonight. You're fully dilated."

"Can I have an epidural? I've been in agony for two days."

The doctor gently rested his hand on Lisa's arm. "I'm going to break your water and notify anesthesiology. In the meantime, just do what you've been doing. Your husband is doing a good job."

A nurse came in about an hour later. "Where is my epidural? I can't take this anymore. Please."

"I'm sorry. The anesthesiologist is with an emergency surgery. He'll be here as soon as he can. Just hang in there."

"Please don't leave." Lisa grasped the nurse's hand.

"I'm not going anywhere. Okay. Here comes a big one. Now breathe."

The anesthesiologist never came. Two hours later, Lisa delivered a seven pound baby girl. The doctor asked, "You picked a name?"

"Yes, Lilith, Please let me hold her. My Lily."

Lisa spent most of the night softly touching the baby's forehead, her cheeks, and her soft hands. She'd entered the world slowly, fighting every inch of the way, and now slept deeply.

David left to make calls and get some sleep. Marika dropped by. "Let me hold her. She is beautiful. Good work, Missy. Good work. Where's the proud Daddy?"

"He left this morning and said he was going to shower, nap, and put the crib together. He'll be back in the early afternoon."

"How'd he do?" Marika wondered.

"He was great. Kept me focused. I think I only screamed at him once."

Marika laughed. "That's good. At least he came through."

"He doesn't want it to be this way and yet, he can't seem to extricate himself. He eats, sleeps, and drinks guilt." Lisa furrowed her brows.

"Enough about that. Who wants to think about that today? When can everybody come and bring your gifts?"

"I'll be home as soon as she's nursing well. Why don't you tell them to come later in the week?" Lisa looked down and smiled at her perfect little girl.

"Done. I'm going to pick up Amber and we'll be back. She is so excited."

"Great. Big sister time for Amber! See you later." Lisa blew her a kiss.

A nurse took the baby. Lisa closed her eyes and slept lightly. She heard her parents in the hall.

"Jack, be careful. The umbrella's dripping water all over the place."

Lisa was all smiles. "Mom. Dad. Did you see her? Isn't she the most beautiful baby girl you've ever seen? She was with me all night — they just took her to be weighed and measured."

"Second most beautiful. You were born with a full head of hair, too. No cue balls in this family!" Jack beamed.

"Oh, Daddy. I bet you say that to all the girls."

"David told us you named her Lilith. Lillian was Mama's name, not Lilith," her mother corrected.

"Yes, I know. But in my dreams she was Lilith, the first woman and I like that. She wanted to be Adam's equal and he wouldn't allow it. If you believe in the Bible stories, she was the first woman and wasn't created from his rib. Adam and Lilith were both created by God."

"No, she's bad luck. She was dark in the Bible. A demon," her mother said.

"There is new interpretation, Mom. I don't remember the whole thing but a rabbi wrote a poem. I only remember this part: *The sky received her smiling/ Lilith embraced all of life/ her wings of fire/ not knowing / where the sky began and her own self ended.* That's the legacy I want to give to her. Mom, call her Lily, then. Like Grandma."

"And the middle name?" she asked.

"What do you think? I think it needs to be short. But maybe not. I'm not settled on anything yet."

There was a crash of thunder and the lights flickered.

"That's some storm. It's coming down in sheets, her mother said. "We lost power for a while and the streets are flooding." Rose sat down by the bed. "Let's see. Daddy's mother was Elsie."

"I don't think so." Lisa laughed. "Ellen? Too ordinary. Elena? Maybe too exotic. Emily? No. I think you need to bring me a baby name book unless we can come up with a name starting with M."

"Who's M?" her mother asked. Her father and mother exchanged glances.

The phone rang. "Mom, can you answer it?"

"Sure, honey." She stroked Lisa's forehead. "Hi, David. Yes, she is beautiful. We'll stay until you come. Oh, you're not sure? What do you mean, you're not sure? Don't be a bum today. Don't disappoint her. Not today."

Scowling, Lisa's mother shook her head and handed Lisa the phone.

"Hi, new Daddy." Lisa tried to sound light.

Her mother read Lisa's face and whispered to her father, "This can't be good."

Lisa slammed down the phone and pushed away the tears.

"What happened?" her father asked.

"The storm knocked out power at Ivy's house. There's a downed line in their yard, a live wire is on the lawn. Poor Ivy and Joy are scared. He's on his way to save the day. Even today."

"It's not going to come to any good. He's stuck. I don't know why, but he's stuck," Lisa's father said, shaking his head.

She blew her nose. "Yes. We will definitely give Lilith a good middle name. Lilith MacKenzie Stern. Named after the first woman and Mac, this child will hold the world in her hands."

Found

֍

> ## Shadowbox: Inherently Buoyant
>
> The back of the box is painted in waves of blue with frothy white surf. Buoys shaped from papier-mâché are painted in a rainbow of colors and sit on the water. There are smiling faces drawn to represent Lisa, Marika, Ivy, Isabela, Rose, Grandma, and Aunt Kate. Off to the side are three stick figure children depicting Amber, Lily, and Joy. They hold their arms open and upward, looking at the sea of faces.

Lily runs along the shoreline picking up shells and chasing birds. For the past few summers, she and Lisa have spent July in Provincetown. Lisa works the counter alongside the summer kids and Lily alternately entertains and annoys the customers. The summer humidity makes Isabela's hip ache, making it too hard for her to stand for long periods of time. Lisa rubs liniment on it every night to give her some relief.

Isabela closes the bakery during the winter months and lives in the upstairs flat with Lisa and Lily in Albany. She helps out at the Center, bakes wedding cakes for a local caterer, and baby sits. The bakery has been up for sale for almost two years but Isabela has not found the right buyer. After all, she would be handing over her life's (and Stefan's) work and nothing has compelled her to sell. The long summer hours are brightened by Lisa and

Lily, and she enjoys the chaos of the summer season now that she doesn't feel as alone.

After losing her son, all thought of happiness with grandkids died with him. She chuckles now and again, never understanding what possessed her to take Lisa home with her. She smiles about how Lisa made a crusty New Englander turn soft. Bringing her home like a wet puppy was so unlike her. Maybe it was God's will that she would grow to love her as a daughter.

Life certainly takes unexpected turns. Isabela's life had always been hard and it is only as an old woman that she realized happiness comes more easily to those who open their arms to it.

Now, she is teaching little Lily to bake bread and make it puff up from a flat piece of dough. Lily, always awed by the final product squeals, "Look, look, look Mommy at what we made! It's deeeelicibous!"

Lily is surrounded by people who love her — the family, of course, doted on her and she quickly became the center's mascot. She is a happy little girl, quick to laugh, easily amused, curious. Lisa thinks she had the best qualities of both of them — the initial enthusiasm that attracted Lisa to David and Lisa's determination.

Ivy's Aunt Kate died and left her house and property to Ivy and Caroline. When Ivy received her degree in art, she and Joy moved there. She converted the garage into a studio and offers lessons to private students. She also teaches at an after-school program operated by a local gallery. Her paintings have begun to sell. The Woodstock art community is active and she has made many new friends.

She and David are not divorced. The emotional time and distance between them has cooled her anger. In some ways, she feels sorry for him. What did he have in his life? A juggling act — trying to please everyone and, of course, satisfying no one. She has gone on a few dates but is in no hurry to get into a relationship. For now, she likes her life as it is.

Reluctantly, Ivy and Lisa agreed that as sisters, Joy and Lily should know each other. Every couple of months, they get together, either in Woodstock or Albany. After many months of strained conversation with unspoken blame hanging in the air, it began to fall away. Slowly, they became friends. But this could only happen when both of them had made their own peace with David.

Joy was reticent around Lisa and Lily at first, but she likes the idea of having a little sister to boss around — particularly since Lily trails after her as an adoring loyal subject.

Marika and Robert were married and have a son named Joseph. It's hard to believe the woman Lisa first met was even tangentially related to Marika. She seems to balance everything effortlessly — a husband, young children, her work at the center, and her growing design business. Lisa often tells her she is the one who came closest to having it all.

A few weeks after Marika spotted Nicky's lamp and blankets on the second floor, she told Lisa, "I know you feel sorry for him but, Missy, be real. Nicky could burn us down! He could throw a fit and damage the place! He could hurt someone! He could scare people away!"

"For god's sake, don't be ridiculous. It was violence that took his life away."

"Didn't David say Nicky attacked him?" Marika asked.

"Yes, but I don't believe him. Regardless, Nicky stays. We'll make sure he has clean blankets. We'll bring up some of the donated furniture we're not using so he has a place for the kerosene lamp. We'll make sure he has food. We'll wash his things. Take care of him."

He remained with them doing odd jobs. He had a warm place to stay, they kept him stocked with food, and found jobs for him to give him purpose. Lisa called Mrs. Ianelli to tell her not to worry, that if he wasn't home, he was probably at WOW, staying warm.

"My poor boy. Leaving food for him like a stray dog." Then, she perked up. "I'll bring the things he liked to eat as a boy. He loved anything with macaroni. Would eat bowls of it. I never knew where he put it all. He was always skinny."

"That's great, Mrs. Ianelli. Maybe someday he'll come back to us."

At first, Lily was afraid of him and stood behind Lisa's leg when she saw him. "Mommy, that dirty man is scary," she said when she turned three.

"You don't need to be afraid of Nick. He's our friend," Lisa told her. "Just don't make loud noises around him. It hurts his ears."

One afternoon Lily watched him from a distance and then ran over, stopping dead about two feet from him. "Mommy says you're our friend."

Lisa watched and thought she saw him smile.

Of them all, David charted the least progress in moving on with his life. Lisa had no doubt that he loved her. He showed her that in many ways except for the one that mattered. As the years went on, she didn't even want him anymore; instead, she pitied him. He devoted time to his daughters, together and apart. When Ivy moved to Woodstock, he went back to live in the house he'd once shared with her.

WOW was a success and expanded into the adjacent building for a training and daycare center. Lisa and David worked on it together without animosity. His original appeal, she thought, died when he disappointed her so deeply. They fell into the routine they developed while working on the first building. Lisa didn't understand what made him so reluctant to make or break commitments but she knew David would always be in her life and it was enough. After all she'd been through, she believed it when she told herself that she didn't really want it to be anything more.

Lisa thought back to the day she arrived in Boston. All the hope she had. The only thing she thought about back then was becoming a part of the changing world. As it happened, it was by loving Mac and David that she grew into herself. At long last, she realized she was living the life she wanted. While she would never get over how Mac was robbed of his life, how they were both robbed of their life, she feels sadness rather than pain. She couldn't pinpoint when the richness of her memories became comforting to her, but she was glad.

Every once in a while her heart skips a beat and she has to pinch herself to make sure Lily is real; how this child has so thoroughly completed the life she's made.

Lily bends over to put another shell in her pail. "Look how many shells I have, Mommy!"

Keep collecting, darling Lily Mac. Throw out the broken ones, my love. Always remember today and the feel of silky, wet sand between your toes. Feet firmly planted. No goniffs. No waiting for a falling shoe to collapse your happiness. If it drops near you, just throw it back into the ocean.

∾

Acknowledgements

❧

I would never have been able to sustain this seven year effort without the loving support of family, friends, and patient readers.

My thank you list is very long.

Thank you to my devoted readers who helped me shape and reshape this story: Amy Berkowitz, Jodi Ackerman Frank, Kathe Kokolias, Cecele Kraus, and Muriel Wilson. Your careful reading, conversation, and encouragement throughout this very long process were way beyond expectation. I love you all.

Thank you to the second string readers for adding to the layers of good feedback: Shelley Brown, Marilyn Day, Christine Tramontano Faga, Susan Garelik, Joan Harrington, Jeff, Laura, and Muriel Marin, Judith Prest, Howard Silverman, Joan Tramontano, Marisa Tramontano, and Marcia Wyrtzen.

A second thank you to my daughter, Marisa, for the pleasure of reading chapters aloud to one another, her perceptive comments, and her steadfast belief in the worthiness of this story. Talk about role reversal!

Thank you to Preston Browning of Wellspring House and Martha Weller of the Saltonstall Foundation of the Arts for giving me the gift of time to write in a magnificent setting.

Thank you to the writers and readers in my life. I can't imagine my life without you. Maria DeLuca-Evans, Gwen Gould, Scott Hicks, Nick Kling, Mary McCarthy, Suzanne Meyers, Sandra Kay Powley, Terry Royne, Marggie Skinner, and Amy White.

Thank you to Carmen Rau of the Women's Building in Albany whose good advice strengthened Lisa's ideas for a Women's Center.

Thank you to James Hobin, reference librarian of the Albany Public Library's *Albany Room* for giving me the look back into that time through actual scrapbooks of yellowed news clippings. So much better than microfiche...

Thank you to the writers of the following books:

Dime-Store Alchemy, The Art of Joseph Cornell by Charles Simic
The Essential Joseph Cornell by Ingrid Schaeffer
Joseph Cornell Dreams, Catherine Corman, editor
Black Panthers for Beginners by Herb Boyd
The Black Panther Leaders Speak, G. Louis Heath, editor
War and the Soul by Edward Tick
The Other Boston Busing Story by Susan Eaton

Thank you to Dina at First Line Editing and Stacey Marin for her precise proofreading.

My deepest thanks to my family.

To my mother, who taught me about the importance of family first and who made sure we made frequent visits to the Delaware library.

To my father, who jumpstarted some of the ideas for this book as we worked on his own story, **I Am a Fortunate Man.**

To my Grandma Sophie, may she rest in peace, who taught me how to bake bread and whose stories grounded me long ago. One might say the whispering in my head never goes away.

To my cousins who love nothing better than getting together to rehash the old stories as we try to figure out who in the world we are.

To my friends who have become family. You know who you are.

To my children, as Charlotte would say, my true *magnum opus*. To all of you. Love transcends all labels. To Allison, Amelia, Angelo, Brian, Christine, Dave, and Marisa.

And to my husband, Ron, who understands my dreams and supports them despite the costs. What can be said about a man who puts up with all the highs and lows, the time away from home, the need for quiet space, and pretends not to mind? Except when I drag him to readings!

He is truly the love of my life. Thank you, my darling.

Readers Guide

Lisa always worried tragedy would befall her. It was a given according to her grandmother whose voice was in Lisa's head even after she died. Just when Lisa had forgotten all about those negative warnings, she suffered a deep loss — her great love died in a car crash while trying to avoid a deer.

Marika was a struggling black, single mother when she and Lisa met. She still nurtured her dream of becoming a dress designer, yet her prospects were slim. She was working in a daycare center and lived in poverty. She burned with rage and disappointment.

Ivy thinks she is a happily married woman living the life she'd always wanted. She had a husband and daughter she adored and didn't have a hint that anything was wrong. Needless to say, she was shocked when her husband, David, came home from work one day and told her he didn't want to be married anymore.

Change was in the air — there was the possibility of an equal rights amendment; abortion was legalized, the blistering summer of riots and the death of Martin Luther King brought racial tension into the public's consciousness, and there was a belief that the protest over an unjust war would in fact stop it. The music was of hope and change, and just good old rock and roll.

How do these broken-hearted women reconnect to the world around them? Catch a ride on the winds of change? Remake their lives and make new dreams? Find the happiness they thought had eluded them?

1. From the very beginning, we are introduced to a Lisa full of contradictions. Why do you think she internalized the superstition and fatalism of her family — 'you sing in the morning, cry in the afternoon,' and a happiness thief is waiting to pounce — with an optimism born out of the times and her confidence in her ability to change things in the world. What impact do you think her family had in eroding her confidence? What impact does it have on her actions?

2. Family relationships play an important role in all the characters' lives. Lisa and Ivy both have better relationships with their fathers than mothers; as an orphan Marika had no one; Mac has a disappointing mother and no father, in David we get a glimpse of a mother with an authoritative nature. The women find surrogates in Isabela, Aunt Kate, and Mrs. Daniels. What impact did this have on the way they walked through the world?

The relationship with their fathers feels strong and supported. Why then does Lisa let her men choose her rather than the other way around? And why does Ivy make herself subordinate to David?

3. The subject of home is another recurring theme. "Home was home. When you lose that, your life is upended, it changes you forever." Grandma's home was burned down and she was forced to live in a new country; Marika was uprooted from a loving home when her parents died; Lisa's home was unlivable without Mac; Ivy lived in the same house as she did when she was with David, but felt rootless. Lisa tries to make a home for women who need one. What is the nature of home in both psychological and physical terms? What does it take to rebuild the concept of 'home'?"

4. Lisa's grandmother's voice is annoying yet she gives some compelling advice. Why does Lisa need to keep her connection to her grandmother alive? Is she in some way a moral compass for Lisa?

5. Lisa is colorblind. She seems unfazed by the conversations in her house about race. Does Lisa identify with Marika? Why do you think they formed such an immediate bond? What do you think each had to gain from the friendship?

6. The political backdrop of the story is important to the trajectory of the characters' lives. The upheaval in cities was hard to ignore. Lisa tried to overcome her disappointment in political rhetoric by trying to do something specific. How did each of her political activities move her closer to her expectations?

From Marika's point of you, she doubted any good would come of any of it. Certainly, nothing that would make her life better. Ivy tried to maintain the status quo. All of the above was true and not true. What was the real impact of the culture on each of their lives? And what actions did they take to feel they were making a difference?

7. David and Mac have different personalities, yet they share common traits. Why is Lisa drawn to controlling men? What are the reasons for her attraction to them? How can she extricate herself from that pattern? Do you think Lisa would have been happy with Mac had he lived?

8. Why does Lisa keep Nicky Ianelli in her life despite the risks?

9. Albany smolders with racial unrest. All the kindling is there for a huge melee. Homes are bulldozed. There is unequal education. There is a discrepancy in justice between black and white. Previously a leader of the Brothers, Louis Vanderholt is a disappointed old man. How does he change?

10. The idea that women are inherently buoyant, that they find a way to survive whatever has befallen them, is an important theme. How does this manifest itself the different generations of women in this book?

11. The concept of a physical women's center is overlaid with emotional connection. Though the building is the point of contact, what do you see happening in the relationships of the women who have made it their community and why?

12. Each character has found his/her own way. Were any of the decisions surprising? Disappointing? Inevitable?

About the Author

∽

Jan Marin Tramontano, a writer living in upstate New York, is the author of three poetry chapbooks, *Paternal Nocturne, Woman Sitting in a Café and other poems of Paris* and *Floating Islands.* She wrote a memoir about her father, *I Am a Fortunate Man.* and her poems appears in her poetry collective's anthology, *Java Wednesdays.*

Her poetry, stories, book reviews, and interviews have been published in numerous literary journals, magazines, and newspapers. She belongs to the International Women's Writers Guild, served on the board and as program chair of the Hudson Valley Writers Guild, and is a member of Poets House and the American Academy of Poets.

She lives in Albany with her husband and youngest daughter. This is her first novel.

Made in the USA
Charleston, SC
10 April 2012